Memoirs of My Dead Life

George Moore

CONTENTS

APOLOGIA PRO SCRIPTIS MEIS

I. SPRING IN LONDON

II. FLOWERING NORMANDY

III. A WAITRESS

IV. THE END OF MARIE PELLEGRIN

V. LA BUTTE

VI. SPENT LOVES

VII. NINON'S TABLE D'HÔTE

VIII. THE LOVERS OF ORELAY

IX. IN THE LUXEMBOURG GARDENS

X. A REMEMBRANCE

XI. BRING IN THE LAMP

XII. SUNDAY EVENING IN LONDON

XIII. RESURGAM

APOLOGIA PRO SCRIPTIS MEIS

[*The* APOLOGIA *which follows needs, perhaps, a word of explanation, not to clear up Mr. Moore's text—that is as delightful, as irrelevantly definite, as paradoxically clear as anything this present wearer of the Ermine of English Literature has ever written—but to explain why it was written and why it is published. When the present publisher, who is hereinafter, in the words of Schopenhauer, "flattened against the wall of the Wisdom of the East," first read and signified his pride in being able to publish these "Memoirs," the passages now consigned to "the late Lord — —'s library" were not in the manuscript. On the arrival of the final copy they were discovered, and thereby hangs an amusing tale, consisting of a series of letters which, in so far as they were written with a certain caustic, humorous Irish pen, have taken their high place among the "Curiosities of Literature." The upshot of the matter was that the publisher, entangled in the "weeds" brought over by his* Mayflower *ancestors, found himself as against the author in the position of Mr. Coote as against Shakespeare; that is, the matter was so beautifully written that he had not the heart to decline it, and yet in parts so—what shall we say?—so full of the "Wisdom of the East" that he did not dare to publish it in the West. Whereupon he adopted the policy of Mr. Henry Clay, which is, no doubt, always a mistake. And the author, bearing in mind the make-up of that race of Man called publishers, gave way on condition that this* APOLOGIA *should appear without change. Here it is, without so much as the alteration of an Ibsen comma, and if the* Mayflower *"weeds" mere instrumental in calling it forth, then it is, after all, well that they grew.*—THE PUBLISHER.]

Last month the post brought me two interesting letters, and the reader will understand how interesting they were to me when I tell him that one was from Mr. Sears, of the firm of Appleton, who not knowing me personally had written to Messrs. Heinemann to tell them that the firm he represented could not publish the "Memoirs" unless two stories were omitted; "The Lovers of Orelay," and "In the Luxembourg Gardens," —Messrs. Heinemann had forwarded the letter to me; my interest in the other letter was less direct, but the reader will understand that it was not less interesting when I tell that it came from the secretary of a certain charitable institution who had been reading the book in question, and now wrote to consult me on many points of life and conduct. He had been compelled to do so, for the reading of the "Memoirs" had disturbed his mind. The reader will agree with me that disturbed is probably the right word to use.

To say that the book had undermined his convictions or altered his outlook on life would be an exaggeration. "Outlook on life" and "standard of conduct" are phrases from his own vocabulary, and they depict him.

"Your outlook on life is so different from mine that I can hardly imagine you being built of the same stuff as myself. Yet I venture to put my difficulty before you. It is, of course, no question of mental grasp or capacity or artistic endowment. I am, so far as these are concerned, merely the man in the street, the averagely endowed and the ordinarily educated. I call myself a Puritan and a Christian. I run continually against walls of convention, of morals, of taste, which may be all wrong, but which I should feel it wrong to climb over. You range over fields where my make-up forbids me to wander.

"Such frankness as yours is repulsive, forbidding, demoniac! You speak of woman as being the noblest subject of contemplation for man, but interpreted by your book and your experiences this seems in the last analysis to lead you right into sensuality, and what I should call illicit connections. Look at your story of Doris! I *do* want to know what you feel about that story in relation to right and wrong. Do you consider that all that Orelay adventure was put right, atoned, explained by the fact that Doris, by her mind and body, helped you to cultivate your artistic sense? Was Goethe right in looking upon all women merely as subjects for experiment, as a means of training his aesthetic sensibilities? Does it not justify the seduction of any girl by any man? And does not that take us straight back to the dissolution of Society? The degradation of woman (and of man) seems to be inextricably involved. Can you regard imperturbedly a thought of your own sister or wife passing through Doris' Orelay experience?"

The address of the charitable institution and his name are printed on the notepaper, and I experience an odd feeling of surprise whenever this printed matter catches my eye, or when I think of it; not so much a sense of surprise as a sense of incongruity, and while trying to think how I might fling myself into some mental attitude which he would understand I could not help feeling that we were very far apart, nearly as far apart as the bird in the air and the fish in the sea. "And he seems to feel toward me as I feel toward him, for does he not say in his letter that it is difficult for him to imagine me built of the same stuff as himself?" On looking into his letter again I imagined my correspondent as a young man in doubt as to which road he shall take, the free road of his instincts up the mountainside with nothing but the sky line in front of him or the puddled track along which the shepherd drives the meek sheep; and I went to my writing table asking myself if my correspondent's spiritual welfare was my real object, for I might be writing to him in order to exercise myself in a private debate before committing the article to paper, or if I was writing for his views to make use of them. One asks oneself these questions but receives no answer. He would supply me with a point of view opposed to my own, this would be an advantage; so feeling rather like a spy within the enemy's lines on the eve of the battle I began my letter. "My Dear Sir: Let me assure you that we are 'built of the same stuff.' Were it not so you would have put my book aside. I even suspect we are of the same kin; were it otherwise you would not have written to me and put your difficulties so plainly before me." Laying the pen aside I meditated quite a long while if I should tell him that I imagined him as a young man standing at the branching of the roads, deciding eventually that it would not be wise for me to let him see that reading between the lines I had guessed his difficulty to be a personal one. "We must proceed cautiously," I said, "there may be a woman in the background.... The literary compliments he pays me and the interest that my book has excited are accidental, circumstantial. Life comes before literature, for certain he stands at the branching of the roads, and the best way I can serve him is by drawing his attention to the fallacy, which till now he has accepted as a truth, that there is one immutable standard of conduct for all men and all women." But the difficulty of writing a sufficient letter on a subject so large and so intricate puzzled me and I sat smiling, for an odd thought had dropped suddenly into my mind. My correspondent was a Bible reader, no doubt, and it would be amusing to refer him to the chapter in Genesis where God is angry with our first parents because they had eaten of the tree of good and evil. "This passage" I said to myself, "has never been properly understood. Why was God angry? For no other reason except that they had set up a moral standard and could be happy no longer, even in Paradise. According to this chapter the moral standard is the origin of all our woe. God himself summoned our first parents before him, and in what plight did they appear? We know how ridiculous the diminutive fig leaf makes a statue seem in our museums; think of the poor man and woman attired in fig leaves just plucked from the trees! I experienced a thrill of satisfaction that I should have been the first to understand a text that men have been studying for thousands of years, turning each word over and over, worrying over it, all in vain, yet through no fault of the scribe who certainly underlined his intention. Could he have done it better than by exhibiting our first parents covering themselves with fig leaves, and telling how after getting a severe talking to from the Almighty they escaped from Paradise pursued by an angel? The story can have no other meaning, and that I am the first to expound it is due to no superiority of intelligence, but because my mind is free. But I must not appear to my correspondent as an exegetist. Turning to his letter again I read:

"I am sorely puzzled. Is your life all of a piece? Are your 'Memoirs' a pose? I can't think the latter, for you seem sincere and frank to the verge of brutality (or over). But what is your standard of conduct? Is there a right and a wrong? Is everything open to any man? Can you refer me now to any other book of yours in which you view life steadily and view it whole from our standpoint? Forgive my intrusion. You see I don't set myself as a judge, but you sweep away apparently all my standards. And you take your reader so quietly and closely into your confidence that you tempt a response. I see your many admirable points, but your center of living is not mine, and I do want to know as a matter of enormous human interest what your subsumptions are. I cannot analyze or express myself with literary point as you do, but you may see what I aim at. It is a bigger question to me than the value or force of your book. It goes right to the core of the big things, and I approach you as one man of limited outlook to another of wider range."

The reader will not suspect me of vanity for indulging in these quotations; he will see readily that my desire is to let the young man paint his own portrait, and I hope he will catch glimpses as I seem to do of an earnest spirit, a sort of protestant Father Gogarty, hesitating on the brink of his lake. "There is a lake in every man's heart"—but I must not quote my own writings. If I misinterpret him ... the reader will be able to judge, having the letter before him. But if my view of him is right, my task is a more subtle one than merely to point out that he will seek in vain for a moral standard whether he seeks it in the book of Nature or in the book of God. I should not move him by pointing out that in the Old Testament we are told an eye for an eye is our due, and in the New the rede is to turn the left cheek after receiving a blow on the right. Nor would he be moved by referring him to the history of mankind, to the Boer War, for instance, or the massacres which occur daily in Russia; everybody knows more or less the history of mankind, and to know it at all is to know that every virtue has at some time or other been a vice. But man cannot live by negation alone, and to persuade my correspondent over to our side it might be well to tell him that if there be no moral standard he will nevertheless find a moral idea if he looks for it in Nature. I reflected how I would tell him that he must not be disappointed because the idea changes and adapts itself to circumstance, and sometimes leaves us for long intervals; if he would make progress he must learn to understand that the moral world only becomes beautiful when we relinquish our ridiculous standards of what is right and wrong, just as the firmament became a thousand times more wonderful and beautiful when Galileo discovered that the earth moved. Had Kant lived before the astronomer he would have been a great metaphysician, but he would not have written the celebrated passage "Two things fill the soul with undying and ever-increasing admiration, the night with its heaven of stars above us and in our hearts the moral law." The only fault I find with this passage is that I read the word "law" where I expected to read the word "idea," for the word "law" seems to imply a Standard, and Kant knew there is none. Is the fault with the translator or with Kant, who did not pick his words carefully? The metaphysician spent ten years thinking out the "Critique of Pure Reason" and only six months writing it; no doubt his text might be emendated with advantage. If there was a moral standard the world within us would be as insignificant as the firmament was when the earth was the center of the universe and all the stars were little candles and Jehovah sat above them, a God who changed his mind and repented, a whimsical, fanciful God who ordered the waters to rise so that his creatures might be overwhelmed in the flood, all except one family (I need not repeat here the story of Noah's Ark and the doctrine of the Atonement) if there was one fixed standard of right and wrong, applicable to everybody, black, white, yellow, and red men alike, an eternal standard that circumstance could not change. Those who believe in spite of every proof to the contrary that there is a moral standard cannot appreciate the beautiful analogy which Kant drew, the moral idea within the heart and the night with its heaven of stars above us. "It is strange," I reflected, "how men can go on worrying themselves about Rome and Canterbury four hundred years after the discovery that the earth moved, and involuntarily a comparison rose up in my mind of a squabble between two departments in an office after the firm has gone bankrupt.... But how to get all these vagrant thoughts into a sheet of paper? St. Paul himself could not proselytize within such limitations, and apparently what I wrote was not sufficient to lead my correspondent out of the narrow lanes of conventions and prejudices into the open field of inquiry. Turning to his letter, I read it again, misjudging him, perhaps ... but the reader shall form his own estimate.

"I honestly felt and feel a big difficulty in reading and thinking over your 'Memoirs' for you are a propagandist whether you recognize that as a conscious mission or not. There is in your book a challenging standard of life which will not wave placidly by the side of the standard which is generally looked up to as his regimental colors by the average man. One must go down. And it was because I felt the necessity of choosing that I wrote to you.

"'Memoirs' is clearly to me a sincere book. You have built your life on the lines there indicated. And there is a charm not merely in that sincerity but in the freedom of the life so built. I could not, for instance, follow my thoughts as you do. I do not call myself a coward for these limitations. I believe it to be a bit of my build; you say that limitation has no other sanction than convention—race inheritance, at least so I gather. Moral is derived from mos. Be it so. Does not that then fortify the common conviction that the moral is the best? Men have been hunting the best all their history long by a process of trial and error. Surely the build of things condemns the murderer, the liar, the sensualist, and the coward! and how do you come by 'natural goodness' if your moral is merely your customary? No, with all respect for your immense ability and your cultured outlook, I do not recognize the lawless variability of the right and the wrong standard which you posit. How get you your evidence? From human actions? But it is the most familiar of facts that men do things they feel to be wrong. I have known a thief who stole every time in pangs of conscience; not merely in the fear of detection. There is a higher and a lower in morals, but the lower is recognized as a lower, and does not appeal to a surface reading of the code of an aboriginal in discussing morals. That, I think is only fair. Your artistic sense is finely developed, but it is none the less firmly based, although there are Victorian back parlors and paper roses.

"You see you are a preacher, not merely an artist. Every glimpse of the beautiful urges the beholder to imitation and *vice versa*. And that is why your 'Memoirs' are not merely 'an exhibition' of the immoral; they are 'an incitement' to the immoral. Don't you think so? And thinking so would you not honestly admit, that society (in the wide sense, of course—civilization) would relapse, go down, deliquesce, if all of us were George Moores as depicted in your book?"

His letter dropped from my hand, and I sat muttering, "How superficially men think!" How little they trouble themselves to discover the truth! While declaring that truth is all important, they accept any prejudice and convention they happen to meet, fastening on to it like barnacles. How disappointing is that passage about the murderer, the sensualist, the liar, and the coward; but of what use would it be to remind my correspondent of Judith who went into the tent of Holofernes to lie with him, and after the love feast drove a nail into the forehead of the sleeping man. She is in Scripture held up to our admiration as a heroine, the saviour of our nation. Charlotte Corday stabbed Marat in his bath, yet who regards Charlotte Corday as anything else but a heroine? In Russia men know that the fugitives lie hidden in the cave, yet they tell the Cossack soldiers they have taken the path across the hill—would my correspondent reprove them and call them liars? I am afraid he has a lot of leeway to make up, and it is beyond my power to help him.

Picking up his letter I glanced through it for some mention of "Esther Waters," for in answer to the question if I could recommend him to any book of mine in which I viewed life—I cannot bring myself to transcribe that tag from Matthew Arnold—I referred him to "Esther Waters," saying that a critic had spoken of it as a beautiful amplification of the beatitudes. Of the book he makes no mention in his letter, but he writes: "There is a challenging standard of life in your book which will not wave placidly by the side of the standard which is generally looked up to as his regimental colors by the average man." The idea besets him, and he refers to it again in the last paragraph; he says: "You see, you are a preacher, not merely an artist." And very likely he is right; there is a messianic aspect in my writings, and I fell to thinking over "Esther Waters"; and reading between the lines for the first time, I understood that it was that desire to standardize morality that had caused the poor girl to be treated so shamefully. Once Catholicism took upon itself to torture and then to burn all those it could lay hands upon who refused to believe with its doctrines, and now in the twentieth century Protestantism persecutes those who act or think in opposition to its moralities. Even the saintly Mrs. Barfield did not dare to keep Esther; but if she sent her servant away, she spoke kindly, giving her enough money to see her through her trouble; there are good people among Christians. The usual Christian attitude would be to tell

Esther that she must go into a reformatory after the birth of her child, for the idea of punishment is never long out of the Christian's thoughts. It is not necessary to recapitulate here how Esther, escaping from the network of snares spread for her destruction, takes refuge in a workhouse, and lives there till her child is reared; how she works fifteen hours a day in a lodging house, sleeping in corners of garrets, living upon insufficient food; or how, after years of struggle, she meets William, now separated from his wife, and consents to live with him that her child may have a father. For this second "transgression," so said a clergyman in a review of the book, Esther could not be regarded as a moral woman. His moral sense, dwarfed by doctrine, did not enable him to see that the whole evil came out of standard morality and the whole good out of the instinct incarnate in her; and he must have read the book without perceiving its theme, the revelation in the life of an outcast servant girl of the instinct on which the whole world rests.

Not until writing these lines did I ever think of "Esther Waters" as a book of doctrine; but it is one, I see that now, and that there is a messianic aspect in my writings. My correspondent did well to point that out, and no blame attaches to him because he seems to fail to see that I may be an admirable moralist while depreciating Christian morality and advocating a return to Nature's. He belonged to the traditions yesterday, today he is among those who are seekers, and to-morrow I doubt not he will be among those prone to think that perhaps Christianity is, after all, retrograde. His lips will curl contemptuously to-morrow when he hears the cruelty of the circus denounced by men who would, if they were allowed, relight the bon fires of the Inquisition; ... he is a Protestant, I had forgotten. Gladiators have begun to appear to us less cruel than monks, and everybody who can think has begun to think that some return to pagan morality is desirable. That is so; awaking out of the great slumber of Christianity, we are all asking if the qualities which once we deemed our exclusive possession have not been discovered among pagans—pride, courage, and heroism. Our contention has become that no superiority is claimed in any respect but one; it appears that it must be admitted that Christians are more chaste than pagans, at all events that chastity flourishes among Christian communities as it has never flourished among pagan. The Christian's boast is that all sexual indulgence outside of the marriage bed is looked upon as sinful, and he would seem to think that if he proclaims this opinion loudly, its proclamation makes amends for many transgressions of the ethical law. All he understands is the law;

nothing of the subtler idea that the ethical impulse is always invading the ethical law finds a way into his mind. Women are hurried from Regent Street to Vine Street, and his conscience is soothed by these raids; the owners of the houses in which these women live are fined, and he congratulates himself that vice is not licensed in England, that, in fact, its existence is unrecognized. Prostitution thrives, nevertheless; but numbers do not discourage the moralist, and when he reads in the newspapers of degraded females, "unfortunates," he breathes a sigh; and if these reports contain descriptions of miserable circumstance and human grief, he mutters "how very sad!"

But the assurance that the women are wretched and despised soothes his conscience, and he remembers if he has not been able to abolish prostitution, he has at all events divested it of all "glamour." It would appear that practical morality consists in making the meeting of men and women as casual as that of animals. "But what do you wish—you would not have vice respected, would you?" "What you call vice was once respected and honored, and the world was as beautiful then as now, and as noble men lived in it. In many ways the world was more moral than when your ideas began to prevail." He asks me to explain, and I tell him that with the degradation of the courtesan the moral standard has fallen, for as we degrade her we disgrace the act of love. We have come to speak of it as part of our lower nature, permissible, it is true, if certain conditions are complied with, but always looked upon askance; and continuing the same strain of argument, I tell him that the act of love was once deemed a sacred rite, and that I am filled with pride when I think of the noble and exalted world that must have existed before Christian doctrine caused men to look upon women with suspicion and bade them to think of angels instead. Pointing to some poor drab lurking in a shadowy corner he asks, "See! is she not a vile thing?" On this we must part; he is too old to change, and his mind has withered in prejudice and conventions; "a meager mind," I mutter to myself, "one incapable of the effort necessary to understand me if I were to tell him, for instance, that the desire of beauty is in itself a morality." It was, perhaps, the only morality the Greeks knew, and upon the memory of Greece we have been living ever since. In becoming *hetairae*, Aspasia, Lais, Phryne, and Sappho became the distributors of that desire of beauty necessary in a state which had already begun to dream the temples of Minerva and Zeus.

The words of Blake come into my mind, "the daring of the lion or the submission of the ox." With these words I should have headed my letter to the secretary of the charitable institution, and I should have told him that many books which he would regard as licentious are looked upon by me as sacred. "Mademoiselle de Maupin," "the golden book of spirit and sense," Swinburne has called it, I have always looked upon as a sacred book from the very beginning of my life. It cleansed me of the belief that man has a lower nature, and I learned from it that the spirit and the flesh are equal, "that earth is as beautiful as heaven, and that perfection of form is virtue." "Mademoiselle de Maupin" was a great purifying influence, a lustral water dashed by a sacred hand, and the words are forever ringing in my ear, "by exaltation of the spirit and the flesh thou shalt live." This book would be regarded by my correspondent as he regards my "Memoirs," and its publication has been interdicted in England. How could it be permitted to circulate in a country in which the kingdom of heaven is (in theory) regarded as more important than the kingdom of earth? A few pages back the idea came up under my pen that the aim of practical morality was to render illicit love as unattractive as possible, and I suppose, though he has never thought the matter out, the Christian moralist would regard Gautier as the most pernicious of writers, for his theme is always praise of the visible world, of all that we can touch and see; and in this book art and sex are not estranged. I have often wondered if the estrangement of the twain so noticeable in English literature is not the origin of this strange belief that bodily love is part of our lower nature. Our appreciation of the mauve flush dying in the west has been indefinitely heightened by descriptions seen in pictures and read in poems, and I cannot but think that if the lover's exaltation before the curve of his mistress's breast had not been forbidden, the ugly thought that the lover's ardor is inferior to the poet's would never have obtained credence. There is but one energy, and the vital fluid, whether expended in love or in a poem, is the same. The poet and the lover are creators, they participate and carry on the great work begun billions of years ago when the great Breath breathing out of chaos summoned the stars into being. But why do I address myself like this to the average moralist? How little will he understand me! In the Orelay adventure which horrified him there was an appreciation of beauty which he has, I am afraid, rendered himself incapable of. Myself and Doris were spiritual gainers by the Orelay adventure, Doris's rendering of "The Moonlight Sonata," till she went to Orelay, was merely brilliant and effective; and have not all the critics in England agreed that the story in which I relate her contains some of the best pages of prose I have written? But why talk of myself when there is Wagner's experience to speak about? Did he not write to Madame Wasendonck, "I owe you Tristan for all eternity"? She has not left any written record of her debt to Wagner, perhaps because she could not find words to give the reader any idea how great it was.

Histories of human civilization there are in abundance, but I do not know of any history of the human intelligence. But when this comes to be written—if it ever should come to be written—the writer will hesitate, at least I can imagine him hesitating, how much of the genius of artists he would be justified in tracing back to sexual impulses. Goethe, as my correspondent informs me, looked upon love of woman as a means of increasing his aesthetic sensibilities, and my correspondent seems to think that he did them wrong thereby, whereas I think he honored them exceedingly. Balzac held the contrary belief, so Gautier tells us, maintaining that great spiritual elation could be gained by restraint, and when inquiry was made into his precise beliefs on this point he confessed that he could not allow an author more than half an hour once a year with his beloved; he placed no restriction, however, on correspondence, "for that helped to form a style." When Gautier mentioned the names of certain great men whose lives offered a striking refutation of this theory, Balzac answered they would have written better if they had lived chastely. Gautier seems to have left the question there, and so will we, remarking only that Balzac was prone to formulating laws out of his single experience. I remember having written, or having heard somebody say, "in other writers we discover this or that thing, but everything exists in Balzac." And in his conversation with Gautier we do not find him praising chastity as a virtue, but extolling the results that may be gotten from chastity as a Yogi might. It is said that English missionaries in India sometimes drive out in their pony chaises to visit a holy man who has left his womenfolk, plentiful food, and a luxurious dwelling for a cave in some lonely ravine. The pony chaise only takes the parson to the mouth of the ravine, and leaving his wife and children in charge of his servant, the parson ascends the rocky way on foot, meeting, perchance, a fat peasant priest from Maynooth bent on the same mission as himself—the conversion of the Yogi. It is amusing for a moment to imagine these two Western barbarians sitting with the emaciated saint on the ledge in front of the cave. Thinking to win his sympathy, they tell him that on one point they are all agreed. The Brahman's eyes would dilate; how can this thing be? his eyes would seem to ask, and it is easy to imagine how contemptuously he would raise his eyes when he gathered gradually from their discourse that his visitors believed that chastity was incumbent upon all men. "But all men are not the same," he would answer, if he answered his visitors; "I dwell in solitude and in silence, and am chaste, and live upon the rice that the pious leave on the rocks for me, but I do not regard chastity and abstinence as possessed of any inherent merits; as virtues, they are but a means to an end. How would you impose chastity upon all men, since every man brings a different idea into the world with him? There are men who would die if forced to live chaste lives, and there are men who would choose death rather than live unchaste, and many a woman if she were forced to live with one husband would make him very unhappy, whereas if she lived with two men she would make them both supremely happy. But the news has reached me even here that in the West you seek a moral standard, and this quest always fills me with wonder. There are priests among you, I can see that, and soldiers, and fishermen, and artists and princes and folk who labor in the fields—now do you expect all these men, living in different conditions of life, to live under the same rule? I am afraid that the East and the West will never understand each other. The sun is setting, my time for speech is over," and the wise man, rising from the stone on which he has been sitting, enters into the cave, leaving the priest and the parson to descend the rocks together in the twilight, their differences hushed for the moment, to break forth again the next day.

Schopenhauer has a fine phrase, one that has haunted my mind these many years, that the follies of the West flatten against the sublime wisdom of the East like bullets fired against a cliff.

How can it be otherwise? For when we were naked savages the Brahmans were learned philosophers, and had seen as far into every mystery as mortal eyes will ever see. We have progressed a little lately; our universities, it is true, are a few hundred years old, but in comparison with the East we are still savages; our culture is but rudimentary, and my correspondent's letter is proof of it. It is characteristic of the ideas that still flourish on the banks of the Thames, ideas that have changed only a little since the *Mayflower* sailed. It would have been better if Columbus had delayed his discovery for, let us say, a thousand years. I am afraid the *Mayflower* carried over a great many intellectual weeds which have caught root and flourished exceedingly in your States—Massachusetts, Pennsylvania, and Washington. A letter arrived from Washington some two or three months ago. The writer was a lady who used to write to me on all subjects under the sun; about fifteen years ago we had ceased to write to each other, so she began her letter, not unnaturally, by speaking of the surprise she guessed her handwriting would cause me. She had broken the long silence, for she had been reading "The Lake," and had been much interested in the book. It would have been impolite to write to me without alluding to the aesthetic pleasure the book had given her, but her interest was mainly a religious one. About five years ago she had become a Roman Catholic, she was writing a book on the subject of her conversion, and would like to find out from me why I had made Father Gogarty's conversion turn upon his love of woman, "for it seems to me clear, unless I have misunderstood your book, that you intended to represent Gogarty as an intellectual man." It is difficult to trace one's motives back, but I remember the irritation her letter caused me, and how I felt it would not be dignified for me to explain; my book was there for her to interpret or misinterpret, as she pleased; added to which her "conversion" to Rome was an annoying piece of news. Fifteen years ago she was an intelligent woman and a beautiful woman, if photographs do not lie, and it was disagreeable for me to think of her going on her knees in a confessional, receiving the sacraments, wearing scapulars, trying to persuade herself that she believed in the Pope's indulgences. She must now be middle-aged, but the decay of physical beauty is not so sad a spectacle as the mind's declension. "She began to think," I said, "of another world only when she found herself unable to enjoy this one any longer; weariness of this world produces what the theologians call 'faith.' How often have we heard the phrase 'You will believe when you are dying'? She would have had," I said, "Father Gogarty leave his church for doctrinal rather than natural reasons, believing scrolls to be more intellectual than the instincts; Father Gogarty poring over some early edition of the Scriptures in his little house on the hilltop, reading by the light of the lamp at midnight and deciding that he would go out of his parish because, according to recent exegesis, a certain verset in the Gospel had been added three hundred years after the death of Christ." I fell to thinking how dry, common, and uninteresting the tale would be had it been written on these doctrinal lines. Carlyle said that Cardinal Newman had the brain of a half-grown rabbit, and he was right; Newman never got further than a scroll, and man must think with his body, as well as with his brain. To think well the whole man must think, and it seems to me that Father Gogarty thought in this complete way. Rose Leicester revealed to him the enchantment and the grace of life, and his quest became life. Had it been Hose Leicester herself the story would have merely been a sensual incident. The instinct to go rose up within him, he could not tell how or whence it came, and he went as the bird goes, finding his way toward a country where he had never been, led as the bird is led by some nostalgic instinct. And I do not doubt that he found life, whether in the form of political or literary ambition or in some other woman who would remind him of the woman he had lost; perhaps he found it in all these things, perhaps in none. Told as I told it the story seems to me a true and human one, and one that might easily occur in these modern days; much more easily than the story my correspondent would have had me write. The story of a priest abandoning his parish for theological reasons is not an improbable one, but I think such a story would be more typical of the sixteenth century, when men were more interested in the authenticity of the Biblical texts than they are in the twentieth. The Bible has been sifted again and again; its history is known, every word has been weighed, and it is difficult to imagine the most scrupulous exegetist throwing a search light into any unexplored corner. Even Catholic scholarship, if Loisy can be regarded as a Catholic, has abandoned the theory that the gospels were written by the Apostles. The earliest, that of Mark, was written sixty years after the death of Christ, and it is the only one for which any scholar claims the faintest historical value. With this knowledge of history in our possession belief has become in modern times merely a matter of temperament, entirely dissociated from the intellect. Some painter once said that Nature put him out. The theologian can say the same about the intellect—it puts him out. Out of a great deal of temperament and a minimum of intellect he gets a precipitate, if I may be permitted to drop into the parlance of the chemist, for dregs would be an impolite word to use, and the precipitate always delights in the fetich. There will always be men and women, the cleric has discovered, who will barter their souls for the sake of rosaries and scapulars and the Pope's indulgences. The two great enemies of religion, as the clerics know well, are the desire to live and the desire to know. We find this in Genesis: God: i. e., the clerics, was angry because his creatures ate of these different fruits. God's comprehension of the danger of the tree of life is not wonderful, but his foreseeing of the danger of the tree of knowledge was extraordinary foreseeing, for very little of the fruit of this tree had been eaten at the time the text was written. All through the Middle Ages the clerics strove to keep men from it with tortures and burnings at the stake, and they were so anxiously striving for success in protecting their flocks from this tree that they allowed the sheep to wander, the rams to follow the ewes, and to gambol as they pleased. But the efforts of the clerics were vain. There were rams who renounced the ewes, and the succulent herbage that grows about the tree of life, for the sake of the fruit of the tree of knowledge; all the fences that the clerics had erected were broken down one by one; and during the nineteenth century a great feast was held under the tree. But after every feast there are always ailing stomachs; these denouncing the feast go about in great depression of spirit, surfeited feasters, saying the branches of the tree have been plucked bare; others complain they have eaten bitter fruit. This is the moment for the prowling cleric. Hell is remote, it has been going down in the world for some time, and biology, if no conclusions be drawn, serves the clerical purpose almost as well. "The origins of existence are humble enough, my son, but think of the glorious heritage," and the faint-hearted sheep is folded again.... The tree of life is more abundant; whenever a fruit is plucked another instantly takes its place, and all the efforts of the clerics are now directed to keep their flocks from this tree. "Back to the tree of knowledge!" they cry. "Hu! Hu! Hu! Both trees," they mutter among themselves, "are accursed, but this one, from which sweet fruit may always be plucked, is the worser." And they collect together in groups to pass censure on their predecessors. "My predecessors were infallible fools," cries the Pope, "to have permitted praise of this fatal tree, wasting their energies on such men as Bruno, who said the earth was round, and Galileo, whom they forced to say he was mistaken when he said the earth moves. A pretty set of difficulties they have involved us in with their accursed astronomy. Boccaccio and the Troubadours should have been burned instead, and if this had been done all the abominable modern literature which would persuade the faithful that this world is not all sackcloth and ashes would never have been written. Away with him who says that the earth is as beautiful as heaven," and Gautier's phrase, *"Moi, je trouve la terre aussi belle que le ciel, et je pense que la correction de la forme est la vertu,"* has become the heresy more intolerable than any other to the modern cleric, and to me and to all the ardent and intellectual spirits of my generation a complete and perfect expression of doctrine. To some it will always seem absurd to look to Gautier rather than to a Bedouin for light. Nature produces certain attitudes of mind, and among these is an attitude which regards archbishops as more serious than pretty women. These will never be among my disciples. So leaving them in full possession of the sacraments, I pass on.

My generation was in sympathy with "Mademoiselle de Maupin" and it did more than to reveal and clarify the ideas we were seeking. It would be vain for me, as for any other man, to attempt to follow the course of an idea and to try to determine its action upon life. Perhaps the part of the book which interested us the least was that very part which would be read aloud in court if a prosecution were attempted: I am alluding to the scene when Mademoiselle de Maupin comes into Albert's room. This scene was, however, inevitable, and could not be omitted, for does it not contain that vision of beauty which Albert had been seeking and which was vouchsafed to him for a little while? Never did he see Mademoiselle de Maupin afterwards, she was but a phantom of his own imagination made visible by some prodigy to him. For a still briefer space Rosette shared Albert's dream, and man and wife remained faithful to each other. It is easy to imagine the vileness which a prosecuting counsel could extract from these beautiful pages made entirely of vision and ecstasy. How false and shameful is the whole business. We are allowed to state that we prefer pagan morality to Christian, but are interdicted from illustrating our beliefs by incident. So long as we confine ourselves to theory we are unmolested. But these are subtleties which do not trouble the minds of the members of vigilance associations, the men and women who gather together in back parlors with lead pencils to mark out passages which they consider "un-Kur-istean" (a good strong accent on the second syllable). Their thoughts pursue beaten tracks. Books like "Mademoiselle de Maupin" they hold would act directly on the temperament, and we know that they do not do this, we know that the things of the intellect belong to the intellect and the things of the flesh to the flesh. Were it otherwise Rose Leicester, the pretty school mistress, might have been left out of my story entitled "The Lake," and her place taken by a book. My lady correspondent, it will be remembered, was in favor of some doctrinal difficulty. My second correspondent, the secretary of the charitable institution, would have chosen as the cause of Father Oliver's flight a sensual book. His choice might have been Burton's "Arabian Nights"; better still Casanova's "Memoirs," for this is a book written almost entirely with the senses; the intellect hardly ever intrudes itself; and instead of an emaciated priest poring over a dusty folio we should have had an inflamed young man curled up in an armchair reading eagerly, walking up and down the room from time to time, unable to contain himself, and eventually throwing the book aside, he would find his way down to the lake.

These two versions of "The Lake," as it might have been written by my correspondents, will convince, I think, almost anyone, even them, that the desire of life which set Father Gogarty free could have been inspired only by a woman's personality. It was not necessary that he should go after the woman herself—but that point has already been explained. What concerns us now to understand is how the strange idea could have come into men's minds that literature is a more potent influence than life itself. The solving of this problem has beguiled many an hour, but the solution seems as far away as ever, and I have never got nearer than the supposition that perhaps this fear of literature is a survival of the very legitimate fear that prevailed in the Middle Ages against writing. In my childhood I remember hearing an old woman say that writing was an invention of the devil, and what an old woman believed forty years ago in outlying districts was almost the universal opinion of the Middle Ages. Denunciations and burnings of books were frequent, and ideas die slowly, finding a slow extinction many generations after the reason for their existence has ceased. In the famous trial of Gille de Rais we have it on record that the Breton baron was asked by his ecclesiastical judges if pagan literature had inspired the strange crimes of which he was accused, if he had read of them in—I have forgotten the names of the Latin authors mentioned, but I remember Gille de Rais' quite simple answer that his own heart had inspired the crimes. Whereupon the judges not unnaturally were shocked, for the conclusion was forced upon them that if Gille's confession were true they were not trying a man who had been perverted by outward influence but one who had been born perverted. Who then was responsible for his crimes? Lunacy sometimes in these modern days serves as a scapegoat, but the knowledge of lunacy in the fifteenth century was not so complete as it is now and the judges preferred to believe that Gille was lying. And about ten years ago London found itself in the same moral quandary. Three or four little boys were discovered to have planned the murder of one of their comrades—sixpence, I think, was the object of the murder; not one was over eight, yet they planned the crime skillfully and very nearly succeeded in avoiding detection. To credit these little boys with instinctive crime was intolerable, and just as in the Middle Ages a scapegoat had to be found. Apuleius and his Ass were out of the question, but the little boys admitted having read penny dreadfuls; London breathed again, the way now was clear, these newspapers must be prosecuted, and this recrudescence of wickedness in the heart of a little boy would never be heard of again. A little later or maybe it was a little earlier, I relate these things in the order in which they come into my mind, the London Vigilance Association instituted a prosecution against Mr. Henry Vizetelly, a man of letters and the publisher of Zola's novels. With the exception of Mr. Robert Buchanan and myself not a single man of letters could be found to speak in Mr. Vizetelly's defense. Everybody urged some excuse, his wife was ill, his children were at the seaside and he had to go down to see them, or that he had never cared much about naturalistic literature; whereas, if the prosecution had been directed against something romantic, etc.—Stranger still is the fact that it was almost impossible to find a counsel willing to defend Mr. Vizetelly. One man threw up the case, giving as his reason that he would have to read the books, another said that it would be impossible to adequately defend Mr. Vizetelly's case because no one could say what one had a right to put into a book. This remark seemed to me at the time contemptible, but there was more in it than I thought, for will it be believed that when the case came into court the judge ruled that the fact that standard writers had availed themselves of a great deal of license could not be taken as a proof that such license was permissible? Two wrongs do not make a right he said. In these circumstances perhaps counsel was wise to tell Mr. Vizetelly to plead guilty to having published an indecent libel; but the advice seemed so cruel that, justly or unjustly, I suspect the lawyer of a wish to escape the odium that would have attached to him if he had defended a book accused of immorality. The old man was heavily fined. On going out of court he set to work to have the books revised, spending hundreds of pounds having the plates altered, but the Vigilance Association attacked him again, and this time they succeeded in killing him. Mr. Vizetelly was over seventy years of age when he went to prison, and the shame, anxiety, and three months of prison life killed him. Five years afterwards the Authors' Society, who would not say a word in his favor, voted a great banquet for Zola when he came to London. Zola received every homage that could be paid to a man of letters. The Vigilance Association raised no protest, and I do not blame them. None would have been heard. But while the banquets were held and the speeches were published in the newspapers some of the members of the Association must have meditated sadly on the futility of their efforts and the death of Mr. Vizetelly. It requires a heavy blow of a very heavy mallet to get anything into some people's heads, and nothing short of the reception that was given to Zola could have affected the minds of the Vigilance Association. The significance of the judge's words that the fact that classical writers had availed themselves of a certain license could not be taken as proof that such license was permissible escaped them altogether, for some time afterwards the question of immorality in literature arose again—I have forgotten the circumstances of this case—but I remember that Mr. Coote, the secretary of the Association, was asked if Shakespeare had not written many very reprehensible passages. Mr. Coote was obliged to admit that he had, and when asked why the Association he represented did mot proceed against Shakespeare he answered because Shakespeare wrote beautifully. A strangely immoral doctrine, for if the license of expression that Shakespeare availed himself of be harmful, Shakespeare should be prosecuted; that he wrote beautifully is no defense whatever. Life comes before literature, and the Vigilance Association lays itself open to a charge of neglect of duty by not proceeding at once against Shakespeare and against all those who have indulged in the same license of expression. The members and their secretary have indeed set themselves a stiff job, but they must not shrink from it if they would avoid shocking other people's moral sense by exhibiting themselves in the light of mere busybodies with a taste for what boys and old men speak of as "spicy bits." Proceedings will have to be taken against all the literature that Mr. Coote believes to be harmful (I accept him as the representative of the ideas of his Association), and the plea must not be raised again that because a reprehensible passage is well written it should be acquitted. We must consider the question impartially. It is true that a magistrate may be found presiding at Bow Street who will refuse to issue a warrant against the publishers, let us say of Byron, Sterne, the Restoration, and the Elizabethan dramatists. The Association will have to risk the refusal; but I would not discourage the Association from the adventure. It must not abandon the tope of finding a magistrate who, anxious to prove himself no moral laggard, will do all that is asked of him. A very pretty selection of "spicy bits" can be picked from "Don Juan," and toward this compilation every member, male and female, might contribute. The reading of these selections in Bow Street in a crowded court would prove quite a literary entertainment, and if the magistrate refused to issue a warrant he could only do so on the pretext that the book had been published a long while, a pretext which can hardly be held to be more valid than the pretext put forward by Mr. Coote for not prosecuting Shakespeare. Of one thing only would I warn the Society which I seem to be taking under my wing, and that is, even if it should succeed in interdicting two-thirds of English literature its task will still be only half accomplished. The newspaper question will still have to be faced. Books are relatively expensive, but the newspaper can be bought for a halfpenny, and it will be admitted that no author is as indecent as the common reporter. The reader thinks that I am going to draw his attention to some celebrated divorce case, an account of which was reported in full in the columns of some daily paper under a large heading "Painful Details," the details being the account the chambermaid gave the outraged husband of—I will spare my reader.

About fifteen years ago I was asked if I would care to go over to — — College to see the sports. We walked across the downs, and while watching the racing I was accosted by the head master, who asked me if I would like to see the college. The sports were more interesting than refectories and dormitories, but it seemed a little churlish to refuse and we went together. No doubt we visited the kitchens and the chapel, but what I remember was a long hall wainscoted with oak and furnished with oak tables and chairs and benches, In this hall there were some thirty or forty boys, of ages varying from twelve to eighteen, reading the newspapers, reading the reports of the Oscar Wilde trial; each daily paper contained three or four columns of it. I asked the head master if it were right to allow the boys to read such reports and he answered that lately the newspapers contained a great deal of objectionable matter, "But how am I to keep the daily papers out of the college?" Now I am not easily scandalized, but I could not help feeling that a grave scandal was being committed in allowing these boys to read the newspapers during the week of that trial. But if you admit the newspapers one day how can you forbid them on another occasion? And while appreciating the head master's difficulty I walked out into the open air unable to take any further interest in the sports. Nor has time obliterated anything of the shame I felt that day. I don't want to make a fuss, I don't want to pose as a moralist, but I cannot help thinking that while newspapers continue to be published, the Vigilance Society need not trouble lest certain books should fall into the hands of young people. My correspondent forgot that thousands of newspapers are published to-day when he wrote to me saying that my book roused sensuality. I am afraid I omitted the passage in which these words occur, fearing to burden my article with quotation. Here it is:

"The perusal of the episodes (Doris' Orelay experiences) does certainly not ennoble me, it rouses sensuality, it lowers woman from a friend and helpmeet into a convenience and a minister to pleasure. I am less able and less willing to think 'high' after your book; poetry is distasteful, art is narrowed, I look out for the licentious, the suggestive, the low, and the mean; and don't you? You seem in passage after passage to be world-weary in a sense that no sane man ought to be, sated, disgusted, tired of life—is it not so? You see I speak from what I am sure you will regard as a narrow platform, my ideals are certainly not yours but I am simply and frankly curious as to the ultimates in your book and in yourself."

Let us suppose now that the Vigilance Association after a sharp crusade has succeeded in redeeming our literature from all reprehensible matter, and flushed with success has attacked the newspapers and obtained an interdiction against the publication of all reports of sexual crimes and misdemeanors. And having extended our imagination so far we may presume as the sequence a world of such highly developed moral susceptibilities that Miss Austen's novels are beginning to cause uneasiness. Miss Austen's novels are still permitted, but in current literature nothing is said that would lead the reader to suppose that men and women are not of the same sex. But men and women still continue to meet and hold conversation. Only some advanced members of the Association are in favor of that complete separation of the sexes which obtains in Ireland in the rural districts. In the imaginary time of which I am writing the Association has only obtained complete control over literature. The theaters are either closed or given over to the representation of plays on religious subjects; but private life has not been invaded by the Puritan missionary, and waltz tunes are still heard and figures seen whirling past lighted windows in Grosvenor Square and Fifth Avenue. Mr. Coote has at this time become a moderate, he is no longer among the progressives, and is in danger of losing his post, so I have no difficulty in imagining what he would do in such a dilemma. He would disguise himself as a waiter and at the next meeting of the Society tell how he had until now showed some reluctance to—the sentence would be a difficult one to finish, perhaps Mr. Coote would break off and say—reluctance to put restraint on the action of men and women as long as they kept within their own doors, but after what he has seen, he finds himself obliged to pass from the moderates to the progressives. What has Mr. Coote seen. How would he tell his tale?

He would tell of the length and the breadth of the ball room, of the parquet floor usually covered with an aubusson carpet but the carpet had been lifted and the gilded furniture taken away; the windows and the recesses had been filled with flowers, and to keep these fresh, great blocks of ice had been placed in the niches. He would tell of the lighting arrangements, for are not flowers and lights incentives to immorality? But his descriptions of the roses and the lilies would only lead up to his descriptions of the shameless animality that came up the staircase between twelve and one. A half-naked lady, the hostess, stood at the head of the stairs receiving her guests with smiles and words of welcome. The dresses the women wore resembled the dress worn by the hostess; young and old alike went about their pleasure with necks and bosoms and arms uncovered, and he saw these undressed creatures slip into the arms of men who whirled them round and round; it was but a whirling of silk ankles and a shuffling of glazed shoes; and every now and then the men and women looked into each other's eyes, and the whole scene was reflected shamelessly in tall mirrors. Notwithstanding the fact that most of Mr. Coote's time was spent behind the buffet serving out ices, he nevertheless contrived to find a spare moment for investigation. On the pretext of seeking a lady who had dropped a handkerchief he had crossed the ball room and was therefore in a position to give an accurate account of the waltzes he had heard, dulcet, undulating, capricious measures, far more provocative than Beethoven's "Kreutzer Sonata" which Tolstoy has denounced. The lady that Mr. Coote sought was not in the ball room, and so he had an opportunity of investigating all the retiring rooms, and I need not describe the pensive and shocked faces that listened to his descriptions of the shady nooks. Sometimes it was a screen, sometimes it was a palm that was employed to hide the couple from observation. Mr. Coote at last discovered the owner of the handkerchief in one of those shady nooks, she was there with a gentleman.... Mr. Coote, of course, would refuse to relate what he saw, he would hesitate, but the members of his Association would insist upon knowing everything, and he would at last confess: "Well, the gentleman had kissed the lady on the point of her shoulder." From this scandalous incident he would pass to tell all that he remembered of the conversation he had heard at the table round which he had worked till nearly four o'clock in the morning handing cutlets, chicken patties, and other delicacies, the names of which he was not acquainted with.

Mr. Coote's description of what he saw may be ingenuous, but is his description untrue? And when Mr. Coote finished up his speech as I imagine him finishing it, by stating that the dancing, the music, the dresses, the wines, and the meats were arranged and learnedly chosen for one purpose and one only, the stimulation of sexual passion, I cannot imagine anyone accusing him of having spoken an untruth. Mr. Coote added that no one went to the ball for the pleasure of the conversation—he was convinced that old and young derived their pleasure, consciously or unconsciously, from sex.

We will imagine the members of Mr. Coote's Society being greatly moved by his description, and the sudden determination of everybody that dancing must be stopped. Had not Byron declared the waltz to be "half a whore"? Tolstoy has gone one better and asked people to say if a woman can remain chaste if a low dress is permitted and Beethoven's "Kreutzer Sonata" is played. Forgetful, of course, that they have prosecuted "Don Juan," the Society accepts Byron's dictum as their war cry, and henceforth the business of Mr. Coote is to inquire into what is immoral in dress, in music, in wine, and in food. After a long consultation with experts and expensive law proceedings the Vigilance Association has (in our imagination) succeeded in reforming society as completely as it succeeded in reforming literature; and the months go by, October, November, December, January, February, March ... but one night the wind changes, and coming out of our houses in the morning we are taken with a sense of delight, a soft south wind is blowing and the lilacs are coming into bloom. My correspondent says that my book rouses sensuality. Perhaps it does, but not nearly so much as a spring day, and no one has yet thought of suppressing or curtailing spring days. Yet how infinitely more pernicious is their influence than any book! What thoughts they put into the hearts of lads and lasses! and perforce even the moralist has to accept the irrepressible feeling of union and growth, the loosening of the earth about the hyacinth shoots and the birds going about their amorous business, and the white clouds floating up gladly through the blue air. Why, then, should he look askance at my book, which is no more than memories of my spring days? If the thing itself cannot be suppressed, why is it worth while to interfere with the recollection? What strange twist in his mind leads him to decry in art what he accepts in nature? A strange twist indeed, one which may be described as a sort of inverted sexuality, finding its pleasure not in the spring day, but in odd corners of ancient literature read only for the sake of passages which he declares to be disgusting, and in spying on modern literature, seeking out passages and expressions which might be denounced in the newspapers or proceeded against in the police court. The psychology of one of these purity mongers is more interesting to the alienist than to a man of letters. Let us take a typical case, that of the late Lord ——. Forty or fifty years ago he was one of the most strenuous advocates of purity in literature, and more shops were raided at his instigation than at any other; yet when he died his library was found to contain the finest collection of impure literature in Europe, and his executors were left wondering whether the prosecutions were prompted by a desire to increase the value of his collection by the destruction of rare books, copies of which were in his possession, or whether he had been moved by conscientious scruples; a man might bamboozle himself in this way: "I am a man of letters and possess these books because they are rare, a curious corner of literature, but it would be highly inexpedient for others to possess them." His conscience might take a still more curious turn, leading to a dizzier height: "I am a sinner; that, alas! is so; but I can prevent others from sinning likewise." No doubt the greater part of the literature which the noble lord collected with so much industry was of that frankly indecent kind which is debarred from every library, Continental as well as English and American. There is a literature which does not come within the scope of the present inquiry, and there is what may perhaps be called a border literature, books which are found in public libraries in the German, the French, and the Italian texts. It seems pertinent to ask why a little knowledge of French and German and Italian should procure the right to read Brantôme's "Femmes Gallantes." It would be difficult for anybody to say that this book is not frankly obscene, and yet in the French text I suppose every library contains it. Casanova's "Memoirs" is another book of the same kind; I am not aware of any complete translation of Boccaccio's tales, but every library possesses an edition in the original Italian. The only reason that can be put forward for the suppression of a book is that it is harmful, and if Brantôme, Casanova, and Boccaccio are harmful in English, they do harm to those who can read them in the original texts. But perhaps I have pointed out enough inconsistencies, and the reader, growing weary, may say: "Are you so young, then, that you don't know that the world is a mass of contradictions? that life is no more than a tale told by an idiot full of sound and fury, and signifying nothing?" Shakespeare did no more than to put into eloquent language every man's belief, that we are all mad on one subject or another. If this be so, every race is mad on some point, for have we not often heard that what is true of the individual is true of the race? Anglo-Saxon madness is book morality. Madness has been defined as a lack of consequence in ideas, and can anything be less consequent than—we need look no further back than Ibsen? The great genius who died in May last was decried by the English people as one of the most immoral of writers; for twenty years at least this opinion obtained in the press, and even among men of letters; suddenly the opinion disappeared, it went out like the flame of a candle; the text is the same, not a comma has been changed, yet now everybody reads it differently. But I must not allow myself to be drawn into speaking of the moral crusades directed against other writers; the task is tempting, and I hope it will be undertaken one of these days. Here, at all events, my concern is with my own writings, as indicated by the title of the article, and it is doubtful if reference to any book would make my point clearer than the tale of what happened in America to my own book, "Esther Waters." The proof sheets were sent in turn to three leading firms, Scribner, Harper, and Appleton, and all three refused the book on the ground that, while recognizing, etc., they did not think it was exactly the kind of book, etc. Even experts make mistakes; this is not denied; what makes my story so remarkable is that all three firms offered to publish an authorized edition of the book as soon as news of its success in England had been cabled to New York. Mr. Appleton, whom I met in Paris, expressed his regret that expert opinion regarding this book had been at fault. "The book," he said, "was quite a proper book to publish, a most admirable book, which would do honor to any firm." I answered: "Very likely all you say, Mr. Appleton, is true, but three weeks ago the experts thought differently. How is it that an immoral book can become moral in three weeks?" My next book, "Evelyn Innes," disturbed the house of Appleton as much as "Esther Waters," and a gentleman of leisure connected with the firm was deputed to mark out not the passages to which he himself took exception, but to which, being an expert, he felt sure that others would take exception. The gentleman was kind enough to insist on submitting his marked copy to me, and my wonderment increased as I turned over the pages, and it reached a climax when I happened upon the following passage, which had been marked to be omitted by the American printer. The passage was: "... in her stage life Evelyn was an agent of the sensual passion, not only with her voice, but in her arms, her neck, and hair, and in every expression of her face; and it was the craving music that had thrown her into Ulick's arms. If it had subjugated her how much more would it subjugate and hold within its persuasion the listener—the listener, who perceived in the music nothing but its sensuality?" "But for what reason," I asked the expert, "do you suggest the elimination of this passage? This is the Puritan point of view. I thought that your proposal was to draw my attention to the passages to which you thought the Puritan would object." "Ah," he said, "that is how I began, but as I got on with the work I thought it better to mark every passage that might give offense." "And to whom would this passage give offense?" I said.

"Certainly not to any religious body?" "No," he answered, "not to any religious body, but it would give offense to the subscribers to the New Opera House. If parents read that the music of 'Tristan' threw Evelyn Innes into the arms of Ulick Dean, they would not care to bring their daughters to hear the opera, and might possibly discontinue their subscriptions." Everybody will agree that "expert opinion" can hardly go further, yet the folly which this "expert" was betrayed into did not arise from any congenital stupidity; it is the mistake that you and I, every one of us, would make when we seek the truth in our casual experience instead of in our hearts.

One would have thought that my pointing out the absurdity of this expurgation of "Evelyn Innes" to the house of Appleton would have saved it ever afterwards from similar folly, and forgetful that experience is, as Coleridge describes it, only a lamp in a vessel's stern which throws a light on the waters we have passed through, none on those which lie before us, the publication of "The Lake" was issued by Messrs. Appleton with my consent. The book, as the American public already know, is free from all matter to which the most severe moralist could take exception, yet the American edition did not conform entirely with the English; a dedication written in French was omitted, for what reason I do not know, but it was omitted. The matter may seem a small one, and it may seem invidious to allude to it at all, but on an occasion like the present nothing must be passed over. The English proofs of the "Memoirs" were read, and the book was accepted, but when it was set up in America it did not seem quite so moral in the American type as it did in the English and difficulties arose; these have been alluded to in the first paragraph of this article, and perhaps wrongly I agreed that the two stories, "The Lovers of Orelay" and "In the Luxembourg Gardens," should be left out. On September 28th I wrote, suggesting that "In the Luxembourg Gardens" might be retained, that it was only necessary to drop out a few sentences to make it, as the expert would say, "acceptable to the American public," but it never occurred to me that "The Lovers of Orelay" could be published in any form except the form in which I wrote it. This morning I received a letter from Mr. Sears.

October 8, 1906. DEAR MR. MOORE:

Your letter of September 28th has just arrived this morning. I hope that by the time you receive this I shall have the open letter which we are to print in "Memoirs of My Dead Life." The book is all ready, waiting for it. As a matter of fact, we have not cut out either "In the Luxembourg Gardens" or "The Lovers of Orelay." We simply have taken out parts of each. Very truly yours, J. H. SEARS.

"Simply have taken out parts of each!" My book, then, is a sort of unfortunate animal, whose destiny was to be thrown on the American vivisecting table and pieces taken out of it. Well, I raise no objection. The promise that this preface will be published without alteration soothes me (it is the anaesthetic), and after all, is it not an honor to be Bowdlerized? Only the best are deemed dangerous.... I am not aware that anybody ever took liberties with Miss Braddon's texts. And the day of the Bowdlerizer is a brief one! Sooner or later the original text is published. This is the rule, and I am confident I shall not prove an exception to the rule.

GEORGE MOORE.

CHAPTER I

SPRING IN LONDON

As I sit at my window on Sunday morning, lazily watching the sparrows—restless black dots that haunt the old tree at the corner of King's Bench Walk—I begin to distinguish a faint green haze in the branches of the old lime. Yes, there it is green in the branches; and I'm moved by an impulse—the impulse of Spring is in my feet; india-rubber seems to have come into the soles of my feet, and I would see London. It is delightful to walk across Temple Gardens, to stop—pigeons are sweeping down from the roofs—to call a hansom, and to notice, as one passes, the sapling behind St. Clement's Danes. The quality of the green is exquisite on the smoke-black wall. London can be seen better on Sundays than on week-days; lying back in a hansom, one is alone with London. London is beautiful in that narrow street, celebrated for licentious literature. The blue and white sky shows above a seventeenth-century gable, and a few moments after we are in Drury Lane. The fine weather has enticed the population out of grim courts and alleys; skipping-ropes are whirling everywhere. The children hardly escape being run over. Coster girls sit wrapped in shawls, contentedly, like rabbits at the edge of a burrow; the men smoke their pipes in sullen groups, their eyes on the closed doors of the public house. At the corner of the great theatre a vendor of cheap ices is rapidly absorbing the few spare pennies of the neighbourhood. The hansom turns out of the lane into the great thoroughfare, a bright glow like the sunset fills the roadway, and upon it a triangular block of masonry and St. Giles's church rise, the spire aloft in the faint blue and delicate air. Spires are so beautiful that we would fain believe that they will outlast creeds; religion or no religion we must have spires, and in town and country—spires showing between trees and rising out of the city purlieus.

The spring tide is rising; the almond trees are in bloom, that one growing in an area spreads its Japanese decoration fan-like upon the wall. The hedges in the time-worn streets of Fitzroy Square light up—how the green runs along? The spring is more winsome here than in the country. One must be in London to see the spring. One can see the spring from afar dancing in St. John's wood, haze and sun playing together like a lad and a lass. The sweet air, how tempting! How exciting! It melts on the lips in fond kisses, instilling a delicate gluttony of life. It would be pleasant in these gardens walking through shadowy alleys, lit here and there by a ray, to see girls walking hand in hand, catching at branches, as girls do when dreaming of lovers. But alas! the gardens are empty; only some daffodils! But how beautiful is the curve of the flower when seen in profile, and still more beautiful is the starry yellow when the flower is seen full face. That antique flower carries my mind back—not to Greek times, for the daffodil has lost something of its ancient loveliness; it is more reminiscent of a Wedgwood than of a Greek vase. My nonsense thoughts amuse me; I follow my thoughts as a child follows butterflies; and all this ecstasy in and about me, is the joy of health—my health and the health of the world. This April day has set brain and blood on fire. Now it would be well to ponder by this old canal! It looks as if it had fallen into disuse, and that is charming; an abandoned canal is a perfect symbol of—well, I do not know of what. A river flows or rushes, even an artificial lake harbours waterfowl, children sail their boats upon it; but a canal does nothing.

Here comes a boat! The canal has not been abandoned. Ah! that boat has interrupted my dreams, and I feel quite wretched. I had hoped that the last had passed twenty years ago. Here it comes with its lean horse, the rope tightening and stretching, a great black mass with ripples at the prow and a figure bearing against the rudder. A canal reminds me of my childhood; every child likes a canal. A canal recalls the first wonder. We all remember the wonder with which we watched the first barge, the wonder which the smoke coming out of the funnel excited. When my father asked me why I'd like to go to Dublin better by canal than by railroad, I couldn't tell him. Nor could I tell any one to-day why I love a canal. One never loses one's fondness for canals. The boats glide like the days, and the toiling horse is a symbol! how he strains, sticking his toes into the path!

There are visits to pay. Three hours pass—of course women, always women. But at six I am free, and I resume my meditations in declining light as the cab rolls through the old brick streets that crowd round Golden Square; streets whose names you meet in old novels; streets full of studios where Hayden, Fuseli, and others of the rank historical tribe talked art with a big A, drank their despair away, and died wondering why the world did not recognise their genius. Children are scrambling round a neglected archway, striving to reach to a lantern of old time. The smell of these dry faded streets is peculiar to London; there is something of the odour of the original marsh in the smell of these streets; it rises through the pavement and mingles with the smoke. Fancy follows fancy, image succeeds image; till all is but a seeming, and mystery envelops everything. That white Arch seems to speak to me out of the twilight. I would fain believe it has its secret to reveal. London wraps herself in mists; blue scarfs are falling—trailing. London has a secret! Let me peer into her veiled face and read. I have only to fix my thoughts to decipher—what? I know not. Something ... perhaps. But I cannot control my thoughts. I am absorbed in turn by the beauty of the Marble Arch and the perspective of the Bayswater Road, fading like an apparition amid the romance of great trees.

As I turn away, for the wind thrills and obliges me to walk rapidly, I think how fortunate I am to experience these emotions in Hyde Park, whereas my fellows have to go to Switzerland and to climb up Mont Blanc, to feel half what I am feeling now, as I stand looking across the level park watching the sunset, a dusky one. The last red bar of light fades, and nothing remains but the grey park with the blue of the suburb behind it, flowing away full of mist and people, dim and mournful to the pallid lights of Kensington; and its crowds are like strips of black tape scattered here and there. By the railings the tape has been wound into a black ball, and, no doubt, the peg on which it is wound is some preacher promising human nature deliverance from evil if it will forego the spring time. But the spring time continues, despite the preacher, over yonder, under branches swelling with leaf and noisy with sparrows; the spring is there amid the boys and girls, boys dressed in ill-fitting suits of broadcloth, daffodils in their buttonholes; girls hardly less coarse, creatures made for work, escaped for a while from the thraldom of the kitchen, now doing the business of the world better than the preacher; poor servants of sacred Spring. A woman in a close-fitting green cloth dress passes me to meet a young man; a rich fur hangs from her shoulders; and they go towards Park Lane, towards the wilful little houses with low balconies and pendent flower-baskets swinging in the areas. Circumspect little gardens! There is one, Greek as an eighteenth-century engraving, and the woman in the close-fitting green cloth dress, rich fur hanging from her shoulders, almost hiding the pleasant waist, enters one of these. She is Park Lane. Park Lane supper parties and divorce are written in her eyes and manner. The old beau, walking swiftly lest he should catch cold, his moustache clearly dyed, his waist certainly pinched by a belt, he, too, is Park Lane. And those two young men, talking joyously—admirable specimens of Anglo-Saxons, slender feet, varnished boots, health and abundant youth—they, too, are characteristic of Park Lane.

Park Lane dips in a narrow and old-fashioned way as it enters Piccadilly. Piccadilly has not yet grown vulgar, only a little modern, a little out of keeping with the beauty of the Green Park, of that beautiful dell, about whose mounds I should like to see a comedy of the Restoration acted.

I used to stand here, at this very spot, twenty years ago, to watch the moonlight between the trees, and the shadows of the trees floating over that beautiful dell; I used to think of Wycherly's comedy, "Love in St. James's Park," and I think of it still. In those days the Argyle Rooms, Kate Hamilton's in Panton Street, and the Café de la Régence were the fashion. But Paris drew me from these, towards other pleasures, towards the Nouvelle Athènes and the Elysée Montmartre; and when I returned to London after an absence of ten years I found a new London, a less English London. Paris draws me still, and I shall be there in three weeks, when the chestnuts are in bloom.

CHAPTER II

FLOWERING NORMANDY

On my arrival in Paris, though the hour was that stupid hour of seven in the morning, while I walked up the grey platform, my head was filled with memories of the sea, for all the way across it had seemed like a beautiful blue plain without beginning or end, a plain on which the ship threw a little circle of light, moving always like life itself, with darkness before and after. I remembered how we steamed into the long winding harbour in the dusk, half an hour before we were due—at daybreak. Against the green sky, along the cliff's edge, a line of broken paling zigzagged; one star shone in the dawning sky, one reflection wavered in the tranquil harbour. There was no sound except the splashing of paddle-wheels, and not wind enough to take the fishing boats out to sea; the boats rolled in the tide, their sails only half-filled. From the deck of the steamer we watched the strange crews, wild-looking men and boys, leaning over the bulwarks; and I remembered how I had sought for the town amid the shadow, but nowhere could I discover trace of it; yet I knew it was there, smothered in the dusk, under the green sky, its streets leading to the cathedral, the end of every one crossed by flying buttresses, and the round roof disappearing amid the chimney-stacks. A curious, pathetic town, full of nuns and pigeons and old gables and strange dormer windows, and courtyards where French nobles once assembled—fish will be sold there in a few hours. Once I spent a summer in Dieppe. And during the hour we had to wait for the train, during the hour that we watched the green sky widening between masses of shrouding cloud, I thought of ten years ago. The town emerged very slowly, and only a few roofs were visible when the fisher girl clanked down the quays with a clumsy movement of the hips, and we were called upon to take our seats in the train. We moved along the quays, into the suburbs, and then into a quiet garden country of little fields and brooks and hillsides breaking into cliffs. The fields and the hills were still shadowless and grey, and even the orchards in bloom seemed sad. But what shall I say of their beauty when the first faint lights appeared, when the first rose clouds appeared above the hills? Orchard succeeded orchard, and the farmhouses were all asleep. There is no such journey in the world as the journey from Dieppe to Paris on a fine May morning. Never shall I forget the first glimpse of Rouen Cathedral in the diamond air, the branching river, and the tall ships anchored in the deep current. I was dreaming of the cathedral when we had left Rouen far behind us, and when I awoke from my dream we were in the midst of a flat green country, the river winding about islands and through fields in which stood solitary poplar-trees, formerly haunts of Corot and Daubigny. I could see the spots where they had set their easels—that slight rise with the solitary poplar for Corot, that rich river bank and shady backwater for Daubigny. Soon after I saw the first weir, and then the first hay-boat; and at every moment the river grew more serene, more gracious, it passed its arms about a flat, green-wooded island, on which there was a rookery; and sometimes we saw it ahead of us, looping up the verdant landscape as if it were a gown, running through it like a white silk ribbon, and over there the green gown disappearing in fine muslin vapours, drawn about the low horizon.

I did not weary of this landscape, and was sorry when the first villa appeared. Another and then another showed between the chestnut-trees in bloom; and there were often blue vases on the steps and sometimes lanterns in metalwork hung from wooden balconies. The shutters were not yet open, those heavy French shutters that we all know so well, and that give the French houses such a look of comfort, of ease, of long tradition. Suddenly the aspect of a street struck me as a place I had known, and I said, "Is it possible that we are passing through Asnières?" The name flitted past, and I was glad I had recognised Asnières, for at the end of that very long road is the restaurant where we used to dine, and between it and the bridge is the *bal* where we used to dance. It was there I saw the beautiful Blanche D'Antigny surrounded by her admirers. It was there she used to sit by the side of the composer of the musical follies which she sang—in those days I thought she sang enchantingly. Those were the days of L'Oeil, Crevé, and Chilpéric. She once passed under the chestnut-trees of that dusty little *bal de banlieue* with me by her side, proud of being with her. She has gone and Julia Baron has gone; Hortense has outlived them all. She must be very old, eighty-five at least. It would be wonderful to hear her sing "Mon cher amant, je te jure" in the quavering voice of eighty-five; it would be wonderful to hear her sing it because she doesn't know how wonderful she is; the old light of love requires an interpreter, and she has had many; many great poets have voiced her woe and decadence.

Not five minutes from that *bal* was the little house in which Hervé lived, and to which he used to invite us to supper; and where, after supper, he used to play to us the last music he had composed. We listened, but the public would listen to it no longer. Sedan had taken all the tinkle out of it, and the poor *compositeur toqué* never caught the public ear again. We listened to his chirpy scores, believing that they would revive that old nervous fever which was the Empire when Hortense used to dance, when Hortense took the Empire for a spring-board, when Paris cried out, "Cascade ma fille, Hortense, cascade." The great Hortense Schneider, the great goddess of folly, used to come down there to sing the songs which were intended to revive her triumphs. She was growing old then, her days were over, and Hervé's day was over. Vainly did he pile parody upon parody; vainly did he seize the conductor's *bâton*; the days of their glory had gone. Now Asnières itself is forgotten; the modern youth has chosen another suburb to disport himself in; the ballroom has been pulled down, and never again will an orchestra play a note of these poor scores; even their names are unknown. A few bars of a chorus of pages came back to me, remembered only by me, all are gone, like Hortense and Blanche and Julia.

But after all I am in Paris. Almost the same Paris; almost the same George Moore, my senses awake as before to all enjoyment, my soul as enwrapped as ever in the divine sensation of life. Once my youth moved through thy whiteness, O City, and its dreams lay down to dreams in the freedom of thy fields! Years come and years go, but every year I see city and plain in the happy exaltation of Spring, and departing before the cuckoo, while the blossom is still bright on the bough, it has come to me to think that Paris and May are one.

CHAPTER III

A WAITRESS

Feeling that he would never see Scotland again, Stevenson wrote in a preface to "Catriona":—"I see like a vision the youth of my father, and of his father, and the whole stream of lives flowing down there far in the north, with the sound of laughter and tears, to cast me out in the end, as by a sudden freshet, on these ultimate islands. And I admire and bow my head before the romance of destiny." Does not this sentence read as if it were written in stress of some effusive febrile emotion, as if he wrote while still pursuing his idea? And so it reminds us of a moth fluttering after a light. But however vacillating, the sentence contains some pretty clauses, and it will be remembered though not perhaps in its original form. We shall forget the "laughter and the tears" and the "sudden freshet," and a simpler phrase will form itself in our memories. The emotion that Stevenson had to express transpires only in the words, "romance of destiny, ultimate islands." Who does not feel his destiny to be a romance, and who does not admire the ultimate island whither his destiny will cast him? Giacomo Cenci, whom the Pope ordered to be flayed alive, no doubt admired the romance of destiny that laid him on his ultimate island, a raised plank, so that the executioner might conveniently roll up the skin of his belly like an apron. And a hare that I once saw beating a tambourine in Regent Street looked at me so wistfully that I am sure it admired in some remote way the romance of destiny that had taken it from the woodland and cast it upon its ultimate island—in this case a barrow. But neither of these strange examples of the romance of destiny seems to me more wonderful than the destiny of a wistful Irish girl whom I saw serving drinks to students in a certain ultimate café in the Latin Quarter; she, too, no doubt, admired the destiny which had cast her out, ordaining that she should die amid tobacco smoke, serving drinks to students, entertaining them with whatever conversation they desired.

Gervex, Mademoiselle D'Avary, and I had gone to this café after the theatre for half an hour's distraction; I had thought that the place seemed too rough for Mademoiselle D'Avary, but Gervex had said that we should find a quiet corner, and we had happened to choose one in charge of a thin, delicate girl, a girl touched with languor, weakness, and a grace which interested and moved me; her cheeks were thin, and the deep grey eyes were wistful as a drawing of Rossetti; her waving brown hair fell over the temples, and was looped up low over the neck after the Rossetti fashion. I had noticed how the two women looked at each other, one woman healthful and rich, the other poor and ailing; I had guessed the thought that passed across their minds. Each had doubtless asked and wondered why life had come to them so differently. But first I must tell who was Mademoiselle D'Avary, and how I came to know her. I had gone to Tortoni, a once-celebrated cafe at the corner of the Rue Taitbout, the dining place of Rossini. When Rossini had earned an income of two thousand pounds a year it is recorded that he said: "Now I've done with music, it has served its turn, and I'm going to dine every day at Tortoni's." Even in my time Tortoni was the rendezvous of the world of art and letters; every one was there at five o'clock, and to Tortoni I went the day I arrived in Paris. To be seen there would make known the fact that I was in Paris. Tortoni was a sort of publication. At Tortoni I had discovered a young man, one of my oldest friends, a painter of talent—he had a picture in the Luxembourg—and a man who was beloved by women. Gervex, for it was he, had seized me by the hand, and with voluble eagerness had told me that I was the person he was seeking: he had heard of my coming and had sought me in every cafe from the Madeleine to Tortoni. He had been seeking me because he wished to ask me to dinner to meet Mademoiselle D'Avary; we were to fetch her in the Rue des Capucines. I write the name of the street, not because it matters to my little story in what street she lived, but because the name is an evocation. Those who like Paris like to hear the names of the streets, and the long staircase turning closely up the painted walls, the brown painted doors on the landings, and the bell rope, are evocative of Parisian life; and Mademoiselle D'Avary is herself an evocation, for she was an actress of the Palais Royal. My friend, too, is an evocation, he was one of those whose pride is not to spend money upon women, whose theory of life is that "If she likes to come round to the studio when one's work is done, *nous pouvons faire la fête ensemble.*" But however defensible this view of life may be, and there is much to be said for it, I had thought that he might have refrained from saying when I looked round the drawing-room admiring it—a drawing-room furnished with sixteenth-century bronzes, Dresden figures, *étagères* covered with silver ornaments, three drawings by Boucher—Boucher in three periods, a French Boucher, a Flemish Boucher, and an Italian Boucher—that I must not think that any of these things were presents from him, and from saying when she came into the room that the bracelet on her arm was not from him. It had seemed to me in slightly bad taste that he should remind her that he made no presents, for his remark had clouded her joyousness; I could see that she was not so happy at the thought of going out to dine with him as she had been.

It was *chez Foyoz* that we dined, an old-fashioned restaurant still free from the new taste that likes walls painted white and gold, electric lamps and fiddlers. After dinner we had gone to see a play next door at the Odéon, a play in which shepherds spoke to each other about singing brooks, and stabbed each other for false women, a play diversified with vintages, processions, wains, and songs. Nevertheless it had not interested us. And during the *entr'actes* Gervex had paid visits in various parts of the house, leaving Mademoiselle D'Avary to make herself agreeable to me. I dearly love to walk by the perambulator in which Love is wheeling a pair of lovers. After the play he had said, "Allons boire un bock," and we had turned into a students' café, a café furnished with tapestries and oak tables, and old-time jugs and Medicis gowns, a café in which a student occasionally caught up a tall bock in his teeth, emptied it at a gulp, and after turning head over heels, walked out without having smiled. Mademoiselle D'Avary's beauty and fashion had drawn the wild eyes of all the students gathered there. She wore a flower-enwoven dress, and from under the large hat her hair showed dark as night; and her southern skin filled with rich tints, yellow and dark green where the hair grew scanty on the neck; the shoulders drooped into opulent suggestion in the lace bodice. And it was interesting to compare her ripe beauty with the pale deciduous beauty of the waitress. Mademoiselle D'Avary sat, her fan wide-spread across her bosom, her lips parted, the small teeth showing between the red lips. The waitress sat, her thin arms leaning on the table, joining very prettily in the conversation, betraying only in one glance that she knew that she was only a failure and Mademoiselle D'Avary a success. It was some time before the ear caught the slight accent; an accent that was difficult to trace to any country. Once I heard a southern intonation, and then a northern; finally I heard an unmistakable English intonation, and said:

"But you're English."

"I'm Irish. I'm from Dublin."

And thinking of a girl reared in its Dublin conventions, but whom the romance of destiny had cast upon this ultimate café, I asked her how she had found her way here; and she told me she had left Dublin when she was sixteen; she had come to Paris six years ago to take a situation as nursery governess. She used to go with the children into the Luxembourg Gardens and talk to them in English. One day a student had sat on the bench beside her. The rest of the story is easily guessed. But he had no money to keep her, and she had to come to this café to earn her living.

"It doesn't suit me, but what am I to do? One must live, and the tobacco smoke makes me cough." I sat looking at her, and she must have guessed what was passing in my mind, for she told me that one lung was gone; and we spoke of health, of the South, and she said that the doctor had advised her to go away south.

Seeing that Gervex and Mademoiselle D'Avary were engaged in conversation, I leaned forward and devoted all my attention to this wistful Irish girl, so interesting in her phthisis, in her red Medicis gown, her thin arms showing in the long rucked sleeves. I had to offer her drink; to do so was the custom of the place. She said that drink harmed her, but she would get into trouble if she refused drink; perhaps I would not mind paying for a piece of beef-steak instead. She had been ordered raw steak! I have only to close my eyes to see her going over to the corner of the cafe and cutting a piece and putting it away. She said she would eat it before going to bed, and that would be two hours hence, about three. While talking to her I thought of a cottage in the South amid olive and orange trees, an open window full of fragrant air, and this girl sitting by it.

"I should like to take you south and attend upon you."

"I'm afraid you would grow weary of nursing me. And I should be able to give you very little in return for your care. The doctor says I'm not to love any one." We must have talked for some time, for it was like waking out of a dream when Gervex and Mademoiselle D'Avary got up to go, and, seeing how interested I was, he laughed, saying to Mademoiselle D'Avary that it would be kind to leave me with my new friend. His pleasantry jarred, and though I should like to have remained, I followed them into the street, where the moon was shining over the Luxembourg Gardens. And as I have said before, I dearly love to walk by a perambulator in which Love is wheeling a pair of lovers: but it is sad to find oneself alone on the pavement at midnight. Instead of going back to the café I wandered on, thinking of the girl I had seen, and of her certain death, for she could not live many months in that café. We all want to think at midnight, under the moon, when the city looks like a black Italian engraving, and poems come to us as we watch a swirling river. Not only the idea of a poem came to me that night, but on the Pont Neuf the words began to sing together, and I jotted down the first lines before going to bed. Next morning I continued my poem, and all day was passed in this little composition.

> We are alone! Listen, a little while,
> And hear the reason why your weary smile
> And lute-toned speaking are so very sweet,
> And how my love of you is more complete
> Than any love of any lover. They
> Have only been attracted by the grey
> Delicious softness of your eyes, your slim
> And delicate form, or some such other whim,
> The simple pretexts of all lovers;—I
> For other reason. Listen whilst I try
> To say. I joy to see the sunset slope
> Beyond the weak hours' hopeless horoscope,
> Leaving the heavens a melancholy calm
> Of quiet colour chaunted like a psalm,
> In mildly modulated phrases; thus
> Your life shall fade like a voluptuous
> Vision beyond the sight, and you shall die
> Like some soft evening's sad serenity....
> I would possess your dying hours; indeed
> My love is worthy of the gift, I plead
> For them. Although I never loved as yet,
> Methinks that I might love you; I would get
> From out the knowledge that the time was brief,
> That tenderness, whose pity grows to grief,
> And grief that sanctifies, a joy, a charm
> Beyond all other loves, for now the arm
> Of Death is stretched to you-ward, and he claims
> You as his bride. Maybe my soul misnames
> Its passion; love perhaps it is not, yet
> To see you fading like a violet,
> Or some sweet thought, would be a very strange
> And costly pleasure, far beyond the range
> Of formal man's emotion. Listen, I

Memoirs of My Dead Life

> Will chose a country spot where fields of rye
> And wheat extend in rustling yellow plains,
> Broken with wooded hills and leafy lanes,
> To pass our honeymoon; a cottage where
> The porch and windows are festooned with fair
> Green leaves of eglantine, and look upon
> A shady garden where we'll walk alone
> In the autumn summer evenings; each will see
> Our walks grow shorter, till to the orange tree,
> The garden's length, is far, and you will rest
> From time to time, leaning upon my breast
> Your languid lily face, then later still
> Unto the sofa by the window-sill
> Your wasted body I shall carry, so
> That you may drink the last left lingering glow
> Of evening, when the air is filled with scent
> Of blossoms; and my spirits shall be rent
> The while with many griefs. Like some blue day
> That grows more lovely as it fades away,
> Gaining that calm serenity and height
> Of colour wanted, as the solemn night
> Steals forward you will sweetly fall asleep
> For ever and for ever; I shall weep
> A day and night large tears upon your face,
> Laying you then beneath a rose-red place
> Where I may muse and dedicate and dream
> Volumes of poesy of you; and deem
> It happiness to know that you are far
> From any base desires as that fair star
> Set in the evening magnitude of heaven.
> Death takes but little, yea, your death has given
> Me that deep peace and immaculate possession
> Which man may never find in earthly passion.

Good poetry of course not, but good verse, well turned every line except the penultimate. The elision is not a happy one, and the mere suppression of the "and" does not produce a satisfying line.

> Death takes but little, Death I thank for giving
> Me a remembrance, and a pure possession
> Of unrequited love.

And mumbling the last lines of the poem, I hastened to the café near the Luxembourg Gardens, wondering if I should find courage to ask the girl to come away to the South and live, fearing that I should not, fearing it was the idea rather than the deed that tempted me; for the soul of a poet is not the soul of Florence Nightingale. I was sorry for this wistful Irish girl, and was hastening to her, I knew not why; not to show her the poem—the very thought was intolerable. Often did I stop on the way to ask myself why I was going, and on what errand. Without discovering an answer in my heart I hastened on, feeling, I suppose, in some blind way that my quest was in my own heart. I would know if it were capable of making a sacrifice; and sitting down at one of her tables I waited, but she did not come, and I asked the student by me if he knew the girl generally in charge of these tables. He said he did, and told me about her case. There was no hope for her; only a transfusion of blood could save her; she was almost bloodless. He described how blood could be taken from the arm of a healthy man and passed into the veins of the almost bloodless. But as he spoke things began to get dim and his voice to grow faint; I heard some one saying, "You're very pale," and he ordered some brandy for me. The South could not save her; practically nothing could; and I returned home thinking of her.

Twenty years have passed, and I am thinking of her again. Poor little Irish girl! Cast out in the end by a sudden freshet on an ultimate café. Poor little heap of bones! And I bow my head and admire the romance of destiny which ordained that I, who only saw her once, should be the last to remember her. Perhaps I should have forgotten her had it not been that I wrote a poem, a poem which I now inscribe and dedicate to her nameless memory.

CHAPTER IV

THE END OF MARIE PELLEGRIN

Octave Barrès liked his friends to come to his studio, and a few of us who believed in his talent used to drop in during the afternoon, and little by little I got to know every picture, every sketch; but one never knows everything that a painter has done, and one day, coming into the studio, I caught sight of a full-length portrait I had never seen before on the easel.

"It was in the back room turned to the wall," he said. "I took it out, thinking that the Russian prince who ordered the Pegasus decoration might buy it," and he turned away, not liking to hear my praise of it; for it neither pleases a painter to hear his early works praised nor abused. "I painted it before I knew how to paint," and standing before me, his palette in his hand, he expounded his new aestheticism: that up to the beginning of the nineteenth century all painting had been done first in monochrome and then glazed, and what we know as solid painting had been invented by Greuze. One day in the Louvre he had perceived something in Delacroix, something not wholly satisfactory; this something had set him thinking. It was Rubens, however, who had revealed the secret! It was Rubens who had taught him how to paint! He admitted that there was danger in retracing one's steps, in beginning one's education over again; but what help was there for it, since painting was not taught in the schools.

I had heard all he had to say before, and could not change my belief that every man must live in the ideas of his time, be they good or bad. It is easy to say that we must only adopt Rubens's method and jealously guard against any infringement on our personality; but in art our personality is determined by the methods we employ, and Octave's portrait interested me more than the Pegasus decoration, or the three pink Venuses holding a basket of flowers above their heads. The portrait was crude and violent, but so was the man that had painted it; he had painted it when he was a disciple of Manet's, and the methods of Manet were in agreement with my friend's temperament. We are all impressionists to-day; we are eager to note down what we feel and see; and the carefully prepared rhetorical manner of Rubens was as incompatible with Octave's temperament as the manner of John Milton is with mine. There was a thought of Goya in the background, in the contrast between the grey and the black, and there was something of Manet's simplifications in the face, but these echoes were faint, nor did they matter, for they were of our time. In looking at his model he had seen and felt something; he had noted this harshly, crudely, but he noted it; and to do this, is after all the main thing. His sitter had inspired him. The word "inspired" offended him; I withdrew it; I said that he had been fortunate in his model, and he admitted that: to see that thin, olive-complexioned girl with fine delicate features and blue-black hair lying close about her head like feathers—she wore her hair as a blackbird wears his wing—compelled one to paint; and after admiring the face I admired the black silk dress he had painted her in, a black silk dress covered with black lace. She wore grey pearls in her ears, and pearls upon her neck.

I was interested in the quality of the painting, so different from Octave's present painting, but I was more interested in the woman herself. The picture revealed to me something in human nature that I had never seen before, something that I had never thought of. The soul in this picture was so intense that I forgot the painting, and began to think of her. She was unlike any one I had ever met in Octave Barrès's studio; a studio beloved of women; the women one met there seemed to be of all sorts, but in truth they were all of a sort. They began to arrive about four o'clock in the afternoon, and they stayed on until they were sent away. He allowed them to play the piano and sing to him; he allowed them, as he would phrase it, to *grouiller* about the place, and they talked of the painters they had sat to, of their gowns, and they showed us their shoes and their garters. He heeded them hardly at all, walking to and fro thinking of his painting, of his archaic painting. I often wondered if his appearance counted for anything in his renunciation of modern methods, and certainly his appearance was a link of association; he did not look like a modern man, but like a sixteenth-century baron; his beard and his broken nose and his hierarchial air contributed to the resemblance; the jersey he wore reminded one of a cuirass, a coat of mail. Even in his choice of a dwelling-place he seemed instinctively to avoid the modern; he had found a studio in the street, the name of which no one had ever heard before; it was found with difficulty; and the studio, too, it was hidden behind great crumbling walls, in the middle of a plot of ground in which some one was growing cabbages. Octave was always, as he would phrase it, *dans une dèche épouvantable*, but he managed to keep a thoroughbred horse in the stable at the end of the garden, and this horse was ordered as soon as the light failed. He would say, "Mes amis et mes amies, je regrette, mais mon cheval m'attend." And the women liked to see him mount, and many thought, I am sure, that he looked like a Centaur as he rode away.

But who was this refined girl? this—a painting tells things that cannot be translated into words—this olive-skinned girl who might have sat to Raphael for a Virgin, so different from Octave's usual women? They were of the Montmartre kin; but this woman might be a Spanish princess. And remembering that Octave had said he had taken out the portrait hoping that the Russian who had ordered the Pegasus might buy it, the thought struck me that she might be the prince's mistress. His mistress! Oh, what fabulous fortune! What might her history be? I burned to hear it, and wearied of Octave's seemingly endless chatter about his method of painting; I had heard all he was saying many times before, but I listened to it all again, and to propitiate him I regretted that the picture was not painted in his present manner, "for there are good things in the picture," I said, "and the model—you seem to have been lucky with your model."

"Yes, she was nice to paint from, but it was difficult to get her to sit. A *concierge's* daughter—you wouldn't think it, would you?" My astonishment amused him, and he began to laugh. "You don't know her?" he said. "That is Marie Pellegrin," and when I asked him where he had met her he told me, at Alphonsine's; but I did not know where Alphonsine's was.

"I'm going to dine there to-night. I'm going to meet her; she's going back to Russia with the prince; she has been staying in the Quartier Bréda on her holiday. *Sacré nom!* Half-past five, and I haven't washed my brushes yet!"

In answer to my question, what he meant by going to the Quartier Bréda for a holiday, he said:

"I'll tell you all about that in the carriage."

But no sooner had we got into the carriage than he remembered that he must leave word for a woman who had promised to sit to him, and swearing that a message would not delay us for more than a few minutes he directed the coachman. We were shown into a drawing-room, and the lady ran out of her bedroom, wrapping herself as she ran in a *peignoir*, and the sitting was discussed in the middle of a polished *parquet* floor. We at last returned to the carriage, but we were hardly seated when he remembered another appointment. He scribbled notes in the lodges of the *concierges*, and between whiles told me all he knew of the story of Marie Pellegrin. This delicate woman that I had felt could not be of the Montmartre kin was the daughter of a *concierge* on the Boulevard Extérieur. She had run away from home at fifteen, had danced at the Elysée Montmartre.

> Sa jupe avait des trous,
> Elle aimait des voyous,
> Ils ont des yeux si doux.

But one day a Russian prince had caught sight of her, and had built her a palace in the Champs Elysées; but the Russian prince and his palace bored her.

The stopping of the carriage interrupted Octave's narrative. "Here we are," he said, seizing a bell hanging on a jangling wire, and the green door in the crumbling wall opened, and I saw an undersized woman—I saw Alphonsine! And her portrait, a life-sized caricature drawn by Octave, faced me from the white-washed wall of the hen-coop. He had drawn her two cats purring about her legs, and had written under it, "Ils viennent après le mou." Her garden was a gravelled space; I think there was one tree in it. A tent had been stretched from wall to wall; and a seedy-looking waiter laid the tables (there were two), placing bottles of wine in front of each knife and fork, and bread in long sticks at regular intervals. He was constantly disturbed by the ringing of the bell, and had to run to the door to admit the company. Here and there I recognised faces that I had already seen in the studio; Clementine, who last year was studying the part of Elsa and this year was singing, "La femme de feu, la cui, la cui, la cuisinière," in a *café chantant*; and Margaret Byron, who had just retreated from Russia—a disastrous campaign hers was said to have been. The greater number were *hors concours*, for Alphonsine's was to the aged courtesan what Chelsea Hospital is to the aged soldier. It was a sort of human garden full of the sound and colour of October.

I scrutinised the crowd. How could any one of these women interest the woman whose portrait I had seen in Barrès's studio? That one, for instance, whom I saw every morning in the Rue des Martyres, in a greasy *peignoir*, going marketing, a basket on her arm. Search as I would I could not find a friend for Marie among the women nor a lover among the men—neither of those two stout middle-aged men with large whiskers, who had probably once been stockbrokers, nor the withered journalist whom I heard speaking to Octave about a duel he had fought recently; nor the little sandy Scotchman whose French was not understood by the women and whose English was nearly unintelligible to me; nor the man who looked like a head-waiter— Alphonsine's lover; he had been a waiter, and he told you with the air of Napoleon describing Waterloo that he had "created" a certain fashionable café on the Boulevard. I could not attribute any one of these men to Marie; and Octave spoke of her with indifference; she had interested him to paint, and now he hoped she would get the Russian to buy her picture.

"But she's not here," I said.

"She'll be here presently," Octave answered, and he went on talking to Clementine, a fair pretty woman whom one saw every night at the *Rat Mort*. It was when the soup-plates were being taken away that I saw a young woman dressed in black coming across the garden.

It was she, Marie Pellegrin.

She wore a dress similar to the one she wore in her portrait, a black silk covered with lace, and her black hair was swathed about her shapely little head. She was her portrait and something more. Her smile was her own, a sad little smile that seemed to come out of a depth of her being, and her voice was a little musical voice, irresponsible as a bird's, and during dinner I noticed how she broke into speech abruptly as a bird breaks into song, and she stopped as abruptly. I never saw a woman so like herself, and sometimes her beauty brought a little mist into my eyes, and I lost sight of her or very nearly, and I went on eating mechanically. Dinner seemed to end suddenly, and before I knew that it was over we were getting up from table.

As we went towards the house where coffee was being served, Marie asked me if I played cards, but I excused myself, saying that I would prefer to sit and look at her; and just then a thin woman with red hair, who had arrived at the same time as Marie and who had sat next her at dinner, was introduced to me, and I was told that she was Marie's intimate friend, and that the two lived together whenever Marie returned to Montmartre. She was known as *La Glue*, her real name was Victorine, she had sat for Manet's picture of Olympe, but that was years ago. The face was thinner, but I recognised the red hair and the brown eyes, small eyes set closely, reminding one of *des petits verres de cognac*. Her sketch-book was being passed round, and as it came into my hands I noticed that she did not wear stays and was dressed in old grey woollen. She lit cigarette after cigarette, and leaned over Marie with her arm about her shoulder, advising her what cards to play. The game was baccarat, and in a little while I saw that Marie was losing a great deal of money, and a little later I saw *La Glue* trying to persuade her away from the card-table.

"One more deal." That deal lost her the last louis she had placed on the table. "Some one will have to pay my cab," she said.

We were going to the Elysée Montmartre, and Alphonsine lent her a couple of louis, *pour passer sa soirée*, and we all went away in carriages, the little horses straining up the steep streets; the plumes of the women's hats floating over the carriage hoods. Marie was in one of the front carriages, and was waiting for us on the high steps leading from the street to the *bal*.

"It's my last night," she said, "the last night I shall see the Elysée for many a month."

"You'll soon be back again?"

"You see, I have been offered five hundred thousand francs to go to Russia for three years. Fancy three years without seeing the Elysée," and she looked round as an angel might look upon Paradise out of which she is about to be driven. "The trees are beautiful," she said, "they're like a fairy tale," and that is exactly what they were like, rising into the summer darkness, unnaturally green above the electric lights. In the middle of a circle of white globes the orchestra played upon an *estrade*, and everyone whirled his partner as if she were a top. "I always sit over there under the trees in the angle," she said; and she was about to invite me to come and sit with her when her attention was distracted from me; for the people had drawn together into groups, and I heard everybody whispering: "That's Marie Pellegrin." Seeing her coming, her waiter with much ostentation began to draw aside tables and chairs, and in a few minutes she was sitting under her tree, she and *La Glue* together, their friends about them, Marie distributing absinthe, brandy, and cigarettes. A little procession suddenly formed under the trees and came towards her, and Marie was presented with a great basket of flowers, and all her company with bouquets; and a little cheer went up from different parts of the *bal*, "Vive Marie Pellegrin, la reine de l'Elysée."

The music began again, the people rushed to see a quadrille where two women, with ease, were kicking off men's hats; and while watching them I heard that a special display of fireworks had been arranged in Marie's honour, the news having got about that this was her last night at the Elysée. A swishing sound was heard; the rocket rose to its height high up in the thick sky. Then it dipped over, the star fell a little way and burst: it melted into turquoise blue, and changed to ruby red, beautiful as the colour of flowers, roses or tulips. The falling fire changed again and again. And Marie stood on a chair and watched till the last sparks vanished.

"Doesn't she look like my picture now?" said Octave.

"You seemed to have divined her soul."

He shrugged his shoulders contemptuously. "I'm not a psychologist; I am a painter. But I must get a word with her," and with a carelessness that was almost insolence, he pushed his way into the crowd and called her, saying he wanted to speak to her; and they walked round the *bal* together. I could not understand his indifference to her charm, and asked myself if he had always been so indifferent. In a little while they returned.

"I'll do my best," I heard her say; and she ran back to join her companions.

"I suppose you've seen enough of the Elysée?"

"Ah! qu'elle est jolie ce soir; et elle ferait joliment marcher le Russe."

We walked on in silence. Octave did not notice that he had said anything to jar my feelings; he was thinking of his portrait, and presently he said that he was sorry she was going to Russia. "I should like to begin another portrait, now that I have learned to paint."

"Do you think she'll go to Russia?"

"Yes, she'll go there; but she'll come back one of these days, and I'll get her to sit again. It is extraordinary how little is known of the art of painting; the art is forgotten. The old masters did perfectly in two days what we spend weeks fumbling at. In two days Rubens finished his *grisaille*, and the glazing was done with certainty, with skill, with ease in half an hour! He could get more depth of colour with a glaze than any one can to-day, however much paint is put on the canvas. The old masters had method; now there's none. One brush as well as another, rub the paint up or down, it doesn't matter so long as the canvas is covered. Manet began it, and Cézanne has— well, filed the petition: painting is bankrupt."

I listened to him a little wearily, for I had heard all he was saying many times before; but Octave always talked as he wanted to talk, and this evening he wanted to talk of painting, not of Marie, and I was glad when we came to the spot where our ways parted.

"You know that the Russian is coming to the studio to-morrow; I hope he'll buy the portrait."

"I hope he will," I said. "I'd buy it myself if I could afford it."

"I'd prefer you to have something I have done since, unless it be the woman you're after ... but one minute. You're coming to sit to me the day after to-morrow?"

"Yes," I said, "I'll come."

"And then I'll be able to tell you if he has bought the picture."

Three days afterwards I asked Octave on the threshold if the Russian had bought the portrait, and he told me nothing had been definitely settled yet.

Marie had gone to St. Petersburg with the prince, and this was the last news I had of her for many months. But a week rarely passed without something happening to remind me of her. One day a books of travels in Siberia opened at a passage telling how a boy belonging to a tribe of Asiatic savages had been taken from his deserts, where he had been found deserted and dying, and brought to Moscow. The gentleman who had found him adopted and educated him, and the reclaimed savage became in time a fashionable young man about town, betraying no trace of his origin until one day he happened to meet one of his tribe. The man had come to Moscow to sell skins; and the smell of the skins awoke a longing for the desert. The reclaimed savage grew melancholy; his adopted father tried in vain to overcome the original instinct; presents of money did not soothe his homesickness. He disappeared, and was not heard of for years until one day a caravan came back with the news of a man among the savages who had betrayed himself by speaking French. On being questioned, he denied any knowledge of French; he said he had never been to St. Petersburg, nor did he wish to go there. And what was this story but the story of Marie Pellegrin, who, when weary of Russian princes and palaces, returned for her holiday to the Quartier Bréda? A few days afterwards I heard in Barrès's studio that she had escaped from Russia; and that evening I went to Alphonsine's to dinner, hoping to see her there. But she was not there. There was no one there except Clementine and the two stockbrokers; and I waited eagerly for news of her. I did not like to mention her name, and the dreary dinner was nearly over before her name was mentioned. I heard that she was ill; no, not dying, but very ill. Alphonsine gave me her address; a little higher up on the same side as the Cirque Fernando, nearly facing the Elysée Montmartre. The number I could inquire out, she said, and I went away in a cab up the steep and stony Rue des Martyres, noticing the café and then the *brasserie* and a little higher up the fruit-seller and the photographer. When the mind is at stress one notices the casual, and mine was at stress, and too agitated to think. The first house we stopped at happened to be the right one, and the *concierge* said, "The fourth floor." As I went upstairs I thought of *La Glue*, of her untidy dress and her red hair, and it was she who answered the bell and asked me into an unfurnished drawing-room, and we stood by the chimneypiece.

"She's talking of going to the Elysée to-night. Won't you come in? She'd like to see you. There are three or four of us here. You know them. Clementine, Margaret Byron?" And she mentioned some other names that I did not remember, and opening a door she cried: "Marie, here's a visitor for you, a gentleman from Alphonsine's. You know, dear, the Englishman, Octave Barrès's friend."

Memoirs of My Dead Life

She gave me her hand, and I held it a long while.

"Comme les Anglais sont gentils. Dès qu'on est malade—"

I don't think Marie finished the sentence, if she did I did not hear her; but I remember quite well that she spoke of my distaste for cards.

"You didn't play that night at Alphonsine's when I lost all my money. You preferred to look at Victorine's drawings. She has done some better ones. Go and look at them, and let's finish our game. Then I'll talk to you. So you heard about me at Alphonsine's? They say I'm very ill, don't they? But now that I've come back I'll soon get well. I'm always well at Montmartre, amn't I, Victorine?" "Nous ne sommes pas installés encore," Marie said, referring to the scarcity of furniture, and to the clock and candelabra which stood on the floor. But if there were too few chairs, there was a good deal of money and jewellery among the bed-clothes; and Marie toyed with this jewellery during the games. She wore large lace sleeves, and the thin arms showed delicate and slight when she raised them to change her ear-rings. Her small beauty, fashioned like an ivory, contrasted with the coarse features about her, and the little nose with beautifully shaped nostrils, above all the mouth fading at the ends into faint indecisions. Every now and then a tenderness came over her face; Octave had seen the essential in her, whatever he might say; he had painted herself—her soul; and Marie's soul rose up like a water-flower in her eyes, and then the soul sank out of sight, and I saw another Marie, *une grue*, playing cards with five others from Alphonsine's, losing her money and her health. A bottle of absinthe stood on a beautiful Empire table that her prince had given her, and Bijou, Clementine's little dog, slept on an embroidered cushion. Bijou was one of those dear little Japanese or Chinese spaniels, those dogs that are like the King Charles. She was going to have puppies, and I was stroking her silky coat thinking of her coming trouble, when I suddenly heard Clementine's voice raised above the others, and looking up I saw a great animation in her face; I heard that the cards had not been fairly dealt, and then the women threw their cards aside, and *La Glue* told Clementine that she was not wanted, that *elle ferait bien de débarrasser les planches,* that was the expression she used. I heard further accusations, and among them the plaintive voice of Marie begging of me not to believe what they said. The women caught each other by the hair, and tore at each other's faces, and Marie raised herself up in bed and implored them to cease; and then she fell back crying. For a moment it seemed as if they were going to sit down to cards again, but suddenly everybody snatched her own money and then everybody snatched at the money within her reach; and, calling each other thieves, they struggled through the door, and I heard them quarrelling all the way down the staircase. Bijou jumped from her chair and followed her mistress.

"Help me to look," Marie said; and looking I saw her faint hands seeking through the bed-clothes. Some jewellery was missing, a bracelet and some pearls, as well as all her money. Marie fell back among the pillows unable to speak, and every moment I dreaded a flow of blood. She began to cry, and the little lace handkerchief was soon soaking. I had to find her another. The money that had been taken had been paid her by a *fournisseur* in the *Quartier*, who had given her two thousand francs for her *garniture de cheminée*. A few francs were found among the bed-clothes, and these few francs, she said, were sufficient *pour passer sa soirée*, and she begged me to go the dressmaker to inquire for the gown that had been promised for ten o'clock.

"I shall be at the Elysée by eleven. *Au revoir, au revoir!* Let me rest a little now. I shall see you to-night. You know where I always sit, in the left-hand corner; they always keep those seats for me."

Her eyes closed, I could see that she was already asleep, and her calm and reasonable sleep reminded me of her agitated and unreasonable life; and I stood looking at her, at this poor butterfly who was lying here all alone, robbed by her friends and associates. But she slept contentedly, having found a few francs that they had overlooked amid the bedclothes, enough to enable her to pass her evening at the Elysée! The prince might be written to; but he, no doubt, was weary of her inability to lead a respectable life, and knew, no doubt, that if he were to send her money, it would go as his last gift had gone. If she lived, Marie would one day be selling fried potatoes on the streets. And this decadence—was it her fault? Octave would say: "Qu'est ce que cela peut nous faire, une fille plus ou moins fichue ... si je pouvais réussir un peu dans ce sacré métier!" This was how he talked, but he thought more profoundly in his painting; his picture of her was something more than mere sarcasm.

She was going to the Elysée to-night. It was just six o'clock, so she wanted her dress by ten. I must hasten away to the dressmaker at once; it might be wiser not—she lay in bed peaceful and beautiful; at the Elysée she would be drinking absinthe and smoking cigarettes until three in the morning. But I had promised: she wouldn't forgive me if I didn't, and I went.

The dressmaker said that Madame Pellegrin would have her dress by nine, and at half-past ten I was at the Elysée waiting for her.

How many times did I walk round the gravel path, wearying of the unnatural green of the chestnut leaves and of the high kicking in the quadrilles? Now and then there would be a rush of people, and then the human tide would disperse again under the trees among the zinc chairs and tables, for the enjoyment of bocks and cigars. I noticed that Marie's friends spent their evening in the left-hand corner; but they did not call me to drink with them, knowing well that I knew the money they were spending was stolen money.

I left the place discontented and weary, glad in a way that Marie had not come. No doubt the dressmaker had disappointed her, or maybe she had felt too ill. There was no time to go to inquire in the morning, for I was breakfasting with Octave, and in the afternoon sitting to him.

We were in the middle of the sitting, he had just sketched in my head, when we heard footsteps on the stairs.

"Only some women," he said; "I've a mind not to open the door."

"But do," I said, feeling sure the women were Marie's friends bringing news of her. And it was so. She had been found dead on her balcony dressed in the gown that had just come home from the dressmaker.

I hoped that Octave would not try to pass the matter off with some ribald jest, and I was surprised at his gravity. "Even Octave," I said, "refrains, *on ne blague pas la mort.*"

"But what was she doing on the balcony?" he asked. "What I don't understand is the balcony."

We all stood looking at her picture, trying to read the face.

"I suppose she went out to look at the fireworks; they begin about eleven."

It was one of the women who had spoken, and her remark seemed to explain the picture.

CHAPTER V

LA BUTTE

To-morrow I shall drive to breakfast, seeing Paris continuously unfolding, prospect after prospect, green swards, white buildings, villas engarlanded; to-day I drive to breakfast through the white torridities of Rue Blanche. The back of the coachman grows drowsier, and would have rounded off into sleep long ago had it not been for the great paving stones that swing the vehicle from side to side, and we have to climb the Rue Lepic, and the poor little fainting animal will never be able to draw me to the Butte. So I dismiss my carriage, half out of pity, half out of a wish to study the Rue Lepic, so typical is it of the upper lower classes. In the Rue Blanche there are *portes-cochères*, but in Rue Lepic there are narrow doors, partially grated, open on narrow passages at the end of which, squeezed between the wall and the stairs, are small rooms where *concierges* sit, eternally *en camisole*, amid vegetables and sewing. The wooden blinds are flung back on the faded yellow walls, revealing a portion of white bed-curtain and a heavy middle-aged woman, *en camisole*, passing between the cooking stove, in which a rabbit in a tin pail lies steeping, and the men sitting at their trades in the windows. The smell of leather follows me for several steps; a few doors farther a girl sits trimming a bonnet, her mother beside her. The girl looks up, pale with the exhausting heat. At the corner of the next street there is the *marchand de vins*, and opposite the dirty little *charbonnier*, and standing about a little hole which he calls his *boutique* a group of women in discoloured *peignoirs* and heavy carpet slippers. They have baskets on their arms. Everywhere traces of meagre and humble life, but nowhere do I see the demented wretch common in our London streets—the man with bare feet, the furtive and frightened creature, gnawing a crust and drawing a black, tattered shirt about his consumptive chest.

The asphalt is melting, the reverberation of the stones intolerable, my feet ache and burn. At the top of the street I enter a still poorer neighbourhood, a still steeper street, but so narrow that the shadow has already begun to draw out on the pavements. At the top of the street is a stairway, and above the stairway a grassy knoll, and above the knoll a windmill lifts its black and motionless arms. For the mill is now a mute ornament, a sign for the *Bal du Moulin de la Galette*.

As I ascend the street grows whiter, and at the Butte it is empty of everything except the white rays of noon. There are some dusty streets, and silhouetting against the dim sky a dilapidated façade of some broken pillars. Some stand in the midst of ruined gardens, circled by high walls crumbling and white, and looking through a broken gateway I see a fountain splashing, but nowhere the inhabitants that correspond to these houses—only a workwoman, a grisette, a child crying in the dust. The Butte Montmartre is full of suggestion; grand folk must at some time have lived there. Could it be that this place was once country? To-day it is full of romantic idleness and abandonment.

On my left an iron gateway, swinging on rusty hinges, leads on to a large terrace, at the end of which is a row of houses. It is in one of these houses that my friend lives, and as I pull the bell I think that the pleasure of seeing him is worth the ascent, and my thoughts float back over the long time I have known Paul. We have known each other always, since we began to write. But Paul is not at home. The servant comes to the door with a baby in her arms, another baby! and tells me that Monsieur et Madame are gone out for the day. No breakfast, no smoke, no talk about literature, only a long walk back—cabs are not found at these heights—a long walk back through the roasting sun. And it is no consolation to be told that I should have written and warned them I was coming.

But I must rest, and ask leave to do so, and the servant brings me in some claret and a siphon. The study is better to sit in than the front room, for in the front room, although the shutters are closed, the white rays pierce through the chinks, and lie like sword-blades along the floor. The study is pleasant and the wine refreshing. The house seems built on the sheer hillside. Fifty feet—more than that—a hundred feet under me there are gardens, gardens caught somehow in the hollow of the hill, and planted with trees, tall trees, for swings hang out of them, otherwise I should not know they were tall. From this window they look like shrubs, and beyond the houses that surround these gardens Paris spreads out over the plain, an endless tide of bricks and stone, splashed with white when the sun shines on some railway station or great boulevard: a dim reddish mass, like a gigantic brickfield, and far away a line of hills, and above the plain a sky as pale and faint as the blue ash of a cigarette.

I can never look upon this city without strong emotion; it has been all my life to me. I came here in my youth, I relinquished myself to Paris, never extending once my adventure beyond Bas Meudon, Ville d'Avray, Fontainebleau—and Paris has made me. How much of my mind do I owe to Paris? And by thus acquiring a fatherland more ideal than the one birth had arrogantly imposed, because deliberately chosen, I have doubled my span of life. Do I not exist in two countries? Have I not furnished myself with two sets of thoughts and sensations? Ah! the delicate delight of owning *un pays ami*—a country where you may go when you are weary to madness of the routine of life, sure of finding there all the sensations of home, plus those of irresponsible caprice. The pleasure of a literature that is yours without being wholly your own, a literature that is like an exquisite mistress, in whom you find consolation for all the commonplaces of life! The comparison is perfect, for although I know these French folk better than all else in the world, they must ever remain my pleasure, and not my work in life. It is strange that this should be so, for in truth I know them strangely well. I can see them living their lives from hour to hour; I know what they would say on any given occasion.

There is Paul. I understand nothing more completely than that man's mind. I know its habitual colour and every varying shade, and yet I may not make him the hero of a novel when I lay the scene in Montmartre, though I know it so well. I know when he dresses, how long he takes to dress, and what he wears. I know the breakfast he eats, and the streets down which he passes—their shape, their colour, their smell. I know exactly how life has come to him, how it has affected him. The day I met him in London! Paul in London! He was there to meet *une petite fermière* with whom he had become infatuated when he went to Normandy to finish his novel. Paul is *foncièrement bon; he married her*, and this is their abode. There is the *salle-à-manger*, furnished with a nice sideboard in oak, and six chairs to match; on the left is their bedroom, and there is the baby's cot, a present from *le grand, le cher et illustre maître*.

Paul and Mrs. Paul get up at twelve, and they loiter over breakfast; some friends come in and they loiter over les *petits verres*. About four Paul begins to write his article, which he finishes or nearly finishes before dinner. They loiter over dinner until it is time for Paul to take his article to the newspaper. He loiters in the printing office or the cafe until his proof is ready, and when that is corrected he loiters in the many cafés of the Faubourg Montmartre, smoking interminable cigars, finding his way back to the Butte between three and four in the morning. Paul is fat and of an equable temperament. He believes in naturalism all the day, particularly after a breakfast over *les petits verres*. He never said an unkind word to any one, and I am sure never thought one. He used to be fond of grisettes, but since he married he has thought of no one but his wife. *Il écrit des choses raides*, but no woman ever had a better husband. And now you know him as well as I do. Here are his own books, "The End of Lucie Pellegrin," the story that I have just finished writing: I think I must explain how it was that I have come to rewrite one of Paul's stories, the best he ever wrote. I remember asking him why he called her Lucie, and he was surprised to hear her name was Marie; he never knew her, he had never been to Alphonsine's, and he had told the story as he had picked it up from the women who turned into the Rat Mort at midnight for a *soupe à l'oignon*. He said it was a pity he did not know me when he was writing it, for I could have told him her story more sympathetically than the women in the Rat Mort, supplying him with many pretty details that they had never noticed or had forgotten. It would have been easy for me to have done this, for Marie Pellegrin is enshrined in my memory like a miniature in a case. I press a spring, and I see the beautifully shaped little head, the pale olive face, the dark eyes, and the blue-black hair. Marie Pellegrin is really part of my own story, so why should I have any scruple about telling it? Merely because my friend had written it from hearsay? Whereas I knew her; I saw her on her death-bed. Chance made me her natural historian. Now I think that every one will accept my excuses, and will acquit me of plagiarism.

I see the Rougon-Macquart series, each volume presented to him by the author, Goncourt, Huysmans, Duranty, Céard, Maupassant, Hennique, etc.; in a word, the works of those with whom I grew up, those who tied my first literary pinafore round my neck. But here are "Les Moralités Legendaires" by Jules Laforgue, and "Les Illuminations" by Rambaud. Paul has not read these books; they were sent to him, I suppose, for review, and put away on the bookcase, all uncut; their authors do not visit here.

And this sets me thinking that one knows very little of any generation except one's own. True that I know a little more of the symbolists than Paul. I am the youngest of the naturalists, the eldest of the symbolists. The naturalists affected the art of painting, the symbolists the art of music; and since the symbolists there has been no artistic manifestation—the game is played out. When Huysmans and Paul and myself are dead, it will be as impossible to write a naturalistic novel as to revive the megatherium. Where is Hennique? When Monet is dead it will be as impossible to paint an impressionistic picture as to revive the ichthyosaurus. A little world of ideas goes by every five-and-twenty years, and the next that emerges will be incomprehensible to me, as incomprehensible as Monet was to Corot.... Was the young generation knocking at the door of the Opéra Comique last night? If the music was the young generation, I am sorry for it. It was the second time I had gone. I had been to hear the music, and I left exasperated after the third act. A friend was with me and he left, but for different reasons; he suffered in his ears; it was my intelligence that suffered. Why did the flute play the chromatic scale when the boy said, "Il faut que cela soit un grand navire," and why were all the cellos in motion when the girl answered, "Cela ou bien tout autre chose?" I suffered because of the divorce of the orchestra and singers, uniting perhaps at the end of the scene. It was speaking through music, no more, monotonous as the Sahara, league after league, and I lost amid sands. A chord is heard in "Lohengrin" to sustain Elsa's voice, and it performs its purpose; a motive is heard to attract attention to a certain part of the story, and it fills its purpose, when Ortrud shrieks out the motive of the secret, and in its simplest form, at the church door, the method may be criticised as crude, but the crudest melodrama is better than this desert wandering. While I ponder on the music of the younger generation, remembering the perplexity it had caused me, I hear a vagrant singing on the other side of the terrace:

Moi, je m'en fous. Je reste dans mon trou

and I say: "I hear the truth in the mouth of the vagrant minstrel, one who possibly has no *trou* wherein to lay his head." *Et moi aussi, je reste dans mon trou, et mon trou est assez beau pour que j'y reste, car mon trou est*—Richard Wagner. My *trou* is the Ring—the Sacrosanct Ring. Again I fall to musing. The intention of Liszt and Wagner and Strauss was to write music. However long Wotan might ponder on

Mother Earth the moment comes when the violins begin to sing; ah! how the spring uncloses in the orchestra, and the lovers fly to the woods!...

The vagrant continued his wail, and forgetful of Paul, forgetful of all things but the philosophy of the minstrel of the Butte, I picked my way down the tortuous streets repeating:

Moi, je m'en fous, Je reste dans mon trou

CHAPTER VI

SPENT LOVES

I am going to see dear and affectionate friends. The train would take me to them, that droll little *chemin de fer de ceinture*, and it seems a pity to miss the Gare St. Lazare, its Sunday morning tumult of Parisians starting with their mistresses and their wives for a favourite suburb. I never run up these wide stairways leading to the great wide galleries full of bookstalls (charming yellow notes), and pierced with little *guichets* painted round with blue, without experiencing a sensation of happy lightness—a light-headedness that I associate with the month of May in Paris. But the tramway that passes through the Place de la Concorde goes as far as Passy, and though I love the droll little *chemin de fer de ceinture* I love this tramway better. It speeds along the quays between the Seine and the garden of the Champs Elysées, through miles of chestnut bloom, the roadway chequered with shadows of chestnut leaves; the branches meet overhead, and in a faint delirium of the senses I catch at a bloom, cherish it for a moment, and cast it away. The plucky little steamboats are making for the landing-places, stemming the current. I love this sprightly little river better than the melancholy Thames, along whose banks saturnine immoralities flourish like bulrushes! Behold the white architecture, the pillars, the balustraded steps, the domes in the blue air, the monumented swards! Paris, like all pagan cities, is full of statues. A little later we roll past gardens, gaiety is in the air.... And then the streets of Passy begin to appear, mean streets, like London streets. I like them not; but the railway station is compensation; the little railway station like a house of cards under toy trees, and the train steaming out into the fanciful country. The bright wood along which it speeds is like the season's millinery.

It is pleasant to notice everything in Paris, the flymen asleep on their box-seats, the little horses dozing beneath the chestnut trees, the bloused workmen leaning over a green-painted table in an arbour, drinking wine at sixteen sous the litre, the villas of Auteuil, rich woodwork, rich iron railings, and the summer hush about villas engarlanded. Auteuil is so French, its symbolism enchants me. Auteuil is like a flower, its petals opening out to the kiss of the air, its roots feeling for way among the rich earth. Ah, the land of France, its vineyards and orchards, its earthly life! Thoughts come unbidden, my thoughts sing together, and I hardly knowing what they are singing. My thoughts are singing like the sun; do not ask me their meaning; they mean as much and as little as the sun that I am part of—the sun of France that I shall enjoy for thirty days. May takes me to dear and affectionate friends who await me at Auteuil, and June takes me away from them. There is the villa! And there amid the engarlanding trees my friend, dressed in pale yellow, sits in front of his easel. How the sunlight plays through the foliage, leaping through the rich, long grass; and amid the rhododendrons in bloom sits a little girl of four, his model, her frock and cap impossibly white under the great, gaudy greenery.

Year after year the same affectionate welcome, the same spontaneous welcome in this garden of rhododendrons and chestnut bloom. I would linger in the garden, but I may not, for breakfast is ready *et il ne faut pas faire manquer la messe à Madame. La messe*! How gentle the word is, much gentler than our word, mass, and it shocks us hardly at all to see an old lady going away in her carriage *pour entendre la messe*. Religion purged of faith is a pleasant, almost a pretty thing. Some fruits are better dried than fresh; religion is such a one, and religion, when nothing is left of it but the pleasant, familiar habit, may be defended, for were it not for our habits life would be unrecorded, it would be all on the flat, as we would say if we were talking about a picture without perspective. Our habits are our stories, and tell whence we have come and how we came to be what we are. This is quite a pretty reflection, but there is no time to think the matter out—here is the doctor! He lifts his skull-cap, and how beautiful is the gesture; his dignity is the dignity that only goodness gives; and his goodness is a pure gift, existing independent of formula, a thing in itself, like Manet's painting. It was Degas who said, "A man whose profile no one ever saw," and the aphorism reminds us of the beautiful goodness that floats over his face, a light from Paradise. But why from Paradise? Paradise is an ugly ecclesiastical invention, and angels are an ugly Hebrew invention. It is unpardonable to think of angels in Auteuil; an angel is a prig compared to the dear doctor, and an angel has wings. Well, so had this admirable chicken, a bird that was grown for the use of the table, produced like a vegetable. A dear bird that was never allowed to run about and weary itself as our helpless English chicken is; it lived to get fat without acquiring any useless knowledge or desire of life; it became a capon in tender years, and then a pipe was introduced into its mouth and it was fed by machinery until it could hardly walk, until it could only stagger to its bed, and there it lay in happy digestion until the hour came for it to be crammed again. So did it grow up without knowledge or sensation or feeling of life, moving gradually, peacefully towards its predestined end—a delicious repast! What better end, what greater glory than to be a fat chicken? The carcasses of sheep that hang in butchers' shops are beginning to horrify the conscience of Europe. To cut a sheep's throat is an offensive act, but to clip out a bird's tongue with a long pair of scissors made for the purpose is genteel. It is true that it beats its wings for a few moments, but we must not allow ourselves to be disturbed by a mere flutter of feathers. Man is merciful, and saved it from life. It grew like an asparagus! And talking of asparagus, here are some from Argenteuil thick as umbrellas and so succulent! A word about the wine. French red wines in England always seem to taste like ink, but in France they taste of the sun. Melons are better in June—that one comes, no doubt, from Algeria. It is, however, the kind I like best, the rich, red melon that one eats only in France; a thing of the moment, unrememberable; but the chicken will never be forgotten; twenty years hence I shall be talking of a chicken, that in becoming a fat chicken acquired twenty years of immortality—which of us will acquire as many?

As we rise from table the doctor calls me into his studio: for he would give me an excellent cigar before he bids me good-bye, and having lighted it I follow my friend to the studio at the end of the garden, to that airy drawing-room which he has furnished in pale yellow and dark blue. On the walls are examples of the great modern masters—Manet and Monet. That view of a plain by Monet—is it not facile? It flows like a Japanese water-colour: the low horizon evaporating in the low light, the spire of the town visible in the haze. And look at the celebrated "Leçon de Danse" by Degas—that dancer descending the spiral staircase, only her legs are visible, the staircase cutting the picture in twain. On the right is the dancing class and the dancing master; something has gone wrong, and he holds out his hands in entreaty; a group of dancers are seated on chairs in the foreground, and their mothers are covering their shoulders with shawls—good mothers anxious for their daughters' welfare, for their advancement in life.

This picture betrays a mind curious, inquisitive and mordant; and that plaid shawl is as unexpected as an adjective of Flaubert's. A portrait by Manet hangs close by, large, permanent and mysterious as nature. Degas is more intellectual, but how little is intellect compared with a gift like Manet's! Yesterday I was in the Louvre, and when wearied with examination and debate—I had gone there on a special errand—I turned into the Salle Carrée for relaxation, and there wandered about, waiting to be attracted. Long ago the Mona Liza was my adventure, and I remember how Titian's "Entombment" enchanted me; another year I delighted in the smooth impartiality of a Terbourg interior; but this year Rembrandt's portrait of his wife held me at gaze. The face tells of her woman's life, her woman's weakness, and she seems conscious of the burden of her sex, and of the burden of her own special lot—she is Rembrandt's wife, a servant, a satellite, a watcher. The emotion that this picture awakens is an almost physical emotion. It gets at you like music, like a sudden breath of perfume. When I approach, her eyes fade into brown shadow, but when I withdraw they begin telling her story. The mouth is no more than a little shadow, but what wistful tenderness there is in it! and the colour of the face is white, faintly tinted with bitumen, and in the cheeks some rose madder comes through the yellow. She wears a fur jacket, but the fur was no trouble to Rembrandt; he did not strive for realism. It is fur, that is sufficient. Grey pearls hang in her ears, there is a brooch upon her breast, and a hand at the bottom of the picture passing out of the frame, and that hand reminds one, as the chin does, of the old story that God took a little clay and made man out of it. That chin and that hand and arm are moulded without display of knowledge, as Nature moulds. The picture seems as if it had been breathed upon the canvas. Did not a great poet once say that God breathed into Adam? and here it is even so.

The other pictures seem dry, insignificant; the Mona Liza, celebrated in literature, hanging a few feet away, seems factitious when compared with this portrait; I have heard that tedious smile excused on the ground that she is smiling at the nonsense she hears talked about her; that hesitating smile which held my youth in tether has come to seem but a grimace; and the pale mountains no more mysterious than a globe or map seen from a little distance. The Mona Liza is a sort of riddle, an acrostic, a poetical decoction, a ballade, a rondel, a villanelle or ballade with double burden, a sestina, that is what it is like, a sestina or chant royal. The Mona Liza, being literature in intention rather than painting, has drawn round her many poets. We must forgive her many mediocre verses for the sake of one incomparable prose passage. She has passed out of that mysterious misuse of oil paint, that arid glazing of *terre verte*, and has come into her possession of eternal life, into the immortality of

Pater's prose. Degas is wilting already; year after year he will wither, until one day some great prose writer will arise and transfer his spirit into its proper medium—literature. The Mona Liza and the "Leçon de Danse" are intellectual pictures; they were painted with the brains rather than with the temperaments; and what is any intellect compared with a gift like Manet's! Leonardo made roads; Degas makes witticisms. Yesterday I heard one that delighted me far more than any road would, for I have given up bicycling. Somebody was saying he did not like Daumier, and Degas preserved silence for a long while. "If you were to show Raphael," he said at last, "a Daumier, he would admire it, he would take off his hat; but if you were to show him a Cabanel he would say with a sigh 'That is my fault!'"

My reverie is broken by the piano; my friend is playing, and it is pleasant to listen to music in this airy studio. But there are women I must see, women whom I see every time I go to Paris, and too much time has been spent in the studio—I must go.

But where shall I go? My thoughts strike through the little streets of Passy, measuring the distance between Passy and the Arc de Triomphe. For a moment I think that I might sit under the trees and watch the people returning from the races. Were she not dead I might stop at her little house in the fortifications among the lilac trees. There is her portrait by Manet on the wall, the very toque she used to wear. How wonderful the touch is; the beads—how well they are rendered! And while thinking of the extraordinary handicraft I remember his studio, and the tall fair woman like a tea-rose coming into it: Mary Laurant! The daughter of a peasant, and the mistress of all the great men—perhaps I should have said of all the distinguished men. I used to call her *toute la lyre*.

The last time I saw her we talked about Manet. She said that every year she took the first lilac to lay upon his grave. Is there one of her many lovers who brings flowers to her grave? What was so rememberable about her was her pleasure in life, and her desire to get all the pleasure, and her consciousness of her desire to enjoy every moment of her life. Evans, the great dentist, settled two thousand a year upon her, and how angry he was one night on meeting Manet on the staircase! In order to rid herself of her lover she invited him to dinner, intending to plead a sick headache after dinner.... She must go and lie down. But as soon as her guest was gone she took off the *peignoir* which hid her ball dress and signed to

Manet, who was waiting at the street corner, with her handkerchief. But as they went downstairs together whom should they meet but the dentist *qui a oublié ses carnets*. And he was so disappointed at meeting his beautiful but deceitful mistress that he didn't visit her again for three or four days. His anger mattered very little to Mary. Someone else settled two thousand a year more upon her; and having four thousand a year or thereabouts, she dedicated herself to the love and conversation of those who wrote books and music and painted pictures.

We humans are more complicated than animals, and we love through the imagination, at least the imagination stimulates the senses, acting as a sort of adjuvant. The barmaid falls in love with No. 1 because he wipes a glass better than No. 2, and Mary fell in love with Coppée on account of his sonnet "Le Lys," and she grew indifferent when he wrote poems like "La Nourrice" or "Le petit épicier de Montrouge qui cassait le sucre avec mélancolie." And it was at this time when their love story was at wane that I became a competitor. But one day Madame Albazi came to Manet's studio, a splendid creature in a carriage drawn by Russian horses from the Steppes, so she said; but who can tell whether a horse comes from the Steppes or from the horse-dealers? Nor does it matter when the lady is extraordinarily attractive, when she inspires the thought—a mistress for Attila! That is not exactly how Manet saw her: but she looks like that in his pastel. In it she holds a tortoiseshell fan widespread across her bosom, and it was on one of the sticks of the fan that he signed his name. A great painter always knows where to sign his pictures, and he never signs twice in the same place. The merit of these Russians is that they never leave one in doubt. She could not sit that day, she was going to the Bois, and asked me and a young man who happened to be in Manet's studio at the time to go there with her, and we went there drawn by the Russian horses, the young man and I wondering all the while which was going to be the countess's lover; we played hard for her; but that day I was wiser than he; I let him talk and recite poetry and jingle out all the aphorisms that he had been collecting for years, feeling his witticisms were in vain, for she was dark as a raven and I was as gold as a sunflower. It was at the corner of the Rue Pontière that we got rid of him. Some days afterwards she sat to Manet. The pastel now hangs in the room of a friend of mine; I bought it for him.

The picture of a woman one knows is never so agreeable a companion as the picture of a woman one has never seen. One's memory and the painter's vision are in conflict, and I like to think better of the long delicate nose, and the sparkling eyes, and a mouth like red fruit. The pastel once belonged to me; it used to hang in my rooms; for with that grace of mind which never left him, Manet said one day, "I always promised you a picture," and searching among the pastels that lined the wall he turned to me saying, "Now I think that this comes to you by right." When I left Paris hurriedly, and left my things to be sold, the countess came to the sale and bought her picture, and then she sold it years afterwards to a picture-dealer, tempted by the price that Manet's pictures were fetching. Hearing that it was for sale, I bought it, as I have said, for a friend. And now I have told the whole story, forgetting nothing except that it was years afterwards, when I had written "Les Confessions d'un jeune Anglais" in the *Revue Indépendante*, that Mary Laurant asked me—oh! she was very enterprising; she sent the editor of the *Revue* to me; an appointment was made. She was wonderful in the garden. She said the moment I arrived, "Now, my dear ——, you must go," and we walked about, I listening to her aphorisms. Mary was beautiful, but she liked one to love her for her wit, to admire her wit; and when I asked her why she did not leave Evans, the great dentist, she said, "That would be a base thing to do. I content myself by deceiving him," and then—this confidence seemed to have a particular significance—"I am not a woman," she said, "that is made love to in a garden." Her garden was a nook at the fortifications, hidden among lilac bushes. She wished to show me her house, and we talked for a long time in her boudoir. But I knew she was Mallarmé's mistress at the time, so nothing came of this *caprice littéraire*.

My thoughts run upon women, and why not? On what would you have them run? on copper mines? Woman is the legitimate subject of all men's thoughts. We pretend to be interested in other things. In the smoking-rooms I have listened to men talking about hunting, and I have said to myself, "Your interest is a pretence: of what woman are you thinking?" We forget women for a little while when we are thinking about art, but only for a while. The legitimate occupation of man's mind is woman; and listening to my friend who is playing music—music I do not care to hear, Brahms—I fall to thinking which of the women I have known in years past would interest me most to visit.

In the spring weather the walk from Passy to the Champs Elysées would be pleasant and not too far; I like to see the swards and the poplars and the villas, the tall iron railings, and the flower vases hidden in bouquets of trees. These things are Paris; the mind of the country, that mind which comes out of a long past, and which may be defined as a sort of ancestral beauty and energy is manifested everywhere in Paris; and a more beautiful day for seeing the tall, white houses and the villas and the trees and the swards can hardly be imagined. I should be interested in all these things, but my real interest would be in one little hillside, a line of houses, eight or nine, close by the Arc de Triomphe, the most ordinary in the avenue. She liked the ordinary, and I have often wondered what was the link of association? Was it no more than her blonde hair drawn up from the neck, her fragrant skin, or her perverse subtle senses? It was something more, but you must not ask me to explain further. I like to remember the rustle of a flowered dress she wore as she moved, drifting like a perfume, passing from her frivolous bedroom into the drawing-room. A room without taste, stiff and middle-class, notwithstanding the crowns placed over the tall portraits. I see a picture of two children; but she is the fairer, and in her pale eyes and thinly-curved lips there is a mixture of yearning and restlessness. As the child was, so is the woman, and Georgette has lived to paper one entire wall of her bedroom with trophies won in the battlefields of ardently danced cotillons. The other child is of a stricter nature, and even in the picture her slightly darkened ringlets are less wanton than her sister's. Her eyes are more pensive, and any one could have predicted children for one and cotillon favours for the other.

We often sat on her bedroom balcony reading, talking, or watching the sky growing pale beyond Mount Valerian, the shadow drifting and defining and shaping the hill. In hours like the present, dreaming in a studio, we remember those who deceived us, those who made us suffer, and in these hours faces, fragments of faces, rise out of a past, the line of a bent neck, the whiteness of a hand, and the eyes. I remember her eyes; one day in an orchard, in the lush and luxuriance of June, her husband was walking in front with a friend, and I was pleading. "Well," she said, raising her eyes, "you can kiss me now." But her husband was in front, and he was a thick-set man, and there was a stream, and I foresaw a struggle—and an unpleasant one: confess and be done with it!—I didn't dare to kiss her, and I don't think she ever forgave me that lack of courage. All this is twenty years ago, and is it not silly to spend the afternoon thinking of such rubbish? But it is of such rubbish that our lives are made. Shall I go to her now and see her in her decadence? Grey hair has not begun to appear yet in the blonde, it will never turn grey, but she was shrivelling a little the last time I saw her. And next year she will be older. At her age a year counts for double. Others are more worthy of a visit. If I do not go to her this year, shall I go next?

In imagination I go past her house, thinking of a man she used to talk about, "the man she left her 'ome for"; that is how the London street girl would word it. He had been the centre of a disgraceful scandal in his old age, a sordid but characteristic end for the Don Juan of the nineteenth century. Perhaps she loved the big, bearded man whose photograph she had once shown me. He killed himself for not having enough money to live as he wished to live. That was her explanation. I think there was some blackmail; she had to pay some money to the dead man's relations for letters. These sensual American women are like orchids, and who would hesitate between an orchid and a rose? It was twenty years ago since she turned round on me in the gloom of her brougham unexpectedly, and it was as if some sensual spirit had come out of a world of perfume and lace.

In imagination I have descended the Champs Elysées, and have crossed the Place de la Concorde, and the Seine is flowing past just as it flowed when the workmen were building Notre Dame, just as it will flow a thousand years hence. A thousand years hence men will stand watching its current, thinking of little blonde women, and the shudder they can send through the flesh; they can, but not twenty years afterwards. The Reverend Donne has it that certain ghosts do not raise the hair but the flesh; mine do no more than to set me thinking that rivers were not created to bear ships to the sea, but to set our memories flowing. Full many a time have I crossed the Pont Neuf on my way to see another woman—an American! The time comes when desire wilts and dies, but the sexual interest never dies, and we take pleasure in thinking in middle life of those we enjoyed in youth. She, of whom I am thinking, lives far away in the Latin Quarter, in an ill-paven street. How it used to throw my carriage from side to side! I have been there so often that I know all the shops, and where the shops end, and there is a whitewashed wall opposite her house; the street bends there. The *concierge* is the same, a little thicker, a little heavier; she always used to have a baby in her arms, now there are no more babies; her children, I suppose, have grown up and have gone away. There used to be a darkness at the foot of the stairs, and I used to slip on those stairs, so great was my haste; the very tinkle of the bell I remember, and the trepidation with which I waited.

Her rooms looked as if they had never been sat in; even the studio was formal, and the richly-bound volumes on the tables looked as if they had never been opened. She only kept one servant, a little, redheaded girl, and seeing this girl back again after an absence of many years, I spoke to Lizzie of the old days. Lizzie told me her servant's story. She had gone away to be married, and after ten years of misfortune she had returned to her old mistress, this demure, discreet and sly New Englander, who concealed a fierce sensuality under a homely appearance. Lizzie must have had many lovers, but I knew nothing of her except her sensuality, for she had to let me into that secret.

She was a religious woman, a devout Protestant, and thinking of her my thoughts are carried across the sea, and I am in the National Gallery looking at Van Eyke's picture, studying the grave sensuality of the man's face—he speaks with uplifted hand like one in a pulpit, and the gesture and expression tell us as plainly as if we heard him that he is admonishing his wife (he is given to admonition), informing her that her condition—her new pregnancy—is an act of the Divine Will. She listens, but how curiously! with a sort of partial comprehension afloat upon her face, more of the guinea-pig than of the rabbit type. The twain are sharply differentiated, and one of the objects of the painter seems to have been to show us how far one human being may be removed from another. The husband is painfully clear to himself, the wife is happily unconscious of herself. Now everything in the picture suggests order; the man's face tells a mind the same from day to day, from year to year, the same passions, the same prayers; his apparel, the wide-brimmed hat, the cloak falling in long straight folds, the peaked shoon, are an habitual part of him. We see little of the room, but every one remembers the chandelier hanging from the ceiling reflected in the mirror opposite. These reflections have lasted for three hundred years; they are the same to-day as the day they were painted, and so is the man; he lives again, he is a type that Nature never wearies of reproducing, for I suppose he is essential to life. This sober Flemish interior expresses my mistress's character almost as well as her own apartment used to do. I always experienced a chill, a sense of formality, when the door was opened, and while I stood waiting for her in the prim drawing-room. Every chair was in its appointed place, large, gilt-edged, illustrated books lay upon the tables.... There was not much light in her rooms; heavy curtains clung about the windows, and tapestries covered the walls. In the passage there were oak chests, and you can imagine, reader, this woman waiting for me by an oak table, a little ashamed of her thoughts, but unable to overcome them. Once I heard her playing the piano, and it struck me as an affectation. As I let my thoughts run back things forgotten emerge; here comes one of her gowns! a dark-green gown, the very same olive green as the man's cloak. She wore her hair short like a boy's, and though it ran all over her head in little curls, it did not detract at all from the New England type, the woman in whose speech Biblical phraseology still lingers. Lizzie was a miraculous survival of the Puritans who crossed the Atlantic in the *Mayflower* and settled in New England. Paris had not changed her. She was *le grave Puritan du tableau*. The reader will notice that I write *le grave Puritan*, for of his submissive, childlike wife there was nothing in Lizzie except her sex. As her instinct was in conflict with her ideals, her manner was studied, and she affected a certain cheerfulness which she dared not allow to subside. She never relinquished her soul, never fell into confidence, so in a sense we always remained strangers, for it is when lovers tell their illusions and lonelinesses that they know each other, the fiercest spasm tells us little, and it is forgotten, whereas the moment when a woman sighs and breaks into a simple confidence is remembered years afterwards, and brings her before us though she be underground or a thousand miles away. These intimacies she had not, but there was something true and real in her, something which I cannot find words to express to-day; she was a clever woman, that was it, and that is why I pay her the homage of an annual visit. These courteous visits began twenty years ago; they are not always pleasant, yet I endure them. Our conversation is often laboured, there are awkward and painful pauses, and during these pauses we sit looking at each other, thinking no doubt of the changes that time has wrought. One of her chief charms was her figure—one of the prettiest I have ever seen—and she still retains a good deal of its grace. But she shows her age in her hands; they have thickened at the joints, and they were such beautiful hands. Last year she spoke of herself as an old woman, and the remark seemed to me disgraceful and useless, for no man cares to hear a woman whom he has loved call herself old; why call attention to one's age, especially when one does not look it? and last year she looked astonishingly young for fifty-five; that was her age, she said. She asked me my age; the question was unpleasant, and before I was aware of it I had told her a lie, and I hate those who force me to tell lies. The interview grew painful, and to bring it to a close she asked me if I would care to see her husband.

We found the old man alone in his studio, looking at an engraving under the light of the lamp, much more like a picture than any of his paintings. She asked him if he remembered me, and he got up muttering something, and to help him I mentioned that I had been one of his pupils. The dear old man said of course he remembered, and that he would like to show me his pictures, but Lizzie said—I suppose it was nervousness that made her say it, but it was a strangely tactless remark—"I don't think, dear, that Mr. — — cares for your pictures." However celebrated one may be, it is always mortifying to hear that some one, however humble the person may be, does not care for one's art. But I saved the situation, and I think my remarks were judicious and witty. It is not always that one thinks of the right words at the right moment, but it would be hard to improve on the admonition that she did me a wrong, that, like every one who liked art, I had changed my opinion many times, but after many wanderings had come back to the truth, and in order to deceive the old man I spoke of Ingres. I had never failed in that love, and how could I love Ingres without loving him? The contrary was the truth, but the old man's answer was very sweet. Forgetful of his own high position, he answered, "We may both like Ingres, but it is not probable that we like the same Ingres." I said I did not know any Ingres I did not admire, and asked him which he admired, and we had a pleasant conversation about the Apotheosis of Homer, and the pictures in the Musée de Montauban. Then the old man said, "I must show Mr. — — my pictures." No doubt he had been thinking of them all through the conversation about the Musée de Montauban. "I must show you my Virgin," and he explained that the face of the Infant Jesus was not yet finished.

It was wonderful to see this old man, who must have been nearly eighty, taking the same interest in his pictures as he took fifty years ago. Some stupid reader will think, perchance, that it mattered that I had once loved his wife. But how could such a thing matter? Think for a moment, dear reader, for all readers are dear, even the stupidest, and you will see that you are still entangled in conventions and prejudices. Perhaps, dear reader, you think she and I should have dropped on our knees and confessed. Had we done so, he would have thought us two rude people, and nothing more.

What will happen to her when he dies? Will she return to Boston? Shall I ever see her again? Last year I vowed that I would not, and I think it would please her as well if I stayed away.... And she is right, for so long as I am not by her she is with me. But in the same room, amid the familiar furniture, we are divided by the insuperable past, and to retain her I must send her away. The idea is an amusing one; I think I have read it somewhere, it seems to me like something I have read. Did I ever read of a man who sent his mistress away so that his possession might be more complete? Whether I did or didn't matters little, the idea is true to me to-day—in order to possess her I must never see her again. A pretty adventure it would be, nevertheless, to spend a week paying visits to those whom I loved about that time; and I can imagine a sort of Beau Brummel of the emotions going every year to Paris to spend a day with each of his mistresses.

There were others about that time. There was Madame ——. The name is in itself beautiful, characteristically French, and it takes me back to the middle centuries, to the middle of France. I always imagined that tall woman, who thought so quickly and spoke so sincerely, dealing out her soul rapidly, as one might cards, must have been born near Tours. She was so French that she must have come from the very heart of France; she was French as the wine of France; as Balzac, who also came from Tours; and her voice, and her thoughts, and her words transported one; by her side one was really in France; and, as her lover, one lived through every circumstance of a French love story. She lived in what is called in Paris an hotel; it had its own *concierge*, and it was nice to hear the man say, "Oui, monsieur, Madame la Marquise est chez elle," to walk across a courtyard and wait in a boudoir stretched with blue silk, to sit under a Louis XVI. rock crystal chandelier. She said one day, "I'm afraid you're thinking of me a great deal," and she leaned her hands on the back of the chair, making it easy for me to take them. She said her hands had not done any kitchen work for five hundred years, and at the time that seemed a very witty thing to say. The drawing-room opened onto a conservatory twenty feet high; it nearly filled the garden, and the marquise used to receive her visitors there. I do not remember who was the marquise's lover when the last fête was given, nor what play was acted; only that the ordinary guests lingered over their light refreshments, scenting the supper, and that to get rid of them we had to bid the marquise ostentatiously goodnight. Creeping round by the back of the house, we gained the bedrooms by the servants' staircase, and hid there until the ordinary guests in decency could delay no longer. As soon as the last one was gone the stage was removed, and the supper tables were laid out. Shall I ever forget the moment when the glass roof of the conservatory began to turn blue, and the shrilling of awakening sparrows! How haggard we all were, but we remained till eight in the morning. That fête was paid for with the last remnant of the poor marquise's fortune. Afterwards she was very poor, and Suzanne, her daughter, went on the stage and discovered a certain talent for acting which has been her fortune to this day. I will go to the Vaudeville tonight to see her; we might arrange to go together to see her mother's grave. To visit the grave, and to strew azaleas upon it, would be a pretty piece of sentimental mockery. But for my adventure there should be seven visits; Madame —— would make a fourth; I hear that she is losing her sight, and lives in a chateau about fifty miles from Paris, a chateau built in the time of Louis XIII., with high-pitched roofs and many shutters, and formal gardens with balustrades and fish-ponds, yes *et des charmilles—charmilles* —what is that in English?—avenues of clipped limes. To walk in an avenue of clipped limes with a woman who is nearly blind, and talk to her of the past, would be indeed an adventure far "beyond the range of formal man's emotion."

Madame —— interrupted our love story. She would be another—that would be five—and I shall think of two more during dinner. But now I must be moving on; the day has ended; Paris is defining itself upon a straw-coloured sky. I must go, the day is done; and hearing the last notes trickle out—somebody has been playing the prelude to "Tristan"—I say: "Another pretty day passed, a day of meditation on art and women—and what else is there to meditate about? Tomorrow will happily be the same as to-day, and to-morrow I shall again meditate on art and women, and the day after I shall be occupied with what I once heard dear old M'Cormac, Bishop of Galway, describe in his sermon as 'the degrading passion of "loave."'"

CHAPTER VII

NINON'S TABLE D'HÔTE

The day dies in sultry languor. A warm night breathes upon the town, and in the exhaustion of light and hush of sound, life strikes sharply on the ear and brain.

It was early in the evening when I returned home, and, sitting in the window, I read till surprised by the dusk; and when my eyes could no longer follow the printed page, holding the book between finger and thumb, my face resting on the other hand, I looked out on the garden, allowing my heart to fill with dreams. The book that had interested me dealt with the complex technique of the art of the Low Countries—a book written by a painter. It has awakened in me memories of all kinds, heartrending struggles, youthful passion, bitter disappointments; it has called into mind a multitude of thoughts and things, and, wearied with admiring many pictures and arguing with myself, I am now glad to exchange my book for the gentle hallucinations of the twilight.

I see a line of leafage drawn across the Thames, but the line dips, revealing a slip of grey water with no gleam upon it. Warehouses and a factory chimney rise ghostly and grey, and so cold is that grey tint that it might be obtained with black and white; hardly is the warmth of umber needed. Behind the warehouses and the factory chimney the sky is murky and motionless, but higher up it is creamy white, and there is some cloud movement. Four lamps, two on either side of the factory chimney, look across the river; one constantly goes out—always the same lamp—and a moment after it springs into its place again. Across my window a beautiful branch waves like a feather fan. It is the only part of the picture worked out in detail. I watch its soft and almost imperceptible swaying, and am tempted to count the leaves. Below it, and a little beyond it, between it and the river, night gathers in the gardens; and there, amid serious greens, passes the black stain of a man's coat, and, in a line with the coat, in the beautifully swaying branch, a belated sparrow is hopping from twig to twig, awakening his mates in search for a satisfactory resting-place. In the sharp towers of Temple Gardens the pigeons have gone to sleep. I can see the cots under the conical caps of slate.

The gross, jaded, uncouth present has slipped from me as a garment might, and I see the past like a little show, struggles and heartbreakings of long ago, and watch it with the same indifferent curiosity as I would the regulated mimicry of a stage play. Pictures from the past come and go without an effort of will; many are habitual memories, but the one before me rises for the first time—for fifteen years it has lain submerged, and now like a water weed or flower it rises—the Countess Ninon de Calvador's boudoir! Her boudoir or her drawing-room, be that as it may, the room into which I was ushered many years ago when I went to see her. I was then a young man, very thin, with sloping shoulders, and that pale gold hair that Manet used to like to paint. I had come with a great bouquet for Ninon, for it was *son jour de fête*, and was surprised and somewhat disappointed to meet a large brunette with many creases in her neck, a loose and unstayed bosom; one could hardly imagine Ninon dressed otherwise than in a *peignoir*—a blue *peignoir* seemed inevitable. She was sitting by a dark, broad-shouldered young man when I came in; they were sitting close together; he rose out of a corner and showed me an impressionistic picture of a railway station. He was one of the many young men who at that time thought the substitution of dots of pink and yellow for the grey and slate and square brushwork of Bastien Lepage was the certain way to paint well. I learned afterwards, during the course of the evening, that he was looked at askance, for even in Montmartre it was regarded as a dishonour to allow the lady with whom you lived to pay for your dinner. Villiers de L'Isle Adam, who had once been Ninon's lover, answered the reproaches levelled against him for having accepted too largely of her hospitality with, "Que de bruit pour quelques côtelettes!" and his transgressions were forgiven him for the sake of the *mot* which seemed to summarise the moral endeavour and difficulties of the entire quarter. When Villiers was her lover Villiers was middle-aged, and Ninon was a young woman; but when I knew her she was interested in the young generation, yet she kept friends with all her old lovers, never denying them her board. How funny was the impressionist's indignation against Villiers! He charged him with having squandered a great part of Ninon's fortune, but Villiers's answer to the young man was, "He talks like the *concierge* in my story of 'Les Demoiselles de Bienfillatre.'"

Poor Villiers was not much to blame; it was part of Ninon's temperament to waste her money, and the canvases round the room testified that she spent a great deal on modern art. She certainly had been a rich woman; rumour credited her with spending fifty thousand francs a year, and in her case rumour said no more than the truth, for it would require that at least to live as she lived, keeping open house to all the literature, music, painting, and sculpture done in Montmartre. At first sight her hospitality seems unreasonable, but when one thinks one sees that it conforms to the rules of all hospitality. There must be a principle of selection, and were the *ratés* she entertained less amusing than the people one meets in Grosvenor Square or the Champs Elysées? Any friend could introduce another, that is common practice, but at Ninon's there was a restriction which I never met elsewhere—no friend could bring another unless the newcomer was a *raté*—in other words, unless he had written music or verse, or painted or carved, in a way that did not appeal to the taste of the ordinary public; inability to reach the taste of the general public was the criterion that obtained there.

The windows of Ninon's boudoir opened upon the garden, and on my expressing surprise at its size and at the large trees that grew there, she gave me permission to admire and investigate; and I walked about the pond, interested in the numerous ducks, in the cats, in the companies of macaws and cockatoos that climbed down from their perches and strutted across the swards. I came upon a badger and her brood, and at my approach they disappeared into an enormous excavation, and behind the summer-house I happened upon a bear asleep and retreated hurriedly. But on going towards the house I heard a well-known voice. "That is Augusta Holmes singing her opera," I said; "she sings all the different parts—soprano, contralto, tenor, and bass." At this time we were all talking about her, and I stood by the window listening until suddenly a well-known smell interrupted her. It was Ninon's cat that had misconducted herself. A window was thrown open, but the ventilation did not prove sufficient. Augusta and her admirers had to leave the piano, and they came from the house glad to breathe the evening air. How dear to me are flowered gowns and evening skies and women with scarfs about their shoulders. Ah! what a beautiful evening it was! And how well do I remember the poet comparing the darkening sky to a blue veil with the moon like a gold beetle upon it. One of the women had brought a guitar with her, and again Augusta's voice streamed up through the stillness, till, compelled by the beauty of the singing, we drew nearer; as the composer sang her songs attitudes grew more abandoned, and hands fell pensively. Among the half-seen faces I caught sight of a woman of exceeding fairness; her hair had only a faint tinge of gold in it; and Ninon remembered that she was a cousin of hers, one whom she had not seen for many years. How Clare had discovered her in the Rue la Moine she could not tell. It was whispered that she was the wife of a rich *commerçant* at Tours. This added to the mystery, and later in the evening the lady told me she had never been in artistic society before, and begged me to point out to her the celebrities present, and to tell her why they were celebrated.

"Who is he—that one slouching towards the pond, that one wearing grey trousers and a black jacket?—oh!"

My companion's exclamation was caused by a new sight of Verlaine; at that moment he had lifted off his hat (the evening was still warm), and the great bald skull, hanging like a cliff over the shaggy eyebrows, shaggy as furze bushes, frightened her. The poet continued his walk round the pond, and, turning suddenly towards us, he stopped to speak to me. I was but a pretext; he clearly wished to speak to my companion. But how strangely did he suit his conversation to her, yet how characteristic of his genius were the words I heard as I turned away, thinking to leave them together—"If I were in love with a young girl or with a young man?" My companion ran forward quickly and seized my arm. "You must not leave me with him," she said. On account of his genius Verlaine was a little slow to see things outside of himself—all that was within him was clear, all without him obscure; so we had some difficulty in getting rid of him, and as soon as he was out of hearing my companion inquired eagerly who he was, and I was astonished at the perception she showed. "Is he a priest? I mean, was he ever a priest?" "A sort of cross between a thieves' kitchen and a presbytery. He is the poet Verlaine. The singer of the sweetest verses in the French language—a sort of ambling song like a robin's. You have heard the robin singing on a coral hedge in autumn-tide; the robin confesses his little soul from the topmost twig; his song is but a tracery of his soul, and so is Verlaine's. His gift is a vision of his own soul, and he makes a tracery as you might of a drawing with a lead pencil, never troubling himself to inquire if what he traces is good or ill. He knows that society regards him as an outcast, but society's point of view is not the only one, that he knows too, and also, though he be a lecher, a crapulous and bestial fellow at times, at other times he is a poet, a visionary, the only poet that Catholicism has produced since Dante. Huysmans, the apologist of Gilles de Rais,—there he is over yonder, talking to the impressionist painter, that small thin man with hair growing thickly, low down on his forehead—Huysmans somewhere in his description of the trial of the fifteenth-century monster, the prototype, so it is said, of the nursery tale of Blue Beard, speaks of the white soul of the Middle Ages; he must have had Verlaine on his mind, for Verlaine has spoken of himself as a mediaeval Catholic, that is to say a Catholic in whom sinning and repentance alternates regularly as night and day. Verlaine has not cut the throats of so many little boys as Gilles de Rais, but Gilles de Rais always declared himself to be a good Catholic. Verlaine abandons himself to the Church as a child to a fairy tale; he does trouble to argue whether the Conception of the Virgin was Immaculate; the mediaeval sculptors have represented her attired very prettily in cloaks with long folds, they have put graceful crowns upon her head, and Verlaine likes these things; they inspire him to write, he feels that belief in the Church is part of himself, and his poetical genius is to tell his own story; he is one of the great soul-tellers. From a literary point of view there is a good deal to be said in favour of faith when it is not joined with practice; acceptance of dogma shields one from controversy; it allows Verlaine to concentrate himself entirely upon things; it weans him away from ideas—the curse of modern literature—and makes him a sort of divine vagrant living his life in the tavern and in the hospital. It is only those who have freed themselves from all prejudice that get close to life, who get the real taste of life—the aroma as from a wine that has been many years in bottle. And Verlaine is aware that this is so. Sometimes he thinks he might have written a little more poetry, and he sighs, but he quickly recovers. 'After all, I have written a good many volumes.' 'And what would art be without life, without love?' He has a verse on that subject; I wish I could remember it for you. His verse is always so winsome, so delicate, slender as the birch tree, elegiac like it; a birch bending over a lake's edge reminds me of Verlaine. He is a lake poet, but the lake is in a suburb not far from a casino. What makes me speak about the lake is that for a long time I thought these verses,

> Ton âme est un lac d'amour
> Dont mes pensées sont les cygnes.
> Vois comme ils font le tour....

were Verlaine's, but they are much less original; their beauty, for they are beautiful, is conventional; numbers of poets might have written them, whereas nobody but Verlaine could have written any of his, really his own, poetry. His desires go sometimes as high as the crucifix; very often they are in the gutter, hardly poetry at all, having hardly any beauty except that of truth, and of course the beauty of a versification that haunts in his ear, for he hears a song in French verse that no French poet has ever heard before, and a song so fluent, ranging from the ecstasy of the nightingale to the robin's little homily.

> Oui, c'était par un soir joyeux de cabaret,
> Un de ces soirs plutôt trop chauds où l'on dirait
> Que le gaz du plafond conspire à notre perte
> Avec le vin du zinc, saveur naïve et verte.
> On s'amusait beaucoup dans la boutique et on
> Entendait des soupirs voisins d'accordéon
> Que ponctuaient des pieds frappant presque en cadence.
> Quand la porte s'ouvrit de la salle de danse
> Vomissant tout un flot dont toi, vers où j'étais,
> Et de ta voix fait que soudain je me tais,
> S'il te plaît de me donner un ordre péremptoire.
> Tu t'écrias 'Dieu, qu'il fait chaud! Patron, à boire!'

"She was from Picardy; and he tells of her horrible accent, and in elegy number five he continues the confession, telling how his well beloved used to get drunk.

> "Tu fis le saut de ... Seine et, depuis morte-vive,
> Tu gardes le vertige et le goût du néant."

"But how can a man confess such things?" my companion asked me, and we stood looking at each other in the midst of the gardens until an ape, cattling prettily, ran towards me and jumped into my arms, and looking at the curious little wizened face, the long arms covered with hair, I said:

"Verlaine has an extraordinary power of expression, and to be ashamed of nothing; but to be ashamed is his genius, just as it was Manet's. It is to his shamelessness that we owe his most beautiful poems, all written in garrets, in taverns, in hospitals—yes, and in prison."

"In prison! But he didn't steal, did he?" and the *commerçant's* wife looked at me with a frightened air, and I think her hand went towards her pocket.

"No, no; a mere love story, a dispute with Rambaud in some haunt of vice, a knife flashed, Rambaud was stabbed, and Verlaine spent three years in prison. As for Rambaud, it was said that he repented and renounced love, entered a monastery, and was digging the soil somewhere on the shores of the Red Sea for the grace of God. But these hopes proved illusory; only Verlaine knows where he is, and he will not tell. The last certain news we had of him was that he had joined a caravan of Arabs, and had wandered somewhere into the desert with these wanderers, preferring savagery to civilization. Verlaine preferred civilized savagery, and so he remained in Paris; and so he drags on, living in thieves' quarters, getting drunk, writing beautiful poems in the hospitals, coming out of hospitals and falling in love with drabs."

>Dans ces femmes d'ailleurs je n'ai pas trouvé l'ange
>Qu'il eût fallu pour remplacer ce diable, toi!
>L'une, fille du Nord, native d'un Crotoy,
>Etait rousse, mal grasse et de prestance molle;
>Elle ne m'adressa guère qu'une parole
>Et c'était d'un petit cadeau qu'il s'agissait,
>En revanche, dans son accent d'ail et de poivre,
>Une troisième, recemment chanteuse au Havre,
>Affectait de dandinement des matelots
>Et m'... enguelait comme un gabier tancant les flots,
>Mais portrait beau vraiment, sacrédié, quel dommage
>La quatrième était sage comme une image,
>Châtain clair, peu de gorge et priait Dieu parfois:
>Le diantre soit de ses sacrés signes de croix!
>Les seize autres, autant du moins que ma mémoire
>Surnage en ce vortex, contaient toutes l'histoire
>Connue, un amant chic, puis des vieux, puis "l'îlot"
>Tantôt bien, tantôt moins, le clair café falot
>Les terasses l'été, l'hiver les brasseries
>Et par degrés l'humble trottoir en théories
>En attendant les bons messieurs compatissants
>Capables d'un louis et pas trop repoussants
>*Qutorum ego parva pars erim*, me disais-je.
>Mais toutes, comme la première du cortège,
>Dès avant la bougie éteinte et le rideau
>Tiré, n'oubliaient pas le "mon petit cadeau."

"In the verses I have just quoted, you remember, he says that the fourth was chaste as an image, her hair was pale brown, she had scarcely any bosom, and prayed to God sometimes. He always hated piety when it interfered with his pleasure, and in the next verse he says, 'The devil take those sacred signs of the Cross!'"

"But do you know any of these women?"

"Oh, yes; we all know the terrible Sara. She beats him."

The *commerçante's* wife asked if she were here.

"He wanted to bring her here, in fact he did bring her once, only she was so drunk that she could not get beyond the threshold, and Ninon's lover, the painter you saw painting the steam engines, was charged to explain to the poet that Sara's intemperance rendered her impossible in respectable society. 'I know Sara has her faults,' he murmured in reply to all argument, and it was impossible to make him see that others did not see Sara with his eyes. 'I know she has her faults,' he repeated, 'and so have others. We all have our faults.' And it was a long time before he could be induced to come back: hunger has brought him."

"And who is that hollow-chested man? How pathetic he looks with his goat-like beard."

"That is the celebrated Cabaner. He will tell you, if you speak to him, that his father was a man like Napoleon, only more so. He is the author of many aphorisms; 'that three military bands would be necessary to give the impression of silence in music' is one. He comes every night to the Nouvelle Athènes, and is a sort of rallying-point; he will tell you that his ballad of 'The Salt Herring' is written in a way that perhaps Wagner would not, but which Liszt certainly would understand."

"Is his music ever played? Does it sell? How does he live? Not by his music, I suppose?"

"Yes, by his music, by playing waltzes and polkas in the Avenue de la Motte Piquet. His earnings are five francs a day, and for thirty-five francs a month he has a room where many of the disinherited ones of art, many of those you see here, sleep. His room is furnished — ah, you should see it! If Cabaner wants a chest of drawers he buys a fountain, and he broke off the head of the Vénus de Milo, saying that now she no longer reminded him of the people he met in the streets; he could henceforth admire her without being troubled by any sordid recollection. I could talk to you for hours about his unselfishness, his love of art, his strange music, and his stranger poems, for his music accompanies his own verses."

"Is he too clever for the public, or not clever enough?"

"Now you're asking me the question we've been asking ourselves for the last ten years.... The man fumbling at his shirt collar over yonder is the celebrated Villiers de L'Isle Adam."

And I remember how it pleased me to tell this simple-minded woman all I knew about Villiers.

"He has no talent whatever, only genius, and that is why he is a raté," I said.

But the woman was not so simple as I had imagined, and one or two questions she put to me led me to tell her that Villiers's genius only appeared in streaks, like gold in quartz.

"The comparison is an old one, but there is no better one to explain Villiers, for when he is not inspired his writing is very like quartz."

"His great name——"

"His name is part of his genius. He chose it, and it has influenced his writings. Have I not heard him say, 'Car je porte en moi les richesses stériles d'un grand nombre de rois oubliés.'"

"But is he a legitimate descendant?"

"Legitimate in the sense that he desired the name more than any of those who ever bore it legitimately."

At that moment Villiers passed by me, and I introduced him to her, and very soon he began to tell us that his *Eve* had just been published, and the success of it was great.

"On m'a dit hier de passer à la caisse ... l'edition était épuisée, vous voyez—il paraît, la fortune est venue ... même à moi."

But Villiers was often tiresomely talkative about trifles, and as soon as I got the chance I asked him if he were going to tell us one of his stories, reminding him of one I had heard he had been telling lately in the *brasseries* about a man in quest of a quiet village where he could get rest, a tired composer, something of that kind. Had he written it? No, he had not written it yet, but now that he knew I liked it he would get up earlier to-morrow. Some one took him away from us, and I had to tell my companion the story.

"Better," I said, "he should never write it, for half of it exists in his voice, and in his gestures, and every year he gets less and less of himself onto the paper. One has to hear him tell his stories in the café—how well he tells them! You must hear him tell how a man, recovering from a long illness, is advised by his doctor to seek rest in the country, and how, seeing the name of a village on the map that touches his imagination, he takes the train, feeling convinced he will find there an Arcadian simplicity. But the village he catches sight of from the carriage window is a morose and lonely village, in the midst of desolate plains. And worse than Nature are the human beings he sees at the station; they lurk in corners, they scrutinise his luggage, and gradually he believes them all to be robbers and assassins.

"He would escape but he dare not, for he is being followed, so turning on his pursuers he asks them if they can direct him to a lodging. The point of Villiers's story is how a suspicion begins in the man's mind, how it grows like a cancer, and very soon the villagers are convinced he is an anarchist, and that his trunks are full of material for the manufacture of bombs. And this is why they dare not touch them. So they follow him to the farmhouse whither they have directed him, and tell their fears to the farmer and his wife. Villiers can improvise the consultations in the kitchen; at midnight in the café, but when morning comes he cannot write, his brain is empty. You must come some night to the Nouvelle Athènes to hear him; leaning across the table he will tell the terror of the hinds and farmer, how they are sure the house is going to be blown up. The sound of their feet on the staircase inspires terror in the wretched convalescent. He sits up in bed, listening, great drops of sweat collected on his forehead. He dare not get out of bed, but he must; and Villiers can suggest the sound of feet on the creaking stairs—yes, and the madness of the man piling furniture against the door, and the agony of those outside hearing the noise within. When they break into the room they find a dead man; for terror has killed him. You must come to the Nouvelle Athènes to hear Villiers tell his story. I'll meet you there to-morrow night.... Will you dine with me? The dinner there is not really too bad; perhaps you'll be able to bear with it."

The *commerçant's* wife hesitated. She promised to come, and she came; but she did not prove an interesting mistress; why, I cannot remember, and I am glad to put her out of my mind, for I want to think of the strange poet whom we heard reciting verses, under the aspen, in which one of the apes had taken refuge. Through the dimness of the years I can see his fair hair floating about his shoulders, his blue eyes and his thin nose. Didn't somebody once describe him as a sort of sensual Christ? He, too, was after the *commerçant's* wife. And didn't he select her as the subject of his licentious verses—reassure yourself, reader, licentious merely from the point of view of prosody.

> "Ta nuque est de santal sur les vifs frissons d'or.
> Mais c'est une autre, que j'adore."

The *commerçant's* wife, forgetful of me, charmed by the poet, by the excitement of hearing herself made a subject of a poem, drew nearer. Strange, is it not, that I should remember a few words here and there?

> "Il m'aime, il m'aime pas, et selon l'antique rite
> Elle effleurait la Marguerite."

The women still sit, circlewise, as if enchanted, the night inspires him, and he improvises trifle after trifle. One remembers fragments. Some time afterwards Cabaner was singing the song of "The Salt Herring."

> "He came along holding in his hands dirty, dirty, dirty,
> A big nail pointed, pointed, pointed,
> And a hammer heavy, heavy, heavy.
> He placed the ladder high, high, high,
> Against the wall white, white, white.
> He went up the ladder high, high, high,

Placed the nail pointed, pointed, pointed
Against the wall—toc! toc! toc!
He tied to the nail a string long, long, long,
And at the end of it a salt herring, dry, dry, dry,
And letting fall the hammer heavy, heavy, heavy,
He got down from the ladder high, high, high,
And went away, away, away.
Since then at the end of the string long, long, long,
A salt herring dry, dry, dry,
Has been swinging slowly, slowly, slowly.
Now I have composed this story simple, simple, simple,
To make all serious men mad, mad, mad,
And to amuse children, little, little, little."

This was the libretto on which Cabaner wrote music "that Wagner would not understand, but which Liszt certainly would." Dear, dear Cabaner, how well I can see thee with thy goat-like beard, and the ape in the tree interrupting thee; he was not like Liszt, he chattered all night. Poor ape, he broke his chain earlier in the evening, and it was found impossible to persuade him to come down. The brute seemed somehow determined that we should not hear Cabaner. Soon after the cocks began answering each other, though it was but midnight; and so loud was their shrilling that I awoke, surprised to find myself sitting at my window in King's Bench Walk. A moment ago I was in Madame Ninon de Calvador's garden, and every whit as much as I am now in King's Bench Walk. Madame Ninon de Calvador—what has become of her?

Is the rest of her story unknown? As I sit looking into the darkness, a memory suddenly springs upon me. Villiers, who came in when dinner was half over, brought a young man with him. Fumbling at his shirt collar, apologising for being late, assuring us that he had dined, he introduced his friend to the company as a young man of genius, of extraordinary genius. Don't I remember Villiers's nervous, hysterical voice! Don't I remember the journalist's voice when he asked Ninon's lover if he sold his pictures, creating at once a bad impression? By some accident a plate was given to him, out of which one of the cats had been fed. The plate might have been given to any one else: Villiers would not have minded, and as for Cabaner, he never knew what he was eating; but it was given to the journalist. Now I remember the young man misconducted himself badly; he struck the table with his fist, and said, "Et bien, je casse tout." Yes, it was he who wrote the article entitled "Ninon's Table d'hôte" in the

Gil Blas, and from it she learned for the first time how the world viewed her hospitality, how misinterpreted were her efforts to benefit the arts and the artists. Somebody told me this story: who I cannot tell; it is all so long ago. But it seems to me that I remember hearing that it was this article that killed her.

The passing of things is always a moving subject for meditation, and it is strange how accident will bring back a scene, explicit in every detail—a tree taking shape upon the dawning sky, the hairy ugliness of the ape in its branches, and along the grey grass a waddling squad of the ducks betaking themselves to the pond, a poet talking to a *commerçant's* wife, Madame de Calvador leaning on a lover's arm.

Had I a palette I could match the blue of the *peignoir* with the faint grey sky. I could make a picture out of that dusky suburb. Had I a pen I could write verses about these people of old time, but the picture would be a shrivelled thing compared with the dream, and the verses would limp. The moment I sought a pen the pleasure of the meditation, which is still with me, which still endures, would vanish. Better to sit by my window and enjoy what remains of the mood and the memory. The mood has nearly passed, the desire of action is approaching.... I would give much for another memory, but memory may not be beckoned, and my mind is dark now, dark as that garden; the swaying, fan-like bough by my window is nearly one mass of green; the last sparrow has fallen asleep. I hear nothing.... I hear a horse trotting in the Strand.

CHAPTER VIII

THE LOVERS OF ORELAY

I had come a thousand miles—rather more, nearly fifteen hundred—in the hope of picking up the thread of a love story that had got entangled some years before and had been broken off abruptly. A strange misadventure our love story had been; for Doris had given a great deal of herself while denying me much, so much that at last, in despair, I fled from a one-sided love affair; too one-sided to be borne any longer, at least by me. And it was difficult to fly from her pretty, inveigling face, delightful and winsome as the faces one finds on the panels of the early German masters. One may look for her face and find it on an oak panel in the Frankfort Gallery, painted in pale tints, the cheeks faintly touched with carmine. In the background of these pictures there are all sorts of curious things; very often a gold bower with roses clambering up everywhere. Who was that master who painted cunning virgins in rose bowers? The master of Cologne, was it not? I have forgotten. No matter. Doris's hair was darker than the hair of those virgins, a rich gold hair, a mane of hair growing as luxuriously as the meadows in June. And the golden note was continued everywhere, in the eyebrows, in the pupils of the eyes, in the freckles along her little nose so firmly and beautifully modelled about the nostrils; never was there a more lovely or affectionate mouth, weak and beautiful as a flower; and the long hands were curved like lilies.

There is her portrait, dear reader, prettily and truthfully and faithfully painted by me, the portrait of a girl I left one afternoon in London more than seventeen years ago, and whom I had lost sight of, I feared for ever. Thought of her? Yes, I thought of her occasionally. Time went by, and I wondered if she were married. What her husband was like, and why I never wrote. It were surely unkind not to write.... Reader, you know those little regrets. Perhaps life would be all on the flat without regret. Regret is like a mountaintop from which we survey our dead life, a mountaintop on which we pause and ponder, and very often looking into the twilight we ask ourselves whether it would be well to send a letter or some token. Now we had agreed upon one which should be used in case of an estrangement—a few bars of Schumann's melody, "The Nut

Bush," should be sent, and the one who received it should at once hurry to the side of the other and all difference should be healed. But this token was never sent by me, perhaps because I did not know how to scribble the musical phrase: pride perhaps kept her from sending it; in any case five years are a long while, and she seemed to have died out of my life altogether; but one day the sight of a woman who had known her, brought her before my eyes, and I asked if Doris married. The woman could not tell me; she had not seen her for many years; they, too, were estranged, and I went home saying to myself: "Doris must be married. What sort of a husband has she chosen? Is she happy? Has she a baby? Oh, shameful thought!"

Do you remember, dear reader, how Balzac, when he had come to the last page of "Massimilla Doni," declares that he dare not tell you the end of this adventure. One word, he says, will suffice for the worshippers of the ideal: "Massimilla Doni was expecting." Then in a passage that is pleasanter to think about than to read—for Balzac when he spoke about art was something of a sciolist, and I am not sure that the passage is altogether grammatical—he tells how the ideas of all the great artists, painters, and sculptors—the ideas they have wrought on panels and in stone—escaped from their niches and their frames—all these disembodied maidens gathered round Massimilla's bed and wept. It would be as disgraceful for Doris to be "expecting" as it was for Massimilla Doni, and I like to think of all the peris, the nymphs, the sylphs, the fairies of ancient legend, all her kinsfolk gathering about her bed, deploring her condition, regarding her as lost to them—were such a thing to happen I should certainly kneel there in spirit with them. And feeling just as Balzac did about Massimilla Doni, that it was a sacrilege that Doris should be "expecting" or even married, I wrote, omitting, however, to tell her why I had suddenly resolved to break silence; I sent her a little note, only a few words, that I was sorry not to have heard of her for so long a time; but though we had been estranged she had not been forgotten; a little commonplace note, relieved perhaps by a touch of wistfulness, of regret. And this note was sent by a messenger duly instructed to ask for an answer. The news the messenger brought back was somewhat disappointing. The lady was away, but the letter would be forwarded to her. "She is not married," I thought; "were she married her name would be sent to me.... Perhaps not." Other thoughts came into my mind, and I did not think of her again for the next two days, not till a long telegram was put into my hand. Doris! It had come from her. It had come more than a thousand miles, "regardless of expense." I said, "This telegram must have cost her ten or twelve shillings at the least." She was delighted to hear from me; she had been ill, but was better now, and the telegram concluded with the usual "Am writing." The letter that arrived, two days afterwards, was like herself, full of impulse and affection; but it contained one phrase which put black misgiving into my heart. In her description of her illness and her health, which was returning, and how she had come to be staying in this far-away Southern town, she alluded to its dulness, saying that if I came there virtue must be its own reward. "Stupid of her to speak to me of virtue," I muttered, "for she must know well enough that it was her partial virtue that had separated us and caused this long estrangement." And I sat pondering, trying to discover if she applied the phrase to herself or to the place where she was staying. How could it apply to the place? All places would be a paradise if— —

At the close of a long December evening I wrote a letter, the answer to which would decide whether I should go to her, whether I should undertake the long journey. "The journey back will be detestable," I muttered, and taking up the pen again I wrote: "Your letter contains a phrase which fills me with dismay: you say, 'Virtue must be its own reward,' and this would seem that you are determined to be more aggressively Platonic than ever. Doris, this is ill news indeed; you would not have me consider it good news, would you?"

Other letters followed, but I doubt if I knew more of Doris's intentions when I got into the train than I did when I sat pondering by my fireside, trying to discover her meaning when she wrote that vile phrase, "Virtue must be its own reward." But somehow I seemed to have come to a decision, and that was the main thing. We act obeying a law deep down in our being, a law which in normal circumstances we are not aware of. I asked myself as I drove to the station, if it were possible that I was going to undertake a journey of more than a thousand miles in quest—of what? Doris's pretty face! It might be pretty no longer; yet she could not have changed much. She had said she was sure that in ten minutes we should be talking just as in old times. Even so, none but madmen travel a thousand miles in search of a pretty face. And it was the madman that is in us all that was propelling me, or was it the primitive man who crouches in some jungle of our being? Of one thing I was sure, that I was no longer a conventional citizen of the nineteenth century; I had gone back two or three thousand years, for all characteristic traits, everything whereby I knew myself, had disappeared! Yet I seemed to have met myself somewhere, in some book or poem or opera.... I could not remember at first, but after some time I began to perceive a shadowy similarity between myself and—dare I mention the names?—the heroes of ancient legend—Menelaus or Jason—which? Both had gone a thousand miles on Beauty's quest. The colour of Helen's hair isn't mentioned in either the "Iliad" or the "Odyssey." Jason's quest was a golden fleece, and so was mine. And it was the primitive hero that I had discovered in myself that helped me to face the idea of the journey, for there is nothing that wearies me so much as a long journey in the train.

When I was twenty I started with the intention of long travel, but the train journey from Calais to Paris wearied me so much that I had rested in Paris for eight years, to return home then on account of some financial embarrassments. During those eight years I thought often of Italy and the south of France, but the train journey of sixteen or seventeen or eighteen hours to the Italian frontier always seemed so much like what purgatory must be, that the heaven of Italy on the other side never tempted me sufficiently to undertake it. A companion would be of no use; one cannot talk for fifteen or sixteen hours, and while debating with myself whether I should go to Plessy, I often glanced down the long perspective of hours. Everything, pleasure and pain alike, are greater in imagination than in reality—there is always a reaction, and having anticipated more than mortal weariness, I was surprised to find that the first two hours in the train passed very pleasantly. It seemed that I had only been in the train quite a little while when it stopped, yet Laroche is more than an hour from Paris, quite a countryside station, and it seems strange that the *Côte d'Azur* should stop there. That was the grand name of the train that I was travelling by. Think of any English company running a train and calling it "The Azure Shore"! Think of going to Euston or to Charing Cross, saying you are going by "The Azure Shore"! So long as the name of this train endures, it is impossible to doubt that the French mind is more picturesque than the English, and one no longer wonders why the French school of painting, etc.

A fruit seller was crying his wares along the platform, and just before we started from Laroche breakfast was preparing on board the train; I thought a basket of French grapes—the grapes that grow in the open air, not the leathery hot-house grapes filled with lumps of glue that we eat in England—would pass the time. I got out and bought a basket from him. On journeys like these one has to resort to many various little expedients. Alas! The grapes were decaying; only the bunch on the top was eatable; nor was that one worth eating, and I began to think that the railway company's attention should be directed to the fraud, for in my case a deliberate fraud had been effected. The directors of the railway would probably think that passengers should exercise some discrimination; it were surely easy for the passenger to examine the quality of a basket of grapes before purchasing—that would be the company's answer to my letter. The question of a letter to the newspaper did not arise, for French papers are not like ours—they do not print all the letters that are sent to them. The French public has no means of ventilating its grievances; a misfortune no doubt, but not such a misfortune as it seems, when one reflects on how little good a letter addressed to the public press does in the way of remedying abuses.

I don't think we stopped again till we got to Lyons, and all the way there I sat at the window looking at the landscape—the long, long plain that the French peasant cultivates unceasingly. Out of that long plain came all the money that was lost in Panama, and all the money invested in Russian bonds—fine milliards came out of the French peasants' stockings. We passed through La Beauce. I believe it was there that Zola went to study the French peasant before he wrote "La Terre." Huysmans, with that benevolent malice so characteristic of him, used to say that Zola's investigation was limited to going out once for a drive in a carriage with Madame Zola. The primitive man that had risen out of some jungle of my being did not view this immense and highly cultivated plain sympathetically. It seemed to him to differ little from the town, so utterly was nature dominated by man and portioned out. On a subject like this one can meditate for a long time, and I meditated till my meditation was broken by the stopping of the train. We were at Lyons. The tall white-painted houses reminded me of Paris—Lyons, as seen from the windows of *La Côte d'Azur* at the end of a grey December day might be Paris. The climate seemed the same; the sky was as sloppy and as grey. At last the train stopped at a place from which I could look down a side street, and I decided that Lyons wore a more provincial look than Paris, and I thought of the great silk trade and the dull minds of the merchants ... their dinner parties, etc. I noticed everything there was to notice in order to pass the time; but there was so little of interest that I wrote out a telegram and ran with it to the office, for Doris did not know what train I was coming by, and it is pleasant to be met at a station, to meet one familiar face, not to find oneself amid a crowd of strangers. Very nearly did I miss the train; my foot was on the footboard when the guard blew his whistle. "Just fancy if I had missed the train," I said, and settling myself in my seat I added, "now, let us study the landscape; such an opportunity as this may never occur again."

The long plain cultivated with tedious regularity that we had been passing through before we came to Lyons, flowed on field after field; it seemed as if we should never reach the end of it, and looking on those same fields, for they were the same, I said to myself: "If I were an economist that plain would interest me, but since I got Doris's letter I am primitive man, and he abhors the brown and the waving field, and 'the spirit in his feet' leads him to some grassy glen where he follows his flocks, listening to the song of the wilding bee that sings as it labours amid the gorse. What a soulless race that plain must breed," I thought; "what soulless days are lived there; peasants going forth at dusk to plough, and turning home at dusk to eat, procreate and sleep." At last a river appeared flowing amid sparse and stunted trees and reeds, a great wide sluggish river with low banks, flowing so slowly that it hardly seemed to flow at all. Rooks flew past, but they are hardly wilding birds; a crow—yes, we saw one; and I thought of a heron rising slowly out of one of the reedy islands; maybe an otter or two survives the persecution of the peasant, and I liked to think of a poacher picking up a rabbit here and there; hares must have almost disappeared, even the flock and the shepherd. France is not as picturesque a country as England; only Normandy seems to have pasturage, there alone the shepherd survives along the banks of the Seine. Picardy, though a swamp, never conveys an idea of the wild; and the middle of France, which I looked at then for the first time, shocked me, for primitive man, as I have said, was uppermost in me, and I turned away from the long plain, "Dreary," I said, "uneventful as a boarding-house."

But it is a long plain that has no hill in it, and when I looked out again a whole range showed so picturesquely that I could not refrain, but turned to a travelling companion to ask its name. It was the Esterelles; and never shall I forget the picturesqueness of one moment—the jagged end of the Esterelles projecting over the valley, showing against what remained of the sunset, one or two bars of dusky red, disappearing rapidly amid heavy clouds massing themselves as if for a storm, and soon after night closed over the landscape.

"Henceforth," I said, "I shall have to look to my own thoughts for amusement," and in my circumstances there was nothing reasonable for me to think of but Doris. Some time before midnight I should catch sight of her on the platform. It seemed to me wonderful that it should be so, and I must have been dreaming, for the voice of the guard, crying out that dinner was served awoke me with a start.

It is said to be the habit of my countrymen never to get into conversation with strangers in the train, but I doubt if that be so. Everything depends on the tact of him who first breaks silence; if his manner inspires confidence in his fellow-traveller he will receive such answers as will carry the conversation on for a minute or two, and in that time both will have come to a conclusion whether the conversation should be continued or dropped. A pleasant little book might be written about train acquaintances. If I were writing such a book I would tell of the Americans I once met at Nuremberg, and with whom I travelled to Paris; it was such a pleasant journey. I should have liked to keep up their acquaintance, but it is not the etiquette of the road to do so. But I am writing no such book; I am writing the quest of a golden fleece, and may allow myself no further deflection in the narrative; I may tell, however, of the two very interesting people I met at dinner on board *La Côte d'Azur*, though some readers will doubt if it be any integral part of my story. The woman was a typical French woman, pleasant and agreeable, a woman of the upper middle classes, so she seemed to me, but as I knew all her ideas the moment I looked at her, conversation with her did not flourish; or would it be more true to say that her husband interested me more, being less familiar? His accent told me he was French; but when he took off his hat I could see that he had come from the tropics—Algeria I thought; not unlikely a soldier. His talk was less stilted than a soldier's, and I began to notice that he did not look like a Frenchman, and when he told me that he lived in an oasis in the desert, and was on his way home, his Oriental appearance I explained by his long residence among the Arabs. He had lived in the desert since he was fourteen. "Almost a Saharian," I said to him. And during dinner, and long after dinner we sat talking of the difference between the Oriental races and the European; of the various Arab *patois*. He spoke the Tunisean *patois* and wrote the language of the Koran, which is understood all over the Sahara and the Soudan, as well as in Mecca. What interested me, perhaps even more than the language question, was the wilding's enterprise in attempting to cultivate the desert. He had already enlarged his estate by the discovery of two ancient Roman wells, and he had no doubt that all that part of the desert lying between the three oases could be brought into cultivation. In ancient times there were not three oases but one; the wells had been destroyed, and hundreds of thousands of acres had been laid waste by the Numidians in order, I think he told me, to save themselves from the Saracens who were following them. He spent eight months of every year in his oasis, and begged of me, as soon as I had wearied of Cannes, to take the boat from Marseilles—I suppose it was from Marseilles—and spend some time with him in the wild.

"Visitors," he said, "are rare. You'll be very welcome. The railway will take you within a hundred miles; the last hundred miles will be accomplished on the back of a dromedary; I shall send you a fleet one and an escort."

"Splendid," I answered. "I see myself arriving sitting high up on the hump gathering dates—I suppose there are date palms where you are? Yes?—and wearing a turban and a bournous."

"Would you like to see my bournous?" he said, and opening his valise he showed me a splendid one which filled me with admiration, and only shame forbade me to ask him to allow me to try it on. Ideas haunt one. When I was a little child I insisted on wearing a turban and going out for a ride on the pony, flourishing a Damascus blade which my father had brought home from the East. Nothing else would have satisfied me; my father led the pony, and I have always thought this fantasy exceedingly characteristic; it must be so, for it awoke in me twenty years afterwards; and fanciful and absurd as it may appear, I certainly should have liked to have worn my travelling companion's bournous in the train if only for a few minutes. All this is twelve years ago, and I have not yet gone to visit him in his oasis, but how many times have I done so in my imagination, seeing myself arriving on the back of a dromedary crying out, "Allah! Allah! And Mohammed is his prophet!" But though one can go on thinking year after year about a bournous, one cannot talk for more than two or three hours about one; and though I looked forward to spending at least a fortnight with my friends, and making excursions in the desert, finding summer, as Fromentin says, *chez lui*, I was glad to say good-bye to my friends at Marseilles.

I was still quite far from the end of my journey, and so weary of talk that at first I was doubtful whether or not it would be worth while to engage again in conversation, but a pleasant gentleman had got into my carriage, and he required little encouragement to tell me his story. His beginnings were very humble, but he was now a rich merchant. It is always interesting to hear how the office boy gets his first chance; the first steps are the interesting ones, and I should be able to tell his story here if we had not been interrupted in the middle of it by his little girl. She had wearied of her mother, who was in the next carriage, and had come in to sit on her father's knee. Her hair hung about her shoulders just as Doris's had done five years ago, taking the date from the day that I journeyed in quest of the golden fleece. She was a winsome child, with a little fluttering smile about her lips and a curious intelligence in her eyes. She admitted that she was tired, but had not been ill, and her father told me that long train journeys produced the same effect on her as a sea journey. She spoke with a pretty abruptness, and went away suddenly, I thought for good, but she returned half an hour afterwards looking a little faint, I thought, green about the mouth, and smiling less frequently. One cannot remember everything, and I have forgotten at what station these people got out; they bade me a kindly farewell, telling me that in about two hours and a half I should be at Plessy, and that I should have to change at the next station, and this lag end of my journey dragged itself out very wearily.

Plessy is difficult to get at; one has to change, and while waiting for the train I seemed to lose heart; nothing seemed to matter, not even Doris. But these are momentary capitulations of the intellect and the senses, and when I saw her pretty face on the platform I congratulated myself again on my wisdom in having sent her the telegram. How much pleasanter it was to walk with her to the hotel than to walk there alone! "She is," I said to myself, "still the same pretty girl whom I so bitterly reproached for selfishness in Cumberland Place five years ago." To compliment her on her looks, to tell her that she did not look a day older, a little thinner, a little paler, that was all, but the same enchanting Doris, was the facile inspiration of the returned lover. And we walked down the platform talking, my talk full of gentle reproof—why had she waited up? There was a reason.... My hopes, till now buoyant as corks, began to sink. "She is going to tell me that I cannot come to her hotel. Why did I send that telegram from Lyons?" Had it not been for that telegram I could have gone straight to her hotel. It was just the telegram that had brought her to the station, and she had come to tell me that it was impossible for me to stay at her hotel.

After thirty hours of travel it mattered little which hotel I stayed at, but to-morrow and the next day, the long week we were to spend together passed before my eyes, the tedium of the afternoons, the irritation and emptiness of Platonic evenings—"Heavens! what have I let myself in for," I thought, and my mind went back over the long journey and the prospect of returning *bredouille*, as the sportsmen say. But to argue about details with a woman, to get angry, is a thing that no one versed in the arts of love ever does. We are in the hands of women always; it is they who decide, and our best plan is to accept the different hotel without betraying disappointment, or as little as possible. But we had not seen each other for so long that we could not part at once. Doris said that I must come to her hotel and eat some supper. No; I had dined on board the train, and all she could persuade me to have was a cup of chocolate. Over that cup of chocolate we talked for an hour, and then I had to bid her goodnight. The moon looked down the street coldly; I crossed from shadow to light, feeling very weary in all my body, and there was a little melancholy in my heart, for after all I might not win Doris. There was sleep, however, and sleep is at times a good thing, and that night it must have come quickly, so great was the refreshment I experienced in the morning when my eyes opened and, looking through mosquito curtains (themselves symbols of the South), were delighted by the play of the sunlight flickering along the flower-papered wall. The impulse in me was to jump out of bed at once and to throw open *les croisées*. And what did I see? Tall palm trees in the garden, and above them a dim, alluring sky, and beyond them a blue sea in almost the same tone as the sky. And what did I feel? Soft perfumed airs moving everywhere. And what was the image that rose up in my mind? The sensuous gratification of a vision of a woman bathing at the edge of a summer wood, the intoxication of the odour of her breasts.... Why should I think of a woman bathing at the edge of a summer wood? Because the morning seemed the very one that Venus should choose to rise from the sea.

Forgive my sensuousness, dear reader; remember it was the first time I breathed the soft Southern air, the first time I saw orange trees; remember I am a poet, a modern Jason in search of a golden fleece. "Is this the garden of the Hesperides?" I asked myself, for nothing seemed more unreal than the golden fruit hanging like balls of yellow worsted among dark and sleek leaves; it reminded me of the fruit I used to see when I was a child under glass shades in lodging-houses, but I knew, nevertheless, that I was looking upon orange trees, and that the golden fruit growing amid the green leaves was the fruit I used to pick from the barrows when I was a boy; the fruit of which I ate so much in boyhood that I cannot eat it any longer; the fruit whose smell we associate with the pit of a theatre; the fruit that women never grow weary of, high and low. It seemed to me a wonderful thing that at last I should see oranges growing on trees; I so happy, so singularly happy, that I am nearly sure that happiness is, after all, no more than a faculty for being surprised. Since I was a boy I never felt so surprised as I did that morning. The *valet de chambre* brought in my bath, and while I bathed and dressed I reflected on the luck of him who in middle age can be astonished by a blue sky, and still find the sunlight a bewitchment. But who would not be bewitched by the pretty sunlight that finds its way into the gardens of Plessy? I knew I was going to walk with Doris by a sea blue as any drop-curtain, and for a moment Doris seemed to be but a figure on a drop-curtain. Am I very cynical? But are we not all figures on drop-curtains, and is not everything comic opera, and "La Belle Hélène" perhaps the only true reality? Amused by the idea of Jason or Paris or Menelaus in Plessy, I asked Doris what music was played by the local orchestra, and she told me it played "The March of Aïda" every evening. "Oh, the cornet," I said, and I understood that the mission of Plessy was to redeem one from the coil of one's daily existence, from Hebrew literature and its concomitants, bishops, vicars, and curates—all these, especially bishops, are regarded as being serious; whereas French novels and their concomitants, pretty girls, are supposed to represent the trivial side of life. A girl becomes serious only when she is engaged to be married; the hiring of the house in which the family is reared is regarded as serious; in fact all prejudices are serious; every deflection from the normal, from the herd, is looked upon as trivial; and I suppose that this is right: the world could not do without the herd nor could the herd do without us—the eccentrics who go to Plessy in quest of a golden fleece instead of putting stoves in the parish churches (stoves and organs are always regarded as too devilishly serious for words).

Once I had a long conversation with my archbishop concerning the Book of Daniel, and were I to write out his lordship's erudition I might even be deemed sufficiently serious for a review in the *Church Gazette*. But looking back on this interview and judging it with all the impartiality of which my nature is capable, I cannot in truth say that I regard it as more serious than pretty Doris's fluent conversation, or the melancholy aspect of his lordship's cathedral as more serious than the pretty Southern sunlight glancing along the seashore, lighting up the painted houses, and causing Doris to open her parasol. What a splendid article I might write on the trivial side of seriousness, but discussion is always trivial; I shall be much more serious in trying to recall the graceful movement of the opening of her parasol, and how prettily it enframed her face. True that almost every face is pretty against the distended silk full of sunlight and shadow, but Doris's, I swear to you, was as pretty as any medieval virgin despite its modernness. Memline himself never designed a more appealing little face. Think of the enchantment of such a face after a long journey, by the sea that the Romans and the Greeks used to cross in galleys, that I used to read about when I was a boy. There it was, and on the other side the shore on which Carthage used to stand; there it was, a blue bay with long red hills reaching out, reminding me of hills I had seen somewhere, I think in a battle piece by Salvator Rosa. It seemed to me that I had seen those hills before—no, not in a picture; had I dreamed them, or was there some remembrance of a previous existence struggling in my brain? There was a memory somewhere, a broken memory, and I sought for the lost thread as well as I could, for Doris rarely ceased talking.

"And there is the restaurant," she said, flinging up her parasol, "built at the end of those rocks."

We were the first swallows to arrive; the flocks would not be here for about three weeks. So we had the restaurant to ourselves, the waiter and doubtless the cook; and they gave us all their attention. Would we have breakfast in the glass pavilion? How shall I otherwise describe it, for it seemed to be all glass? The scent of the sea came through the window, and the air was like a cordial—it intoxicated; and looking across the bay one seemed to be looking on the very thing that Whistler had sought for in his Nocturnes, and that Steer had nearly caught in that picture of children paddling, that dim, optimistic blue that allures and puts the world behind one, the dream of the opium-eater, the phrase of the syrens in "Tannhäuser," the phrase which begins like a barcarolle; but the accompaniment tears underneath until we thrill with expectation.

As I looked across the bay, Doris seemed but a little thing, almost insignificant, and the thought came that I had not come for nothing even if I did not succeed in winning her.

"Doris, dear, forgive me if I am looking at this bay instead of you, but I've never seen anything like this before," and feeling I was doing very poor justice to the emotions I was experiencing, I said: "Is it not strange that all this is at once to me new and old? I seem, as it were, to have come into my inheritance."

"Your inheritance! Am I not——"

"Dearest, you are. Say that you are my inheritance, my beautiful inheritance; how many years have I waited for it?" As I took her in my arms she caught sight of the waiter, and turning from her I looked across the bay, and my desire nearly died in the infinite sweetness blowing across the bay.

"Azure hills, not blue; hitherto I have only seen blue."

"They're blue to-day because there is a slight mist, but they are in reality red."

"A red-hilled bay," I said, "and all the slopes flecked with the white sides of villas."

"Peeping through olive trees."

"Olive trees, of course. I have never yet seen the olive; the olive begins at Avignon or thereabouts, doesn't it? It was dark night when we passed through Avignon."

"You'll see very few trees here; only olives and ilex."

"The ilex I know, and there is no more beautiful tree than the ilex."

> "Were not the crocuses that grew
>   Under that ilex tree,
> As beautiful in scent and hue
>   As ever fed the bee?"

"Whose verses are those?"

"Shelley's. I know no others. Are the lines very wonderful? They seem no more than a statement, yet they hang about my memory. I am glad I shall see the ilex tree."

"And the eucalyptus—plenty of eucalyptus trees."

"That was the scent that followed us this morning as we came through the gardens."

"Yes, as we passed from our hotel one hung over the garden wall, and the wind carried its scent after us."

The arrival of the waiter with *hors d'oeuvres* distracted our attention from the olive tree to its fruit, I rarely touch olives, but that morning I ate many. Should we have mutton cutlets or lamb? Doris said the Southern mutton was detestable. "Then we'll have lamb." An idea came into my head, and it was this, that I had been mistaken about Doris's beauty. Hers was not like any face that one may find in a panel by Memline. She was like something, but I could not lay my thoughts on what she was like.

"A sail would spoil the beauty of the bay," I said when the waiter brought in the coffee, and left us—we hoped for the last time. Taking hands and going to the window we sat looking across the sailless bay. "How is it that no ships come here? Is the bay looked upon as a mere ornament and reserved exclusively for the appreciation of visitors? Those hills, too, look as if they had been designed in a like intent.... How much more beautiful the bay is without a sail—why I cannot tell, but——"

"But what?"

"A great galley rowed by fifty men would look well in this bay.... The bay is antiquity, and those hills; all the morning while talking to you a memory or a shadow of a memory has fretted in my mind like a fly on a pane. Now I know why I have been expecting a nymph to rise out of those waves during breakfast. For a thousand years men believed that nymphs came up on those rocks, and that satyrs and their progeny might be met in the woods and on the hillsides. Only a thin varnish has been passed over these beliefs. One has only to come here to look down into that blue sea-water to believe that nymphs swim about those rocks; and when we go for a drive among those hillsides we'll keep a sharp lookout for satyrs. Now I know why I like this country. It is heathen. Those mountains—how different from the shambling Irish hills from whence I have come! And you, Doris, you might have been dug up yesterday, though you are but two-and-twenty. You are a thing of yester age, not a bit like the little Memline head which I imagined you to be like when I was coming here in the train, nor like anything done by the Nuremberg painters. You are a Tanagra figure, and one of the finest. In you I read all the winsomeness of antiquity. But I must look at the bay now, for I may never see anything like it again; never have I seen anything like it before. Forgive me, remember that three days ago I was in Ireland, the day before yesterday I was in England, yesterday I was in Paris. I have come out of the greyness of the North. When I left Paris all was grey, and when the train passed through Lyons a grey night was gathering; now I see no cloud at all: the change is so wonderful. You cannot appreciate my admiration. You have been looking at the bay for the last three weeks, and *La côte d'azur* has become nothing to you now but palms and promenades. To me it is still quite different. I shall always see you beautiful, whereas Plessy may lose her beauty in a few days. Let me enjoy it while I may."

"Perhaps I shall not outlast Plessy."

"Yes, you will. Do you know, Doris, that you don't look a day older since the first time I saw you walking across the room to the piano in your white dress, your gold hair hanging down over your shoulders. It has darkened a little, that is all."

"It is provoking you should see me when I am thin. I wish you had seen me last year when I came from the rest cure. I went up more than a stone in weight. Every one said that I didn't look more than sixteen. I know I didn't, for all the women were jealous of me."

As I sat watching the dissolving line of the horizon, lost in a dream, I heard my companion say:

"Of what are you thinking?"

"I'm thinking of something that happened long ago in that very bay."

"Tell me about it;" and her hand sought mine for a moment.

"Would you like to hear it? I'd like to tell it, but it's a long, long story, and to remember it would be an effort. The colour of the sea and the sky is enough; the warmth of the sunlight penetrates me; I feel like a plant; the only difference between me and one of those palm trees——"

"I am sure those poor palms are shivering. There is not enough heat here for them; they come from the south, and you come from the north."

"I suppose that is so. They grow, but they don't flourish here. However, my mood is not philanthropic; I cannot pity even a palm tree at the present moment. See how my cigar smoke curls and goes out! It is strange, Doris, that I should meet you here, for some years ago it was arranged that I should come here— —"

"With a woman?"

"Yes, of course. How can it be otherwise? Our lives are woven along and across with women. Some men find the reality of their lives in women, others, as we were saying just now, in bishops."

"Tell me about the woman who asked you to come here? Did you love her? And what prevented you from coming here with her?"

"It is one of the oddest stories—odd only because it is like myself. Every character creates it own stories; we are like spools, and each spool fills itself up with a different-coloured thread. The story, such as it is, began one evening in Victoria Street at the end of a long day's work. A letter began it. She wrote asking me to dine with her, and her letter was most welcome, for I had no plans for that evening. I do not know if you know that curious dread of life which steals through the twilight; it had just laid its finger on my shoulder when the bell rang, and I said: 'My visitor is welcome, whoever she or he may be.' The visitor would have only spent a few minutes perhaps with me, but Gertrude's letter—that was her name—was a promise of a long and pleasant evening, for it was more than a mere invitation to dinner. She wrote: 'I have not asked any one to meet you, but you will not mind dining alone with me. I hope you will be able to come, for I want to consult you on a matter about which I think you will be able to advise me.' As I dressed I wondered what she could have to propose, and with my curiosity enkindled I walked to her house. The evening was fine—I remember it—and she did not live far from me; we were neighbours. You see I knew Gertrude pretty well, and I liked her. There had been some love passages between us, but I had never been her lover; our story had got entangled, and as I went to her I hoped that this vexatious knot was to be picked at last. To be Gertrude's lover would be a pleasure indeed, for though a woman of forty, a natural desire to please, a witty mind, and pretty manners still kept her young; she had all the appearance of youth; and French gowns and underwear that cost a little fortune made her a woman that one would still take a pleasure in making love to. It would be pleasant to be her lover for many reasons. There were disadvantages, however, for Gertrude, though never vulgar herself, liked vulgar things. Her friends were vulgar; her flat, for she had just left her husband, was opulent, overdecorated; the windows were too heavily curtained, the electric light seemed to be always turned on, and as for the pictures—well, we won't talk of them; Gertrude was the only one worth looking at. And she was rather like a Salon picture, a Gervex, a Boldeni—I will not be unjust to Gertrude, she was not as vulgar as a Boldeni. She had a pretty cooing manner, and her white dress fell gracefully from her slender flanks. You can see her, can't you, coming forward to meet me, rustling a little, breathing an odour of orris root, taking my hand and very nearly pressing it against her bosom? Gertrude knew how to suggest, and no sooner had the thought that she wished to inspire passed through my mind than she let go my hand, saying: 'Come, sit down by me, tell me what you have been doing'; and her charm was that it was impossible to say whether what I have described, dress, manner, and voice, was unconscious or intentional."

"Probably a little of both," Doris said.

"I see you understand. You always understand."

"And to make amends for the familiarity of pressing your hand to her bosom she would say: 'I hope you will not mind dining alone with me,' and immediately you would propound a little theory that two is company and three is a county council, unless indeed the three consist of two men and one woman. A woman is never really happy unless she is talking to two men, woman being at heart a polyandrist."

"Doris, you know me so well that you can invent my conversations."

"Yes, I think I can. You have not changed; I have not forgotten you though we have not seen each other for five years; and now go on, tell me about Gertrude."

"Well, sitting beside her on the sofa——"

"Under the shaded electric light," interrupted Doris.

"I tried to discover—not the reason of this invitation to dinner; of course it was natural that old friends should dine together, but she had said in her letter that she wished to talk to me about some matter on which she thought I could advise her. The servant would come in a moment to announce that dinner was ready, and if Gertrude did not tell me at once I might, if the story were a long one, have to wait till dinner was over; her reluctance to confide in me seemed to point to pecuniary help. Was it possible that Gertrude was going to ask me to lend her money! If so, the loan would be a heavy one, more than I could afford to lend. That is the advantage of knowing rich people; when they ask for money they ask for more than one can afford to lend, and one can say with truth: 'Were I to lend you five hundred pounds, I should not be able to make ends meet at the end of the year.' Her reluctance to confide in me seemed incomprehensible, unless indeed she wanted to borrow money. But Gertrude was not that kind, and she was a rich woman. At last, just before the servant came into the room, she turned round saying that she had sent for me because she wished to speak to me about a yacht. Imagine my surprise. To speak to me about a yacht! If it had been about the picture.

"The door opened, the servant announced that dinner was ready, and we had to talk in French during dinner, for her news was that she had hired a yacht for the winter in order that she might visit Greece and the Greek Islands. But she did not dare to travel in Greece alone for six months, and it was difficult to find a man who was free and whom one could trust. She thought she could trust me, and remembering that I had once liked her, it had occurred to her to ask me if I would like to go with her. I shall never forget how Gertrude confided her plan to me, the charming modesty with which she murmured: 'Perhaps you do still, and you will not bore me by claiming rights over me. I don't mind your making love to me, but I don't like rights. You know what I mean. When we return to England you will not pursue me. You know what I have suffered from such pursuits; you know all about it?' Is it not curious how a woman will sometimes paint her portrait in a single phrase; not paint, but indicate in half-a-dozen lines her whole moral nature? Gertrude exists in the words I have quoted just as God made her. And now I have to tell you about the pursuit. When Gertrude mentioned it I had forgotten it; a blankness came into my face, and she said: 'Don't you remember?' 'Of course, of course,' I said, and this is the story within the story.

"One day after lunch Gertrude, getting up, walked unconsciously towards me, and quite naturally I took her in my arms, and when I had told her how much I liked her, and the pleasure I took in her company, she promised to meet me at a hotel in Lincoln. We were to meet there in a fortnight's time; but two days before she sent for me, and told me that she would have to send me away. I really did like Gertrude, and I was quite overcome, and a long hour was spent begging of her to tell why she had come to this determination. One of course says unjust things, one accuses a woman of cruelty; what could be the meaning of it? Did she like to play with a man as a cat plays with a mouse? But Gertrude, though she seemed distressed at my accusations, refused to give me any explanation of her conduct; tears came into her eyes—they seemed like genuine tears—and it was difficult to believe that she had taken all this trouble merely to arrive at this inexplicable and most disagreeable end. Months passed without my hearing anything of Gertrude, till one day she sent me a little present, and in response to a letter she invited me to come to see her in the country. And, walking through some beautiful woods, she told me the reason why she had not gone to Lincoln. A Pole whom she had met at the gambling tables at Monte Carlo was pursuing her, threatening her that if he saw her with any other man he would murder her and her lover. This at first seemed an incredible tale, but when she entered into details, there could be no doubt that she was telling the truth, for had she not on one occasion very nearly lost her life through this man? They were in Germany together, she and the Pole, and he had locked her up in her room without food for many hours, and coming in suddenly he had pressed the muzzle of a pistol against her temple and pulled the trigger. Fortunately, it did not go off. 'It was a very near thing,' she said; 'the cartridge was indented, and I made up my mind that if things went any further, I should have to tell my husband.' 'But things can't go further than an indented cartridge,' I answered. 'What you tell me is terrible'; and we talked for a long time, walking about the woods, fearing that the Pole might spring from behind every bush, the pistol in his hand. But he did not appear; she evidently knew where he was, or had made some compact with him. Nevertheless, at the close of the day, I drove through the summer evening not having got anything from Gertrude except a promise that if she should find herself free, she would send for me. Weeks and months went by during which I saw Gertrude occasionally; you see love stories, once they get entangled, remain entangled; that is what makes me fear that we shall never be able to pick the knot that you have tied our love story into. Misadventure followed misadventure. It seems to me that I behaved very stupidly on many occasions; it would take too long to tell you how—when I met her at the theatre I did not do exactly what I should have done; and on another occasion when I met her driving in a suburb, I did not stop her cab, and so on and so on until, resolved to bring matters to a crisis, Gertrude had sent me an invitation to dinner, and her plan was the charming one which I have told you, that we should spend six months sailing about the Greek Islands in a yacht. We left the dining-room and returned to the drawing-room, she telling me that the yacht had been paid for—the schooner, the captain, the crew, everything for six months; but I not unnaturally pointed out to her that I could not accept her hospitality for so long a time, and the greater part of the evening was spent in trying to persuade her to allow me to pay—Gertrude was the richer—at least a third of the upkeep of the yacht must come out of my pocket.

"The prospect of a six months' cruise among the Greek Islands kindled my imagination, and while listening to Gertrude I was often in spirit far away, landing perchance at Cyprus, exalted at the prospect of visiting the Cyprians' temple; or perchance standing with Gertrude on the deck of the yacht watching the stars growing dim in the east; the sailors would be singing at the time, and out of the ashen stillness a wind would come, and again we would hear the ripple of the water parting as the jib filled and drew the schooner eastward. I imagined how half an hour later an island would appear against the golden sky, a lofty island lined with white buildings, perchance ancient fanes. 'What a delicious book my six months with Gertrude will be!' I said as I walked home, and the title of the book was an inspiration, 'An Unsentimental Journey.' It was Gertrude's own words that had suggested it. Had she not said that she did not mind my making love to her, but she did not like rights? She couldn't complain if I wrote a book, and I imagined how every evening when the lover left her, the chronicler would sit for an hour recording his impressions. Very often he would continue writing until the pencil dropped from his hand, till he fell asleep in the chair. An immediate note-taking would be necessary, so fugitive are impressions, and an analysis of his feelings, their waxing and their waning; he would observe himself as an astronomer observes the course of a somewhat erratic star, and his descriptions of himself and of her would be interwoven with descriptions of the seas across which Menelaus had gone after Helen's beauty—beauty, the noblest of men's quests.

"For once Nature seemed to me to put into the hands of the artist a subject perfect in its every part; the end especially delighted me, and I imagined our good-byes at Plymouth or Portsmouth or Hull, wherever we might land. 'Well, Gertrude, goodbye. We have spent a very pleasant six months together; I shall never forget our excursion. But this is not a rupture; I may hope to see you some time during the season? You will allow me to call about tea-time?' And she would answer: 'Yes, you may call. You have been very nice.' Each would turn away sighing, conscious of a little melancholy in the heart, for all partings are sad; but at the bottom of the heart there would be a sense of relief, of gladness—that gladness which the bird feels when it leaves its roost: there is nothing more delicious perhaps than the first beat of the wings. I forget now whether I looked forward most to the lady or to the book.... If the winds had been more propitious, I might have written a book that would have compared favourably with the eighteenth-century literature, for the eighteenth century was cynical in love; while making love to a woman, a gallant would often consider a plan for her subsequent humiliation. Gouncourt——"

"But, dear one, finish about the yacht."

"Well, it seemed quite decided that Gertrude and I were to go to Marseilles to meet the schooner; but the voyage from the Bay of Biscay is a stormy and a tedious one; the weather was rough all the way, and she took a long time to get to Gibraltar. She passed the strait signalling to Lloyd's; we got a telegram; everything was ready; I had ordered yachting clothes, shoes, and quantities of things; but after that telegram no news came, and one evening Gertrude told me she was beginning to feel anxious; the yacht ought to have arrived at Marseilles. Three or four days passed, and then we read in the paper—the *Evening Standard*, I think it was—the *Ring-Dove*, a large schooner, had sunk off the coast while making for the Bay of Plessy. Had she passed that point over yonder, no doubt she would have been saved; all hands were lost, the captain, seven men, and my book."

"Good heavens, how extraordinary! And what became of Gertrude? Were you never her lover?"

"Never. We abstained while waiting for the yacht. Then she fell in love with somebody else; she married her lover; and now he deplores her; she found an excellent husband, and she died in his arms."

At every moment I expected Doris to ask me how it was that, for the sake of writing a book, I had consented to go away for a six months' cruise with a woman whom I didn't love. But there was a moment when I loved her—the week before Lincoln. Whether Doris agreed tacitly that my admiration of Gertrude's slender flanks and charm of manner and taste in dress justified me in agreeing to go away with her, I don't know; she did not trouble me with the embarrassing question I had anticipated. Isn't it strange that people never ask the embarrassing questions one foresees? She asked me instead with whom I had been in love during the past five years, and this too embarrassed me, though not to the extent the other question would have done. To say that since I had seen Doris I had led a chaste life would be at once incredible and ridiculous. Sighing a little, I spoke of a *liaison* that had lasted many years and had come to an end at last. Fearing that Doris would ask if it had come to an end through weariness, it seemed well to add that the lady had a daughter growing up, and it was for the girl's sake we had agreed to bring our love story to a close. We had, however, promised to remain friends.

Doris's silence embarrassed me a little, for she didn't ask any questions about the lady and her daughter; and it was impossible to tell from her manner whether she believed that this lady comprised the whole of my love life for the last five years, and if she thought I had really broken with her. For a moment or two I did not dare to look at Doris, and then I felt that her disbelief mattered little, so long as it did not enter as an influencing factor into the present situation. Under a sky as blue and amid nature poetical as a drop-curtain, one's moral nature dozes. No doubt that was it. There is an English church at Plessy, but really! Dear little town, town of my heart, where the local orchestra plays "The March of Aida" and "La Belle Hélène"! If I could inoculate you, reader, with the sentiment of the delicious pastoral you would understand why, all the time I was at Plessy, I looked upon myself as a hero of legend, whether of the Argonauts or the siege of Troy matters little. Returning from Mount Ida after a long absence, after presenting in imagination the fairest of women with the apple, I said:

"You asked me whom I had been in love with; now tell me with whom have you been in love?"

"For the last three years I have been engaged to be married."

"And you are still engaged?"

She nodded, her eyes fixed on the blue sea, and I said laughing, that it was not of a marriage or an engagement to be married that I spoke, but of the beautiful, irrepressible caprice.

"You wouldn't have me believe that no passion has caught you and dragged you about for the last five years, just as a cat drags a little mouse about?"

"It is strange that you should ask me that, for that is exactly what happened."

"Really?"

"Only that I suffered much more than any mouse ever suffered."

"Doris, tell me. You know how sympathetic I am; you know I shall understand. All things human interest me. If you have loved as much as you say, your story will ... I must hear it."

"Why should I tell it?" and her eyes filled with tears. "I suffered horribly. Don't speak to me about it. What is the good of going over it all again?"

"Yes, there is good; very much good comes of speaking, if this love story is over, if there is no possibility of reviving it. Tell it, and in telling, the bitterness will pass from you. Who was this man? How did you meet him?"

"He was a friend of Albert's. Albert introduced him."

"Albert is the man you are engaged to? The old story, the very oldest. Why should it always be the friend? There are so many other men, but it is always the friend who attracts." And I told Doris the story of a friend who had once robbed me, and my story had the effect of drying her tears. But they began again as soon as she tried to tell her own story. There could be no doubt that she had suffered. Things are interesting in proportion to the amount of ourselves we put into them; Doris had clearly put all her life into this story; a sordid one it may seem to some, a story of deception and lies, for of course Albert was deceived as cruelly as many another good man. But Doris must have suffered deeply, for at the memory of her sufferings her face streamed with tears. As I looked at her tears I said: "It is strange that she should weep so, for her story differs nowise from the many stories happening daily in the lives of men and women. She will tell me the old and beautiful story of lovers forced asunder by cruel fate, and this spot is no doubt a choice one to hear her story." And raising my eyes I admired once again the drooping shore, the serrated line of mountains sweeping round the bay. And the colour was so intense that it overpowered the senses like a perfume, "like musk," I thought. When I turned to Doris I could see she was wholly immersed in her own sorrow, and it took all my art to persuade her to tell it, or it seemed as if all my art of persuasion were necessary.

"As soon as you knew you loved him, you resolved to see him no more?"

Doris nodded.

"You sent him away before you yielded to him?"

She nodded, and looking at me her eyes filled with tears, but which only seemed to make them still more beautiful, she told me that they had both felt that it was impossible to deceive Albert.

All love stories are alike in this; they all contain what the reviewers call "sordid details." But if Tristan had not taken advantage of King Mark's absence on a hunting expedition, the world would have been the poorer of a great love story; and what, after all, does King Mark's happiness matter to us—a poor passing thing, whose life was only useful in this, that it gave us an immortal love story? And if Wagner had not loved Madame Wasendonck, and if Madame Wasendonck had not been unfaithful to her husband, we should not have had "Tristan." Who then would, for the sake of Wasendonck's honour, destroy the score of "Tristan"? Nor is the story of "Tristan" the only one, nor the most famous. There is also the story of Helen. If Menelaus's wife had not been unfaithful to him, the world would have been the poorer of the greatest of all poems, the "Iliad" and the "Odyssey." Dear me, when one thinks of it, one must admit that art owes a great deal to adultery. Children are born of the marriage, stories of the adulterous bed, and the world needs both—stories as well as children. Even my little tale would not exist if Doris had been a prudent maiden, nor would it have interested me to listen to her that day by the sea if she had naught to tell me but her unswerving love for Albert. Her story is not what the world calls a great story, and it would be absurd to pretend that if a shorthand writer had taken it down his report would compare with the stories of Isolde and Helen, but I heard it from her lips, and her tears and her beauty replaced the language of Wagner and of Homer; and so well did they do this that I am not sure that the emotion I experienced in listening to her was less than that which I have experienced before a work of art.

"Do you know," she began, "perhaps you don't, perhaps you've never loved enough to know the anxiety one may feel for the absent. We had been together all day once, and when we bade each other good-bye we agreed that we should not see each other for two days, till Thursday; but that night in bed an extraordinary desire took hold of me to know what had become of him. I felt I must hear from him; one word would be enough. But we had promised. It was stupid, it was madness, yet I had to take down the telephone, and when I got into communication what do you think the answer was?—'Thank God you telephoned! I've been walking about the room nearly out of my mind, feeling that I should go mad if the miracle did not happen.'"

"If you loved Ralph better than Albert——"

"Why didn't I give up Albert? Albert's life would have been broken and ruined if I had done that. You see he has loved me so many years that his life has become centred in me. He is not one of those men who like many women. Outside of his work nothing exists but me. He doesn't care much for reading, but he reads the books I like. I don't know that he cares much about music for its own sake, but he likes to hear me sing just because it is me. He never notices other women; I don't think that he knows what they wear, but he likes my dresses, not because they are in good taste, but because I wear them.

One can't sacrifice a man like that. What would one think of oneself? One would die of remorse. So there was nothing to be done but for Ralph to go away. It nearly killed me."

"I'm afraid I can give you no such love; my affection for you will prove very tepid after such violent emotions."

"I don't want such emotions again; I could not bear them, they would kill me; even a part would kill me. Two months after Ralph left I was but a little shadow. I was thinner than I am now, I was worn to a thread, I could hardly keep body and skirt together."

We laughed at Doris's little joke; and we watched it curling and going out like a wreath of cigarette smoke.

"But did you get no happiness at all out of this great love?"

"We were happy only a very little while."

"How long?"

Doris reflected.

"We had about six weeks of what I should call real happiness, the time while Albert was away. When he came back the misery and remorse began again. I had to see him—not Albert, the other—every day; and Albert began to notice that I was different. We used to go out together, we three, and at last the sham became too great and Albert said he could not stand it any longer. 'I prefer you should go out with him alone, and if it be for your happiness I'll give you up.'"

"So you nearly died of love! Well, now you must live for love, liking things as they go by. Life is beautiful at the moment, sad when we look back, fearful when we look forward; but I suppose it's hopeless to expect a little Christian like you to live without drawing conclusions, liking things as they go by as the nymphs do. Dry those tears; forget that man. You tell me it is over and done. Remember nothing except that the sky and the sea are blue, that it is a luxury to feel alive here by the sea-shore. My happiness would be to make you happy, to see you put the past out of your mind, to close your eyes to the future. That will be easy to do by this beautiful sea-shore, under those blue skies with flowers everywhere and drives among the mountains awaiting us. We create our own worlds. Chance has left you here and sent me to you. I want you to eat a great deal and to sleep and to get fatter and to dream and to read Theocritus, so that when we go to the mountains we shall be transported into antiquity. You must forget Albert and him who made you unhappy—he allowed you to look back and forwards."

"I think I deserve some happiness; you see I have sacrificed so much."

At these words my hopes rose—shall I say like a balloon out of which a great weight of ballast has been thrown?—and so high did they go that failure seemed like a little feather swimming in the gulf below. "She deserved some happiness," and intends to make me her happiness. Her words could bear no other interpretation; she had spoken without thought, and instinctively. Albert was away; why should she not take this happiness which I offered her? Would she understand that distance made a difference, that it was one thing to deceive Albert if he were with her, and another when she was a thousand miles away? It was as if we were in a foreign country; we were under palm trees, we were by the Mediterranean. With Albert a thousand miles away it would be so easy for her to love me. She had said there was no question of her marrying any one but Albert—and to be unfaithful is not to be inconstant. These were the arguments which I would use if I found that I had misunderstood her; but for the moment I did not dare to inquire; it would be too painful to hear I had misunderstood her; but at last, feeling she might guess the cause of my silence, I said, not being able to think of anything more plausible:

"You spoke, didn't you, of going for a drive?"

"We were speaking of happiness—but if you'd like to go for a drive. There's no happiness like driving."

"Isn't there?"

She pinched my arm, and with a choking sensation in the throat I asked her if I should send for a carriage.

"There will be time for a short drive before the sun setting. You said you admired the hills—one day we will go to a hill town. There is a beautiful one—Florac is the name of it—but we must start early in the morning. To-day there will be only time to drive as far as the point you have been admiring all the morning. The road winds through the rocks, and you want to see the ilex trees."

"My dear, I want to see you."

"Well, you're looking at me. Come, don't be disagreeable."

"Disagreeable, Doris! I never felt more kindly in my life. I'm still absorbed in the strange piece of luck which has brought us together, and in such a well-chosen spot; no other would have pleased me as much."

"Now why do you like the landscape? Tell me."

"I cannot think of the landscape now, Doris: I'm thinking of you, of what you said just now."

"What did I say?"

"You said—I tried to remember the words at the time, but I have forgotten them, so many thoughts have passed through my mind since—you said—how did you word it?—after having suffered as much as you did, some share of happiness——"

"No, I didn't say that; I said, having sacrificed so much, I thought I deserved a little happiness."

"So she knew what she was saying," I said to myself. "Her words were not casual," but not daring to ask her if she intended to make me her happiness, I spoke about the landscape. "You ask me why I like the landscape? Because it carries me back into past times when men believed in nymphs and in satyrs. I have always thought it must be a wonderful thing to believe in the dryad. Do you know that men wandering in the woods sometimes used to catch sight of a white breast between the leaves, and henceforth they could love no mortal woman? The beautiful name of their malady was nympholepsy. A disease that every one would like to catch."

"But if you were to catch it you wouldn't be able to love me, so I'll not bring you to the mountains. Some peasant girl——"

"Fie! Doris, I have never liked peasant girls."

"Your antiquity is eighteenth-century antiquity. There are many alcoves in it."

"I don't know that the alcove was an invention of the eighteenth century. There were alcoves at all times. But, Doris, good heavens! what are those trees? Never did I see anything so ghastly; they are like ghosts. Not only have they no leaves, but they have no bark nor any twigs; nothing but great white trunks and branches."

"I think they are called plantains."

"That won't do, you are only guessing; I must ask the coachman."

"I think, sir, they are called plantains."

"You only think. Stop and I'll ask those people."

"Sont des plantains, Monsieur."

"Well, I told you so," Doris said, laughing.

Beyond this spectral avenue, on either side of us there were fields, and Doris murmured:

"See how flat the country is, to the very feet of the hills, and the folk working in the fields are pleasant to watch."

I declared that I could not watch them, nor could you, reader, if you had been sitting by Doris. I had risen and come away from long months of toil; and I remember how I told Doris as we drove across those fields towards the hills, that it was not her beauty alone that interested me; her beauty would not be itself were it not illumed by her wit and her love of art. What would she be, for instance, if she were not a musician? Or would her face be the same face if it were robbed of its mirth? But mirth is enchanting only when the source of it is the intelligence. Vacuous laughter is the most tiresome of things; a face of stone is more inveigling. But Doris prided herself on her beauty more than on her wit, and she was disinclined to admit the contention that beauty is dependent upon the intelligence. Our talk rambled on, now in one direction, now in another.

Lovers are divided into two kinds, the babbling and the silent.

We meet specimens of the silent kind on a Thames back-water—the punt drawn up under the shady bank with the twain lying side by side, their arms about each other all the afternoon. When evening comes, and it is time to return home, her fellow gets out the sculls, and they part saying: "Well, dear, next Sunday, at the same time." "Yes, at the same time next Sunday."

We were of the babbling kind, as the small part of our conversation that appears in this story shows.

"My dear, my dear, remember that we are in an open carriage."

"What do those folks matter to us?"

"My dear, if I don't like it?"

To justify my desire of her lips I began to compare her beauty with that of a Greek head on a vase, saying that hers was a cameo-like beauty, as dainty as any Tanagra figure.

"And to see you and not to claim you, not to hold your face in my hands just as one holds a vase, is— —"

"Is what?"

"A kind of misery. What else shall I say? Fancy my disappointment if, on digging among these mountains, I were to find a beautiful vase, and some one were to say: 'You can look at it but not touch it.'"

"Do you love me as well as that?" she answered, somewhat moved, for my words expressed a genuine emotion.

"I do indeed, Doris."

"We might get out here. I want you to see the view from the hilltop."

And, telling the driver that he need not follow us, to stay there and rest his panting horse, we walked on. Whether Doris was thinking of the view I know not; I only know that I thought only of kissing Doris. To do so would be pleasant—in a way—even on this cold hillside, and I noticed that the road bent round the shoulder of the mount. We soon reached the hilltop, and we could see the road enter the village in the dip between the hills, a double line of houses—not much more—facing the sea, a village where we might go to have breakfast; we might never go there; however that might be, we certainly should remember that village and the road streaming out of it on the other side towards the hills. Now and then we lost sight of the road; it doubled round some rock or was hidden behind a group of trees; and then we caught sight of it a little farther on, ascending the hills in front of us, and no doubt on the other side it entered another village, and so on around the coast of Italy. Even with the thought of Doris's kisses in my mind, I could admire the road and the curves of the bay. I felt in my pocket for a piece of paper and a pencil. The colour was as beautiful as a Brabizon; there were many tints of blue, no doubt, but the twilight had gathered the sea and sky into one tone, or what seemed to be one tone.

"You wanted to see olive trees—those are olives."

"So those are olives! Do I at last look upon olives?"

"Are you disappointed?"

"Yes and no. The white gnarled trunk makes even the young trees seem old. The olive is like an old man with skimpy legs. It seems to me a pathetic tree. One does not like to say it is ugly; it is not ugly, but it would be puzzling to say wherein lies its charm, for it throws no shade, and is so grey—nothing is so grey as the olive. I like the ilex better."

Where the road dipped there was a group of ilex trees, and it was in their shade that I kissed Doris, and the beauty of the trees helps me to appreciate the sentiment of those kisses. And I remember that road and those ilex trees as I might remember a passage in Theocritus. Doris—her very name suggests antiquity, and it was well that she was kissed by me for the first time under ilex trees; true that I had kissed her before, but that earlier love story has not found a chronicler, and probably it never will. I like to think that the beauty of the ilex is answerable, perhaps, for Doris's kisses—in a measure. Her dainty grace, her Tanagra beauty, seemed to harmonise with that of the ilex, for there is an antique beauty in this tree that we find in none other. Theocritus must have composed many a poem beneath it. It is the only tree that the ancient world could have cared to notice; and if it were possible to carve statues of trees, I am sure that the ilex is the tree sculptors would choose. The beech and the birch, all the other trees, only began to be beautiful when men invented painting. No other tree shapes itself out so beautifully as the ilex, lifting itself up to the sky so abundantly and with such dignity—a very queen in a velvet gown is the ilex tree; and we stood looking at the group, admiring its glossy thickness, till suddenly the ilex tree went out of my mind, and I thought of the lonely night that awaited me.

"Doris, dear, it is more than flesh and blood can bear. My folly lay in sending the telegram. Had I not sent it you wouldn't have known by what train I was coming; you would have been fast asleep in your bed, and I should have gone straight to your hotel."

"But, darling, you wouldn't compromise me. Every one would know that we stayed at the same hotel."

"Dearest, it might happen by accident, and were it to happen by accident what could you do?"

"All I can say is that it would be a most unfortunate accident."

"Then I have come a thousand miles for nothing. This is worse than the time in London when I left you for your strictness. Can nothing be done?"

"Am I not devoted to you? We have spent the whole day together. Now I don't think it's at all nice of you to reproach me with having brought you on a fool's errand."

"I didn't say that," and we quarrelled a little until we reached the carriage. Doris was angry, and when she spoke again it was to say:

"If you are not satisfied, you can go back. I'm sorry. I think it's most unreasonable that you should ask me to compromise myself."

"And I think it's unkind of you to suggest that I should go back, for how can I go back?"

She did not ask me why—she was too angry at the moment—and it was well she did not, for I should have been embarrassed to tell her that I was fairly caught.

I had come a thousand miles to see her, and I could not say I was going to take the *Côte d'azur* back again, because she would not let me stay at her hotel; to do so would be too childish, too futile. The misery of the journey back would be unendurable. There was nothing to do but to wait, and hope that life, which is always full of accidents, would favour us. Better think no more about it. For it is thinking that makes one miserable.

There were many little things which helped to pass the time away. Doris went every evening to a certain shop to fetch two eggs that had been laid that morning. It was necessary for her health that she should eat eggs beaten up with milk between the first and second breakfast. We went there, and it was amusing to pick my way through the streets, carrying her eggs back to the hotel for her. She knew a few people—strange folk, I thought them—elderly spinsters living *en pension* at different hotels. We dined with her friends, and after dinner Doris sang, and when she had played many things that she used to play to me in the old days, it was time for her to go to bed, for she rarely slept after six o'clock, so she said.

"Good-night. Ah, no, the hour is ill," I murmured to myself as I wended my lonely way, and I lay awake thinking if I had said anything that would prejudice my chances of winning her, if I had omitted to say anything that might have inclined her to yield. One lies awake at night thinking of the mistakes one has made; thoughts clatter in one's head. Good heavens! how stupid it was of me not to have used a certain argument. Perhaps if I had spoken more tenderly, displayed a more Christian spirit—all that paganism, that talk about nymphs and dryads and satyrs and fauns frightened her. In the heat of the moment one says more than one intends, though it is quite true that, as a rule, it is well to insist that there is no such thing as our lower nature, that everything about us is divine. So constituted are we that the mind accepts the convention, and what we have to do is to keep to the convention, just as in opera. Singing appears natural so long as the characters do not speak. Once they speak they cannot go back to music; the convention has been broken.

As in Art so it is in Life. Tell a woman that she is a nymph, and she must not expect any more from you than she would from a faun, that all you know is the joy of the sunlight, that you have no dreams beyond the worship of the perfect circle of her breast, and the desire to gather grapes for her, and she will give herself to you unconscious of sin. I must have fallen asleep thinking of these things, and I must have slept soundly, for I remembered nothing until the servant came in with my bath, and I saw again the pretty sunlight flickering along the wall-paper. Before parting the previous night, Doris and I had arranged that I was to call an hour earlier than usual at the hotel; I was to be there at half-past ten. She had promised to be ready. We were going to drive to Florac, to one of the hill towns, and it would take two hours to get there. We were going to breakfast there, and while I dressed, and in the carriage going there, I cherished the hope that perhaps I might be able to persuade Doris to breakfast in a private room, though feeling all the while that it would be difficult to do so, for the public room would be empty, and crowds of waiters would gather about us like rooks, each trying to entice us towards his table.

The village of Florac is high up among the hills, built along certain ledges of rock overlooking the valley, and going south in the train one catches sight of many towns, like it built among mountain declivities, hanging out like nests over the edge of precipices, showing against a red background, crowning the rocky hill. No doubt these mediaeval towns were built in these strange places because of the security that summit gives against raiders. One can think of no other reason, for it is hard to believe that in the fifteenth century men were so captivated with the picturesque that for the sake of it they would drag every necessary of life up these hills, several hundred feet above the plain, probably by difficult paths— the excellent road that wound along the edge of the hills, now to the right, now to the left, looping itself round every sudden ascent like a grey ribbon round a hat, did not exist when Florac was built. On the left the ground shelves away into the valley, down towards the sea, and olives were growing down all these hillsides. Above us were olive trees, with here and there an orange orchard, and the golden fruit shining among the dark leaves continued to interest me. Every now and again some sudden aspect interrupted our conversation; the bay as it swept round the carved mountains, looking in the distance more than ever like an old Italian picture of a time before painters began to think about values and truth of effect, when the minds of men were concerned with beauty; as mine was, for every time I looked at Doris it occurred to me that I had never seen anything prettier, and not only her face but her talk still continued to enchant me. She was always so eager to tell me things, that she must interrupt, and these interruptions were pleasant. I identified them with her, and so closely that I can remember how our talk began when we got out of the suburbs. By the last villa there was a eucalyptus tree growing; the sun was shining, and Doris had asked me to hold her parasol for her; but the road zigzagged so constantly that I never shifted the parasol in time, and a ray would catch her just in the face, adding perhaps to the freckles—there were just a few down that little nose which was always pleasant to look upon. I was saying that I still remember our talk as we passed that eucalyptus tree. Doris had begun one of those little confessions which are so interesting, and which one hears only from a woman one is making love to, which probably would not interest us were we to hear them from any one else. It delighted me to hear Doris say: "This is the first time I have ever lived alone, that I have ever been free from questions. It was a pleasure to remember suddenly as I was dressing that no one would ask me where I was going, that I was just like a bird by myself, free to spring off the branch and to fly. At home there are always people round one; somebody is in the dining-room, somebody is in the drawing-room; and if one goes down the passage with one's hat on there is always somebody to ask where one is going, and if you say you don't know they say, 'Are you going to the right or to the left, because if you are going to the left I should like you to stop at the apothecary's and to ask——?'" How I agreed with her! Family life I said degrades the individual, and is only less harmful than socialism, because one can escape from it....

"But, Doris, you're not ill! You are looking better."

"I weighed this morning, and I have gone up two pounds. You see I am amused, and a woman's health is mainly a question whether she is amused, whether somebody is making love to her."

"Making love! Doris, dear, there is no chance of making love to anybody here. That is the only fault I find with the place; the sea, the bay, the hill towns, everything I see is perfect in every detail, only the essential is lacking. I was thinking, Doris, that for the sake of your health we might go and spend a few days at Florac."

"My dear, it would be impossible. Everybody would know that I had been there."

"Maybe, but I don't agree. However, I am glad that you have gone up two pounds.... I am sure that what you need is mountain air. The seaside is no good at all for nerves. I have a friend in Paris who suffers from nerves and has to go every year to Switzerland to climb the Matterhorn."

"The Matterhorn!"

"Well, the Matterhorn or Mont Blanc; he has to climb mountains, glaciers, something of that kind. I remember last year I wrote to him saying that I did not understand the three past tenses in French, and would he explain why—something, I have forgotten what—and he answered: 'Avec mes pieds sur des glaciers je ne puis m'arrêter pour vous expliquer les trois passés.'"

Doris laughed and was interested, for I had introduced her some years ago to the man who had written this letter; and then we discussed the *fussent* and the *eussent*, *été*, and when our language of the French Grammar was exhausted we returned to the point whence we had come, whether it was possible to persuade Doris to pass three days in the hotel at Florac—in the interests of her health, of course.

"I'm not sure at all that mountain air would not do me good. Plessy lies very low and is very relaxing."

"Very."

But though I convinced her that it would have been better if she had gone at once to stop at Florac, I could do nothing to persuade her to pass three days with me in the inn there. As we drove up through the town the only hope that remained in my mind was that I might induce her to take breakfast in a private room. But the *salle du restaurant* was fifty feet long by thirty feet wide, it contained a hundred tables, maybe more, the floor was polished oak, and the ceilings were painted and gilded, and there were fifty waiters waiting for the swallows that would soon arrive from the north; we were the van birds.

"Shall we breakfast in a private room?" I whispered humbly.

"Good heavens! no! I wouldn't dare to go into a private room before all these waiters."

My heart sank again, and when Doris said, "Where shall we sit?" I answered, "Anywhere, anywhere, it doesn't matter."

It had taken two hours for the horses to crawl up to the mountain town, and as I had no early breakfast I was ravenously hungry. A box of sardines and a plate of butter, and the prospect of an omelette and a steak, put all thoughts of Doris for the moment out of my head, and that was a good thing. We babbled on, and it was impossible to say which was the more interested, which enjoyed talking most; and the pleasure which each took in talking and hearing the other talk became noticeable.

"I didn't interrupt you just now, I thought it would be cruel, for you were enjoying yourself so much," said Doris, laughing.

"Well, I promise not to interrupt the next time—you were in the midst of one of your stories."

It was not long before she was telling me another story, for Doris was full of stories. She observed life as it went by, and could recall what she had seen. Our talk had gone back to years before, to the evening when I first saw her cross the drawing-room in a white dress, her gold hair hanging over her shoulders; and in that moment, as she crossed the room, I had noticed a look of recognition in her eyes; the look was purely instinctive; she was not aware of it herself, but I could not help understanding it as a look whereby she recognised me as one of her kin. I had often spoken to her of that look, and we liked speaking about it, and about the time when we became friends in Paris. She had written asking me to go to see her and her mother. I had found them in a strange little hotel, just starting for some distant suburb, going there to buy presents from an old couple, dealers in china and glass, from whom, Doris's mother explained, she would be able to buy her presents fifty per cent, cheaper than elsewhere. She was one of those women who would spend three shillings on a cab in order to save twopence on a vase.

"It took us two hours to get to that old, forgotten quarter, to the old quaint street where they lived. They were old-world Jews who read the Talmud, and seemed to be quite isolated, out of touch with the modern world. It was like going back to the Middle Ages; this queer old couple moving like goblins among the china and glass. Do you ever see them now? Are they dead?"

"Let me tell you," cried Doris, "what happened. The old man died two years ago, and his wife, who had lived with him for forty years, could not bear to live alone, so what do you think she did? She sent for her brother-in-law— —"

"To marry him?"

"No, not to marry him, but to talk to him about her husband. You see this couple had lived together for so many years that she had become ingrained, as it were, in the personality of her late husband, her habits had become his habits, his thoughts had become hers. The story really is very funny," and Doris burst out laughing, and for some time she could not speak with laughing. "I am sorry for the poor man," she said at last.

"For whom? For the brother-in-law?"

"Yes; you see he is dyspeptic, and he can't eat the dishes at all that his brother used to like, but the wife can't and won't cook anything else."

"In other words," I said, "the souvenir of brother Isaac is poisoning brother Jacob."

"That is it."

"What a strange place this world is!" And then my mind drifted back suddenly. "O Doris, I'm so unhappy—this place—I wish I had never come."

"Now, now, have a little patience. Everything comes right in the end."

"We shall never be alone." "Yes, we shall. Why do you think that?"

"Because I can't think of anything else."

"Well, you must think of something else. We're going to the factory where they make perfume, and I'm going to buy a great many bottles of scent for myself, and presents for friends. We shall be able to buy the perfume twenty-five per cent. or fifty per cent. cheaper."

"Don't you think we might go to see the pictures? There are some in a church here."

On inquiry we heard that they had been taken away, and I followed Doris through the perfume factory. Very little work was doing; the superintendent told us that they were waiting for the violets. A few old women were stirring caldrons, and I listened wearily, for it did not interest me in the least, particularly at that moment, to hear that the flowers were laid upon layers of grease, that the grease absorbed the perfume, and then the grease was got rid of by means of alcohol. The workrooms were cold and draughty, and the choice of what perfumes we were to buy took a long time. However, at last, Doris decided that she would prefer three bottles of this, three bottles of that, four of these, and two of those. Her perfume was heliotrope; she always used it.

"And you like it, don't you dear?"

"Yes, but what does it matter what I like?"

"Now, don't be cross. Don't look so sad."

"I don't mind the purchase you made for your friends, but the purchase of heliotrope is really too cynical."

"Cynical! Why is it cynical?"

"Because, dear, it is evocative of you, of that slender body moving among fragrances of scented cambrics, and breathing its own dear odour as I come forward to greet you. Why do you seek to torment me?"

"But, dear one— —"

I was not to be appeased, and sat gloomily in the corner of the carriage away from her. But she put out her hand, and the silken palm calmed my nervous irritation, and we descended the steep roads, the driver putting on and taking off the brake. The evening was growing chilly, so I asked Doris if I might tell the coachman to stop his horses and to put up the hood of the carriage. In a close carriage one is nearly alone. But every moment I was reminded that people were passing, and between her kisses the thought passed that I must go back to Paris, however unkind it might be. It would be unkind to leave her, for she was not very strong; she would require somebody to look after her. As I was debating the question in my mind Doris said:

"You don't mind, dear, but before we go back to the hotel, I have a visit to pay."

In the three weeks' time she had spent at Plessy before I came there, Doris had made the acquaintance of all kinds of elderly spinsters, who lived in the different hotels *en pension*, and who would go away as soon as the visitors arrived, to seek another "resort" where the season had not yet commenced, and where they could be boarded and bedded for ten francs a day. I had made the acquaintance of Miss Tubbs and Miss Whitworth, and we were dining with them that night. Doris had explained that we could not refuse to dine with them at least once.

"But as we're going to spend the evening with them, I don't see the necessity — —"

"Of course not, dear, but don't you remember you promised to go to see the Formans with me?"

Miss Forman had dined with us last night, but her mother had not been able to come, and that was a relief to me whatever it may have been to Doris; I had heard that Mrs. Forman was a very old woman, and as her daughter struck me as an ineffectual person, I said as I sat down to dinner, "One of the family is enough." What her mother's age could be I could not guess, for Miss Forman herself might pass for seventy. But after speaking to her for a little while one saw that she was not so old as she looked at first sight. Nothing saddens me more than those who have aged prematurely, for the cause of premature ageing is generally a declension of the mind. As soon as the mind begins to narrow and wither the body follows suit; prejudices and conventions age us more than years do. Before speaking a word it was easy to see from Miss Forman's appearance that no new idea had entered into her life for a long while, and I imagined her at once to be one of those daughters that one finds abroad in different provincial towns, living with their mothers on small incomes. "The daughter's tragedy is written all over her face," I said, and while speaking to her I scrutinised her, reading in her everything that goes to make up that tragedy. She had the face of those heroines, for they are heroines—the broad low brow, the high nose, the sympathetic eyes, grey and expressive of duty and sacrifice of self. Her dress and her manners were as significant as her face, and seemed to hint at the life she had lived. She wore a black silk gown which looked old-fashioned—why I cannot say. Was it the gown or the piece of black lace that she wore on her head, or the Victorian earrings that hung from her ears down her dust-coloured neck, that gave her a sort of bygone appearance, the look of an old photograph? Her manners took me farther back in the century even than the photograph did; she seemed to have come out of the pages of some trite and uninteresting novel, a rather listless book written at the end of the eighteenth century, before the art of novel-writing had been found out. She listened, and her listening was in itself a politeness, and she never lost her politeness, though she seldom understood what I said. When I finished speaking she answered what I had said indirectly, like one whose mind was not quite capable of following any conversation except the most trite. She laughed if she thought I had said anything humourous, and sometimes looked a little embarrassed; she only seemed to be at her ease when speaking of her mother. If, for instance, we were speaking of books, she would break in with her mother's opinions, thinking it wonderful that her mother had read—shall we say, "The Three Musketeers?" three times. She was interested in all her mother's characteristics, and her habit was to speak of her mother as her mamma. She seemed to delight in the word, and every time she pronounced it a light came into her old face, and I began to understand her and to feel that I could place her, to use a colloquialism which is so expressive that perhaps its use may be forgiven. "The daughter's tragedy," I muttered, and considering it, philosophising according to my wont, I tried to reconcile myself to this visit. "After all," I said, "I am on my own business, therefore I have no right to grumble."

I wished to see what Miss Forman was like in her own house; above all, I wished to see if her mother were as typical of the mother who accepts her daughter's sacrifice, as Miss Forman was of the daughter that has been sacrificed. From the daughter's appearance I had imagined Mrs. Forman to be a tall, good-looking, distinguished woman, lying upon a sofa, wearing a cap upon her white hair, her feet covered with a shawl, and Miss Forman arranging it from time to time. Nature is always surprising; she follows a rhythm of her own; we beat one, two, three, four, but the invisible leader of the orchestra sets a more subtle rhythm. But though Nature's rhythm is irregular, its irregularity is more apparent than real, for when we listen we hear that everything goes to a beat, and in looking at Mrs. Forman I recognised that she was the inevitable mother of such a daughter, and that Nature's combination was more harmonious than mine. The first thing that struck me was that the personal energy I had missed in the daughter survived in the mother, notwithstanding her seventy-five years. The daughter reminded me now of a tree that had been overshadowed; Miss Forman had remained a child, nor could she have grown to womanhood unless somebody had taken her away; no doubt somebody had wanted to marry her; there is nobody that has not had her love affair, very few at least, and I imagined Miss Forman giving up hers for the sake of her mamma, and I could hear her mamma—that short, thick woman, looking more like a ball of lard than anything else in the world, alert notwithstanding her sciatica, with two small beady eyes in the glaring whiteness of her face—forgetful of her daughter's sacrifice, saying to her some evening as they warmed their shins over the fire:

"Well, Caroline, I never understood how it was that you didn't marry Mr. So-and-so, I think he would have suited you very well."

My interest in these two women who had lived side by side all their lives was slight; it was just animated by a slight curiosity to see if Miss Forman would be as much interested in her mother in her own house by her mother's side as she had been in the hotel among strangers. I waited to hear her call her mother mamma; nor had I to wait long, for as soon as the conversation turned on the house which the Formans had lately purchased, and the land which Mrs. Forman was buying up and planting with orange trees, Miss Forman broke in, and in her high-pitched voice she told us enthusiastically that mamma was so energetic; she never could be induced to sit down and be quiet; even her sciatica could not keep her in her chair. A few moments after Miss Forman told us that they did not leave Plessy even during the summer heat. Mamma could not be induced to go away. The last time they had gone to a hill village intending to spend some three or four weeks there, but the food did not suit mamma at all, and Miss Forman explained how the critical moment came and she had said to her mamma, "Well, mamma, this place does not suit you; I think we had better go home again"; and they had come home after six days in the hill village, probably never to leave Plessy again; and turning to her mother with a look of admiration on her face Miss Forman said: "I always tell mamma that she will never be able to get away from here until balloon travelling comes into fashion. If a balloon were to come down to mamma's balcony, mamma might get into it and be induced to go away for a little while for a change of air. She would not be afraid. I don't think mamma was ever afraid of anything." Her voice seemed to me to attain a certain ecstasy in the words, "I don't think mamma was ever afraid of anything," and I said, "She is proud of her ideal, and it is well that she should be, for there is no other in the world, not for her at least," and noticing that the three women were talking together, that I was no longer observed, I got up with a view to studying the surroundings in which Mrs. Forman and her daughter lived.

On the wall facing the fireplace there were two portraits—two engravings—and I did not need to look at the date to know that they had been done in 1840; one was her Majesty Queen Victoria, the other her Royal Consort, Prince Albert. Shall I be believed if I say that in my little excursions round the room and the next room I discovered a small rosewood table on which stood some wax fruit, a small sofa covered with rep and antimacassars, just as in old days? More characteristic still was the harmonium, with a hymn-book on the music rest, and every Sunday, no doubt, Miss Forman played hymns with her stiff, crooked fingers, and they said prayers together, the same old-fashioned English prayers for which I always hanker a little.

Satisfied with the result of my quest, and fearing that it might be regarded as an impertinence if I stayed away any longer, I returned to the back drawing-room, only to accompany the Formans and Doris back again to the front drawing-room. There was a piano there. The Formans had persuaded Doris to sing, and she was going to do so to please them. "They don't know anything about singing," she whispered to me; "but what does that matter? You see, poor things, they have so little to distract them in their lives; it will be quite a little event for them to hear me sing," and she went to the piano and sang song after song.

"It is kind indeed of you to sing to us, to an old woman and a middle-aged woman," Mrs. Forman said, "and I hope you will come to see us again, both of you."

"What should bring me to see them again?" I asked myself as I tried to get Doris away, for she lingered about the doorway with them, making impossible plans, asking them to come to see her when they came to England, telling them that if her health required it and she came to Plessy again she would rush to see them. "Why should she go on like that, knowing well that we shall never see them again, never in this world?" I thought. Mrs. Forman insisted that her daughter should accompany us to the gate, and all the way there Doris begged of Miss Forman to come to dine with us; we were dining with Miss Tubbs and Miss Whitworth, friends of hers; it would be so nice if she would come. The carriage would be sent back for her; it would be so easy to send it back. I offered up a prayer that Miss Forman might refuse, and she did refuse many times; but Doris was so pressing that she consented; but when we got into the carriage a thought struck her. "No," she said, "I cannot go, for the dressmaker is coming this evening to try on mamma's dress, and mamma is very particular about her gowns; she hates any fulness in the waist; the last time the gown had to go back—you must excuse me."

"Good-bye, dear, good-bye," I heard Doris crying, and I said to myself, "How kind she is!"

"Now, my dear, aren't you glad that you came to see them? Aren't they nice? Isn't she good? And you like goodness."

"Dear Doris, I like goodness, and I like to discover your kind heart. Don't you remember my saying that your pretty face was dependent upon your intelligence; that without your music and without your wit your face would lose half its charm? Well, now, do you know that it seems to me that it would only lose a third of its charm; for a third of my love for you is my admiration of your good heart. You remember how, years ago, I used to catch you doing acts of kindness? What has become of the two blind women you used to help?"

"So you haven't forgotten them. You used to say that it was wonderful that a blind woman should be able to get her living."

"Of course it is. It has always seemed to me extraordinary that any one should be able to earn his living."

"You see, dear, you have not been forced to get yours, and you do not realise that ninety per cent of men and women have to get theirs."

"But a blind woman! To get up in the morning and go out to earn enough money to pay for her dinner; think of it! Getting up in the dark, knowing that she must earn four, five, ten shillings a day, whatever it is. Every day the problem presents itself, and she always in the dark."

"Do you remember her story?"

"I think so. She was once rich, wasn't she? In fairly easy circumstances, and she lost her fortune. It all went away from her bit by bit. It is all coming back to me, how Fate in the story as you told it seemed like a black shadow stretching out a paw, grabbing some part of her income again and again till the last farthing was taken. Even then Fate was not satisfied, and your friend must catch the smallpox and lose her eyes. But as soon as she was well she decided to come to England and learn to be a masseuse. I suppose she did not want to stop in Australia, where she was known. How attractive courage is! And where shall we find an example of courage equal to that of this blind woman coming to England to learn to be a masseuse? What I don't understand is bearing with her life in the dark, going out to her work every day to earn her dinner, and very often robbed by the girl who led her about?

"How well you remember, dear."

"Of course I do. Now, how was it? Her next misfortune was a sentimental one. There was some sort of a love story in this blind woman's life, not the conventional, sentimental story which never happens, but a hint, a suggestion, of that passion which takes a hundred thousand shapes, finding its way even to a blind woman's life. Now don't tell me; it's all coming back to me. Something about a student who lived in the same house as she did; a very young man; and they made acquaintance on the stairs; they took to visiting each other; they became friends, but it was not with him she fell in love. This student had a pal who came to share his rooms, an older man with serious tastes, a great classical scholar, and he used to go down to read to the blind woman in the evening. It really was a very pretty story, and very true. He used to translate the Greek tragedies aloud to her. I wonder if she expected him to marry her?"

"No, she knew he could not marry her, but that made no difference."

"You're quite right. It was just the one interest in her life, and it was taken from her. He was a doctor, wasn't he?"

Doris nodded, and I remembered how he had gone out to Africa. "No sooner did he get there than he caught a fever, one of the worst kinds. The poor blind masseuse did not hear anything of her loss for a long time. The friend upstairs didn't dare to come down to tell her. But at last the truth could be hidden from her no longer. It's extraordinary how tragedy follows some."

"Isn't it?"

"And now she sits alone in the dark. No one comes to read to her. But she bears with her solitude rather than put up with the pious people who would interest themselves in her. You said there were no interesting books written for the blind, only pieties. The charitable are often no better than Shylocks, they want their money's worth. I only see her, of course, through your description, but if I see her truly she was one of those who loved life, and life took everything from her!"

"Do you remember the story of the other blind woman?"

"Yes and no, vaguely. She was a singer, wasn't she?" Doris nodded. "And I think she was born blind, or lost her sight when she was three or four years old. You described her to me as a tall, handsome woman with dark, crinkly hair, and a mouth like red velvet."

"I don't think I said like red velvet, dear."

"Well, it doesn't sound like a woman's description of another woman, but I think you told me that she had had love affairs, and it was that that made me give her a mouth like red velvet. Why should she not have love affairs? She was as much a woman as another; only one doesn't realise until one hears a story of this kind what the life of the blind must be, how differently they must think and feel about things from those who see. Her lover must have been a wonder to her, something strange, mysterious; the blind must be more capable of love than anybody else. She wouldn't know if he were a man of forty or one of twenty. And what difference could it make to her?"

"Ah, the blind are very sensitive, much more so than we are."

"Perhaps."

"I think Judith would have known the difference between a young man and a middle-aged. There was little she didn't know."

"I daresay you're quite right. But still everything must have been more intense and vague. When the blind woman's lover is not speaking to her he is away; she is unable to follow him, and sitting at home she imagines him in society surrounded by others who are not blind. She doesn't know what eyes are, but she imagines them like— what? anyhow she imagines them more beautiful than they are. No, Doris, no eyes are more beautiful than yours; she imagines every one with eyes like yours. I have not thought of her much lately, but I used to think of her when you told me the story, as standing on a platform in front of the public, calm as a caryatid. She must have had a beautiful voice to have been able to get an engagement; and the great courage that these blind women have! Fancy the struggle to get an engagement, a difficult thing to do in any circumstances—but in hers! And when her voice began to fail her she must have suffered, for her voice was her one possession, the one thing that distinguished her from others, the one thing she knew herself by, her personality as it were. She didn't know her face as other women know theirs; she only knew herself when she sang, then she became an entity, as it were. Nor could teaching recompense her for what she had lost, however intelligent her pupils might be, or however well they paid her. How did she lose her pupils?"

"I don't think there was any reason. She lost her pupils in the ordinary way; she was unlucky. As you were just saying, it was more difficult for her to earn her living than for those who could see, and Judith is no longer as young as she was; she isn't old, she is still a handsome woman, but in a few years.... If old-age pensions are to be granted to people, they surely ought to be granted to blind women."

"Yes, I remember; the sentiment of the whole story is in my mind; only I am a little confused about the facts. I remember you wrote a lot of letters—how was it?"

"Well, I just felt that the thing to do was to get an annuity for Judith; I could not afford to give her one myself; so after a great deal of trouble I got into communication with a rich woman who was interested in the blind and wanted to found one."

"You are quite right, that was it. You must have written dozens of letters."

"Yes, indeed, and all to no purpose. Judith knew the trouble I was taking, but she couldn't bear with her loneliness any longer; the dread of the long evenings by herself began to prey upon her nerves, and she went off to Peckham to marry a blind man—quite an elderly man; he was over sixty. They had known each other for some time, and he taught music like her; but though he only earned forty or fifty pounds a year, still she preferred to have somebody to live with than the annuity."

"But I don't see why she should lose her annuity."

"Don't you remember, dear? This to me is the point of the story. The charitable woman drew back, not from any sordid motive, because she regretted her money, but for a fixed idea; she had learned from somebody that blind people shouldn't marry, and she did not feel herself justified in giving her money to encouraging such marriages."

"Was there ever anything so extraordinary as human nature? Its goodness, its stupidity, its cruelty! The woman meant well; one can't even hate her for it; it was just a lack of perception, a desire to live up to principles. That is what sets every one agog, trying to live up to principles, abstract ideas. If they only think of what they are and what others are! The folly of it! This puzzle-headed woman—I mean the charitable woman pondering over the fate of the race, as if she could do anything to advance or retard its destiny!"

"You always liked those stories, dear. You said that you would write them."

"Yes, but I'm afraid the pathos is a little deeper than I could reach; only Turgenieff could write them. But here we are at the Dog's Home."

"Don't talk like that—it's unkind."

"I don't mean to be unkind, but I have to try to realise things before I can appreciate them."

It seemed not a little incongruous that these two little spinsters should pay for our dinners, and I tried to induce Doris to agree to some modification in the present arrangements, but she said it was their wish to entertain us.

The evening I spent in that hotel hearing Doris sing, and myself talking literature to a company of about a dozen spinsters, all plain and elderly, all trying to live upon incomes varying from a hundred and fifty to two hundred pounds a year, comes up before my mind, every incident. Life is full of incidents, only our intelligence is not always sufficiently trained to perceive them; and the incident I am about to mention was important in the life I am describing. Miss Tubbs had asked me what wine I would drink. And in a moment of inadvertence I said "Vin Ordinaire," forgetting that the two shillings the wine would cost would probably mean that Miss Tubbs would very likely have to go without her cup of tea at five o'clock next day in order that her expenditure should not exceed her limit, and I thought how difficult life must be on these slippery rocks, incomes of one hundred and fifty a year. Poor little gentlefolk, roving about from one boarding-house to another, always in search of the cheapest, sometimes getting into boarding-houses where the cheapness of the food necessitates sending for the doctor, so the gain on one side is a loss on the other. Poor little gentlefolk, the odds-and-ends of existence, the pence and threepenny bits of human life!

That Doris's singing should have provoked remarks painfully inadequate, mattered little. Inadequate remarks about singing and about the other arts are as common in London drawing-rooms as in hotels and boarding-houses (all hotels are boarding-houses; there is really no difference), and the company I found in these winter resorts would have interested me at any other time. I can be interested in the woman who collects stamps, in the gentle soul who keeps a botany book in which all kinds of quaint entries are found, in the lady who writes for the papers, and the one who is supposed to have a past. Wherever human beings collect there is always to be found somebody of interest, but when one's interest is centred in a lady, everybody else becomes an enemy; and I looked upon all these harmless spinsters as my enemies, and their proposals for excursions, and luncheons, and dinners caused me much misgiving, not only because they separated me from Doris, but because I felt that any incident, the proposed picnic, might prove a shipwrecking reef. One cannot predict what will happen. Life is so full of incidents; a woman's jealous tongue or the arrival of some acquaintance might bring about a catastrophe. A love affair hangs upon a gossamer thread, you know, and that is why I tried to persuade Doris away from her friends.

She was very kind and good and didn't inflict the society of these people too much upon me. Perhaps she was conscious of the danger herself, and we only visited the boarding-houses in the evening. But these visits grew intolerable. The society of Miss Tubbs and Miss Whitworth jarred the impressions of a long day spent in the open air, in a landscape where once the temples of the gods had been, where men had once lived who had seen, or at all events believed, in the fauns and the dryads, in the grotto where the siren swims.

One afternoon I said to Doris: "I'm afraid I can't go to see Miss Tubbs this evening. Can't we devise something else? Another dinner in a boarding-house would lead me to suicide, I think."

"You would like to drown yourself in that bay and join the nymphs. Do you think they would prove kinder than I?"

I did not answer Doris. I suddenly seemed to despair; the exquisite tenderness of the sky, and the inveigling curves of the bay seemed to become detestable to me, theatrical, absurd. "Good God!" I thought: "I shall never win her love. All my journey is in vain, and all this love-making." The scene before me was the most beautiful in shape and colour I had ever seen; but I am in no mood to describe the Leonardo-like mountains enframing the azure bay. The reader must imagine us leaning over a low wall watching the sea water gurgling among the rocks. We had come to see some gardens. The waiter at my hotel had told me of some, the property of a gentleman kind enough to throw them open to the public twice a week; and I had taken his advice, though gardens find little favour with me—now and again an old English garden, but the well-kept horticultural is my abhorrence. But one cannot tell a coachman to drive along the road, one must tell him to go somewhere, so we had come to see what was to be seen. And all was as I had imagined it, only worse; the tall wrought-iron gate was twenty feet high, there was a naked pavilion behind it, and a woman seated at a table with a cash-box in front of her. This woman took a franc apiece, and told us that the money was to be devoted to a charitable purpose; we were then free to wander down a gravel walk twenty feet wide branching to the right and the left, along a line of closely clipped shrubs, with a bunch of tall grasses here and a foreign fir there; gardens that a painter would turn from in horror. I said to Doris:

"This is as tedious as a play at the *Comédie*, as tiresome as a tragedy by Racine, and very like one. Let us seek out one of the external walks overlooking the sea; even there I'm afraid the knowledge that these shrubs are behind us will spoil our pleasure."

Doris laughed; that was one of her charms, she could be amused; and it was in this mood that we sat down on a seat placed in a low wall overlooking the bay, looking at each other, basking in the rays of the afternoon sun, and there we sat for some little while indolent as lizards. Pointing to one at a little distance I said:

"It is delightful to be here with you, Doris, but the sunlight is not sufficient for me. Doris, dear, I am very unhappy. I have lain awake all night thinking of you, and now I must tell you that yesterday I was sorely tempted to go down to that bay and join the nymphs there. Don't ask me if I believe that I should find a nymph to love me; one doesn't know what one believes, I only know that I am unhappy."

"But why, dear, do you allow yourself to be unhappy? Look at that lizard. Isn't he nice? Isn't he satisfied? He desires nothing but what he has got, light and warmth."

"And, Doris, would you like me to be as content as that lizard—to desire nothing more than light and warmth?"

Doris looked at me, and thinking her eyes more beautiful even than the sunlight, I said:

> "'And the sunlight clasps the earth,
>   And the moonbeams kiss the sea,
> But what are all those kissings worth,
>   If thou kiss not me?'

"That is the eternal song of the spheres and of the flowers. If I don't become part of the great harmony, I must die."

"But you do kiss me," Doris answered wilfully, "when the evening turns cold and the coachman puts up the hood of the carriage."

"Wilful Doris! Pretty puss cat!"

"I'm not a puss cat; I'm not playing with you, dear. I do assure you I feel the strain of these days; but what am I to do? You wouldn't have me tell you to stay at my hotel and to compromise myself before all these people?"

"These people! Those boarding-houses are driving me mad! That Miss Forman!"

"I thought you liked her. You said she is good, 'a simple, kind person, without pretensions.' And that is enough, according to yesterday's creed. You were never nicer than you were yesterday speaking of her (I remember your words): you said the flesh fades, the intellect withers, only the heart remembers. Do you recant all this?"

"No, I recant nothing; only yesterday's truth is not to-day's. One day we are attracted by goodness, another day by beauty; and beauty has been calling me day after day: at first the call was heard far away like a horn in the woods, but now the call has become more imperative, and all the landscape is musical. Yesterday standing by those ancient ruins, it seemed to me as if I had been transported out of my present nature back to my original nature of two thousand years ago. The sight of those ancient columns quickened a new soul within me; or should I say a soul that had been overlaid began to emerge? The dead are never wholly dead; their ideas live in us. I am sure that in England I never appreciated you as intensely as I do here. Doris, I have learned to appreciate you like a work of art. It is the spirit of antiquity that has taken hold of me, that has risen out of the earth and claimed me. That hat I would put away——"

"Don't you like my hat?"

"Yes, I like it, but I am thinking of the Doris that lived two thousand years ago; she did not wear a hat. In imagination I see the nymph that is in you, though I may never see her with mortal eyes."

"Why should you not see her, dear?"

"I have begun to despair. All these boarding-houses and their inhabitants jar the spirit that this landscape has kindled within me. I want to go away with you where I may love you. I am afraid what I am saying may seem exaggerated, but it is quite true that you remind me of antiquity, and in a way that I cannot explain though it is quite clear to me."

"But you do possess me, dear?"

"No, Doris, not as I wish. This journey will be a bitter memory that will endure for ever; we must think not only of the day that we live, but of the days in front of us; we must store our memories as the squirrel stores nuts, we must have a winter hoard. If some way is not found out of this horrible dilemma, I shall remember you as a collector remembers a vase which a workman handed to him and which slipped and was broken, or like a vase that was stolen from him; I cannot find a perfect simile, at least not at this moment; my speech is imperfect, but you will understand."

"Yes, I understand, I think I understand."

"If I do not get you, it will seem to me that I have lived in vain."

"But, dear one, things are not so bad as that. We need not be in Paris for some days yet, and though I cannot ask you to my hotel, there is no reason why — —"

"Doris, do not raise up false hopes."

"I was only going to say, dear, that it does not seem to be necessary that we should go straight back to Paris."

"You mean that we might stop somewhere at some old Roman town, at Arles in an eighteenth-century house. O Doris, how enchanting this would be! I hardly dare to think lest — —"

"Lest what, dear? Lest I should deceive you?"

There was a delicious coo in her voice, the very love coo; it cannot be imitated any more than the death-rattle, and exalted and inspired by her promise of herself, of all herself, I spoke in praise of the eighteenth century, saying that it had loved antiquity better than the nineteenth, and had reproduced its spirit.

"Is it not strange that, in the midst of reality, artistic conceptions always hang about me; but shall I ever possess you, Doris? Is it my delicious fate to spend three days with you in an old Roman town?"

"There is no reason why it shouldn't be. Where shall it be?"

"Any town would be sufficient with you, Doris; but let us think of some beautiful place"; and looking across the bay into the sunset, I recalled as many names as I could; many of those old Roman towns rose up before my eyes, classic remains mingling with mediaeval towers, cathedral spires rising over walls on which Roman sentries had once paced. We could only spend our honeymoon in a town with a beautiful name—a beautiful name was essential—a name that it would be a delight to remember for ever after; the name would have to express by some harmonious combination of syllables the loves that would be expended there. Rocomadour imitated too obviously the sound of sucking doves, and was rejected for that reason. Cahor tempted us, but it was too stern a name; its Italian name, Devona, appealed to us; but, after all, we could not think of Cahor as Devona. And for many reasons were rejected Armance, Vezelay, Oloron, Correz, Valat, and Gedre. Among these, only Armance gave us any serious pause. Armance! That evening and the next we studied *L'Indicateur des Chemins de fer*. "Armance," I said, interrupting Doris, who was telling me that we should lose our tickets by the *Côte d'Azur*. For in Doris's opinion it was necessary that we should leave Plessy by the *Côte d'Azur*. Her friends would certainly come to the station to see her off. "That is a matter of no moment," I said. "At Marseilles we can catch an express train, which will be nearly as good. There are two excellent trains; either will do, if you have decided to spend three days at Armance."

She asked me if Armance were a village or a town, and I answered, "What matter?"—for everywhere in France there are good beds and good food and good wine—ay, and omelettes. We should do very well in any village in the south of France for three days. But suddenly two names caught my eye, Orelay and Verlancourt, and we agreed that we preferred either of these names to Armance.

"Which name shall give shelter to two unfortunate lovers flying in search of solitude?"

"Orelay is a beautiful name."

"Orelay it shall be," I said. "We shall be able to get there from Marseilles in a few hours."

"You see, dear, it would be impossible for me to travel all the way to Paris—a journey of at least twenty-four hours would kill me, and I'm not strong; nothing tires me more than railway traveling. We must stop somewhere. Why not at Orelay?"

As this history can have only one merit, that of absolute truth, I must confess that the subterfuge whereby Doris sought to justify herself to herself, delighted me. Perhaps no quality is more human than that of subterfuge. She might unveil her body, but she could not unveil her soul. We may only lift a corner of the veil; he who would strip human nature naked and exhibit it displays a rattling skeleton, no more: where there is no subterfuge there is no life.

This story will be read, no doubt, by the young and the old, the wise and the foolish, by the temperate and the intemperate, but the subject matter is so common to all men that it will interest every one, even ecclesiastics, every one except certain gentlemen residing chiefly in Constantinople, whose hostility to the lover on his errand is so well known, and so easily understandable, that I must renounce all hope of numbering them among the admirers of my own or Doris's frailty. But happily these gentlemen are rare in England, though it is suspected that one or two may be found among the reviewers on the staff of certain newspapers; otherwise how shall we account for the solitary falsetto voices in the choir of our daily and weekly press, shouting abstinence from the housetops? But with the exception of these few critics every one will find pleasure in this narrative; even in aged men and women enough sex is left to allow them to take an interest in a love story; in these modern days when the novel wanders even as far as the nuns in their cells (I have good authority for making this statement), perhaps I may be able to count upon an aged Mother Abbess to be, outwardly perhaps a disapproving, but at heart a sympathetic reader. Indeed, I count upon the ascetic more than upon any other class for appreciation, for the imagination of those who have had no experience in love adventures will enkindle, and they will appreciate perhaps more intensely than any other the mental trouble that a journey to Orelay with Doris would entail.

It would take nearly five hours according to the time table to get from Marseilles to Orelay; and these five hours would wear themselves wearily away in conversation with Doris, in talking to her of every subject except the subject uppermost in my mind. I should have kept a notebook, just as I had arranged to do when I thought I was going on the yachting excursion among the Greek Islands with Gertrude; but, having no notes, I can only appeal to the reader's imagination. I must ask him to remember the week of cruel abstinence I had been through, and to take it into his consideration. My dear, dear reader, I am sure you can see me if you try (in your mind's eye, of course) walking about the corridors, seeking the guard, asking every one I meet:

"How far away are we now from Orelay?"

"Orelay? Nearly two hours from Orelay."

Our heavy luggage had been sent on before, but we had a number of dressing cases and bags with us, and there might not be time to remove all these. The guard, who had promised to take them out of the carriage for us, might not arrive in time. However this might be, he was not to be found anywhere, and I sought him how many times up and down the long length of the train. You can see me, reader, can you not? walking about the train, imagining all kinds of catastrophes—that the train might break down, or that it might not stop at Orelay; or, a still more likely catastrophe, that the young lady might change her mind. What if that were to happen at the last moment! Ah, if that were to happen I should have perchance to throw myself out of the train, unless peradventure I refrained for the sake of writing the story of a lover's deception. The transitional stage is an intolerable one, and I wondered if Doris felt it as keenly, and every time I passed our carriage on my way up and down in search of the guard, I stopped a moment to study her face; she sat with her eyes closed, perhaps dozing. How prosaic of her to doze on the way to Orelay! Why was she not as agitated as I?

And the question presented itself suddenly, Do women attach the same interest to love adventures as we do? Do women ask themselves as often as we do if God, the Devil, or Calamitous Fate will intervene between us and our pleasure? Will it be snatched out of our arms and from our lips? Perhaps never before, only once in any case, did I experience an excitement so lancinating as I experienced that day. And as I write the sad thought floats past that such expectations will never be my lot again. The delights of the moment are perhaps behind me, but why should I feel sad for that? Life is always beautiful, in age as well as in youth; the old have a joy that the youths do not know—recollection. It is through memory we know ourselves; without memory it might be said we have hardly lived at all, or only like animals.

This is a point on which I would speak seriously to every reader, especially to my young readers; for it is of the utmost importance that every one should select adventures that not only please them at the moment, but can be looked back upon with admiration, and for which one can offer up a mute thanksgiving. My life would not have been complete, a corner-stone would have been lacking if Doris had not come to Orelay with me. Without her I should not have known the joy that perfect beauty gives; that beauty which haunted in antiquity would never have been known to me. But without more, as the lawyers say, we will return to Doris. I asked her if she had been asleep? No, she had not slept, only it rested her to keep her eyes closed, the sunlight fatigued her. I did not like to hear her talk of fatigue, and to hide from her what was passing in my mind I tried to invent some conversation. Orelay—what a lovely name it was! Did she think the town would vindicate or belie its name? She smiled faintly and said she would not feel fatigued as soon as she got out of the train, and there was some consolation in the thought that her health would not allow her to get farther that day than Orelay.

We decided to stay at the Hôtel des Valois. One of the passengers had spoken to me of this hotel; he had never stayed there himself, but he believed it to be an excellent hotel. But it was not his recommendation that influenced me, it was the name—the Hôtel des Valois. How splendid! And when we got out at Orelay I asked the porters and the station-master if they could recommend a hotel. No, but they agreed that the Hôtel des Valois was as good as any other. We drove there wondering what it would be like. Everything had turned out well up to the present, but everything would go for naught if the Hôtel des Valois should prove unworthy of its name. And the first sight of it was certainly disappointing. Its courtyard was insignificant, only saved by a beautiful ilex tree growing in one corner. The next moment I noticed that the porch of the hotel was pretty and refined—a curious porch it was, giving the hotel for a moment the look of an eighteenth-century English country house. There were numerous windows with small panes, and one divined the hall beyond the porch. The hall delighted us, and I said to Doris as we passed through that the hotel must have been a nobleman's house some long while ago, when Orelay had a society of its own, perhaps a language, for in the seventeenth or the eighteenth century Provençal or some other dialect must have been written or spoken at Orelay. We admired the galleries overlooking the hall, and the staircase leading to them. We seemed to have been transported into the eighteenth century; the atmosphere was that of a Boucher, a provincial Boucher perhaps, but an eighteenth-century artist for all that. The doves that crowd round Aphrodite seemed to have led us right; and we foresaw a large quiet bedroom with an Aubusson carpet in the middle of a parquet floor, writing-tables in the corners of the room or in the silken-curtained windows.

This was the kind of room I had imagined—one as large as a drawing-room, and furnished like a drawing-room, with sofas and arm-chairs that we could draw around the fire, and myself and Doris sitting there talking. Love is composed in a large measure of desire of intimacy, and if the affection that birds experience in making their nest be not imitated, love descends to the base satisfaction of animals which merely meet in obedience to an instinct, and separate as soon as the instinct has been served. Birds understand love better than all animals, except man. Who has not thought with admiration of the weaver-birds, and of our own native wren? But the rooms that were offered to us corresponded in no wise with those that we had imagined the doors of the beautiful galleries would lead us into. The French words *chambre meublée* will convey an idea of the rooms we were shown into; for do not the words evoke a high bed pushed into the corner, an eider-down on top, a tall dusty window facing the bed, with skimpy red curtains and a vacant fireplace? There were, no doubt, a few chairs—but what chairs!

The scene was at once tragic and comic. It was of vital importance to myself and Doris to find a room such as I have attempted to describe, and it was of equal indifference to the waiter whether we did or didn't. The appearance of each contributed to the character of the scene. Doris's appearance I have tried to make clear to the reader; mine must be imagined; it only remains for me to tell what the waiter was like; an old man, short and thick, slow on the feet from long service, enveloped in an enormous apron; one only saw the ends of his trousers and his head; and the head was one of the strangest ever seen, for there was not a hair upon it; he was bald as an egg, and his head was the shape of an egg, and the colour of an Easter egg, a pretty pink all over. The eyes were like a ferret's, small and restless and watery, a long nose and a straight drooping chin, and a thick provincial accent—that alone amused me.

"Have you no other rooms?"

"Nous n'avons que cela."

I quote his words in the language in which they were spoken, for I remember how brutal they seemed, and how entirely in keeping with the character of the room. No doubt the words will seem flat and tame to the reader, but they never can seem that to me. "*Nous n'avons que cela*" will always be to me as pregnant with meaning as the famous *to be or not to be*. For it really amounted to that. I can see Doris standing by me, charming, graceful as a little Tanagra statuette, seemingly not aware of the degradation that the possession of her love would mean in such a room as that which we stood in; and I think I can honestly say that I wished we had never come to Orelay, that we had gone straight on to Paris. It were better even to sacrifice her love than that it should be degraded by vulgar circumstances; and, instead of a holy rite, my honeymoon had come to seem to me what the black mass must seem to the devout Christian.

"The rooms will look better," Doris said, "when fires have been lighted, and when our bags are unpacked. A skirt thrown over the arm of a chair furnishes a room."

Taking her hands in mine I kissed them, and was almost consoled; but at that moment my eyes fell upon the beds, and I said:

"Those beds! O Doris, those beds! yours is no better than mine." Women are always satisfied, or they are kind, or they are wise; and accept the inevitable without a murmur.

"Dearest, ask the waiter to bring us some hot water."

I did so, and while he was away I paced the room, unable to think of anything but the high bed; it was impossible to put out of my sight the ridiculous spectacle of a couple in a nightgown and pyjama suit climbing into it. The vision of myself and Doris lying under that eider-down, facing that tall window, with nothing to shut out the light but those vulgar lace curtains, pursued me, and I paced the room till the pink waiter returned with two jugs; and then, feeling very miserable, I began to unpack my bag without getting further than the removal of the brushes and comb; Doris unpacked a few things, and she washed her hands, and I thought I might wash mine; but before I had finished washing them I left the dreadful basin, and going to Doris with dripping hands I said:

"There is very little difference in the rooms. Perhaps you would like to sleep in mine?"

"I can see no difference. I think I'll remain where I am."

Which room she slept in may seem insignificant to the reader, but this is not so, for had we changed rooms this story would never have been written. I can see myself even now walking to and fro like a caged animal vainly seeking for a way of escape, till suddenly—my adventure reminds me very much of the beginning of many romantic novels—the tapestry that the wind had blown aside, the discovery of the secret door—suddenly I discovered a door in the wall paper; it was unlatched, and pushing through it I descended two steps, and lo! I was in the room of my heart's desire; a large, richly-coloured saloon with beautifully proportioned windows and red silk damask curtains hanging from carved cornices, and all the old gilding still upon them. And the silk fell into such graceful folds that the proportions of the windows were enhanced. And the walls were stretched with silk of a fine romantic design, the dominant note of which was red to match the curtains. There were wall lights, and a curious old clock on the marble chimney-piece amid branching candelabra. I stayed a moment to examine the clock, deciding very soon that it was not of much value ... it was made in Marseilles a hundred years ago.

"A beautiful room in its proportions and in its colour," I said, and seeing another door ajar I went through it and discovered a bedroom likewise in red with two beds facing each other. The beds were high, it is true, and a phrase from a letter I had written to Doris, "aggressively virtuous," rose up in my mind as I looked upon them. But the curtains hung well from *les ciels de lit* (one cannot say *cieux de lit*, I suppose)—the English word is, I think, "tester." "This room is far from the bedroom of my dreams," I muttered, "but *à la rigueur ça peut marcher*." But pursuing my quest a little farther, I came upon a spacious bedroom with two windows looking out on the courtyard—a room which would have satisfied the most imaginative lover, a room worthy of the adorable Doris, and I can say this as I look back fondly on her many various perfections. A great bed wide and low, "like a battlefield as our bed should be," I said, for the lines of the old poet were running in my head:

"Madame, shall we undress you for the fight?
The wars are naked that you make to-night."

And, looking upon it, I stood there like one transfigured, filled with a great joy; for the curtains hanging from a graceful tester like a crown would have satisfied the painter Boucher.... He rarely painted bedrooms. I do not remember any at this moment; but I remember many by Fragonard, and Fragonard would have said: "I have no fault to find with that bed." The carpet was not Aubusson, but it was nevertheless a finely-designed carpet, and its colour was harmonious; the sofa was shapely enough, and the Louis XVI. arm-chairs were filled with deep cushions. I turned to the toilet-table fearing it might prove an incongruity, but it was in perfect keeping with the room, and I began at once to look forward to seeing it laid out with all the manifold ivories and silver of Doris's dressing-case.

Imagine my flight, dear reader, if you can, back to Doris, whom I had left trying to make the best of that miserable square room; more like a prison cell than a bedroom.

"What is the matter, dearest?" she asked.

But without answering her I said, "Give me your hand," and led her as a prince leads his betrothed, in a fairy tale, through the richly-coloured salon, lingering a moment for her to admire it, and then I took her through my room, the double-bedded room, saying: "All this is nothing; wait till you see your room." And Doris paused overcome by the beauty of the bed, of the curtains falling from the tester gracefully as laburnum or acacia branches in June.

"The rooms are beautiful, but a little cheerless."

"Doris, Doris, you don't deserve to lie there! The windows of course must be opened, fresh air must be let in, and fires must be lighted. But think of you and me sitting here side by side talking before our bedtime."

Fires were lighted quickly, servants came in bearing candelabra in their hands, and among them, and with Doris by my side, I imagined myself a prince, for who is a prince but he who possesses the most desirable thing in the world, who finds himself in the most delectable circumstances? And what circumstance is more delightful than sitting in a great shadowy bedroom, watching the logs burning, shedding their grateful heat through the room, for the logs that were brought to us, as we soon discovered, were not the soft wood grown for consumption in Parisian hotels; the logs that warmed our toes in Orelay were dense and hard as iron, and burned like coal, only more fragrantly, and very soon the bareness of the room disappeared; a petticoat, as Doris had said, thrown over a chair gives an inhabited look to a room at once; and the contents of her dressing-case, as I anticipated, took the room back to one hundred years ago, when some great lady sat there in a flowered silk gown before one of those inlaid dressing tables, filled with pigments and powders and glasses.

There was one of those tables in the room, and I drew it from the corner and raised its lid, the lid with the looking-glass in it. And I liked the unpacking of her dressing-case, the discovery of a multitude of things for bodily use, the various sponges; the flat sponge for the face, the round sponge for the body, and the little sponges; all the scissors and the powder for the nails, and the scents, the soft silks, the lace scarfs, and the long silk nightgown soon to droop over her shoulders. My description by no means exhausts the many things she produced from her dressing-case and bags, nor would the most complete catalogue convey an impression of Doris's cleanliness of her little body! One would have to see her arranging her things, with her long curved hands and almond nails carefully cut—they were her immediate care, and many powders and ointments and polishers were called into requisition. Some reader will cry that all this is most unimportant, but he is either hypocritical or stupid, for it is only with scent and silk and artifices that we raise love from an instinct to a passion.

"I am longing," said Doris, "to see that beautiful red drawing-room with all the candelabra lighted and half a dozen logs blazing on the hearth. It is extraordinary how cold it is."

To procure an impartial mind, bodily ease is necessary, and we sat on either side of a splendid fire warming our toes. At the bottom of his heart every Christian feels, though he may not care to admit it in these modern days, that every attempt to make love a beautiful and pleasurable thing is a return to paganism. In his eyes the only excuse for man's love of woman is that without it the world would come to an end. Why he should consider the end of the world a misfortune I have never been able to find out, for if his creed be a true one the principal use of this world is to supply Hell with fuel. He is never weary of telling us that very few indeed may hope to get to Heaven.

"But France is not a Christian country, and yet you see the high bed has not become extinct," said Doris.

Doris, who was doubtless feeling a little tired, sat looking into the fire. Her attitude encouraged reverie; dream linked into dream till at last the chain of dreams was broken by the entrance of the pink waiter bringing in our dinner. In the afternoon I had called him an imbecile, which made him very angry, and he had explained that he was not an imbecile, but if I hurried him he lost his head altogether. Of course one is sorry for speaking rudely to a waiter; it is a shocking thing to do, and nothing but the appearance of the bedroom we were shown into would excuse me. His garrulousness, which was an irritation in the afternoon, was an amusement as he laid the cloth and told me the bill of fare; moreover, I had to consult him about the wine, and I liked to hear him telling me in his strong Southern accent of a certain wine of the country, as good as Pomard and as strong, and which would be known all over the world, only it did not bear transportation. Remembering how tired we were, and the verse—

"Quand on boit du Pomard on devient bon on aime,
On devient aussi bon que le Pomard lui-même—"

we drank, hoping that the wine would awaken us. But the effect of that strong Southern wine seemed to be more lethargic than exhilarating, and when dinner was over and we had returned to our seats by the fireside we were too weary to talk, and too nervous.

The next morning, the coffee and the rolls and butter were ready before Doris, and the vexation of seeing the breakfast growing cold was recompensed by the pleasure of teasing her, urging her to pass her arms into her dressing-gown, to come as she was, it did not matter what she had on underneath. The waiter did not count; he was not a man, he was a waiter, a pink creature, pinker than anything in the world, except a baby's bottom, and looking very like that.

"Hasten, dear, hasten!" and I went back to the salon and engaged in chatter with the old provincial, my English accent contrasting strangely with his. It was the first time I had heard the Southern accent. At Plessy I had heard all accents, Swiss, German, Italian; there was plenty of Parisian accent there, and I had told a Parisian flower-woman, whose husband was a Savoyard, that I declined to believe any more in the Southern accent *"C'est une blague qu'on m'a faite"*; but at Orelay I had discovered the true accent, and I listened to the old man for the sake of hearing it. He was asking me for my appreciation of the wine we had drunk last night when Doris entered in a foamy white dressing-gown.

"You liked the wine, dear, didn't you? He wants to know if we will have the same wine for twelve-o'clock breakfast."

"Dear me, it's eleven o'clock now," Doris answered, and she looked at the waiter.

"Monsieur and Madame will go for a little walk; perhaps you would like to breakfast at one?"

We agreed that we could not breakfast before one, and our waiter suggested a visit to the cathedral—it would fill up the time pleasantly and profitably; but Doris, when she had had her coffee, wanted to sit on my knee and to talk to me; and then there was a piano, and she wanted to play me some things, or rather I wanted to hear her. But the piano was a poor one; the notes did not come back, she said, and we talked for some hours without perceiving that the time was passing. After lunch the waiter again inquired if we intended to go for a little walk; there were vespers about four in the cathedral.

"It would do Monsieur and Madame good."

"The walk or the cathedral?" we inquired, and, a little embarrassed, the old fellow began to tell us that he had not been to the cathedral for some years, but the last time he was there he had been much impressed by the darkness. It was all he could do to find his way from pillar to pillar; he had nearly fallen over the few kneeling women who crouched there listening to the clergy intoning Latin verses. According to his account there were no windows anywhere except high up in the dome. And leaning his hands on the table, looking like all the waiters that ever existed or that will ever exist, his *tablier*, reaching nearly to his chin, upheld by strings passed over the shoulders, he told us that it was impossible to see what was happening in the chancel; but there had seemed to be a great number of clergy seated in the darkness at the back, for one heard voices behind the tall pieces of furniture singing Latin verses; one only heard the terminations of the words, an "us" and a "noster," and words ending in "e," and the organ always coming in a little late.

"My good man," I said, "your description leaves nothing to be desired. Why should I go to the cathedral unless to verify your impressions? I am sure the service is exactly as you describe it, and I would not for the world destroy the picture you have evoked of those forgotten priests intoning their vespers in the middle of the granite church behind a three-branched candlestick."

The poor man left the room very much disconcerted, feeling, Doris said, as if he had lost one of the forks.

"Thank Heaven that matter is done with—a great weight is off my mind."

"But there is the museum. You would like to see that?" said Doris, and a change came into my face.

"Well, Doris, the waiter has told us that there is a celebrated study by David in the museum, 'The Nymph of Orelay.'"

"But, dear one, am I not your nymph of Orelay?" and Doris slipped on her knees and put her arms about me. "Will I not do as well as the painted creature in the museum?"

"Far better," I said, "far better. Now we are free, Doris, freed from the cathedral and from the museum. All the day belongs to us, and to-morrow we may pass as we like."

"And so we will," Doris said meditatively; and so we did, dear reader, and I consider the time was well spent, for by so doing we avoided catching cold, a thing easy to do when a mistral is blowing. It was not until the following evening we remembered that time was always on the wing, that our little bags would have to be packed. Next morning we were going.

"Going away by the train," Doris said regretfully. "Would we were going away in a carriage! We shall leave Orelay knowing nothing of it but this suite of apartments."

"There is no reason why we should not drive," and I stopped packing my bag, and stood looking at her.

"I wonder if we should have stayed three days if we had not discovered these rooms? Dear one, I think I should not have meant so much to you in those humbler rooms: you attach much importance to these cornices and hangings."

"I should have loved you always, Doris, but I think I can love you better here," and with our bags in our hands we wandered from the bedroom into the drawing-room and stood admiring its bygone splendour. "Doris, dear, you must play me 'The Nut Bush.' I want to hear it on that old piano. Tinkle it, dear, tinkle it, and don't play 'The Nut Bush' too sentimentally, nor yet too gaily."

"Which way will you have it?" she asked; "'a true love's truth or a light love's art'?"

"I would have it dainty and fantastic as Schumann wrote it, 'only the song of a secret bird.'"

"With a pathos of loneliness in it?"

"That is it," I cried, "that is the right time to play it in, without stress on either side.... No, you mustn't leave the piano, Doris. Sing me some songs. Go on singing Schumann or Schubert; there are no other songs. Let me hear you sing 'The Moonlight' or 'The Lotus-flower.' Schumann and Schubert were the singing birds of the fifties; I love their romantic sentimentalities, orange gardens, south winds, a lake with a pinnace upon it, and a nightingale singing in a dark wood by a lonely shore; that is how they felt, how they dreamed." And resigning herself to my humour, she sang song after song till at last, awaking from a long reverie of music and old association of memories, I said, "Play me a waltz, Doris; I would hear an old-time waltz played in this room; its romantic flourishes will evoke the departed spirits." And very soon, sitting in my chair with half-closed eyes, it seemed to me that I saw crinolines faintly gliding over the floor, and white-stockinged feet, sloping shoulders and glistening necks with chignons—swan-like women, and long-whiskered cavaliers wearing peg-top trousers and braided coats dancing or talking with them.... The music suddenly stopped and Doris said:

"If we are to catch our train we must go on with our packing."

"You mustn't talk to me of trains," and overcome with a Schumann-like longing and melancholy I took her in my arms, overcome by her beauty. She was perfection. No Chelsea or Dresden figure was ever more dainty, gayer, or brighter. She was Schumann and Dresden, but a Dresden of an earlier period than Schumann; but why compare her to anything? She was Doris, the very embodiment of her name.

"Ah, Doris, why are we leaving here? Why can't we remain here for ever?"

"It is strange," she said; "I feel the charm of those old stately rooms as much as you do. But, dearest, we have missed the train."

The pink waiter came up, I promised to hasten, but my love of Doris delayed us unduly, and we arrived at the station only to hear that the train had gone away some ten minutes before. The train that had left was the only good train in the day, and missing it had given us another twenty-four hours in Orelay; but Doris was superstitious. "Our three days are done," she said; "if we don't go today we shall go to-morrow, and to go on the fourth day would be unlucky. What shall we do all day? The spell has been broken. We have left our hotel. Let us take a carriage," she pleaded, "and drive to the next station. The sun is shining, and the country is beautiful; we saw it from the railway, a strange red country grey with olives, olive orchards extending to the very foot of the mountains, and mingling with the pine trees descending the slopes."

"The slopes!" I said, "the precipitous sides of that high rock! Shall I ever forget it, beginning like the tail of a lion and rising up to the sky, towering above the level landscape like a sphinx."

"The drive would be delightful!"

"And it would be a continuation of the romance of the old Empire drawing-room. A post-chaise would be the thing if we could discover one."

Sometimes Nature seems to conspire to carry out an idea, and though no veritable post-chaise of old time was discovered in the coach-house behind the courtyard in which the ilex trees flourished, we happened to catch sight of a carriage some twenty-five or thirty years old, a cumbersome old thing hung upon C springs, of the security of which the coachman seemed doubtful. He spoke disparagingly, telling us that the proprietor had been trying to sell it, but no one would buy it, so heavy was it on the horses' backs, so out of fashion one was ashamed to go out in it. The coachman's notions of beauty did not concern us, but Doris dreaded lest one of the wheels should come off; however, on examination it was found to be roadworthy, and I said to Doris as I helped her into it:

"If it be no post-chaise, at all events ladies wearing crinolines have sat inside it, that is certain, and gentlemen wearing peg-top trousers with braid upon them. Good God, Doris, if you were to wear a crinoline I should love you beyond hope of repentance. Don't I remember when I was a boy every one wore white stockings; I had only heard of black ones, and I always hoped to meet a lady wearing black stockings... now my hope is to meet one wearing white."

"We might have searched the town for a crinoline and a pair of white stockings."

"Yes, and I might have discovered a black silk stock. I wonder how I should have looked in it. Doris," I said, "we have missed the best part of our adventure. We forgot to dress for the part we are playing, the lovers of Orelay."

Who will disagree with me when I say that no adventure is complete unless it necessitates an amount of ceremonial, the wearing of wigs, high bodices, stockings, and breeches? Every one likes to dress himself up, whether for a masquerade ball or to be enrolled in some strange order. Have you, reader, ever seen any one enrolled in any of these orders? If you have, you will excuse the little comedy and believe it to be natural—the comedy that Doris and I played in the old carriage driving from Orelay to Verlancourt, where we hoped to breakfast.

We could hardly speak for excitement. Doris thought of how she would look in a crinoline, and I remembered the illustrations in an early edition of Balzac of which I am the happy possessor. How nice the men looked in the light trousers and the black stockings of the period; and crossing my legs I followed with interest the line of my calf. Somebody did that in "Les Illusions Perdues." She and I lay back thinking which story in "The Human Comedy" was the most applicable to our case; and the only one we could think of was when Madame Bargeton, a provincial blue-stocking, left Angoulême for Paris with Lucien de Rubempré. There were no railways in the forties; they must have travelled in a post-chaise. Yes, I remember their journey, faintly it is true, but I remember it. Madame Bargeton was a woman of five-and-thirty at least, and Doris was much younger. Lucien was only one-and-twenty, and even at that time I was more than that. The names of these people and of the people they met at the theatre and in the Tuileries Gardens—Rastignac, Madame d'Espard, the Duchess of Chaulieu, Madame de Rochefide, and Canalis—carried my mind back from crinolines and white stockings, from peg-top trousers and braided coats, to the slim trousers that were almost breeches and to the high-breasted gowns of the Restoration. Our mothers and fathers wore the crinolines and the peg-top trousers, and our grandfathers the tight trousers and the black silk stocks. The remembrance of these costumes filled me with a tenderness and a melancholy I could not subdue, and I could see that Doris was thinking of the same subject as myself.

We were thinking of that subject which interested men before history began, the mutability of human things, the vanishing of generations.

Young as she was, Doris was thinking of death; nor is it the least extraordinary she should, for as soon as any one has reached the age of reflection the thought of death may come upon him at any moment, though he be in the middle of a ballroom or lying in the arms of his mistress. If the scene be a ballroom he has only to look outside, and the night will remind him that in a few years he will enter the eternal night; or if the scene be a bedroom the beautiful face of his mistress may perchance remind him of another whose face was equally beautiful and who is now under the earth; lesser things will suffice to recall his thoughts from life to death, a rose petal falling on a marble table, a dead bird in the path as he walks in his garden. And after the thought of death the most familiar thought is the decay of the bodily vesture. The first grey hair may seem to us an amusing accident, but very few years will pass before another and yet another appear, and if these do not succeed in reminding us that decay has begun, a black speck on a tooth cannot fail to do so; and when we go to the dentist to have it stopped we have begun to repair artificially the falling structure. The activity of youth soon passes, and its slenderness. I remember still the shock I felt on hearing an athlete say that he could no longer run races of a hundred yards; he was half a second or a quarter of a second slower than he was last year. I looked at him saying, "But you are only one-and-twenty," and he answered, "Yes, that is it." A football player I believe is out of date at eight-and-twenty. Out of date! What a pathos there is in the words—out of date! *Suranné*, as the French say. How are we to render it in English? By the beautiful but artificial word "yester-year"? Yester-year perhaps, for a sorrow clings about it; it conveys a sense of autumn, of "the long decline of roses." There is something ghostlike in the out-of-date. The landscape about Plessy had transported us back into antiquity, making us dream of nymphs and dryads, but the gilt cornices and damask hangings and the salon at Orelay had made us dream of a generation ago, of the youth of our parents. Ancient conveys no personal meaning, but the out-of-date transports us, as it were, to the stern of the vessel, throws us into a mournful attitude; we lean our heads upon our hands and, looking back, we see the white wake of the vessel with shores sinking in the horizon and the crests of the mountains passing away into the clouds.

While musing on these abstract questions raised by my remark that we had not managed our adventure properly, since we had forgotten to provide ourselves with proper costumes, the present suddenly thrust itself upon me.

"Good God!" I said to Doris, "let us look back, for we shall never see Orelay again!" and she from one window, and I from the other, saw the spires of Orelay for the last time. We could not tear ourselves away, but fortunately the road turned; Orelay was blotted out from our sight for ever, and we sank back to remember that a certain portion of our lives was over and done, a beautiful part of our lives had been thrown into the void, into the great rubble-heap of emotions that had been lived through, that are no more.

"Of what are you thinking, dear? You have been far away. This is the first time we have been separated, and we are not yet five miles from Orelay."

"Five miles! Ah, if it were only five!"

We did not speak for a long time, and watching the midday sun, I thought that peradventure it was not farther from us than yesterday. Were I to say so to Doris she would answer, "It will be the same in Paris," but if she did it would be the first falsehood she had told me, for we both knew that things are never the same; things change—for better or worse, but they change.

This last sentence seems to me somewhat trite, and if I were to continue this story any further my pen would run into many other superficial and facile observations, for my mind is no longer engrossed with the story. I no longer remember it; I do not mean that I do not remember whether we got to Verlancourt, whether we had breakfast, or whether we drove all the way to Paris with relays of horses. I am of course quite certain about the facts: we breakfasted at Verlancourt, and after breakfast we asked the coachman whether he would care to go on to Paris with us; he raised his eyes—"The carriage is a very old one, surely, Monsieur——" Doris and I laughed, for, truth to tell, we had been so abominably shaken that we were glad to exchange the picturesque old coach of our fathers' generation for the train.

These stories are memories, not inventions, and an account of the days I spent in Paris would interest nobody; all the details are forgotten, and invention and remembrance do not agree any better than the goat and the cabbage. So, omitting all that does not interest me—and if it does not interest me how can it interest the reader?—I will tell merely that my adventure with Doris was barren of scandal or unpleasant consequences. Her mother, a dear unsuspicious woman—whether her credulity was the depth of folly or the depth of wisdom I know not; there are many such mothers, my blessing be upon them!—took charge of her daughter, and Doris and her mother returned to England. I am afraid that when I confess that I did not speak to Doris of marriage I shall forfeit the good opinion of my reader, who will, of course, think that a love story with such an agreeable creature as Doris merited a lifetime of devotion; but I pray the reader to discover an excuse for me in the fact that Doris had told me when we were at Plessy that there was no question of her marrying any one but Albert. Had she not sacrificed the great love of her life in order that she might remain constant to Albert? Is it to be expected, then, that having done that, she would put Albert aside and throw her lot in with mine? She might have done this; men and women act inconsequently. Having on one occasion refused to drop the mutton chop for the shadow, on the next occasion they would drop it for the shadow of the shadow; but Doris was made of sterner stuff, and some months afterwards she wrote me a steady, sensible little letter telling me that she was going to be married, and that it seemed to her quite natural that she should marry Albert. Years have passed away, and nothing has happened to lead me to believe that she has not proved a true and loving wife. Albert has always told me that he found all the qualities in her which he had foreseen from the first time he looked upon her pretty, sparkling face. Frown not, reader; accuse me not of superficial cynicism! Albert is part of the world's inheritance. You may be Albert yourself—every one has been or will be Albert; Albert is in us all, just as I am in you all. Doris, too, is in you, dear lady who sit reading my book—Doris my three-days mistress at Orelay, and Doris the faithful spouse of Albert for twenty years in a lonely London suburb.

Study and boudoir would like to know if Doris had any children. About two years afterwards I heard that she was "expecting." The word came up spontaneously in my mind, perhaps because I had written it in the beginning of the story. Reader, do you remember in "Massimilla Doni" how Balzac, when he came to the last pages, declares that he dare not tell you the end of the adventure. One word, he says, will suffice for the worshippers of the ideal— *Massimilla Doni* was "expecting." I have not read the story for many years, but the memory of it shines in my mind bright—well, as the morning star; and I looked up this last paragraph when I began to write this story, but had to excuse myself for not translating it, my pretext being that I was baffled by certain grammatical obscurities, or what seemed to me such. I seemed to understand and to admire it all till I came to the line that *"les peuplades de cent cathédrales gothiques"* (which might be rendered as the figured company of a hundred Gothic cathedrals), *"tout le peuple des figures qui brisent leur forme pour venir à vous, artistes compréhensifs, toutes ces angéliques filles incorporelles accoururent autour du lit de Massimilla, et y pleurèrent!"* What puzzles me is why statues should break their forms (*form* I suppose should be translated by *mould*)—break their moulds—the expression seems very inadequate—break their moulds "in order to go to you, great imaginative artists." How could they break their moulds or their forms to go to the imaginative artists, the mould or the form being the gift of the imaginative artists? I should have understood Balzac better if he had said that the statues escape from their niches and the madonnas and the angels from their frames to gather round the bed of *Massimilla* to weep. Balzac's idea seems to have got a little tangled, or maybe I am stupid to-day. However, here is the passage:

"Les péris, les ondines, les fées, les sylphides du vieux temps, les muses de la Grèce, les vierges de marbre de la Certosa di Pavia, le Jour et la Nuit de Michel Ange, les petits anges que Bellini le premier mit au bas des tableaux d'église, et que Raphaël a faits si divinement au bas de la vierge au donataire, et de la madone qui gèle a Dresde, les délicieuses filles d'Orcagna, dans l'église de San-Michele à Florence, les choeurs célestes du tombeau de Saint Sébald à Nuremberg, quelques vierges du Duomo de Milan, les peuplades de cent cathédrales gothiques, tout le peuple des figures qui brisent leur forme pour venir à vous, artistes compréhensifs, toutes ces angéliques filles incorporelles accoururent autour du lit de Massimilla, et y pleurèrent."

CHAPTER IX

IN THE LUXEMBOURG GARDENS

There was a time when my dream was not literature, but painting; and I remember an American giving me a commission to make a small copy of Ingres's "Perseus and Andromeda," and myself sitting on a high stool in the Luxembourg, trying to catch the terror of the head thrown back, of the arms widespread, chained to the rock, and the beauty of the foot advanced to the edge of the sea. Since my copying days the picture has been transferred to the Louvre. What has become of my copy, whether I ever finished it and received the money I had been promised, matters very little. Memories of an art that one has abandoned are not pleasant memories. Maybe the poor thing is in some Western state where the people are ignorant enough to accept it as a sketch for the original picture. My hope is that it has drifted away, and become part of the world's rubbish and dust. But why am I thinking of it at all? Only because a more interesting memory hangs upon it.

After working at it all one morning, I left the museum feeling half satisfied with my drawing, but dreading the winged monster that awaited me after lunch. In those days I was poor, though rich for the Quarter. I moved in a society of art students, and we used to meet for breakfast in a queer little café; the meal cost us about a shilling. On my return from this café soon after twelve—I had breakfasted early that morning—I remember how, overcome by a sudden idleness, I could not go back to my work, and feeling that I must watch the birds and the sunlight (they seemed to understand each other so well), I threw myself on a bench and began to wonder if there was anything better in the world worth doing than to sit in an alley of clipped limes, smoking, thinking of Paris and of myself.

Every one, or nearly every one, except perhaps the upper classes, whose ideas of Paris are the principal boulevards—the Rue de Rivoli, the Rue de la Paix—knows the Luxembourg Gardens; and watching April playing and listening to water trickling from a vase that a great stone Neptune held in his arms at the end of the alley, my thoughts embraced not only the garden, but all I know of Paris, of the old city that lies far away behind the Hôtel de Ville and behind the

Boulevard St. Antoine. I thought of a certain palace now a museum, rarely visited, of its finely proportioned courtyard decorated with bas-reliefs by Jean Goujon. I had gone there a week ago with Mildred; but finding she had never heard of Madame de Sévigné, and did not care whether she had lived in this palace or another, I spoke to her of the Place des Vosges, saying we might go there, hoping that she would feel interested in it because it had once been the habitation of the old French nobility. As I spoke, its colour rose up before my eyes, pretty tones of yellow and brown brick, the wrought-iron railings and the high-pitched roofs and the slim chimneys. As I walked beside her I tried to remember if there were any colonnades. It is strange how one forgets; yes, and how one remembers. The Place des Vosges has always seemed to me something more than an exhibition of the most beautiful domestic architecture in France. The mind of a nation shapes itself, like rocks, by a process of slow accumulation, and it takes centuries to gather together an idea so characteristic as the Place des Vosges. One cannot view it—I cannot, at least—without thinking of the great monarchical centuries, and of the picturesque names which I have learned from Balzac's novels and from the history of France. In his "Étude de Catherine de Médicis," Balzac speaks of Madame de Sauve, and I am sure she must have lived in the Place des Vosges. Monsieur de Montresser might have occupied a flat on the first floor. Le Comte Bouverand de la Loyère, La Marquise d'Osmond, Le Comte de Coëtlogon, La Marquise de Villefranche, and Le Duc de Cadore, and many other names rise up in my mind, but I will not burden this story with them. I suppose the right thing to do would be to find out who had lived in the Place des Vosges; but the search, I am afraid, would prove tedious and perhaps not worth the trouble. For if none of the bearers of the names I have mentioned lived in the Place des Vosges, it is certain that others bearing equally noble names lived there.

Its appearance is the same to-day as it was in the seventeenth century, but it is now inhabited by the small tradespeople of the Quarter; the last great person who lived there was Victor Hugo; his house has been converted into a museum, and it is there that the most interesting relics of the great poet are stored. I unburdened my mind to Mildred, and my enthusiasm enkindled in her an interest sufficient to induce her to go there with me, for I could not forgo a companion that day, though she was far from being the ideal companion for such sentimental prowling as mine. Afterwards we visited Notre Dame together, and the quays, and the old streets; but

Mildred lacked the historical sense, I am afraid, for as we returned in the glow of the sunset, when the monumented Seine is most beautiful, she said that Paris wasn't bad for an old city, and it was the memory of this somewhat crude remark that caused a smile to light up my lips as I looked down the dark green alley through which the April sunlight flickered.

But I did not think long of her; my attention was distracted by the beauty of a line of masonry striking across the pale spring sky, tender as a faded eighteenth-century silk, only the blue was a young blue like that of a newly opened flower; and it seemed to me that I could detect in the clouds going by, great designs for groups and single figures, and I compared this aerial sculpture with the sculpture on the roofs. In every angle of the palace there are statues, and in every corner of the gardens one finds groups or single figures. Ancient Rome had sixty thousand statues—a statue for every thirty-three or thirty-four inhabitants; in Paris the proportion of statues to the people is not so great, still there are a great many; no city has had so many since antiquity; and that is why Paris always reminds me of those great days of Greece and Rome when this world was the only world.

When one tires of watching the sunlight there is no greater delight than to become absorbed in the beauty of the balustrades, the stately flights of steps, the long avenues of clipped limes, the shapely stone basins, every one monumented in some special way. "How shapely these gardens are," I said, and I fell to dreaming of many rocky hills where, at the entrance of cool caves, a Neptune lies, a vase in his arms with water flowing from it. Yesterevening I walked in these gardens with a sculptor; together we pondered Carpeau's fountain, and, after admiring Frémiet's horses, we went to Watteau's statue, appropriately placed in a dell, among greenswards like those he loved to paint. At this moment my meditation was broken.

"I thought I should find you in the museum painting, but here you are, idling in this pretty alley, and in the evening you'll tell us you've been working all day."

"Will you come for a walk?" I said, thinking that the gardens might interest her, and, if they did not, the people we should meet could not fail to amuse her. It was just the time to see the man who came every morning to feed the sparrows; he had taught them to take bread from his lips, and I thought that Mildred would like to see the funny little birds hopping about his feet, so quaint, so full of themselves, seeming to know all about it. Then if we had luck we might meet Robin Hood, for in those days a man used to wander in the gardens wearing the costume of the outlaw, and armed with a bow and quiver. The strange folk one meets in the Luxembourg Gardens are part of their charm. Had I not once met a man in armour, not plate, but the beautiful chain armour of the thirteenth century, sitting on a bench eating his lunch, his helmet beside him?—a model no doubt come from a studio for the lunch hour, or maybe he was an *exalté* or a *fumist*; a very innocent *fumist* if he were one, not one of the Quarter certainly, for even the youngest among us would know that it would take more than a suit of armour to astonish the frequenters of the gardens. As we came down a flight of steps we met an old man and his wife, an aged couple nearly seventy years of age, playing football, and the gambols of this ancient pair in the pretty April sunlight were pathetic to watch. I called her attention to them, telling her that in another part of the garden three old women came to dance; but seeing that Mildred was not interested, I took the first opportunity to talk of something else. She was more interested in the life of the Quarter, in *le bal Bullier*, in my stories of grisettes and students; and I noticed that she considered every student as he passed, his slim body buttoned tightly in a long frock-coat, with hair flowing over his shoulders from under his slouched hat, just as she had considered each man on board the boat a week ago as we crossed from Folkestone to Boulogne. We had met on the boat; I noticed her the moment I got on board; her quiet, neat clothes were unmistakably French, though not the florid French clothes Englishwomen so often buy and wear so badly. The stays she had on I thought must be one of those little ribbon stays with very few bones, and as she walked up and down she kept pressing her leather waistband still more neatly into its place, looking first over one shoulder and then over the other. She reminded me of a bird, so quick were her movements, and so alert. She was nice-looking, not exactly pretty, for her lips were thin, her mouth too tightly closed, the under lip almost disappearing, her eyes sloped up very much at the corners, and her eyebrows were black, and they nearly met.

The next time I saw her she was beside me at dinner—we had come by chance to the same hotel, a small hotel in the Rue du Bac. Her mother was with her, an elderly, sedate Englishwoman, to whom the girl talked very affectionately, "Yes, dearest mamma"; "No, dearest mamma." She had a gay voice, though she never seemed to laugh or joke; but her face had a sad expression, and she sighed continually.

After dinner her mother went to the piano and played with a great deal of accent and noise the "Brooklyn Cake Walk."

"We used to dance that at Nice. Oh, dear mamma, do you remember that lovely two-step?"

Her mother nodded and smiled, and began playing a Beethoven sonata, but she had not played many bars before her daughter said:

"Now, mother, don't play any more; come and talk to us."

I asked her if she did not like Beethoven. She shrugged her shoulders; an expression of irritation came into her face. She either did not want to talk of Beethoven then, or she was incapable of forming any opinion about him, and, judging from her interest in the "Brooklyn Cake Walk," I said:

"The Cake Walk is gayer, isn't it?"

The sarcasm seemed lost upon her; she sat looking at me with a vague expression in her eyes, and I found it impossible to say whether it was indifference or stupidity.

"Mildred plays Beethoven beautifully. My daughter loves music. She plays the violin better than anybody you ever heard in your life."

"Well, she must play very well indeed, for I've heard Sarasate and ——"

"If Mildred would only practise," and she pressed her daughter to play something for me.

"I haven't got my keys—they're upstairs. No, mother ... leave me alone; I'm thinking of other things."

Her mother went back to the piano and continued the sonata. Mildred looked at me, shrugged her shoulders, and then turned over the illustrated papers, saying they were stupid. We began to talk about foreign travel, and I learned that she and her mother spent only a small part of every year in England. She liked the Continent much better; English clothes were detestable; English pictures she did not know anything about, but suspected they must be pretty bad, or else why had I come to France to paint? She admitted, however, she had met some nice Englishmen, but Yankees—oh! Yankees! There was one at Biarritz. Do you know Biarritz? No, nor Italy. Italians are nice, are they not? There was one at Cannes.

"Don't think I'm not interested in hearing about pictures, because I am, but I must look at your ring, it's so like mine. This one was given to me by an Irishman, who said the curse of Moreen Dhu would be upon me if I gave it away."

"But who is Moreen Dhu? I never heard of her."

"You mustn't ask me; I'm not a bit an intelligent woman. People always get sick of me if they see me two days running."

"I doubt very much if that is true. If it were you wouldn't say it."

"Why not? I shouldn't have thought of saying it if it weren't true."

Next evening at dinner I noticed that she was dressed more carefully than usual; she wore a cream-coloured gown with a cerise waistband and a cerise bow at the side of her neck. I noticed, too, that she talked less; she seemed preoccupied. And after dinner she seemed anxious; I could not help thinking that she wished her mamma away, and was searching for an excuse to send her to bed.

"Mamma, dear, won't you play us the 'Impassionata'?"

"But, Milly dear, you know quite well that I can't play it."

Mamma was nevertheless persuaded to play not only the "Impassionata" but her entire repertoire. She was not allowed to leave the piano, and had begun to play Sydney Smith when the door opened, and a man's face appeared for a second. Remembering her interest in men, I said:

"Did you see that man? What a nice, fresh-looking young man!"

She put her finger on her lip, and wrote on a piece of paper:

"Not a word. He's my fiancé, and mother doesn't know he's here. She does not approve; he hasn't a bean." ... "Thank you, mother, thank you; you played that sonata very nicely."

"Won't you play, my dear?"

"No, mother dear, I'm feeling rather tired; we've had a long day."

And the two bade me good-night, leaving me alone in the sitting-room to finish a letter. But I had not quite got down to the signature when she came in looking very agitated, even a little frightened.

"Isn't it awful?" she said. "I was in the dining-room with my fiancé, and the waiter caught us kissing. I had to beg of him not to tell mamma. He said 'Foi de gentilhomme,' so I suppose it's all right."

"Why not have your fiancé in here? I'm going to bed."

"Oh, no, I wouldn't think of turning you out. I'll see him in my bedroom; it's safer, and if one's conscience is clear it doesn't matter what people say."

A few days afterwards, as I was slinging my paintbox over my shoulders, I heard some one stop in the passage, and speaking to me through the open door she said:

"You were so awfully decent the other night when Donald looked in. I know you will think it cheek; I am the most impudent woman in the world; but do you mind my telling mamma that I am going to the Louvre with you to see the pictures? You won't give me away, will you?"

"I never split on any one."

"My poor darling ought to go back. He's away from the office without leave, and he may get the sack; but he's going to stay another night. Can you come now? Mamma is in the salon. Come just to say a word to her and we will go out together. Donald is waiting at the corner."

Next morning as I was shaving I heard a knock at my door.

"*Entré!*"

"Oh, I beg your pardon, but I didn't want to miss you. I'll wait for you in the salon."

When I came downstairs she showed me a wedding ring. She had married Donald, or said she had.

"Oh, I am tired. I hate going to the shops, and now mamma wants me to go shopping with her. Can't you stay and talk to me, and later on we might sneak out together and go somewhere?... Are you painting to-day?"

"Well, no, I'm going to a museum a long way from here. I have never seen Madame de Sévigné's house."

"Who is she?"

"The woman who wrote the famous letters."

"I am afraid I shall only bore you, because I can't talk about books."

"You had better come; you can't stay in this hotel by yourself all the morning."

There was some reason which I have forgotten why she could not go out with Donald, and I suppose it was my curiosity in all things human that persuaded me to yield to her desire to accompany me, though, as I told her, I was going to visit Madame de Sévigné's house. The reader doubtless remembers that we visited not only Madame de Sévigné's house, but also Victor Hugo's in the Place des Vosges, and perhaps her remark as we returned home in the evening along the quays, that "Paris wasn't bad for an old city," has not yet slipped out of the reader's memory. For it was a strange remark, and one could hardly hear it without feeling an interest in the speaker; at least, that was how I felt. It was that remark that drew my attention to her again, and when we stopped before the door of our hotel, I remembered that I had spent the day talking to her about things that could have no meaning for her. Madame de Sévigné and Jean Goujon, old Paris and its associated ideas could have been studied on another occasion, but an opportunity of studying Mildred might never occur again. I was dining out that evening; the next day I did not see her, and the day after, as I sat in the Luxembourg Gardens, beguiled from my work by the pretty April sunlight and the birds in the alley (I have spoken already of these things), as I sat admiring them, a thought of Mildred sprang into my mind, a sudden fear that I might never see her again; and it was just when I had begun to feel that I would like to walk about the gardens with her that I heard her voice. These coincidences often occur, yet we always think them strange, almost providential. The reader knows how I rose to meet her, and how I asked her to come for a walk in the gardens. Very soon we turned in the direction of the museum, for, thinking to propitiate me, Mildred suggested I should take her there, and I did not like to refuse, though I feared some of the pictures and statues might distract me from the end I now had in view, which was to find out if Donald had been her first lover, and if her dear little mamma suspected anything.

"So your mother knows nothing about your marriage?"

"Nothing. He ought to go back, but he's going to stay another night. I think I told you. Poor dear little mamma, she never suspected a bit."

As we walked to the museum I caught glimpses of what Donald's past life had been, learning incidentally that his father was rich, but since Donald was sixteen he had been considered a ne'er-do-well. He had gone away to sea when he was a boy, and had been third mate on a merchant ship; in a hotel in America he had been a boot-black, and just before he came to Paris he fought a drunken stoker and won a purse of five pounds.

She asked me which were the best pictures, but she could not keep her attention fixed, and her attempts to remember the names of the painters were pathetic. "Ingres, did you say? I must try to remember.... Puvis de Chavannes? What a curious name! but I do like his picture. He has given that man Donald's shoulders," she said, laying her hand on my arm and stopping me before a picture of a young naked man sitting amid some grey rocks, with grey trees and a grey sky. The young man in the picture had dark curly hair, and Mildred said she would like to sit by him and put her hands through his hair. "He has got big muscles, just like Donald. I like a man to be strong: I hate a little man."

We wandered on talking of love and lovers, our conversation occasionally interrupted, for however interested I was in Mildred, and I was very much interested, the sight of a picture sometimes called away my attention. When we came to the sculpture-room it seemed to me that Mildred was more interested in sculpture than in painting, for she stopped suddenly before Rodin's "L'age d'arain," and I began to wonder if her mind were really accessible to the beauty of the sculptor's art, or if her interest were entirely in the model that had posed before Rodin. Sculpture is a more primitive art than painting; sculpture and music are the two primitive arts, and they are therefore open to the appreciation of the vulgar; at least, that is how I tried to correlate Mildred with Rodin, and at the same moment the thought rose up in my mind that one so interested in sex as Mildred was could not be without interest in art. For though it be true that sex is antecedent to art, art was enlisted in the service of sex very early in the history of the race, and has, if a colloquialism may be allowed here, done yeoman service ever since. Even in modern days, notwithstanding the invention of the telephone and the motor car, we are still dependent upon art for the beginning of our courtships. To-day the courtship begins by the man and the woman sending each other books. Before books were invented music served the purpose of the lover. For when man ceased to capture woman, he went to the river's edge and cut a reed and made it into a flute and played it for her pleasure; and when he had won her with his music he began to take an interest in the tune for its own sake. Amusing thoughts like these floated through my mind in the Luxembourg galleries—how could it be otherwise since I was there with Mildred?—and I began to argue that it was not likely that one so highly strung as Mildred could be blind to the sculptor's dream of a slender boy, and that boy, too, swaying like a lily in some ecstasy of efflorescence.

"The only fault I find with him is that he is not long enough from the knee to the foot, and the thigh seems too long. I like the greater length to be from the knee to the foot rather than from the knee to the hip. Now, have I said anything foolish?"

"Not the least. I think you are right. I prefer your proportions. A short tibia is not pretty."

A look of reverie came into her eyes. "I don't know if I told you that we are going to Italy next week?"

"Yes, you told me."

Her thoughts jerked off at right angles, and turning her back on the statue, she began to tell me how she had made Donald's acquaintance. She and her mother were then living in a boarding-house in the same square in which Donald's father lived, and they used to walk in the square, and one day as she was running home trying to escape a shower, he had come forward with his umbrella. That was in July, a few days before she went away to Tenby for a month. It was at Tenby she had become intimate with Toby Wells; he had succeeded for a time in putting Donald out of her mind. She had met Toby at Nice.

"But you like Donald much better than Toby?"

"Of course I do; he came here to marry me. Oh, yes, I've forgotten all about Toby. You see, I met Donald when I went back to London. But do look at that woman's back; see where her head is. I wonder what made Rodin put a woman in that position."

She looked at me, and there was a look of curious inquiry on her face. Overcome with a sudden shyness, I hastened to assure her that the statue was "La Danaide."

"Rodin often introduces a trivial voluptuousness into art; and his sculpture may be sometimes called *l'article de Paris*. It is occasionally soiled by the sentiment, of which Gounod is the great exponent, a base soul who poured a sort of bath-water melody down the back of every woman he met, Margaret or Madeline, it was all the same."

"Clearly this is not a day to walk about a picture-gallery with you. Come, let us sit down, and we'll talk about lighter things, about lovers. You won't mind telling me; you know you can trust me. One of these days you will meet a man who will absorb you utterly, and all these passing passions will wax to one passion that will know no change."

"Do you think so? I wonder."

"Do you doubt it?"

"I don't think any one man could absorb me; no one man could fill my life."

"Not even Donald?"

"Donald is wonderful. Do you remember that morning, a few days after we arrived?"

"Your wedding night?"

"Yes, my wedding night."

We are interested in any one who is himself or herself, and this girl was certainly herself and nothing but herself. Travelling about as she did with her quiet, respectable mother, who never suspected anything, she seemed to indicate a type—type is hardly the word, for she was an exception. Never had I seen any one like her before, her frankness and her daring; here at least was one who had the courage of her instincts. She was man-crazy if you will, but now and then I caught sight of another Mildred when she sighed, when that little dissatisfied look appeared in her face, and the other Mildred only floated up for a moment like a water-flower or weed on the surface of a stream.

"... You know I do mean to be a good girl. I think one ought to be good. But really, if you read the Bible——Oh, must you go?—it has been such a relief talking things over with you. Shall I see you to-night? There is no one else in the hotel I can talk to, and mamma will play the piano, and when, she plays Beethoven it gets upon my nerves."

"You play the violin, don't you?"

"Yes, I play," and that peculiar sad look which I had begun to think was characteristic of her came into her face, and I asked myself if this sudden misting of expression should be ascribed to stupidity or to a sudden thought or emotion. "I am sorry you're not dining at the hotel."

"I am sorry, too; I'm dining with students in the Quarter; they would amuse you."

"I wish I were a grisette."

"If you were I would take you with me. Now I must say good-bye; I have to get on with my painting."

That night I returned to the hotel late and went away early in the morning. But the next day she came upon me again in the gardens, and as we walked on together she told me that Donald had gone away.

"He was obliged to return, you see; he left the office without leave, and he had only two pounds, the poor darling. I don't know if I told you that he had to borrow two pounds to come here." "No, you omitted that little fact. You see, you are so absorbed in yourself that you think all these things are as interesting to everybody else as they are to you."

"Now you're unkind," and she looked at me reproachfully. "It is the first time you have been unsympathetic. If I talked to you it was because I thought my chatter interested you. Moreover, I believed that you were a little interested in me, and I have come all this way—"

My heart was touched, and I begged of her to believe that my remark was only uttered in sport, to tease her. But it was a long time before I could get her to finish the sentence. "You have come a long way, you said—"

"I came to tell you that we are going to Rome tomorrow. I didn't like to go away without seeing you, but it seems as if I were mistaken; it would not have mattered to you if I had."

She had her fiddle-case with her; and to offer to carry it for her seemed an easy way out of my difficulty; but she would not surrender it for a while. I asked her if she had been playing at a concert, or if she were coming from a lesson. No; well, then, why had she her fiddle-case with her?

"Don't ask me; leave me in peace. It doesn't matter. I cannot play now, and ten minutes ago my head was full of it."

These little ebullitions of temper were common in Mildred, and I knew that the present one would soon pass away. In order that its passing might be accomplished as rapidly as possible, I suggested we should sit down, and I spoke to her of Donald.

"I don't want to talk about him. You have offended me."

"I'm sorry you are leaving Paris. This is the beautiful month. How pleasant it is here, a soft diffused warmth in the air, the sunlight flickering like a live thing in the leaves, and the sound of water dripping at the end of the alley. We are all alone here, Mildred. Come, tell me why you brought your fiddle-case."

"Well," she said, "I brought it on the chance of meeting you. I thought you might like to hear me play. We are going away to-morrow morning. I can't play in that hotel, in that stuffy little room; mamma would want to accompany me."

"Play to me in the Luxembourg Gardens!"

"One can do anything one likes here; no one pays any attention to anybody else," and she pointed with her parasol to a long poet, with hair floating over his shoulders, who walked up and down the other end of the alley reciting his verses.

"Perhaps your playing will interrupt him."

"Oh, if he doesn't like it he'll move away. But I don't want to play; I can't play when I'm out of humour, and I was just in the very humour for playing until your remark about—"

"About what?"

"You know very well," she answered.

The desire to hear her play the fiddle in the gardens gained upon me. The moment was an enchanting one, the light falling through the translucid leaves and the poet walking up and down carried my thoughts into another age. I began to see a picture—myself, the poet, and this girl playing the violin for us; other figures were wanting to make up the composition. Cabanel's picture of the Florentine poet intruded itself, interrupting my vision, the picture of Dante reading his verses at one end of a stone bench to a frightened girl whose lover is drawing her away from him who had been to Hell and witnessed the tortures of the damned, who had met the miserable lovers of Rimini whirling through space and heard their story from them. Lizard-like, a man lies along a low wall, listening to the poet's story. But why describe a picture so well known? Why mention it at all? Only because its design intruded itself, spoiling my dream, an abortive idea that I dimly perceived in Nature without being able to grasp it; an illusive suggestion for a picture was passing by me, and so eager was my pursuit of the vision that there was no strength in me to ask Mildred to play. True that the sound of her violin might help me, but it must happen accidentally, just as everything else was happening, without sequence, without logic. At that moment my ear caught the sound of violin-playing; some dance measure of old time was being played, and in the sunlit interspace three women appeared dancing a gavotte, advancing and retiring through the light and shade. The one who played the violin leaned sometimes against a tree, and sometimes she joined the others, playing as she danced.

"I know that gavotte. Come, let us go to them. I'll play for them if they'll let me."

Very soon the woman who played the violin seemed to recognise Mildred as a better player than herself. She handed her fiddle to a bystander and the gavotte proceeded, the three old ladies bowing and holding up their skirts and pointing their toes with the grace of bygone times. Never, I think, did reality seem more like a dream. "But who are these three women?" I asked myself, and, sinking on a bench like one enchanted, I dreamed that these were three sisters, the remnant of a noble family who had lost its money during several generations till at last nothing remained, and the poor old women had to devise some mode of earning their living. I imagined the scene in some great house which they would have to leave on the morrow, and they talking together, thinking they must go forth to beg, till she who played the fiddle said that something would happen to save them from the shame of mendicancy. I imagined her saying that their last crust of bread would not be eaten before some one would come to tell them that a fortune awaited them. And it so happened that the day they divided this crust the one to whom faith had been given came upon an old letter. She stood reading till the others asked her what she was reading with so much interest. "I told you," she said, "that we should be saved, that God in His great mercy would not turn us out into the streets to beg. This letter contains explicit directions how the gavotte used to be danced when our ancestors lived in the Place des Vosges."

"But what help to us to know the true step of the gavotte?" cried the youngest sister.

"A great deal," the eldest answered gravely; "I can play the fiddle, and we can all learn to dance; we'll go to dance the gavotte in the Luxembourg Gardens whenever it is fine—the true gavotte as it was danced when Madame de Sévigné drove up in a painted coach drawn by six horses, and entered the courtyard of her hotel decorated with bas-reliefs by Jean Goujon."

This is the story that I dreamed as I sat on the bench listening to the pretty, sprightly music flowing like a live thing. Under the fingers of the old woman the music scratched along like dead leaves along a pathway, without accent, without rhythm; now the old gavotte tripped like the springtime, pretty as the budding trees, as the sunlight along the swards. Mildred brought out the contrast between the detached and the slurred notes. How gaily it went! Full of the fashion of the time—the wigs, the swords, the bows, the gallantry! How sedate! How charming! How well she understood it! How well the old women danced to it! How delighted every one was! She played on until the old women, unable to dance any more, sat down to listen to her. After trying some few things which I did not know, I heard her playing a piece of music which I could not but think I had heard before—in church! Beginning it on the low string, she poured out the long, long phrase that never seems to end, so stern and so evocative of Protestantism that I could not but think of a soul going forth on its way to the Judgment Seat, telling perforce as it goes how it has desired and sought salvation, pleading almost defiantly. But Mildred could not appreciate such religious exaltation, yet it was her playing that had inspired the thought in me. Had she been taught to play it? Was she echoing another's thought? Her playing did not sound like an echo; it seemed to come from the heart, or out of some unconscious self, an ante-natal self that in her present incarnation only emerged in music, borne up by some mysterious current to be sucked down by another.

She played other things, not certain what she was going to play; and then, as if suddenly moved to tell us about other things, she began to play a very simple, singing melody, interrupted now and again, so it seemed to me, by little fluttering confessions. I seemed to see a lady in white, at the close of day, in a dusky boudoir, one of Alfred Stevens's women, only much more refined, one whose lover has been unfaithful to her, or maybe a woman who is weary of lovers and knows not what to turn her mind to, hesitating between the convent and the ball-room. Ah, the beautiful lament—how well Mildred played it!—followed by the slight crescendo, and then the return of the soul upon itself, bewailing its weakness, confessing its follies in elegant, lovely language, seemingly speaking in a casual way, yet saying such profound things, profound even as Bach. The form is different, more light, more graceful, apparently more superficial, but just as deep; for when we go to the bottom of things all things are deep, one as deep as another, just as all things are shallow, one as shallow as another; for have not mystics of every age held that things exist not in themselves, but in the eye that sees and the ear that hears?

A crowd had collected to hear her, for she was playing out of the great silence that is in every soul, in that of the light-o'-love as well as of the saint, and she went on playing, apparently unaware of the number of people she had collected about her. She stopped playing and returned to me.

"You play beautifully; why did you say you didn't like Beethoven?"

"I didn't say I didn't like Beethoven; you know very well mamma can't play the 'Impassionata.'"

"Why aren't you always like this?"

"I don't know. One can't always be the same. I feel differently when I play; the mood only comes over me sometimes. I used to play a great deal; I only play occasionally now, just when I feel like it."

We walked through the alleys by the statues, seeing them hardly at all, thinking of the music.

"I must be getting back," she said. "You see, I've got to pack up. Mother can't do any packing; I've to do hers for her. I hope we shall meet again some day."

"What good would it be? I only like you when you're playing, and you're not often in the mood."

"I'm sorry for that; perhaps if you knew me better——"

"Now you're married, and I suppose Donald will come to Rome to fetch you?"

"Oh, I don't think he'll be able. He has got no money."

"And you'll fall in love with some one else?"

"Well, perhaps so; I don't feel that I ever could again after this week." Stopping suddenly in front of a hosier's shop, she said: "I like those collars; they have just come out—those turned-down ones. Do you like them as well as the great high stand-up collars about three inches deep? When they were the fashion men could hardly move their heads." Then she made some remarks about neckties and the colour she liked best—violet. "Yes, there's a nice shade of violet. Poor Donald! He's so handsome."

After the hosier's shop she spoke no more about music. And long before we reached the hotel she who had played—I cannot say for certain what she played that day in the Luxembourg Gardens; my love of music was not then fully awakened; could it have been?—the names of Bach and Chopin come up in my mind—"I can't speak about music," she said, as we turned into the Rue du Bac, and she ran up the stairs of the hotel possessed completely by the other Mildred. She asked her mother to play the "Brooklyn Cake Walk," and she danced "the lovely two-step," as she had learned it at Nice, for my enjoyment. I noticed that she looked extraordinarily comic as she skipped up and down the room, the line of her chin deflected, and that always gives a slightly comic look to a face. She came downstairs with me, and, standing at the hotel door, she told me of something that had happened yesterday.

"Mother and I went to Cook's to get the tickets. When we went into the office I saw a Yank—oh, so nicely dressed! Lovely patent-leather boots. And I thought, 'Oh, dear, he'll never look at me.' But presently he did, and took out his card-case and folded up a card and put it on the ledge behind him, and gave me a look and moved away. So I walked over and took it up. Mamma never saw, but the clerks did."

I have reported Mildred's story truthfully at a particular moment of her life. Those who travel meet people now and again whose individuality is so strong that it survives. Mildred's has survived many years, and I have written this account of it because it seems to me to throw a gleam into the mystery of life without, however, doing anything to destroy the mystery.

CHAPTER X

A REMEMBRANCE

It was in the vastness of Westminster Hall that I saw her for the first time—saw her pointed face, her red hair, her brilliant teeth. The next time was in her own home—a farm-house that had been rebuilt and was half a villa. At the back were wheat-stacks, a noisy thrashing-machine, a pigeon-cote, and stables whence, with jangle of harness and cries of yokels, the great farm-horses always seemed to be coming from or going to their work on the downs. In a garden planted with variegated firs she tended her flowers all day; and in the parlour, where we assembled in the evening, her husband smoked his pipe in silence; the young ladies, their blonde hair hanging down their backs, played waltzes; she alone talked. Her conversation was effusive, her laughter abundant and bright. I had only just turned eighteen, and was deeply interested in religious problems, and one day I told her the book I carried in my pocket, and sometimes pretended to study, was Kant's "Critique of Pure Reason." My explanation of the value of the work did not seem to strike her, and her manifest want of interest in the discussion of religious problems surprised me, for she passed for a religious woman, and I failed to understand how mere belief could satisfy any one. One day in the greenhouse, whither I had wandered, she interrupted some allusion to the chapter entitled "The Deduction of the Categories" with a burst of laughter, and declared that she would call me Kant. The nickname was not adopted by the rest of the family—another was invented which appealed more to their imagination—but she held to the name she had given me, and during the course of our long friendship never addressed me by any other.

There was no reason why I should have become the friend of these people. We were opposed in character and temperament, but somehow we seemed to suit. There was little reflection on either side; certainly there was none on mine; at that time I was incapable of any; my youth was a vague dream, and my friends were the shadows on the dream. I saw and understood them only as one sees and understands the summer clouds when, lying at length in the tall grass, one watches the clouds curl and uncurl. In such mood, visit succeeded visit, and before I was aware, the old Squire who walked about the downs in a tall hat died, and my friends moved into the family place, distant about a hundred yards—an Italian house, sheltered among the elms that grew along the seashore. And in their new house they became to me more real than shadows; they were then like figures on a stage, and the building of the new wing and the planting of the new garden interested me as might an incident in a play; and I left them as I might leave a play, taking up another thread in life, thinking very little of them, if I thought at all. Years passed, and after a long absence abroad I met them by chance in London.

Again visit succeeded visit. My friends were the same as when I had left them; their house was the same, the conduct of their lives was the same. I do not think I was conscious of any change until, one day, walking with one of the girls in the garden, a sensation of home came upon me. I seemed always to have known these people; they seemed part and parcel of my life. It was a sudden and enchanting awaking of love; life seemed to lengthen out like the fields at dawn, and to become distinct and real in many new and unimagined ways. Above all, I was surprised to find myself admiring her who, fifteen years ago, had appeared to me not a little dowdy. She was now fifty-five, but such an age seemed impossible for so girl-like a figure and such young and effusive laughter. I was, however, sure that she was fifteen years older than when I first saw her, but those fifteen years had brought each within range of the other's understanding and sympathy. We became companions. I noticed what dresses she wore, and told her which I liked her best in. She was only cross with me when I surprised her in the potting-shed wearing an old bonnet out of which hung a faded poppy. She used to cry: "Don't look at me, Kant. I know I'm like an old gipsy woman."

"You look charming," I said, "in that old bonnet."

She put down the watering-can and laughingly took it from her head. "It is a regular show."

"Not at all. You look charming when working in the greenhouse.... I like you better like that than when you are dressed to go to Brighton."

"Do you?... I thought you liked me best in my new black silk."

"I think I like you equally well at all times."

We looked at each other. There was an accent of love in our friendship. "And strange, is it not," I said, "I did not admire you half as much when I knew you first?"

"How was that? I was quite a young woman then."

"Yes," I said, regretting my own words; "but, don't you see, at that time I was a mere boy—I lived in a dream, hardly seeing what passed around me."

"Yes, of course," she said gaily, "you were so young then, all you saw in me was a woman with a grown-up son."

Her dress was pinned up, she held in her hand the bonnet which she said made her look like an old gipsy woman, and the sunlight fell on the red hair, now grown a little thinner, but each of the immaculate teeth was an elegant piece of statuary, and not a wrinkle was there on that pretty, vixen-like face. Her figure especially showed no signs of age, and if she and her daughters were in the room it was she I admired.

One day, while seeking through the store-room for a sheet of brown paper to pack up a book in, I came across a pile of old *Athenaeums*. Had I happened upon a set of drawings by Raphael I could not have been more astonished. Not one, but twenty copies of the *Athenaeum* in a house where never a book was read. I looked at the dates— three-and-thirty years ago. At that moment she was gathering some withering apples from the floor.

"Whoever," I cried, "could have left these copies of the *Athenaeum* here?"

"Oh, they are my *Athenaeums*," she said. "I always used to read the *Athenaeum* when I was engaged to be married to Mr. Bartlett. You must have heard of him—he wrote that famous book about the Euphrates. I was very fond of reading in those days, and he and I used to talk about books in the old garden at Wandsworth. It is all built over now."

Memoirs of My Dead Life

This sudden discovery of dead tastes and sympathies seemed to draw us closer together, and in the quietness of the store-room, amid the odour of the apples, her face flushed with all the spirit of her girlhood, and I understood her as if I had lived it with her.

"You must have been a delightful girl. I believe if I had known you then I should have asked you to marry me."

"I believe you would, Kant.... So you thought because I never read books now that I had never read any? You have no idea how fond of books I was once, and if I had married Mr. Bartlett I believe I should have been quite a blue-stocking. But then Dick came, and my father thought it a more suitable match, and I had young children to look after. We were very poor in those days; the old Squire never attempted to help us."

At this time I seemed to be always with my friends; I came to see them when I pleased, and sometimes I stayed a week, sometimes I stayed six months: but however long my visit they said it was not long enough. The five-o'clock from London brought me down in time for dinner, and I used to run up to my room just as if I were a member of the family. If I missed this train and came down by the six-o'clock, I found them at dinner, and then the lamplight seemed to accentuate our affectionate intimacy, and to pass round the table shaking hands with them all was in itself a peculiar delight. On one of these occasions, missing her from her place, I said: "Surely you have not allowed her to remain till this hour in the garden?"

I was told that she was ill, and had been for the last fortnight confined to her room. Several days passed; allusion to her illness became more frequent; and then I heard that the local doctor would accept the responsibility no longer, and had demanded a consultation with a London physician. But she would not hear of so much expense for her sake, and declared herself to be quite sufficiently well to go to London.

The little pony-carriage took her to the station, and I saw her in the waiting-room wrapped up in shawls. She was ashamed to see me, but in truth the disease had not changed her as she thought it had. There are some who are so beautiful that disease cannot deform them, and she was endowed with such exquisite life that she would turn to smile back on you over the brink of the grave.

We thought the train was taking her from us for ever, but she came back hopeful. Operation had been pronounced unnecessary, but she remained in her room many days before the medicine had reduced her sufficiently to allow her to come downstairs. Nearly a month passed, and then she appeared looking strangely well, and every day she grew better until she regained her girlish figure and the quick dance of movement which was a grace and a joy in the silent peacefulness of the old house. Her grace and lightness were astonishing, and one day, coming down dressed to go in the carriage, she raced across the library, opened her escritoire, hunting through its innumerable drawers for one of the sums of money which she kept there wrapped up in pieces of paper.

"How nice you look! You are quite well now, and your figure is like a girl of fifteen."

She turned and looked at me with that love in her face which an old woman feels for a young man who is something less and something more to her than her son. As a flush of summer lingers in autumn's face, so does a sensation of sex float in such an affection. There is something strangely tender in the yearning of the young man for the decadent charms of her whom he regards as the mother of his election, and who, at the same time, suggests to him the girl he would have loved if time had not robbed him of her youth. There is a waywardness in such an affection that formal man knows not of.

I remember that day, for it was the last time I saw her beautiful. Soon after we noticed that she did not quite recover, and we thought it was because she did not take her medicine regularly. She spent long hours alone in her greenhouse, the hot sun playing fiercely on her back, and we supplicated—I was the foremost among her supplicators—that she would not carry the heavy flower-pots to and fro, nor cans of water from the tank at the bottom of the garden, and to save her I undertook to water her flowers for her. But she was one of those who would do everything herself—who thought that if she did not shut the door it was not properly shut. She was always speaking of her work. "If I leave my work," she would say, "even for one week, everything gets so behind-hand that I despair of ever being able to make up the arrear. The worst of it is that no one can take up my work where I leave off." And as she grew worse this idea developed until it became a kind of craze. At last, speculating on the strength of our friendship, I told her her life belonged to her husband and children, and that she had no right to squander it in this fashion. I urged that with ordinary forbearance she might live for twenty years, but at the present rate of force-expenditure she could not hope to live long. I spoke brutally, but she smiled, knowing how much I loved her; and, looking back, it seems to me she must have known she could not be saved, and preferred to give the last summer of her life entirely to her flowers. It was pathetic to see her, poor moribund one, sitting through the long noons alone, the sun beating in upon her through the fiery glass, tending her flowers. I remember how she used to come in in the evenings exhausted, and lie down on the little sofa. Her husband, with an anxious, quiet, kindly look in his eyes, used to draw the skirt over her feet and sit down at her feet, tender, loving, soliciting the right to clasp her hand, as if they had not been married thirty years, but were only sweethearts. At that time we used all to implore her to allow us to send for the London doctor, and I remember how proud I was when she looked up and said, "Very well, Kant, it shall be as you wish it." I remember, too, waiting by the little wood at the corner of the lane, where I should be sure to meet the doctor as he came up from the station. The old elms were beautiful with green, the sky was beautiful with blue, and we lingered, looking out on the fair pasturage where the sheep moved so peacefully, and, with the exquisite warmth of summer in our flesh, we talked of her who was to die.

"Is it then incurable?"

"There is no such thing as cure.... We cannot create, we can only stimulate an existent force, and every time we stimulate we weaken, and so on until exhaustion. Our drugs merely precipitate the end."

"Then there is no hope?"

"I'm afraid not."

"Can she live for five years?"

"I should think it extremely improbable."

"What length of life do you give her?"

"You are asking too much.... I should say about a year."

The doctor passed up the leafy avenue. I remained looking at the silly sheep, seeing in all the green landscape only a dark, narrow space. That day I saw her for the last time. She was sitting on a low chair, very ill indeed, and the voice, weak, but still young and pure, said: "Is that you, Kant? Come round here and let me look at you." Amid my work in London, I used to receive letters from my friends, letters telling me of the march of the disease, and with each letter death grew more and more realisable until her death seemed to stand in person before me. It could not be much longer delayed, and the letter came which told me that "Mother was not expected to live through the winter." Soon after came another letter: "Mother will not live another month"; and this was followed by a telegram: "Mother is dying; come at once."

It was a bleak and gusty afternoon in the depth of winter, and the Sunday train stopped at every station, and the journey dragged its jogging length of four hours out to the weary end. The little station shivered by an icy sea, and going up the lane the wind rattled and beat my face like an iron. I hurried, looking through the trees for the lights that would shine across the park if she were not dead, and welcome indeed to my eyes were the gleaming yellow squares. Slipping in the back way, and meeting the butler in the passage, I said: "How is she?"

"Very bad indeed, sir."

She did not die that night, nor the next, nor yet the next; and as we waited for death, slow but sure of foot, to come and take what remained of her from us, I thought often of the degradation that these lingering deaths impose upon the watchers, and how they force into disgraceful prominence all that is animal in us. For, however great our grief may be, we must eat and drink, and must even talk of other things than the beloved one whom we are about to lose; for we may not escape from our shameful nature. And, eating and drinking, we commented on the news that came hourly from the sickroom: "Mother will not live the week." A few days after, "Mother will hardly get over Sunday"; and the following week, "Mother will not pass the night." Lunch was the meal that shocked me most, and I often thought, "She is dying upstairs while we are eating jam tarts."

One day I had to ride over the downs for some letters, and when, on my return, I walked in from the stables, I met her son. He was in tears, and sobbing he said: "My dear old chap, it is all over; she is gone." I took his hand and burst into tears. Then one of her daughters came downstairs and I was told how she had passed away. A few hours before she died she had asked for a silk thread; for thirty years, before sleeping, she always passed one between her beautiful teeth. Her poor arms were shrunken to the very bone and were not larger than a little child's. Haggard and over-worn, she was lifted up, and the silk was given to her and the glass was held before her; but her eyes were glazed with death, and she fell back exhausted. Then her breathing grew thicker, and at last and quite suddenly, she realised that she was about to die; and looking round wildly, not seeing those who were collected about her bed, she said, "Oh, to die when so much remains undone! How will they get on without me!"

I helped to write the letters, so melancholy, so conventional, and expressing so little of our grief, and the while the girls sat weaving wreaths for the dead, and at every hour wreaths and letters of sympathy arrived. The girls went upstairs where the dead lay, and when they returned they told me how beautiful their mother looked. And during those dreadful days, how many times did I refuse to look on her dead! My memory of her was an intensely living thing, and I could not be persuaded to sacrifice it. We thought the day would never come, but it came. There was a copious lunch, cigars were smoked, the crops, the price of lambs, and the hunting, which the frost had much interfered with, were alluded to furtively, and the conversation was interspersed with references to the excellent qualities of the deceased. I remember the weather was beautiful, full of pure sunlight, with the colour of the coming spring in the face of the heavens. And the funeral procession wound along the barren sea road, the lily-covered coffin on a trolley drawn by the estate labourers. That day every slightest line and every colour of that bitter, barren coast impressed themselves on my mind, and I saw more distinctly than I had ever done before the old church with red-brown roofs and square dogmatic tower, the forlorn village, the grey undulations of the dreary hills, whose ring of trees showed aloft like a plume. In the church the faces of the girls were discomposed with grief, and they wept hysterically in each other's arms. The querulous voice of the organ, the hideous hymn, and the grating voice of the aged parson standing in white surplice on the altar-steps! Dear heart! I saw thee in thy garden while others looked unto that sunless hole, while old men, white-haired and tottering, impelled by senile curiosity, pressed forward and looked down into that comfortless hole.

The crowd quickly dispersed; the relatives and the friends of the deceased, as they returned home, sought those who were most agreeable and sympathetic, and matters of private interest were discussed. Those who had come from a distance consulted their watches, and an apology to life was implicit in their looks, and the time they had surrendered to something outside of life evidently struck them as being strangely disproportionate. The sunlight laughed along the sea, and the young corn was thick in the fields; leaves were beginning in the branches, larks rose higher and higher, disappearing in the pale air, and, as we approached the plantations, the amorous cawing of the rooks sounded pleasantly in the ear. The appearance of death in the springtime, at the moment when the world renews its life, touched my soul with that anguish which the familiar spectacle has always and will never fail to cause as long as a human heart beats beneath the heavens. And, dropping behind the chattering crowd that in mourning-weed wended its way through the sad spring landscape, I thought of her whom I had loved so long and should never see again. I thought of memory as a shrine where we can worship without shame, of friendship, and of the pure escapement it offers us from our natural instincts; I remembered that there is love other than that which the young man offers to her he would take to wife, and I knew how much more intense and strangely personal was my love of her than the love which that day I saw the world offering to its creatures.

CHAPTER XI

BRING IN THE LAMP

For many days there has not been a wind in the trees, and the landscape reminds me of a somnambulist—the same silence, the same mystery, the same awe. The thick foliage of the ash never stirs; even the fingery leaves hanging out from the topmost twigs are still. The hawthorns growing out of a tumbled wall are turning yellow and brown, the hollyhocks are over, the chrysanthemums are beginning. Last night a faint pink sky melted into the solemn blue of midnight. There were few stars; Jupiter, wearisomely brilliant, sailed overhead; red Mars hung above the horizon under a round, decorative moon.... The last days of September! and every day the light dies a few minutes earlier. At half-past five one perceives a chilliness about one's feet; no doubt there is a touch of frost in the air; that is why the leaves hang so plaintively. There is certainly a touch of frost in the air, and one is tempted to put a match to the fire. It is difficult to say whether one feels cold or whether one desires the company of the blaze. Tea is over, the dusk gathers, and the brute Despondency lurks in the corners. At the close of day, when one's work is over, benumbing thoughts arise in the study and in the studio. Think of a painter of architecture finishing the thirty-sixth pillar (there are forty-three). The dusk has interrupted his labour, and an ache begins in his heart as he rises from the easel. Be his talent great or little, he must ask himself who will care should he leave the last seven pillars unfinished? Think of the writer of stories! Two, three, or four more stories are required to make up a requisite number of pages. The dusk has interrupted his labour, and he rises from his writing-table asking who will care whether the last stories are written or left unwritten? If he write them his ideas will flicker green for a brief springtime, they will enjoy a little summer; when his garden is fading in the autumn his leaves will be well-nigh forgotten; winter will overtake them sooner than it overtakes his garden, perhaps. The flowers he deemed immortal are more mortal than the rose. "Why," he asks, "should any one be interested in my stories any more than in the thousand and one stories published this year? Mine are among the number of trivial things that compose the tedium which we call life." His thoughts will flit back over the past, and his own life will seem hardly more real than the day's work on the easel if he be a painter, on the secretaire if he be a writer. He will seem to himself like a horse going round and round a well. But the horse is pumping water—water is necessary; but art, even if his work is good enough to be called art, is not, so far as he knows, necessary to any one. Whosoever he may be, proof is not wanting that the world can do well without his work. But however sure he may feel that that is so, and in the hours I describe it seems sure indeed, he will have to continue his labour. Man was born to labour, as the oldest texts say; he must continue to drive his furrow to the end of the field, otherwise he would lie down and die of sheer boredom, or go mad. He asks himself why he became a maker of idols. "An idol-maker, an idol-maker," he cries, "who can find no worshippers for his wares! Better the sailor before the mast or the soldier in the field." His thoughts break away, and he begins to dream of a life of action. It would be a fine thing, he thinks, to start away in a ship for South America, where there are forests and mountain ranges almost unknown. He has read of the wild shepherds of the Pampas. So inured are they to horseback that they cannot walk a mile without resting; and sitting by the fire at the end of the autumn day, he can see them galloping through the long grass of the Pampas, whirling three balls attached by leather thongs. The weapon is called the bolus, and flying through the air it encircles the legs of the guana, bringing it to the earth. But if he went to America, would he find content in a hunter's life? Can the artist put by his dreams and find content in the hunter's life? His dreams would follow him, and sitting by the camp-fire in the evening he would begin to think how he might paint the shadows or tell of the uncouth life of those who sat around him eating of jerked meat. No, there is nothing for him but to follow the furrow; he will have to write stories till his brain fades or death intervenes. And what story shall he write to complete his book, since it must be completed, it forming part of the procession of things? The best part of story-writing is the seeking for the subject. Now there is a sound of church bells in the still air, beautiful sounds of peace and long tradition, and he likes to listen, thinking of the hymns and the homely sermons of the good minister. Shall he get up and go? Perhaps the service would soothe his despondency; but there is not courage enough in his heart. He can do no more than strike a match; the fire lights up. It is one of those autumn afternoons with just that touch of frost in the air which makes a fire welcome, and as he crouches in his arm-chair the warmth soothes the spirit and flesh, and in the doze of the flesh the spirit awakes. What—is the story coming now? Yes; it is forming independently of his will, and he says, "Let it take shape." And the scene that rises up in his mind is a ball-room; he sees women all arow, delicate necks and arms of young girls, and young men in black collected about the doorways. Some couples are moving to the rhythm of a languorous waltz, a French imitation of Strauss, a waltz never played now, forgotten perhaps by everybody but him—a waltz he heard twenty long years ago. That waltz has lain ever since forgotten in his brain, but now he hears it all; never before was he able to remember that *coda*, and it comes with a scent of violets in it—the perfume of a little blond woman who dreams as she dances with the young man blond as herself. Let it be that the choice was made by her rather than by him, and let her wear *crêpe de chime*, with perhaps a touch of white somewhere, and a white frill about her neck. Let her be a widow whose husband died six months after marriage, six months ago. Let her have come from some distant part of the world, from America—Baltimore will do as well as any other, perhaps better, for the dreamer by the fire has no faintest notion whether Baltimore lies in the middle of a plain or surrounded by mountains, whether it be built of marble or brick or stone. Let her come from Baltimore, from some prettily named street—Cathedral Street—there must be a Cathedral Street in Baltimore. The sound of the church bells in the air no doubt led the dreamer to choose Cathedral Street for her to live in.... The dance would have to be an informal one, some little dance that she might come to though her husband was dead only six months. Coming from America, she would be dancing the sliding Boston step, and the two together would pass between the different groups sliding forward and back, avoiding the dancer here, and reappearing from behind a group of French men and women bumping up and down, hammering the floor, the men holding the women as if they were guitars. An American widow dances, her hand upon her partner's shoulder, fitting herself into him, finding a nook between his arm and side, and her head is leaned upon his shoulder. She follows his every step; when he reverses there is never a hitch or jolt; they are always going to the same rhythm. How delicious are these moments of sex and rhythm, and how intense if the woman should take a little handkerchief edged with black and thrust it into her dancer's cuff with some little murmur implying that she wishes him to keep it. To whomsoever these things happen life becomes a song. A little event of this kind lifts one out of the humdrum of material existence. I suppose the cause of our extraordinary happiness is that one is again, as it were, marching in step; one has dropped into the Great Procession and is actively doing the great Work. There is no denying it, that in these moments of sex one does feel more conscious than at any other time of rhythm, and, after all, rhythm is joy. It is rhythm that makes music, that makes poetry, that makes pictures; what we are all after is rhythm, and the whole of the young man's life is going to a tune as he walks home, to the same tune as the stars are going over his head. All things are singing together. And he sings as he passes the *concierge's* lodge, pitying the poor couple asleep—what do they know of love? Humble beasts unable to experience the joy of rhythm. Exalted he goes upstairs; he is on rhythm bent, words follow ideas, rhymes follow words, and he sits down at his writing-table and drawing forth a sheet of paper he writes. A song moves within him, a fragrant song of blond hair and perfume—the handkerchief inspires him, and he must get the rondel perfect: a rondel, or something like a rondel, which he will read to her tomorrow, for she has appointed to meet him—where? No better place for lovers than the garden of L'Église de la Trinité. His night passes in shallow sleep; but his wakings are delicious, for at every awaking he perceives a faint odour of violets. He dreams of blond hair and how carefully he will dress himself in the morning! Would she like him better in his yellow or his grey trousers? Or should he wear a violet or a grey necktie? These are the questions that are important; and what more important questions are there for a young man of twenty-five going to meet a delicious little Dresden figure with blond hair and forget-me-not eyes in the garden of L'Église de la Trinité? He knows she will come, only he hopes not to be kept too long waiting, and at ten o'clock he is there for sure, walking up and down watching the nursemaids and the perambulators drawn up in the shade. On another occasion he might have looked at the nursemaids, but this day the prettiest is plain-featured; they are but the ordinary bread of existence; to-day he is going to partake of more extraordinary fare. He hopes so, at least, and the twenty years that have gone by have done nothing to obliterate the moment when he saw her walk across the gravelled space, a dainty little woman with blond hair, dressed in black, coming to her appointment. The dreamer sees her and her lover going together out of the garden. He follows them down the street, hearing them talking, trying to decide where they shall go to breakfast. To take her to a Parisian restaurant would be a common pleasure. He is bent on taking her to the country. Both want to sit on the warm grass and kiss each other peradventure. All souls dream of the country when they are in love; and she would hear him tell her that he loves her under the shade of trees. She is Chloe, and he is whomsoever was Chloe's lover. Whither are they going? Are they going to Bougeval? Many things may be said in its favour, but he has been there; and he has been to Meudon; he would go with her to some place where he has never been before, and where perchance he will never be again. Vincennes? The name is a pretty one, and it lures him. And they go there, arriving about eleven o'clock, a little early for breakfast.

The sun is shining, the sky is blue, white clouds are unfolding—like gay pennants they seem to him. He is glad the sun is shining—all is omen, all is oracle, the clouds are the love pennants of the sky. What a chatter of thoughts and images are going on in his brain, perchance in hers, too! Moreover, there is her poem in his pocket—he must read it to her, and that she may hear it they sit upon the grass. Twenty years ago there was some rough grass facing the villas, and some trees and bushes, with here and there a bench for lovers to sit upon—for all kinds of people to sit upon, but lovers think that this world is made only for lovers. Only love is of serious account, and the object of all music and poetry, of pictures and sculpture, is to incite love, to praise love, to make love seem the only serious occupation. Vincennes, its trees and its white clouds lifting themselves in the blue sky, were regarded that day by these lovers as a very suitable setting for their gallantries. The dear little woman sits—the dreamer can see her on the warm grass—hidden as well as she can hide herself behind some bushes, the black crêpe dress hiding her feet or pretending to hide them. White stockings were the fashion; she wears white stockings, and how pretty and charming they look in the little black shoes! The younger generation now only knows black stockings; the charms of white are only known to the middle-aged. But the young man must read her his poem. He wants her to hear it because the poem pleases him, and because he feels that his poem will aid him to her affections. And when she asks him if he has thought of her during the night, he has to answer that her violet-scented handkerchief awoke him many times, that the wakings were delicious. What time did he go to bed? Very late; he had sat up writing a poem to her telling of the beauty of her blond hair.

> "Lady, unwreath thy hair,
> That is so long and fair.
> May flowers are not more sweet
> Than the shower of loosened hair
> That will fall around my feet.
> Lady, unwreath thy hair,
> That is so long and fair.

"The golden curls they paint,
Round the forehead of a saint,
Ne'er glittered half so bright
As thy enchanted hair,
Full of shadow, full of light.
Lady, unwreath thy hair,
That is so long and fair.

"Lady, unwreath thy hair,
That is so long and fair,
And weave a web of gold
Of thy enchanted hair,
Till all be in its hold.
Lady, unwreath thy hair,
That is so long and fair."

"Do let me see your poem.... It is charming. But what do you mean by 'enchanted hair'? Is it that my hair has enchanted you? 'And weave a web of gold.'... 'Unwreath'—do you mean unloose my hair?"

"Dames, tressez vos cheveux blonds
Qui sont si lourds et si longs.

"How well it goes with French!"

"I don't understand French, but I like your poem in English. Do you know, I like it very much!"

It is easy to obtain appreciation for poetry in such circumstances. Horace's best ode would not please a young woman as much as the mediocre verses of the young man she is in love with. It is well that it should be so, and this is the dreamer's criticism of life as he sits lost in shadow, lit up here and there by the blaze. He remembers the warmth of the grass and the scanty bushes; there was hardly sufficient cover that spring day for lovers in Vincennes, and he tries to remember if he put his hand on her white ankle while she was reading the poem. So far as he can remember he did, and she checked him and was rather cross, declaring just like the puss-cat that he must not do such things, that she would not have come out with him had she thought he was going to misbehave himself in that way. But she is not really angry with him. How can she be? Was it not he who wrote that her hair was enchanted? And what concern is it of hers that the phrase was borrowed from another poet? Her concern is that he should think her hair enchanted, and her hands go up to it. The young man prays to unloose it, to let it fall about her shoulders. He must be paid for his poem, and the only payment he will accept is to see her hair unwreathed.

"But I cannot undo my hair on the common. Is there no other payment?" and she leans a little forward, her eyes fixed upon him. The dreamer can see her eyes, clear young eyes, but he cannot remember her mouth, how full the lips were or how thin; ah, but he remembers kissing her! On such a day a young man kisses his young woman, and it may be doubted if the young woman would ever go out with him again if he refrained, the circumstances being as I describe. But the lovers of Vincennes have to be careful. The lady with the enchanted hair has just spied a middle-aged gentleman with his two sons sitting on a bench at a little distance.

"Do be quiet, I beg of you. I assure you, he saw us."

"If he did it would matter little; he would remember his young days, before his children were born. Moreover, he looks kindly disposed."

Later on the lovers address themselves to him, for time wears away even with lovers, and the desire of breakfast has come upon them both. The kindly disposed gentleman tells them the way to the restaurant. He insists even on walking part of the way with them, and they learn from him that the restaurant has only just been opened for the season; the season is not yet fairly begun, but no doubt they will be able to get something to eat, an omelette and a cutlet.

Now the accomplished story-teller would look forward to this restaurant; already his thoughts would fix themselves on a *cabinet particulier*, and his fancy, if he were a naturalistic writer, would rejoice in recording the fact that the mirror was scrawled over with names of lovers, and he would select the ugliest names. But, dear reader, if you are expecting a *cabinet particulier* in this story, and an amorous encounter to take place therein, turn the page at once—you will be disappointed if you do not; this story contains nothing that will shock your—shall I say your "prudish susceptibilities"? When the auburn-haired poet and the corn-coloured American lunched at

Vincennes they chose a table by the window in the great long *salle* lined with tables, and they were attended by an army of waiters weary of their leisure.

There was a lake at Vincennes then, I am sure, with an island upon it and tall saplings, through which the morning sun was shining. The eyes of the lovers admired the scene, and they admired too the pretty reflections, and the swans moving about the island. The accomplished story-teller cries, "But if there is to be no scene in the restaurant, how is the story to finish?" Why should stories finish? And would a sensual *dénouement* be a better end than, let us say, that the lovers are caught in a shower as they leave the restaurant? Such an accident might have happened: nothing is more likely than a shower at the end of April or the beginning of May, and I can imagine the lovers of Vincennes rushing into one of the *concierge's* lodges at the gates of the villas.

"For a few minutes," they say; "the rain will be over soon."

But they are not long there when a servant appears carrying three umbrellas; she gives one to Marie, one to me; she keeps one for herself.

"But who is she? You told me you knew no one at Vincennes."

"No more I do."

"But you must know the people who live here; the servant says that Monsieur (meaning her master) knows Monsieur (meaning you)."

"I swear to you I don't know anybody here; but let's go—it will be rather fun."

"But what shall we say in explanation? Shall we say we're cousins?"

"Nobody believes in cousins; shall we say we're husband and wife?"

The dreamer sees two figures; memory reflects them like a convex mirror, reducing them to a tenth their original size, but he sees them clearly, and he follows them through the rain up the steps of the villa to the *perron*—an explicit word that the English language lacks. The young man continues to protest that he never was at Vincennes before, that he knows no one living there, and they are both a little excited by the adventure. Who can be the owner of the house? A man of ordinary tastes, it would seem, and while waiting for their host the lovers examine the Turkey carpet, the richly upholstered sofas and chairs.

A pretty little situation from which an accomplished story-teller could evolve some playful imaginings. The accomplished story-teller would see at once that *le bon bourgeois et sa dame* and the children are learning English, and here is an occasion of practice for the whole family. The accomplished story-teller would see at once that the family must take a fancy to the young couple, and in his story the rain must continue to fall in torrents; these would prevent the lovers from returning to Paris. Why should they not stay to dinner? After dinner the accomplished story-teller would bring in a number of neighbours, and set them dancing and singing. What easier to suppose than that it was *la bourgeoise's* evening at home? The young couple would sit in a distant corner oblivious to all but their own sweet selves. *Le bourgeois et sa dame* would watch them with kindly interest, deeming it a kindness not to tell them that there were no trains after twelve; and when the lovers at last determined that they must depart, *le bourgeois* and *la bourgeoise* would tell them that their room was quite ready, that there was no possibility of returning to Paris that night. A pretty little situation that might with advantage be placed on the stage—on the French stage. A pretty, although a painful, dilemma for a young woman to find herself in, particularly when she is passionately in love with the young man. "Bitterly," the accomplished story-teller would say, "did the young widow regret the sacrifice to propriety she had made in allowing her young man to pass her off as his wife!" The accomplished story-teller would then assure his reader that the pretty American had acted precisely as a lady should act under the circumstances. But not being myself an accomplished story-teller, I will not attempt to say how a lady should act in such a situation, and it would be a fatuous thing for me to suggest that the lady was passionately in love. The situation that my fancy creates is ingenious; and I regret it did not happen. Nature spins her romances differently; and I feel sure that the lovers returned from Vincennes merely a little fluttered by their adventure. The reader would like to know if any appointment was made to meet again; if one was made it must have been for the next day or the next, for have we not imagined the young widow's passage already taken? Did she not tell that she was going back to America at the end of the week? He had said: "In a few days the Atlantic will be between us," and this fact had made them feel very sad, for the Atlantic is a big thing and cannot be ignored, particularly in love affairs. It would have been better for the poet if he had accepted the bourgeois' invitation to dinner; friends, as I suggested, might have come in, an impromptu dance might have been arranged, or the rain might have begun again; something would certainly have happened to make them miss the train; and they would have been asked to stay the night. The widow did not speak French, the young man did; he might have arranged it all with the *bourgeois et sa dame*, and the dear little widow might never have known her fate—O happy fate!—until the time came for them to go to their room. But he, foolish fellow, missed the chance the rain gave him, and all that came of this outing was a promise to come back next year, and to dance the Boston with him again; meanwhile he must wear her garter upon his arm. Did the suggestion that she should give him her garter come from her or from him? Was the garter given in the cab when they returned from Vincennes, or was it given the next time they met in Paris? To answer these questions would not help the story; suffice it to say that she said that the elastic would last a year, and when she took his arm and found it upon it she would know that he had been faithful to her. There was the little handkerchief which she had given him, and this he must keep in a drawer. Perhaps some of the scent would survive this long year of separation. I am sure that she charged him to write a letter to the steamer she had taken her passage in, and, careless fellow! instead of doing so he wrote verses, and the end of all this love affair, which began so well, was an angry letter bidding him good-bye for ever, saying he was not worthy because he had missed the post. All this happened twenty years ago; perhaps the earth is over her charming little personality, and it will be over me before long. Nothing endures; life is but change. What we call death is only change. Death and life always overlapping, mixed inextricably, and no meaning in anything, merely a stream of change in which things happen. Sometimes the happenings are pleasant, sometimes unpleasant, and in neither the pleasant nor the unpleasant can we detect any purpose. Twenty long years ago, and there is no hope, not a particle.

I have come to the end of my mood; an ache in my heart brings me to my feet, and looking round I cry out: "How dark is the room! Why is there no light? Bring in the lamp!"

CHAPTER XII

SUNDAY EVENING IN LONDON

Married folk always know, only the bachelor asks, "Where shall I dine? Shall I spend two shillings in a chop-house, or five in my club, or ten at the Café Royal?" For two or three more shillings one may sit on the balcony of the Savoy, facing the spectacle of evening darkening on the river, with lights of bridge and wharf and warehouse afloat in the tide. Married folk know their bedfellows; bachelors, and perhaps spinsters, are not so sure of theirs: this is a side issue which we will not pursue; an allusion to it will suffice to bring before the reader the radical difference between the lives of the married and the unmarried. O married ones, from breakfast to six, only, do our lives resemble yours! At that hour we begin to experience a sense of freedom and, I confess it, of loneliness. Perhaps life is essentially a lonely thing, and the married and the unmarried differ only in this, that we are lonely when we are by ourselves, and they are lonely when they are together.

At half-past six the bachelor has to tidy up after the day's work, to put his picture away if he be a painter, to put his writings away if he be a writer, and then the very serious question arises, with whom shall he dine? His thoughts fly through Belgravia and Mayfair, and after whisking round Portman Square, and some other square in the northern neighbourhood, they soar and go away northward to Regent's Park, seeking out somebody living in one of those stately terraces who will ask him to stay to dinner. At So-and-So's there is always a round of beef and cold chicken-pie, whereas What-do-you-call-them's begin with soup. But really the food is not of much consequence; it is interesting company he seeks.

It was last week that I realised, and for the first time, how different was the life of the married from the unmarried. The day was Sunday, and I had been writing all day, and in the hush that begins about six o'clock I remembered I had no dinner engagement that evening. The cup of tea I generally take about half-past four had enabled me to do another hour's work, but a little after six sentences refused to form themselves, a little dizziness began in the brain, and the question not only "Where shall I dine?" but "Where shall I pass the hour before dinner?" presented itself. The first thing to do was to dress, and while dressing I remembered that I had not wandered in St. James's Park for some time, and that that park since boyhood had fascinated me. St. James's Park and the Green Park have never been divided in my admiration of their beauty. The trees that grow along the Piccadilly railings are more beautiful in St. James's Park, or seem so, for the dells are well designed. The art of landscape-gardening is more akin to the art of a musician than to that of a painter; it is a sort of architecture with colour added. The formal landscape-gardening of Versailles reminds one of a tragedy by Racine, but the romantic modulations of the green hills along the Piccadilly areas are as enchanting as Haydn. There was a time when a boy used to walk from Brompton to Piccadilly to see, not the dells, but the women going home from the Argyle Rooms and the Alhambra, but after a slight hesitation he often crossed from the frequented to the silent side, to stand in admiration of the white rays of moonlight stealing between the trunks of the trees, allowing him to perceive the shapes of the hollows through the darkness. The trees grow so beautifully about these mounds, and upon the mounds, that it is easy to fill the interspaces with figures from Gainsborough's pictures, ladies in hoops and powdered hair, elegant gentlemen wearing buckled shoes, tail-coats, and the swords which made them gentlemen. Gainsborough did not make his gentlemen plead—that was his fault; but Watteau's ladies put their fans to their lips so archly, asking the pleading lover if he believes all he says, knowing well that his vows are only part of the gracious entertainment. But why did not the great designer of St. James's Park build little Greek temples—those pillared and domed temples which give such grace to English parks? Perhaps the great artist who laid out the Green Park was a moralist and a seer, and divining the stream of ladies that come up from Brompton to Piccadilly he thought—well, well, his thoughts were his own, and now the earth is over him, as Rossetti would say.

Five-and-twenty years ago the white rays slanted between the tree-trunks, and the interspaces lengthened out, disappearing in illusive lights and shades, and, ascending the hill, the boy used to look over the empty plain, wondering at the lights of the Horse Guards shining far away like a village. Perhaps to-night, about midnight, I may find myself in Piccadilly again, for we change very little; what interested us in our youth interests us almost to the end. St. James's Park is perhaps more beautiful in the sunset—there is the lake, and, led by remembrance of some sunsets I had seen on it, I turned out of Victoria Street last Sunday, taking the eastern gate, my thoughts occupied with beautiful Nature, seeing in imagination the shapes of the trees designing themselves grandly against the sky, and the little life of the ponds—the ducks going hither and thither, every duck intent upon its own business and its own desire. I was extremely fortunate, for the effect of light in the Green Park was more beautiful last Sunday than anything I had ever seen; the branches of the tall plane trees hung over the greensward, the deciduous foliage hardly stirring in the pale sunshine, and my heart went out to the ceremonious and cynical garden, artificial as eighteenth-century couplets. Wild Nature repels me; and I thought how interesting it was to consider one's self, to ponder one's sympathies. Our antipathies are not quite so interesting to consider, but they are interesting, too, in a way, for they belong to one's self, and self is man's main business: all outside of self is uncertain; all comes from self, all returns to self. The reason I desired St. James's Park last Sunday was surely because it was part of me—not that part known to my friends; our friends understand only those margins of themselves which they discover in us. Never did I meet one who discovered for himself or herself that I loved trees better than flowers, or was deeply interested in the fact when attention was called to it....

I watch the trees and never weary of their swaying—solemnly silent and strangely green they are in the long, rainy days, excited when a breeze is blowing; in fine weather they gossip like frivolous girls! In their tremulous decline they are more beautiful than ever, far more beautiful than flowers. Now, I am telling myself, the very subconscious soul is speaking. And with what extraordinary loveliness did the long branches hang out of the tall, stately plane trees like plumes; in the hush of sound and decline of light the droop of the deciduous foliage spoke like a memory. I seemed to have known the park for centuries; yon glade I recognised as one that Watteau had painted. But in what picture? It is difficult to say, so easily do his pictures flow one into the other, always the same melancholy, the melancholy of festival, that pain in the heart, that yearning for the beyond which all suffer whose business in life is to wear painted or embroidered dresses, and to listen or to plead, with this for sole variation, that they who listen to-day will plead to-morrow. Watteau divined the sorrow of those who sit under colonnades always playing some part, great or small, in love's comedy, listening to the murmur of the fountain, watching a gentleman and lady advancing and bowing, bowing and retiring, dancing a pavane on a richly coloured carpet. Pierrot, the white, sensual animal, the eighteenth-century modification of the satyr, of the faun, plays a guitar; the pipe of Pan has been exchanged for a guitar.

As the twilight gathered under the plane trees my vision became more mixed and morbid, and I hardly knew if the picture I saw was the picture in the Dulwich Gallery or the exquisite picture in the Louvre, "Une Assemblée dans la Parc." We all know that picture, the gallants and the ladies by the water-side, and the blue evening showing through the tall trees. The picture before me was like that picture, only the placing of the trees and the slope of the greensward did not admit of so extended a composition. A rough tree-trunk, from which a great branch had been broken or lopped off, stood out suddenly in very nineteenth-century naturalness, awaking the ghost of a picture which I recognised at once as Corot. Behind the tree a tender, evanescent sky, pure and transparent as the very heart of a flower, rose up, filling the park with romance, and as the sunset drooped upon the water, my soul said, "The Lake!" Ah, the pensive shadow that falls from the hills on either side of "The Lake," leaving the middle of the picture suffused with a long stream of light, narrowing as it approached the low horizon. But the line of the trees on the hither side of this London lake was heavier than the spiritual trees in the picture entitled "By the Water-side," and there was not anywhere the beauty of the broken birch that leans over the lake in "Le Lac de Garde." Then I thought of "The Ravine," for the darkening island reminded me of the hillside in the picture. But the St. James's Park sky lacked the refined concentration of light in "The Ravine," so beautifully placed, low down in the picture, behind some dark branches jutting from the right. The difference between Nature and Corot is as great as the difference between a true and a false Corot. Not that there is anything untrue in Nature, only Nature lacks humanity—self! Therefore not quite so interesting as a good Corot.

So did I chatter to myself as I walked toward the bridge, that dear bridge, thrown straight as a plank across the lake, with numerous water-fowl collected there, a black swan driving the ducks about, snatching more than his due share of bread, and little children staring stolidly, afraid of the swan, and constantly reproved by their mothers for reasons which must always seem obscure to the bachelor. A little breeze was blowing, and the ducks bobbed like corks in the waves, keeping themselves in place with graceful side-strokes of their webbed feet. Sometimes the ducks rose from the water and flew round the trees by Queen Anne's Mansions, or they fled down the lake with outstretched necks like ducks on a Japanese fan, dropping at last into the water by the darkening island, leaving long silver lines, which the night instantly obliterated.

An impression of passing away, of the effacement of individual life. One sighs, remembering that it is even so, that life passes, sunrise after sunrise, moonlight upon moonlight, evening upon evening, and we like May-flies on the surface of a stream, no more than they for all our poets and priests.

The clock struck seven, reminding me of the dinner-hour, reminding me that I should have to dine alone that evening. To avoid dining alone I should not have lingered in St. James's Park, but if I had not lingered I should have missed an exquisite hour of meditation, and meditations are as necessary to me as absinthe to the absinthe-drinker. Only some little incident was wanting—a meeting with one whom one has not seen for a long time, a man or a woman, it would not matter which, a peg whereon to hang the description of the dusk among the trees, but I had met no friend in the Park. But one appeared on the threshold of St. James's Street. There I met a young man, a painter, one whose pictures interested me sometimes, and we went to a restaurant to talk art.

"After dinner," I said, "we will get the best cigars and walk about the circus. Every Sunday night it is crowded; we shall see the women hurrying to and fro on love's quest. The warm night will bring them all out in white dresses, and a white dress in the moonlight is an enchantment. Don't you like the feather boas reaching almost to the ground? I do. Lights-o'-love going about their business interest me extraordinarily, for they and the tinkers and gipsies are the last that remain of the old world when outlawry was common. Now we are all socialists, more or less occupied with the performance of duties which obtain every one's approval. Methinks it is a relief to know that somebody lives out of society. I like all this London, this midnight London, when the round moon rises above the gracious line of Regent Street, and flaming Jupiter soars like a hawk, following some quest of his own. We on our little, he on his greater quest."

The night was hot and breathless, like a fume, and upon a great silken sky the circular and sonorous street circled like an amphitheatre.... I threw open my light overcoat, and, seizing the arm of my friend, I said:

"He reminds me of a Turk lying amid houris. The gnawing, creeping sensualities of his phrase—his one phrase—how descriptive it is of the form and whiteness of a shoulder, the supple fulness of the arm's muscle, the brightness of eyes increased by kohl! Scent is burning on silver dishes, and through the fumes appear the subdued colours of embroidered stuffs and the inscrutable traceries of bronze lamps. Or, maybe, the scene passes on a terrace overlooking a dark river. Behind the domes and minarets a yellow moon dreams like an odalisque, her hand on the circle of her breast; and through the torrid silence of the garden, through the odour of over-ripe fruit and the falling sound thereof, comes the melancholy warble of a fountain. Or is it the sorrow of lilies rising through the languid air to the sky? The night is blue and breathless; the spasms of the lightning are intermittent among the minarets and the domes; the hot, fierce fever of the garden waxes in the almond scent of peaches and the white odalisques advancing, sleek oracles of mood.... He reminds me of the dark-eyed Bohemian who comes into a tavern silently, and, standing in a corner, plays long, wild, ravishing strains. I see him not, I hardly hear him; my thoughts are far away; my soul slumbers, desiring nothing. I care not to lift my head. Why should I break the spell of my meditations? But I feel that his dark eyes are fixed upon me, and little by little, in spite of my will, my senses awake; a strange germination is in progress within me; thoughts and desires that I dread, of whose existence in myself I was not aware, whose existence in myself I would fain deny, come swiftly and come slowly, and settle and absorb and become part of me.... Fear is upon me, but I may not pause; I am hurried on; repudiation is impossible, supplication and the wringing of hands are vain; God has abandoned me; my worst nature is uppermost. I see it floating up from the depths of my being, a viscous scum. But I can do nothing to check or control.... God has abandoned me.... I am the prey to that dark, sensual-eyed Bohemian and his abominable fiddle; and seizing my bank-notes, my gold and my silver, I throw him all I have. I bid him cease, and fall back exhausted. Give me "The Ring," give me "The Ring." Its cloud palaces, its sea-caves and forests, and the animality therein, its giants and dwarfs and sirens, its mankind and its godkind—surely it is nearer to life! Or go into the meadows with Beethoven, and listen to the lark and the blackbird! We are nearer life lying by a shady brook, hearing the quail in the meadows and the yellow-hammer in the thicket, than we are now, under this oppressive sky. This street is like Klinsor's garden; here, too, are flower-maidens—patchouli, jessamine, violet. Here is the languorous atmosphere of "Parsifal." Come, let us go; let us seek the country, the moon-haunted dells we shall see through Piccadilly railings. Have you ever stood in the dip of Piccadilly and watched the moonlight among the trees, and imagined a comedy by Wycherley acted there, a goodly company of gallants and fine ladies seated under the trees watching it? Every one has come there in painted sedan-chairs; the bearers are gathered together at a little distance."

"My dear friend, you're talking so much that you don't see those who are passing us. That girl, she who has just turned to look back, favours heliotrope; it is delicious still upon the air; she is as pretty a girl as any that ever came in a sedan-chair to see a comedy by Wycherley. The comedy varies very little: it is always the same comedy, and it is always interesting. The circus in a sultry summer night under a full moon is very like Klinsor's garden. Come, if you be not *Parsifal*."

CHAPTER XIII

RESURGAM

I was in London when my brother wrote telling me that mother was ill. She was not in any immediate danger, he said, but if a change for the worse were to take place, and it were necessary for me to come over, he would send a telegram. A few hours after a telegram was handed to me. It contained four words: *"Come at once.—Maurice."* "So mother is dying," I muttered to myself, and I stood at gaze, foreseeing myself taken into her room by a nurse and given a chair by the bedside, foreseeing a hand lying outside the bed which I should have to hold until I heard the death-rattle and saw her face become quiet for ever.

This was my first vision, but in the midst of my packing, I remembered that mother might linger for days. The dear friend who lies in the church-yard under the downs lingered for weeks; every day her husband and her children saw her dying under their eyes: why should not this misfortune be mine? I know not to what God, but I prayed all night in the train, and on board the boat; I got into the train at the Broadstone praying. It is impossible, at least for me, to find words to express adequately the agony of mind I endured on that journey. Words can only hint at it, but I think that any one possessed of any experience of life, or who has any gift of imagination, will be able to guess at the terror that haunted me— terror of what?—not so much that my mother might die, nor hope that she might live, but just that I might arrive in time to see her die. In this confession I am afraid I shall seem hard and selfish to some; that will be because many people lack imagination, or the leisure to try to understand that there are not only many degrees of sensibility, but many kinds, and it is doubtful if any reader can say with truth any more than that my sensibility is not his or hers. It is my privilege to be sympathetic with ideas I do not share, and in certain moods I approach those who take a sad pleasure in last words, good-byes, and at looking on the dead. In my present mood it seems to me that it is not unlikely that my mother's last good-bye and her death appeared to me more awful in imagination than it would have ever done in reality. Indeed, there can be hardly any doubt that this is so, for we are only half-conscious of what is happening. Reality clouds, our actions mitigate, our perception; we can see clearly only when we look back or forwards. There is something very merciful about reality; if there were not, we should not be able to live at all.

But to the journey. How shall I tell it? The third part must have been the most painful, so clearly do I remember it: the curious agony of mind caused by a sudden recognition of objects long forgotten—a tree or a bit of bog-land. The familiar country, evocative of a great part of my childhood, carried my thoughts hither and thither. My thoughts ranged like the swallows; the birds had no doubt just arrived, and in swift elliptical flights they hunted for gnats along the banks of the old weedy canal. That weedy canal along which the train travelled took my thoughts back to the very beginning of my life, when I stood at the carriage window and plagued my father and mother with questions regarding the life of the barges passing up and down. And it was the sudden awakenings from these memories that were so terrible—the sudden thrust of the thought that I was going westward to see my mother die, and that nothing could save her from death or me from seeing her die. Perhaps to find one's self suddenly deprived of all will is the greatest suffering of all. How many times did I say to myself, "Nothing can save me unless I get out at the next station," and I imagined myself taking a car and driving away through the country! But if I did such a thing I should be looked upon as a madman. "One is bound on a wheel," I muttered, and I began to think how men under sentence of death must often wonder why they were selected especially for such a fate, and the mystery, the riddle of it all, must be perhaps the greatest part of their pain.

The morning was one of the most beautiful I had ever seen, and I used to catch myself thinking out a picturesque expression to describe it. It seemed to me that the earth might be compared to an egg, it looked so warm under the white sky, and the sky was as soft as the breast feathers of a dove. This sudden bow-wowing of the literary skeleton made me feel that I wanted to kick myself. Nature has forgotten to provide us with a third leg whereby we may revenge ourselves on instincts that we cannot control. A moment afterward I found myself plunged in reflections regarding the impossibility of keeping one's thoughts fixed on any one subject for any considerable length of time. At the end of these reflections I fell back, wondering, again asking if I were really destined to watch by my mother's death-bed. That day I seemed to become a sheer mentality, a sort of buzz of thought, and I could think of myself only as of a fly climbing a glass dome. It seemed to me that I was like a fly climbing and falling back, buzzing, and climbing again. "Never," I said to myself, "have I been more than a fly buzzing in a glass dome. And, good Lord, who made the glass dome?" How often did I ask myself that question, and why it was made, and if it were going to endure for ever!

In such sore perplexity of mind questions from anybody would be intolerable, and I shrank back into the corner of the carriage whenever a passer-by reminded me, however vaguely, of anybody I had ever known; the mental strain increased mile after mile, for the names of the stations grew more familiar. I began to try to remember how many there were before we arrived at Claremorris, the station at which I was going to get out. Half an hour afterward the train slackened, the porter cried out "Ballyhaunis." The next would be Claremorris, and I watched every field, foreseeing the long road, myself on one side of the car, the driver on the other; a two hours' drive in silence or in talk—in talk, for I should have to tell him my errand.... He might be able to tell me about my mother, if the news of her illness had got as far as Claremorris. At the public-house where I went to get a car I made inquiries, but nothing was known. My mother must have fallen ill suddenly—of what? I had not heard she was ailing; I did not remember her ever to have been ill. At that moment some trees reminded me that we were close to Ballyglass, and my thoughts wandered away to the long road on the other side of the hill, and I saw there (for do we not often see things in memory as plainly as if they were before us?) the two cream-coloured ponies, Ivory and Primrose, she used to drive, and the phaeton, and myself in it, a little child in frocks, anxious, above all things, to see the mail-coach go by. A great sight it was to see it go by with mail-bags and luggage, the guard blowing a horn, the horses trotting splendidly, the lengthy reins swinging, and the driver, his head leaned a little on one side to save his hat from being blown away—he used to wear a grey beaver hat. The great event of that time was the day that we went to Ballyglass, not to see the coach go by, but to get into it, for in those days the railway stopped at Athenry. And that was the day I saw the canal, and heard with astonishment that there was a time long ago, no doubt in my father's youth, when people used to go to Dublin in a barge. Those memories were like a stupor, and awaking suddenly I saw that more than two and a half miles lay between me and my mother. In half an hour more I should know whether she were alive or dead, and I watched the horse trotting, interested in his shambling gait, or not at all interested in it—I do not know which.

On occasions of great nervous tension one observes everything.... Everything I remembered best appeared with mechanical regularity; now it was a wood, a while afterward somebody's farmyard, later on a line of cottages, another wood, one of my own gate lodges. An old sawyer lived in it now—looking after it for me; and I hoped that the wheels of the car would not bring him out, for it would distress me to see him. The firs in the low-lying land had grown a little within the last thirty years, but not much. We came to the bridge; we left it behind us; the gate lodge and the drive from it; the plantation that I knew so well, the lilac bushes, the laburnums —good Heavens! How terrible was all this resurrection! Mists hide the mountains from us, the present hides the past; but there are times when the present does not exist at all, when every mist is cleared away, and the past confronts us in naked outline, and that perhaps is why it is so painful to me to return home. The little hill at the beginning of the drive is but a little hill, but to me it is much more, so intimately is it associated with all the pains and troubles of childhood. All this park was once a fairyland to me; now it is but a thin reality, a book which I have read, and the very thought of which bores me, so well do I know it. There is the lilac bush! I used to go there with my mother thirty years ago at this time of year, and we used to come home with our hands full of bloom. Two more turnings and we should be within sight of the house! This is how men feel when condemned to death. I am sure of it. At the last hill the driver allowed his horse to fall into a walk, but I begged of him to drive on the horse, for I saw some peasants about the steps of the hall door; they were waiting, no doubt, for news, or perhaps they had news. "We have bad news for you," they cried in the wailing tones of the West.

"Not altogether bad news," I said to myself; "my mother is dead, but I have been saved the useless pain, the torture of spirit, I should have endured if I had arrived in time." China roses used to grow over the railings; very few blooms were left. I noticed just a few as I ran up the high steps, asking myself why I could not put the past behind me. If ever there was a time to live in the present this was one; but never was the present further from me and the past clearer than when I opened the hall door and stood in the hall paved with grey stones and painted grey and blue. Three generations had played there; in that corner I had learned to spin my first top, and I had kept on trying, showing a perseverance that amazed my father. He said, "If he will show as much perseverance in other things as he does in the spinning of a top, he will not fail." He used to catch me trying and trying to spin that top when he came downstairs on his way to the stables to see his beloved racehorses; that is the very chair on which he used to put his hat and gloves. In those days tall hats were worn in the country, and it was the business of his valet to keep them well brushed. How the little old man used to watch me, objecting in a way to my spinning my top in the hall, fearful lest I should overturn the chair on which the hat stood: sometimes that did happen, and then, oh dear!

In search of some one I opened the drawing-room door. My sister was there, and I found her on a sofa weeping for our mother, who had died that morning. We are so constituted that we demand outward signs of our emotions, especially of grief; we are doubtful of its genuineness unless it is accompanied by sighs and tears; and that, I suppose, is why my sister's tears were welcomed by me, for, truth to tell, I was a little shocked at my own insensibility. This was stupid of me, for I knew through experience that we do not begin to suffer immediately after the accident; everything takes time, grief as well as pain. But in a moment so awful as the one I am describing one does not reflect; one falls back on the convention that grief and tears are inseparable as fire and smoke. If I could not weep it were well that my sister could, and I accepted her tears as a tribute paid to our mother's goodness—a goodness which never failed, for it was instinctive. It even seemed to me a pity that Nina had to dry her eyes so that she might tell me the sad facts—when mother died, of her illness, and the specialist that had not arrived in time. I learned that some one had blundered—not that that mattered much, for mother would not have submitted to an operation.

While listening to her, I unwittingly remembered how we used to talk of the dear woman whose funeral I described in the pages entitled "A Remembrance." We used to talk, her daughters and her son and her husband and I, of her who was dying upstairs. We were greatly moved—I at least appreciated my love of her—yet our talk would drift from her suddenly, and we would speak of indifferent things, or maybe the butler would arrive to tell us lunch was ready. How these incidents jar our finer feelings! They seem to degrade life, and to such a point that we are ashamed of living, and are tempted to regard life itself as a disgrace.

I foresaw that the same interruptions, the same devagations, would happen among ourselves in the square Georgian house standing on a hill-top overlooking a long winding lake, as had happened among my friends in the Italian house under the downs amid bunches of evergreen oaks. Nor had I to wait long for one of these unhappy devagations. My sister had to tell me who was staying in the house: an aunt was there, my mother's sister, and an uncle, my mother's brother, was coming over next day. It is easy to guess how the very mention of these names beguiled us from what should be the subject of our thought. And the room itself supplied plenty of distractions: all the old furniture, the colour of the walls, the very atmosphere of the room took my thought back to my childhood. The sofa on which my sister was sitting had been broken years ago, and I unwittingly remembered how it had been broken. It had been taken away to a lumber-room; somebody had had it mended. I began to wonder who had done this—mother, most likely; she looked after every thing. I have said that I had just arrived after a long journey. I had eaten nothing since the night before. My sister spoke of lunch and we went into the dining-room, and in the middle of the meal my brother came in looking so very solemn that I began to wonder if he had assumed the expression he thought appropriate to the occasion—I mean if he had involuntarily exaggerated the expression of grief he would naturally wear. We are so constituted that the true and the false overlap each other, and so subtly that no analysis can determine where one ends and the other begins. I remembered how the relatives and the friends on the day of the funeral in Sussex arrived, each one with a very grave face, perchance interrupting us in the middle of some trivial conversation; if so, we instantly became grave and talked of the dead woman sympathetically for a few minutes; then on the first opportunity, and with a feeling of relief, we began to talk of indifferent things; and with every fresh arrival the comedy was re-acted. Returning from the past to the present, I listened to my brother, who was speaking of the blunder that had been made: how a wrong doctor had come down owing to—the fault was laid upon somebody, no matter upon whom; the subject was a painful one and might well have been dropped, but he did not dare to talk of anything but our mother, and we all strove to carry on the conversation as long as possible. But my brother and I had not seen each other for years; he had come back from India after a long absence. Nor, I think, had I seen my sister since she was married, and that was a long while ago; she had had children; I had not seen her before in middle age. We were anxious to ask each other questions, to hear each other's news, and we were anxious to see the landscape that we had not seen, at least not together, for many years; and I remember how we were tempted out of the house by the soft sunlight floating on the lawn. The same gentle day full of mist and sunlight that I had watched since early morning had been prolonged, and the evening differed hardly from the morning; the exaltation in the air was a little more intense. My mother died certainly on the most beautiful day I had ever seen, the most winsome, the most white, the most wanton, as full of love as a girl in a lane who stops to gather a spray of hawthorn. How many times, like many another, did I wonder why death should have come to any one on such a bridal-like day. That we should expect Nature to prepare a decoration in accordance with our moods is part of the old savagery. Through reason we know that Nature cares for us not at all, that our sufferings concern her not in the least, but our instincts conform to the time when the sun stood still and angels were about. It was impossible for us not to wonder why the black shadow of death should have fallen across the white radiant day. I say "us," for my brother no doubt pondered the coincidence, though he did not speak his thoughts to me. No one dares to speak such thoughts; they are the foolish substance of ourselves which we try to conceal from others, forgetting that we are all alike. The day moved slowly from afternoon to evening, like a bride hidden within a white veil, her hands and her veil filled with white blossom; but a black bird, tiny like a humming-bird, had perched upon a bunch of blossom, and I seemed to lose sight of the day in the sinister black speck that had intruded itself upon it. No doubt I could think of something better were I to set my mind upon doing so, but that is how I thought the day I walked on the lawn with my brother, ashamed and yet compelled to talk of what our lives had been during the years that separated us. How could one be overpowered with grief amid so many distracting circumstances? Everything I saw was at once new and old. I had come among my brother and sister suddenly, not having seen them, as I have said, for many years; this was our first meeting since childhood, and we were assembled in the house where we had all been born. The ivy grown all over one side of the house, the disappearance of the laburnum, the gap in the woods—these things were new; but the lake that I had not seen since a little child I did not need to look at, so well did I know how every shore was bent, and the place of every island. My first adventures began on that long yellow strand; I did not need to turn my head to see it, for I knew that trees intervened and I knew the twisting path through the wood. That yellow strand speckled with tufts of rushes was my first playground. But when my brother proposed that we should walk there, I found some excuse; why go? The reality would destroy the dream. What reality could equal my memory of the firs where the rabbits burrowed, of the drain where we fished for minnows, of the long strand with the lake far away in summertime? How well I remember that yellow sand, hard and level in some places as the floor of a ball-room. The water there is so shallow that our governess used to allow us to wander at will, to run on ahead in pursuit of a sandpiper. The bird used to fly round with little cries; and we often used to think it was wounded; perhaps it pretended to be wounded in order to lead us away from its nest. We did not think it possible to see the lake in any new aspect, yet there it lay as we had never seen it before, so still, so soft, so grey, like a white muslin scarf flowing out, winding past island and headland. The silence was so intense that one thought of the fairy-books of long ago, of sleeping woods and haunted castles; there were the castles on islands lying in misted water, faint as dreams. Now and then a bird uttered a piercing little chatter from the branches of the tall larches, and ducks talked in the reeds, but their talk was only a soft murmur, hardly louder than the rustle of the reeds now in full leaf. Everything was spellbound that day; the shadows of reed and island seemed fixed for ever as in a magic mirror—a mirror that somebody had breathed upon, and, listening to the little gurgle of the water about the limestone shingle, one seemed to hear eternity murmuring its sad monotony.

The lake curves inland, forming a pleasant bay among the woods; there is a sandy spit where some pines have found roothold, and they live on somehow despite the harsh sallies of the wind in winter. Along the shore dead reeds lie in rows three feet deep among the rushes; had they been placed there by hand they could not have been placed with more regularity; and there is an old cart-track, with hawthorns growing out of a tumbled wall. The hillside is planted— beautiful beeches and hollies at one end, and at the other some lawny interspaces with tall larches swaying tasselled branches shedding faint shadows. These were the wonder of my childhood. A path leads through the wood, and under the rugged pine somebody has placed a seat, a roughly hewn stone supported by two upright stones. For some reason unknown to me this seat always suggested, even when I was a child, a pilgrim's seat. I suppose the suggestion came from the knowledge that my grandmother used to go every day to the tomb at the end of the wood where her husband and sons lay, and whither she was taken herself long ago when I was in frocks; and twenty years after my father was taken there.

What a ceaseless recurrence of the same things! A hearse will appear again in a few days, perhaps the same hearse, the horses covered up with black made to look ridiculous with voluminous weed, the coachman no better than a zany, the ominous superior mute directing the others with a wand; there will be a procession of relatives and friends, all wearing crepe and black gloves, and most of them thinking how soon they can get back to their business: that masquerade which we call a funeral!

Fearing premature burial (a very common fear), my mother had asked that her burial should be postponed until a natural change in the elements of her body should leave no doubt that life no longer lingered there. And the interval between her death and her burial I spent along the lake's shore. The same weather continued day after day, and it is almost impossible to find words to express the beauty of the grey reflection of the islands and the reeds, and the faint evanescent shores floating away, disappearing in the sun-haze, and the silence about the shores, a kind of enchanted silence, interrupted, as I have said, only by the low gurgle of the water about the limestone shingle. Now and then the song of a bird would break out, and all was silence again.... "A silence that seems to come out of the very heart of things!" I said, and I stopped to listen, like one at the world's end; I walked on, wondering, through the rushes and tussocked grass and juniper bushes which grew along the wilding shore, along the edge of the wood. Coming from the town, I could not but admire the emptiness of the country; hardly ever did I hear the sound of a human voice or a footstep; only once did I meet some wood-gatherers, poor women carrying bundles of faggots, bent under their loads. And thinking that perchance I knew them—they were evidently from the village; if so, I must have known them when I was a boy—I was suddenly seized by an unaccountable dread or a shyness, occasioned no doubt by the sense of the immense difference that time had effected in us: they were the same, but I was different. The books I had pondered and the pictures I had seen had estranged me from them, simple souls that they were; and the consciousness of the injustice of the human lot made it a pain to me to look into their eyes. So I was glad to be able to pass behind some bushes, and to escape into the wood without their perceiving me.

And coming upon pleasant interspaces, pleasanter even than those that lingered in my memory, I lay down, for, though the days were the first days of May, the grass was long and warm and ready for the scythe, the tasselled branches of the tall larches swung faintly in a delicious breeze, and the words of the old Irish poet came into my mind, "The wood was like a harp in the hands of a harper." To see the boughs, to listen to them, seemed a sufficient delight, and I began to admire the low sky full of cotton-like clouds, and the white flower that was beginning to light up the little leaves of the hedgerow, and I suppose it was the May-flower that drew down upon me a sudden thought of the beloved girl lost to me for ever. My mother's death had closed that wound a little, but in a moment all my grief reappeared, the wound gaped again, and it was impossible to stanch the bleeding.

A man cannot lament two women at the same time, and only a month ago the most beautiful thing that had ever appeared in my life, an idea which I knew from the first I was destined to follow, had appeared to me, had stayed with me for a while, and had passed from me. All the partial loves of my youth seemed to find expression at last in a passion that would know no change. Who shall explain the mystery of love that time cannot change? Fate is the only word that conveys any idea of it, for of what use to say that her hair was blond and thick, that her eyes were grey and blue? I had known many women before her, and many had hair and eyes as fine and as deep as hers. But never one but she had had the indispensable quality of making me feel I was more intensely alive when she was by me than I was when she was away. It is that tingle of life that we are always seeking, and that perhaps we must lose in order to retain. On such a day, under the swaying branches of the larches, the whiteness of the lake curving so beautifully amid low shores could not fail to remind me of her body, and its mystery reminded me of her mystery; but the melancholy line of mountains rippling down the southern sky was not like her at all. One forgets what is unlike, caring only to dwell upon what is like.... Thinking of her my senses grow dizzy, a sort of madness creeps up behind the eyes. What an exquisite despair is this—that one shall never possess that beautiful personality again, sweet-scented as the May-time, that I shall never hold that dainty oval face in my hands again, shall look into those beautiful eyes no more, that all the intimacy of her person is now but a memory never to be renewed by actual presence—in these moments of passionate memory one experiences real grief, a pang that never has found expression perchance except in Niobe; even that concentration of features is more an expression of despair than grief. And it was the grief that this girl inspired that prevented me from mourning my mother as I should like to have mourned her, as she was worthy of being mourned, for she was a good woman, her virtues shone with more admirable light year after year; and had I lived with her, had I been with her during the last years of her life, her death would have come upon me with a sense of personal loss; I should have mourned her the day she died as I mourn her now, intimately; when I am alone in the evening, when the fire is sinking, the sweetness of her presence steals by me, and I realise what I lost in losing her.

We do not grieve for the dead because they have been deprived of the pleasures of this life (if this life be a pleasure), but because of our own loss. But who would impugn such selfishness? It is the best thing we have, it is our very selves. Think of a mistress's shame if her lover were to tell her that he loved her because she wished to be beloved, because he thought it would give her pleasure to be loved—she would hate him for such altruism, and deem him unworthy of her. She would certainly think like this, and turn her face from him for a while until some desire of possession would send her back to him. We are always thinking of ourselves directly or indirectly. I was thinking of myself when shame prevented me from going to meet the poor wood-gatherers; they would not have thought at all of the injustice of having been left to the labour of the fields while I had gone forth to enjoy the world; they would have been interested to see me again, and a few kind words would have made their load seem easier on their backs. Called back by a sudden association of ideas, I began to consider that shameful injustice is undoubtedly a part of our human lot, for we may only grieve passionately for the casual, or what seems the merely casual; perhaps because the ultimate law is hidden from us; I am thinking now of her who comes suddenly into our lives tempting us with colour, fugitive as that of a flower, luring us with light as rapid as the light shed from the wings of a dove. Why, I asked myself, as I lay under the larches, are we to mourn transitory delight so intensely, why should it possess us more entirely than the sorrow that we experience for her who endured the labour of child-bearing, who nourished us perchance at her breast, whose devotion to us was unceasing, and who grew kindlier and more divorced from every thought of self as the years went by? From injustice there can be no escape, not a particle. At best we can, indeed we must, acquiesce in the fact that the only sorrow to be found in our hearts for aged persons is a sort of gentle sorrow, such as the year itself administers to our senses in autumn, when we come home with our hands full of the beautiful single dahlias that the Dutchmen loved and painted, bound up with sprays of reddening creepers; we come home along the sunny roads over which the yellow beeches lean so pathetically, and we are sad for the year, but we do not grieve passionately; our hearts do not break.

Then again we cannot grieve as the conventions would have us grieve—in strange dress; the very fact of wearing crepe and black gloves alienates us from our real selves; we are no longer ourselves, we are mummers engaged in the performance of a masque. I could have mourned my mother better without crêpe. "There never has been invented anything so horrible as the modern funeral," I cried out. A picture of the hearse and the mutes rose up in my mind, and it was at that very moment that the song of the bird broke out again, and just above my head in the larches an ugly, shrilling song of about a dozen notes with an accent on the two last, a stupid, tiresome stave that never varied. "What bird can it be," I cried out, "that comes to interrupt my meditations?" and getting up I tried to discover it amid the branches of the tree under which I had been lying. It broke out again in another tree a little farther away, and again in another. I followed it, and it led me round the wood towards the hilltop to the foot of the steps, two short flights; the second flight, or part of it at least, has to be removed when the vault is opened. It consists, no doubt, of a single chamber with shelves along either side; curiosity leads few into vaults not more than a hundred years old; above the vault is the monument, a very simple one, a sort of table built in, and when my father was buried, a priest scrambled up or was lifted up by the crowd, and he delivered a funeral oration from the top of it.

That day the box edgings were trampled under foot, and all the flowers in the beds. My mother, perhaps, cared little for flowers, or she did not live here sufficiently long to see that this garden was carefully tended; for years there were no children to come here for a walk, and it was thought sufficient to keep in repair the boundary wall so that cattle should not get in. No trees were cut here when the Woods were thinned, and the pines and the yews have grown so thickly that the place is overshadowed; and the sepulchral dark is never lifted even at midday. At the back of the tomb, in the wood behind it, the headstones of old graves show above the ground, though the earth has nearly claimed them; only a few inches show above the dead leaves; all this hillside must have been a graveyard once, hundreds of years ago, and this ancient graveyard has never been forgotten by me, principally on account of something that happened long ago when I was a little child. The mystery of the wood used to appeal to my curiosity, but I never dared to scramble over the low wall until one day, leaving my governess, who was praying by the tomb, I discovered a gap through which I could climb. My wanderings were suddenly brought to an end by the appearance, or the fancied appearance, of somebody in a brown dress—a woman I thought it must be; she seemed to float along the ground, and I hurried back, falling and hurting myself severely in my hurry to escape through the gap. So great was my fear that I spoke not of my hurt to my governess, but of the being I had seen, beseeching of her to come back; but she would not come back, and this fact impressed me greatly. I said to myself, "If she didn't believe somebody was there she'd come back." The fear endured for long afterwards; and I used to beg of her not to cross the open space between the last shift of the wood and the tomb itself. We can re-live in imagination an emotion already experienced. Everything I had felt when I was a child about the mysterious hollows in the beech wood behind the tomb and the old stone there, and the being I had seen clothed in a brown cloak, I could re-live again, but the wood enkindled no new emotion in me. Everything seemed very trivial. The steps leading to the tomb, the tomb itself, the boundary wall, and the enchanted wood was now no more than a mere ordinary plantation. There were a few old stones showing through the leaves, that is all. Marvels never cease; in youth one finds the exterior world marvellous, later on one finds one's inner life extraordinary, and what seemed marvellous to me now was that I should have changed so much. The seeing of the ghost might be put down to my fancy, but how explain the change in the wood—was its mystery also a dream, an imagination? Which is the truth—that experience robs the earth of its mystery, or that we have changed so that the evanescent emanations which we used suddenly to grow aware of, and which sometimes used to take shape, are still there, only our eyes are no longer capable of perceiving them? May not this be so?—for as one sense develops, another declines. The mystic who lives on the hillside in the edge of a cave, pondering eternal rather than ephemeral things, obtains glimpses, just as the child does, of a life outside this life of ours. Or do we think these things because man will not consent to die like a plant? Wondering if a glimpse of another life had once been vouchsafed to me when my senses were more finely wrought, I descended the hillside; the bird, probably a chaffinch, repeated its cry without any variation. I went down the hillside and lay in the shadow of the tasselled larches, trying to convince myself that I had not hoped to see the brown lady, if it were a lady I had seen, bending over the stones of the old burial-ground.

One day the silence of the woods was broken by the sound of a mason's hammer, and on making inquiry from a passing workman—his hodman probably—I learned that on opening the vault it had been discovered that there was not room for another coffin. But no enlargement of the vault was necessary; a couple of more shelves was all that would be wanted for many a year to come. His meaning was not to be mistaken—when two more shelves had been added there would be room for my brothers, myself, and my sister, but the next generation would have to order that a further excavation be made in the hill or look out for a new burial-ground. He stood looking at me, and I watched for a moment a fine young man whose eyes were pale as the landscape, and I wondered if he expected me to say that I was glad that things had turned out very well.... The sound of the mason's hammer got upon my nerves, and feeling the wood to be no longer a place for meditation, I wandered round the shore as far as the old boat-house, wondering how it was that the words of a simple peasant could have succeeded in producing such a strange revulsion of feeling in me. No doubt it was the intensity with which I realised the fact that we are never far from death, none of us, that made it seem as if I were thinking on this subject for the first time. As soon as we reach the age of reflection the thought of death is never long out of our minds. It is a subject on which we are always thinking. We go to bed thinking that another day has gone, that we are another day nearer our graves. Any incident suffices to remind us of death. That very morning I had seen two old blue-bottles huddled together in the corner of a pane, and at once remembered that a term of life is set out for all things—a few months for the blue-bottle, a few years for me. One forgets how one thought twenty years ago, but I am prone to think that even the young meditate very often upon death; it must be so, for all their books contain verses on the mutability of things, and as we advance in years it would seem that we think more and more on this one subject, for what is all modern literature but a reek of regret that we are but bubbles on a stream? I thought that nothing that could be said on this old subject could move me, but that boy from Derryanny had brought home to me the thought that follows us from youth to age better than literature could have done; he had exceeded all the poets, not by any single phrase—it was more his attitude of mind towards death (towards my death) that had startled me—and as I walked along the shore I tried to remember his words. They were simple enough, no doubt, so simple that I could not remember them, only that he had reminded me that Michael Malia, that was the mason's name, had known me since I was a little boy; I do not know how he got it out; I should not have been able to express the idea myself, but without choosing his words, without being aware of them, speaking unconsciously, just as he breathed, he had told me that if my heart were set on any particular place I had only to tell Michael Malia and he would keep it for me; there would be a convenient place for me just above my grandfather when they had got the new shelf up; he had heard we were both writers.

That country boy took it out of me as perhaps no poet had ever done! I shall never forget him as I saw him going away stolidly through the green wood, his bag of lime on his back.

And sitting down in front of the tranquil lake I said, "In twenty or thirty years I shall certainly join the others in that horrible vault; nothing can save me," and again the present slipped away from me and my mind became again clear as glass; the present is only subconscious; were it not so we could not live. I have said all this before; again I seemed to myself like a fly crawling up a pane of glass, falling back, buzzing, and crawling again. Every expedient that I explored proved illusory, every one led to the same conclusion that the dead are powerless. "The living do with us what they like," I muttered, and I thought of all my Catholic relations, every one of whom believes in the intervention of priests and holy water, the Immaculate Conception, the Pope's Indulgences, and a host of other things which I could not remember, so great was my anguish of mind at the thought that my poor pagan body should be delivered helpless into their pious hands. I remembered their faces, I could hear their voices—that of my dear brother, whom I shall always think of as a strayed cardinal rather than as a colonel; I could see his pale eyes moist with faith in the intercession of the Virgin—one can always tell a Catholic at sight, just as one can tell a consumptive. The curving lake, the pale mountains, the low shores, the sunlight, and the haze contributed not a little to frighten me; the country looked intensely Catholic at that moment. My thoughts swerved, and I began to wonder if the face of a country takes its character from the ideas of those living in it. "How shall I escape from that vault?" I cried out suddenly. Michael Malia's hodman had said that they might place me just above my grandfather, and my grandfather was a man of letters, a historian whose histories I had not read; and in the midst of the horror my probable burial inspired in me, I found some amusement in the admission that I should like the old gentleman whose portrait hung in the dining-room to have read my novels. This being so, it was not improbable that he would like me to read his histories, and I began to speculate on what the author of a history of the French Revolution [1] would think of "Esther Waters." The colour of the chocolate coat he wears in his picture fixed itself in my mind's eye, and I began to compare it with the colour of the brown garment worn by the ghost I had seen in the wood. Good Heavens, if it were his ghost I had seen!

1. Still unpublished.

And listening to the lapping of the lake water I imagined a horrible colloquy in that vault. It all came into my mind, his dialogue and my dialogue. "Great God," I cried out, "something must be done to escape!" and my eyes were strained out on the lake, upon the island on which a Welshman had built a castle. I saw all the woods reaching down to the water's edge, and the woods I did not see I remembered; all the larch trees that grew on the hillsides came into my mind suddenly, and I thought what a splendid pyre might be built out of them. No trees had been cut for the last thirty years; I might live for another thirty. What splendid timber there would then be to build a pyre for me!—a pyre fifty feet high, saturated with scented oils, and me lying on the top of it with all my books (they would make a nice pillow for my head). The ancient heroes used to be laid with their arms beside them; their horses were slaughtered so that their spirits might be free to serve them in the aerial kingdoms they had gone to inhabit. My pyre should be built on the island facing me; its flames would be seen for miles and miles; the lake would be lighted up by it, and my body would become a sort of beacon-fire—the beacon of the pagan future awaiting old Ireland! Nor would the price of such a funeral be anything too excessive—a few hundred pounds perhaps, the price of a thousand larches and a few barrels of scented oil and the great feast: for while I was roasting, my mourners should eat roast meat and drink wine and wear gay dresses—the men as well as the women; and the gayest music would be played. The "Marriage of Figaro" and some Offenbach would be pleasing to my spirit, the ride of the Valkyrie would be an appropriate piece; but I am improvising a selection, and that is a thing that requires careful consideration. It would be a fine thing indeed if such a funeral—I hate the word—such a burning as this could be undertaken, and there is no reason why it should not be, unless the law interdicts public burnings of human bodies. And then my face clouded, and my soul too; I grew melancholy as the lake, as the southern mountains that rippled down the sky plaintive as an Irish melody, for the burning I had dreamed of so splendidly might never take place. I might have to fall back on the Public Crematorium in England—in Ireland there is no Crematorium;

Ireland lingers in the belief in the resurrection of the body. "Before I decide," I said to myself, "what my own funeral shall be, I must find out what funeral liberties the modern law and Christian morality permit the citizen," and this I should not be able to discover until I returned to Dublin.

It was by the side of dulcet Lough Cara that I began to imagine my interview with the old family solicitor, prejudiced and white-headed as the king in a certain kind of romantic play, a devout Catholic who would certainly understand very little of my paganism; but I should catch him on two well-sharpened horns—whether he should be guilty of so unbusiness-like an act as to refuse to make a will for theological reasons, or to do a violence to his conscience by assisting a fellow-creature to dispose of his body in a way that would give the Almighty much trouble to bring about the resurrection of the body in the valley of Jehoshaphat. The embarrassment of the family solicitor would be amusing, and if he declined to draw up my will for me there would be plenty of other solicitors who would not hesitate to draw up whatever will I was minded to make. In order to secure the burial of my body, my notion was to leave all my property, lands, money, pictures, and furniture to my brother, Colonel Maurice Moore on the condition that I should be burnt and the ashes disposed of without the humiliation of Christian rites; that if the conditions that the inheritance carried with it were so disagreeable to Colonel Maurice Moore that he could not bring himself to see that the disposal of my remains was carried out according to my wishes, my property, lands, money, pictures, and furniture, should go to my brother Augustus Moore; that in the event of his declining to carry out my wishes regarding the disposal of my remains, all my property should go to my brother Julian Moore; that if he should refuse to carry out my wishes regarding the disposal of my remains, all the said property should go to my friend Sir William Eden, who would, I felt sure, take a sad pleasure in giving effect to the wishes of his old friend. A will drawn up on these lines would secure me against all chance of being buried with my ancestors in Kiltoon, and during the next two days I pondered my own burning. My brother might think that he was put to a good deal of expense, but he would not fail me. He had taken off my hands the disagreeable task of seeing the undertakers and making arrangements for the saying of Masses, etc., arrangements which would be intensely disagreeable to me to make so. I had plenty of time to think out the details of my burning; and I grew happy in the thought that I had escaped from the disgrace of Christian burial—a disgrace which was never, until the last two days, wholly realised by me, but which was nevertheless always suspected. No doubt it was the dread of Kiltoon that had inspired that thought of death from which in late years I had never seemed able to escape. I am of the romantic temperament, and it would be a pity to forgo the burning I had imagined. I delighted in the vision that had come upon me of the felling of the larch trees on the hillside and the building of the pyre about the old castle. It would reach much higher; I imagined it at least fifty feet high. I saw it flaming in imagination, and when half of it was burnt, the mourners would have to take to the boats, so intense would be the heat. What a splendid spectacle! Never did any man imagine a more splendid funeral! It would be a pity if the law obliged me to forgo it. But there was no use hoping that the law would not; there was a law against the burning of human remains, and I might have to fall back on the Public Crematorium: it only remained for me to decide what I would wish to be done with the ashes. In a moment of happy inspiration I conceived the idea of a Greek vase as the only suitable repository for my ashes, and I began to remember all the Greek vases I had seen: all are beautiful, even the Roman Greek; these are sometimes clumsy and heavy, but the sculpture is finely designed and executed. Any Greek vase I decided would satisfy me, provided, of course, that the relief represented Bacchanals dancing, and nearly every Greek vase is decorated in this way. The purchase of the vase would be an additional expense; no doubt I was running my brother in for a good deal of money; it is becoming more and more difficult to buy original Greek sculpture! and in a moment of posthumous parsimony my thoughts turned to a copy of a Greek vase in granite, granite being more durable than marble, and I wanted the vase to last for a long time. It was delightful to take a sheet of paper and a pencil and to draw all that I remembered of the different vases I had seen, different riots of lusty men carrying horns of wine, intermingled with graceful girls dancing gracefully, youths playing on pipes, and amidst them fauns, the lovely animality of the woods, of the landscape ages, when men first began to milk their goats, and when one man out of the tribe, more pensive, more meditative than the others, went down to the river's bank and cut a reed and found music within it. The vase I remembered best has upright handles springing from the necks of swans. It stands about two feet high, perhaps a little more, and its cavity should be capable of containing all that remains of me after my burning. None would have thought, from the happy smile upon my lips, that I was thinking of a Grecian urn and a little pile of white ashes. "O death, where is thy sting?" I murmured, and the pencil dropped from my hand, for my memory was more beautiful than anything I could realise upon paper. I could only remember one side of a youth, that side of him next to an impulsive maiden; her delight gives her wings; his left arm is about her shoulder. She is more impulsive than he, and I wondered at his wistfulness—whether he was thinking of another love or a volume of poems that he loved better. Little by little many of the figures in the dance were remembered, for the sculpture was so well done that the years had only clouded my memory. The clouds dispersed, and I saw this time one whole figure, that of a dancing-girl; her right arm is extended, her left arm is bent, she holds a scarf as she dances, and the muscles of the arms are placed so well, and the breasts too, that one thinks that the girl must have been before the sculptor as he worked. Ingres and Antiquity alone knew how to simplify. There is little, but that little is so correct that detail is unnecessary, and I exulted in remembrance of the dainty design of the belly, half hidden, half revealed by little liquid folds. "How exquisite," I said, "is that thigh! how well it advances! And we poor moderns have lived upon that beauty now well-nigh two thousand years? But how vainly we have attempted to imitate that drapery flowing about the ankles, like foam breaking on the crest of a wave." A slender youth stands next; his shoulders are raised, for the pipes are to his lips, his feet are drawn close together, and by him a satyr dances wildly, clashing cymbals as he dances. He is followed, I think—it is difficult to say whether this be a recollection of another vase or whether the figure is included in the same group—by a faun tempting the teeth and claws of a panther with a bunch of grapes. And it was this winsome faun that decided me to select this vase as the repository of my ashes. And I determined to stipulate in my will that this vase be chosen. But my will must not be too complicated, otherwise it might be contested. All that is not common can easily be argued to be madness by a loquacious lawyer before a stupid jury. Who except a madman, asks the lawyer, would trouble to this extent as to what shall be done with his remains? Everybody in the court agrees with him, for every one in court is anxious to prove to his neighbour that he is a good Christian. Everything is convention, and lead coffins and oak coffins cannot be held as proof of insanity, because men believe still in the resurrection of the body. Were the Pharaohs insane? Was the building of the Great Pyramid an act of madness? The common assurance is that it matters nothing at all what becomes of our remains, yet the world has always been engaged in setting up tombs. It is only those pretty satyrs who do not think of tombs. Satyrs wander away into some hidden place when they feel death upon them. But poor humanity desires to be remembered. The desire to be remembered for at least some little while after death is as deep an instinct as any that might be readily named, and our lives are applied to securing some little immortality for ourselves. What more natural than that every one should desire his death and burial to be, as it were, typical of the ideas which he agreed to accept during life: what other purpose is served by the consecration of plots of ground and the erection of crosses? In this at least I am not different from other people; if I am anxious about my burning, it is because I would to the last manifest and express my ideas, and neither in my prose nor verse have I ever traced out my thoughts as completely or as perfectly as I have done in this order for my tomb. One trouble, however, still remained upon my mind. Where should the vase be placed? Not in Westminster Abbey. Fie upon all places of Christian burial! A museum inspires lofty thoughts in a few; Gouncourt speaks of the icy admiration of crowds. The vase might stand in the stone wall, and in the very corner where I learned to spin my top? But sooner or later a housemaid would break it. The house itself will become the property of another family, and the stranger will look upon the vase with idle curiosity, or perhaps think it depressing to have me in the hall. An order for my removal to a garret might be made out.

The disposal of the vase caused me a great deal of anxiety, and I foresaw that unless I hit upon some idea whereby I could safeguard it from injury for ever, my project would be deprived of half its value. As I sat thinking I heard a noise of feet suddenly on the staircase. "They are bringing down my mother's coffin," I said, and at that moment the door was opened and I was told that the funeral procession was waiting for me. My brother, and various relatives and friends, were waiting in the hall; black gloves were on every hand, crepe streamed from every hat, "All the paraphernalia of grief," I muttered; "nothing is wanting." My soul revolted against this mockery. "But why should I pity my mother? She wished to lie beside her husband. And far be it from me to criticise such a desire!"

The coffin was lifted upon the hearse. A gardener of old time came up to ask me if I wished there to be any crying. I did not at first understand what he meant; he began to explain, and I began to understand that he meant the cries with which the Western peasant follows his dead to the grave. Horrible savagery! and I ordered that there was to be no keening; but three or four women, unable to contain themselves, rushed forward and began a keen. It was difficult to try to stop them. I fancy that every one looked round to see if there were any clouds in the sky, for it was about a mile and a half to the chapel; we would have to walk three miles at least, and if it rained, we should probably catch heavy colds. We thought of the damp of the wood, and the drip from the melancholy boughs of yew and fir growing about that sepulchre on the hillside. But there was no danger of rain; Castle Island lay in the misted water, faint and grey, reminding me of what a splendid burial I might have if the law did not intervene to prevent me. And as we followed the straggling grey Irish road, with scant meagre fields on either side—fields that seemed to be on the point of drifting into marsh land—past the houses of the poor people, I tried to devise a scheme for the safeguarding of the vase. But Rameses the Second had not succeeded in securing his body against violation; it had been unswathed; I had seen his photograph in the Strand, and where he failed, how should I succeed?

Twenty priests had been engaged to sing a Mass, and whilst they chanted, my mind continued to roam, seeking the unattainable, seeking that which Rameses had been unable to find. Unexpectedly, at the very moment when the priest began to intone the Pater Noster, I thought of the deep sea as the only clean and holy receptacle for the vase containing my ashes. If it were dropped where the sea is deepest it would not reach the bottom, but would hang suspended in dark, moveless depths where only a few fishes range, in a cool, deep grave "made without hands, in a world without stain," surrounded by a lovely revel of Bacchanals, youths and maidens, and wild creatures from the woods, man in his primitive animality. But nothing lasts for ever. In some millions of years the sea will begin to wither, and the vase containing me will sink (my hope is that it will sink down to some secure foundation of rocks to stand in the airless and waterless desert that the earth will then be).

Rameses failed, but I shall succeed. Surrounded by dancing youths and maidens, my tomb shall stand on a high rock in the solitude of the extinct sea of an extinct planet. Millions of years will pass away, and the earth, after having lain dead for a long winter, as it does now for a few weeks under frost and snow, will, with all other revolving planets, become absorbed in the sun, and the sun itself will become absorbed in greater suns, Sirius and his like. In the matters of grave moment, millions of years are but seconds; billions convey very little to our minds. At the end of, let us say, some billion years the ultimate moment towards which everything from the beginning has been moving will be reached; and from that moment the tide will begin to flow out again, the eternal dispersal of things will begin again; suns will be scattered abroad, and in tremendous sun-quakes planets will be thrown off; in loud earth-quakes these planets will throw off moons. Millions of years will pass away, the earth will become cool, and out of the primal mud life will begin again in the shape of plants, and then of fish, and then of animals. It is like madness, but is it madder than Christian doctrine? and I believe that billions of years hence, billions and billions of years hence, I shall be sitting in the same room as I sit now, writing the same lines as I am now writing: I believe that again, a few years later, my ashes will swing in the moveless and silent depths of the Pacific Ocean, and that the same figures, the same nymphs, and the same fauns will dance around me again.

THE END